BLADE:

CHING!

The arrow struck the pommel of the raised sword and ricocheted off, embedding itself in the floor a foot away from where Blade lay.

Abigail sagged, her expression dissolving into despair.

Drake carried through the movement without looking up, plunging the sword down into Blade's side. The tip of the sword punched out through Blade's back, striking the tiles beneath with an audible crack. Abigail bit back a scream of horror as she watched Blade gasp, impaled on the end of his own sword.

Game over.

More high octane New Line action from Black Flame

BLADE: TRINITY

A novel by
Natasha Rhodes

Based on the motion picture
written by David S. Goyer

BLACK FLAME

To Marijan, with love.

A Black Flame Publication
www.blackflame.com

First published in 2004 by BL Publishing, Games Workshop Ltd.,
Willow Road, Nottingham NG7 2WS, UK.

Distributed in the US by Simon & Schuster, 1230 Avenue of the
Americas, New York. NY 10020, USA.

10 9 8 7 6 5 4 3 2 1

ISBN 1 84416 106 4

A CIP record for this book is available from the British Library.

Printed in the UK by Bookmarque, Surrey, UK.

PROLOG

South-eastern Iraq,
Dhi Qar Province
Six months ago

It was daybreak in the desert.

The shadows of the night withered under the blow-torch intensity of the first rays of dawn. As the sun crept over the horizon, the creatures of the night scurried away into their burrows, away from the heat and light of what would be another long, blisteringly hot day.

Few things could survive out here for long. The rocky desert stretched to vanishing point in all directions, further than the eye could see or the body could walk, claiming all but the hardiest. There was no shade here, no water, nothing to break the endless desolation.

Nothing, except for the ziggurat.

Towering more than a hundred feet above the barren earth, the massive stepped pyramid dominated the otherwise featureless landscape for miles around. The sheer scale of the ziggurat was mind-boggling, its colossal sides soaring up into the endless blue sky as though seeking to pierce the stratosphere and claim the heavens as its own. Its four-tiered construction was bisected at regular intervals by stone platforms where once there had been sacrifices, renewing humanity's connection to the gods above who, it was believed, would one day return.

The pyramid might once have inspired respect, even awe, but the passing millennia had robbed it of much of its glory. In years gone by, its mud-brick walls had been clad in a colorful riot of glazed pigments. Now, even these had been scoured bare by the desert winds and the merciless heat of the sun. Once the crowning glory of the ancient Sumerian city of Ur, the monument now stood alone, crumbling under the weight of centuries.

Yet it had not been forgotten entirely. A scrawny shepherd knelt at the foot of the ziggurat, his head bowed. The tinny sound of a religious broadcast emanated from the battered radio at his feet, leading the shepherd in the first of his daily prayers. In the near distance, his ragged flock of goats foraged for whatever scrub the harsh environment had to offer. Their bleating and the dull clank of the bells on their collars had a comforting and soporific effect upon the shepherd as he kept half an ear open to their activities. He knew that it wouldn't be long before one of them would wander off and do something stupid that would require his attention.

The shepherd allowed himself a wry smile. That was the problem with goats. They were born stupid, they lived stupid lives, and the only brief spark of excitement they had in their short existences lay in finding new and interesting ways to die.

Sometimes he was sure they did it deliberately, just to annoy him.

A low-pitched hum intruded upon the shepherd's attention. His eyes refocused as he was drawn out of his contemplative reverie. He licked his dry lips and peered up into the dawn sky, shielding his eyes from the morning light with a leathery hand.

Two helicopters flying in from the west. And they were approaching fast.

His prayers forgotten, the shepherd rose to his feet and watched intently as the twin machines roared overhead, circling the ziggurat like predatory dragonflies before dipping and touching down at the base of the pyramid. Their rotors whipped up a tornado of whirling sand as they landed, their sleek curved sides throwing spears of light out of the gathering dust cloud. There was a distinct crunching sound as the full weight of the enormous machines settled into the coarse shale at the foot of the ziggurat. The roar of their engines died away, and their spinning rotors slowed gradually, then drifted to a halt.

An expectant hush fell over the desert.

The shepherd coughed and blinked sand out of his eyes, vaguely aware of the sound of frantic bleating as the last of his flock fled over the dunes.

He hesitated. He should go after his sheep before they ran too far away.

But this was far more interesting...

The shepherd watched in fascination as four armed figures jumped down from the cockpit of the first helicopter and strode purposefully towards the ziggurat. They were clad from head to toe in thick desert camo-gear and moved confidently across the shifting sands, carrying huge silver cases of equipment between them as if they weighed nothing at all.

As far as the shepherd was concerned, these people might as well have been aliens.

As he watched, one of the figures stopped. Turning to face the east, the figure threw back his shoulders and stared up into the sky. Then he lifted a gloved hand and gave a one-finger salute to the new day, the rising sun reflected on the mirrored faceplate of his helmet.

The second figure—a woman, judging by the telltale curves of her camo-suit—waved at him in an irritable fashion, urging him onward. Together, they mounted the steps of the ziggurat's central entry ramp and disappeared into the dark mouth of the shrine. Silence fell over the desert once more, broken only by the sound of the sand whipped up by the helicopters falling back to earth like dry rain.

Unable to curb his curiosity, the shepherd gathered his robes around him and began to follow up the steps behind the figures. He was impressed. These strangers must indeed be very brave, or else very foolish. For it was well known amongst his people that those who went into the great pyramid very rarely came back out again.

The sound of distant bleating drew his attention, and the shepherd gave a sigh. He squinted into the darkness of the ziggurat, wishing heartily that he could stay longer and see if the figures came out again. What a story he would have to tell his family tonight! But for now, he must go and round up his flock before they strayed too far. Left to their own devices for too long, it was likely that they would soon die from terror, or excitement, or possibly both.

Picking up his wind-up radio, the shepherd turned and ambled off after his fleeing charges, gazing back over his shoulder from time to time.

From the mouth of the ziggurat, one of the figures watched the shepherd go, and licked his lips.

Inside the ziggurat it was cool and shady, a welcome relief from the heat of the desert.

Quickly locating the burial tomb, the four-strong team spread out. Despite their obvious profession-alism, a buzz of excitement rippled through them as they secured the area, set down their heavy equip-ment and checked their weaponry.

Danica Talos knelt down on the ground and acti-vated her miniature laptop computer, setting it on top of one of the dusty rocks littering the cave's floor. The laptop sprang to life in a buzz of color and static, emitting a brief series of high-pitched bleeps as it automatically registered itself on the wireless network. A sea of digital color washed over Danica's faceplate as she called up a schematic of the ziggurat. No expression showed on what was visible of her face, but her movements betrayed an intense excitement as she locked in on their current location and called up a 3D wireframe map of the room.

Danica studied the display for a moment, her lips moving soundlessly behind the faceplate of her helmet. Then she turned and traced her fingers along the bricks in the wall until she reached the eighth one, which was a slightly different color to the rest. She flattened her gloved palm against the cold stone and pushed. There was a muffled clanking behind the walls as hidden counterweights shifted, then the floor in front of her dropped away, opening up with a groan.

A stone staircase was revealed, leading downwards into the darkness.

Danica's eyes glinted beneath her faceplate as she stepped towards it, scarcely able to believe her luck. She had found the secret entrance! Finally, all her months of planning were starting to pay off.

She gave a sly glance to the figures standing behind her, who were staring down at the stone steps as though mesmerized. In the months that preceded their little expedition, the rest of the team had grown skeptical that they would find anything here at all. Sure, they had gone along with her research—although it wasn't as if they had any choice in the matter.

But Danica knew that they spoke in whispers behind her back, doubting her, maybe even making fun of her for believing what she did. She didn't blame them for being skeptical. She had felt the same way at first. This entire mission had been based on only the tiniest scraps of evidence, nothing but gossip and conjecture and good old-fashioned rumor scraped together from the four corners of the Earth.

But Danica's belief had been strong enough to carry the mission through, and now here they stood, perhaps ten minutes away from achieving their objective, one that had been Danica's sole and driving ambition for nearly three years.

Salvation.

Danica picked up her laptop and moved forward, motioning to the others to join her. Cautiously, the team followed her as she stepped downwards into the gloom.

It was far darker in the room below. The diffused sunlight from above barely penetrated down here; it seemed to shrink back from the choking thousand-year-old dust and the faint smell of decay that seemed to permeate everything.

Grimwood, the largest and most imposing member of the team, took out a battery-powered lantern and clicked it on. The wash of yellow light illuminated a small sandstone room with a dusty earthen floor, barely big enough to accommodate the four of them with all of their equipment. Grimwood slowly swept the beam of light around the chamber before directing it up onto the walls of the burial vault. The walls were covered from floor to ceiling with some kind of ancient writing, etched into the bare stone with angular precision.

Apart from this, the tomb was empty.

"That's great. We've got dick." Grimwood turned to the others, his voice dripping with disgust. "Is there any reason we had to embark on this fuck-fest during the day?"

Danica removed her helmet with a flourish and looked around, sizing up the situation. Her unusual beauty was apparent even in the dim light, as was the deference with which the others treated her. Her calm demeanor and regal air instantly gave her away as the team's leader. She spoke without looking up, concentrating intently on the details of the room around her, matching them up with those displayed on her laptop. "Night time's too tricky, Grimwood. You know that."

One by one, the other three removed their helmets and looked around. Although striking, the team's faces were subtly different, as though they had each been sculpted by an artist who had heard the human face described in detail, but had never seen one in the flesh. Their features were fractionally elongated, with sharp cheekbones and strong jaw lines. Three sets of eyes flashed and glinted in the darkness, seemingly lit from within by a dim yellow light. The team's fingernails were too pointed, their teeth too sharp to be entirely human.

But they weren't human. They were vampires. And out here, in the middle of the fiery desert, they were nervous as hell.

Grimwood turned away from the others and studied the angular writing on the walls. He touched it with a meaty finger. "What is this chicken-scratch?"

Danica looked up from her computer display. "Cuneiform. Dates back about four thousand years."

Despite his impatience, this made the big man pause. He ran his tongue over the tips of his steel-capped teeth as he considered this. Then he gestured around at the sandy walls, voicing the question that was running through all of their minds. "So why here?"

"Because this was the cradle of civilization." Danica's voice was soft. She fingered the tiny steel crucifix around her neck, a wistful look on her face. "He would've been comfortable here."

Another of the team, Asher, moved over to join Danica. From the similarity of his features, it was clear that he was related to her. He put a hand on her shoulder, shaking his head doubtfully. "I don't know, Dan. Seems like another dead-end."

The fourth member of the team spoke up. "I'm not so sure..."

Wolfe's voice was quiet but he instantly had everyone's attention. In the resultant hush, he studied the portable radar unit set up on the floor near the center of the chamber. He looked up, his face lit with excitement. "There's something beneath us."

The others crowded around the flickering display as Wolfe adjusted the monitor, twisting the dials this way and that. Gradually, an image emerged from the static. A cross-section of the ground was revealed, the subsurface topography clearly showing something large buried in the sand just a couple of feet or so below them.

Something...

"Is that a body?"

Asher's voice was more nervous than he'd meant it to be. Grimwood smirked and gave him a mocking glance, and Asher clenched his jaw in frustration. He really, really didn't want to be here, and he didn't care who knew it. Screw the mission. He just wanted to get out of here, as quickly as possible. As a vampire, he didn't mind being underground, but this subterranean death vault was making him feel claustrophobic. There was a strong air of dread to this place, a prickling feeling in the back of his neck that told him that bad things had happened here, and that he should leave now while he still could.

Biting back his misgivings, Asher stepped forward and watched guardedly as Wolfe made a further few adjustments on his radar unit. The image on the screen slowly drew into focus.

It was definitely a body.

The team was so absorbed by this that they didn't hear the sound of shifting counterweights until it was too late. With a hiss, banks of ropes strung across the stone ceiling sprung taut. A block weight dropped on the other side of the wall with a loud grating sound, sending a huge slab of rock crashing down the stairs, sealing off the exit.

"What the fuck?"

Running over to the slab of stone, Grimwood pounded his fist against it, then tried to shoulder it open using brute strength. It was no good. The stone was solid and must have weighed at least half a ton.

They were trapped.

Asher was the first to break the stunned silence. "Radio backup. See if they can open it from the other—"

"Guys...?" Wolfe pointed down at the ground with a shaking finger. A tiny depression had formed in the floor in front of them. Sand was trickling down into it in a steady stream, vanishing into the ground like a bathtub emptying. Wolfe set his radar unit down and gingerly knelt by the hole, trying to see where the sand was going. Perhaps it was some kind of escape tunnel opening up?

The sand moved faster as the hole expanded, until it was rushing down into the earth like a miniature whirlpool. The hole widened, sucking in more and more sand until it was almost a foot across.

As though hypnotized, Wolfe leaned in closer...

The ground exploded.

Before any of the team could react, a clawed, armored hand burst up out of the sand and grabbed Wolfe by the throat. It held him there for a moment, and then tightened suddenly. The chamber echoed with a gristly crunch, then the hand yanked backwards, dragging Wolfe headfirst down into the sand with unstoppable force. One of his legs lashed out convulsively as he went under, catching the edge of the electric lantern, which tipped over and shorted out.

The tomb was plunged into darkness.

Yelling, Asher and Grimwood rushed to Wolfe's side. Groping around blindly, they managed to grab hold of Wolfe's ankles. They yanked backwards, trying to pull their stricken team member free. Even with their combined strength, Wolfe didn't budge. It was like trying to pull a sword out of solid rock.

The lamp came back on again briefly, flickering on and off with a spasmodic crackling sound as sand grains trickled across its internal electrical contacts. It was clear that they didn't have much time before it went out altogether.

As the team struggled, one of Wolfe's thrashing legs broke free from Asher's grip, catching him in the chest with such force that he was propelled bodily upwards. The young vampire's head struck the ceiling with a crack and he fell back to the floor, stunned.

Danica rushed in to take his place, grabbing Wolfe's leg and pulling with all her might. The sand beneath her appeared to be writhing, lit only by the blue electrical flashes from the crackling lamp. Dark shapes moved beneath the surface like sharks in the ocean, or something far worse...

Abruptly, and to her surprise, Wolfe came free.

His head, however, stayed in the sand.

As Danica dropped Wolfe's headless body with a soundless scream of horror, a geyser of bright red blood erupted from the earth, staining the floor and spurting across the walls, making the inscriptions seem to crawl around like black, angular insects.

Something began to move upwards through the sand—something large and bestial, though undoubtedly humanoid in shape. It bucked and twisted as it unearthed itself, bunching powerful muscles as it fought its way upwards, illuminated in nightmare snapshots by the spastically flickering lamp.

Before any of the team could move, a hideous, armor-plated creature burst up through the blood-stained sand, flinging back its head and roaring triumphantly as though breaking free from the bowels of hell itself. The creature's entire lower face was covered in a tribal mask of bright blood, and its muscular body rippled with long, spiny growths that jutted from its armored skin like living thorns.

Shaking off the last of the clinging sand, the creature whipped its head around to face them, rattlesnake fast. Fixing the team with a baleful glare, the beast opened its armor-plated jaws and howled at them, revealing a set of impossibly long, hinged fangs, drenched in fresh blood and gore.

At that moment, the lantern went out.
For good.

ONE

It had been a quiet night in the meatpacking district until the building exploded.

Seagulls shrieked overhead as the massive explosion ripped through the grimy industrial building, white fire shooting out of its windows and rolling upwards towards the sky. The earth itself seemed to tremble as the shockwave surged outwards like a fiery tsunami, blowing banks of tempered windows out in a shower of shining glass. Oily black smoke belched out in its wake as the ancient brick walls of the building split and crumbled in the intense heat, raining debris down onto the sidewalk below.

Moments later, a second explosion shook the building. A screaming, burning man shot up into the night sky, thrown out of a window by the force of the explosion, trailing fire like a human comet. Below him, the factory door flew open and rebounded off its hinges, revealing a raging inferno within. The cold night air was filled with the sounds of yelling and running as more men raced out, most of them on fire.

Pandemonium reigned.

Then the roiling flames parted for the briefest of moments and a powerful-looking black man strode calmly out of the blaze, seemingly unaffected by the intense heat around him. He was tall and heavily muscled, his impressive silhouette bristled with an arsenal of high-tech weaponry. Leaping flames reflected across his designer wraparound sunshades as he walked away from the conflagration, his footsteps ringing out above the sounds of the fire like the drumming of the damned.

The man's name was Blade, and he was just beginning to enjoy himself.

At the sight of him, the majority of the burning factory's escapees fled even faster into the smoke-filled night. But Blade wasn't interested in them. His sights were currently set on a far greater prize—a small group of figures that were running in the opposite direction to the rest.

For these were vampires.

Blade smiled wickedly and drew his gun. There were always a number of rules governing the chase, he knew. Number one was obvious: don't get caught.

The vampire gang fleeing across the parking lot ahead of him seemed very keen to avoid that fate. Their boots skidded on the wet asphalt as they hurtled across the lot, tripping and tumbling over each other in their efforts to get away from Blade. There were three of them, each one more ugly than the next, and they snapped and snarled at one another as they ran in a desperate bid not to be the one at the back. Had they stopped to think, they might have come up with a better plan, or indeed, any plan at all.

Because after all, if you run, there is always the chance you'll get caught.

Reaching the edge of the parking lot, the trio of vampires jumped a chain-link fence and sprinted towards their double-parked vehicles, two modified street-racing cars. Gedge, the youngest of the trio, leaped into the Eagle Talon car as it started to pull out without him, already commandeered by two fleeter-footed vampires. The other car, an old-style Mustang, did a high-speed three-point turn and zoomed towards the exit to the parking lot. It revved its engine in a mocking salute as it passed the Eagle.

Time to ride.

Gedge slammed the door closed behind him and thumped the lock down, his lips pulled back from his sharpened fangs in fear. He glanced nervously through the cracked windshield as Stone and Campbell, his two workmates, climbed atop their stretched and lowered hardtail chopper motorbikes. They gunned their engines, preparing to flee.

Across the parking lot, Blade's head snapped around at the noise. He started to stride towards them, picking up speed as he went. His hand blurred and suddenly there was an automatic Mach pistol in it, the barrel of which had been fitted with a silencer. He fired the gun without breaking pace, spitting a volley of silver death at the retreating vampires. The streets rang with the aftershocks of the shots, the individual echoes blurring together to create one long explosion.

The driver of the Mustang stamped on the brakes as bullets tore through the car's bodywork, pinging and plinking across the trunk. Cursing, he slammed the Mustang into reverse and viciously floored the accelerator, aiming to grind Blade into the asphalt. Blowing up his buddies was one thing. Shooting the hell out of his beloved car was another. The Daywalker was gonna pay for this.

The racer screamed backwards towards Blade, smoke billowing from its outsized tires as the car swerved towards him, burning rubber.

Before Blade's mind had consciously registered the situation, his body was already airborne. Leaping upwards from a standing start, he athletically arced his body over the hood of the speeding car as it flashed by beneath him, drawing his second pistol as he did so. Hanging upside down in midair, Blade swiftly fired off two sweeping rounds of bullets, one through the Mustang's roof, one through its engine block.

Inside the car, the two vampires screamed as Blade's bullets riddled their bodies. Ordinary bullets wouldn't kill them, but these were something special: hand-cast silver shells filled with a garlic-oil compound. To a vampire, this was a deadly combination. All vampires were severely allergic to allicin, the chemical that gave garlic its pungent taste and smell, and catastrophically allergic to silver. Taken internally, this particular combination caused a chain reaction in a vampire's body that would take a human several dozen pints of ingested gasoline and a flamethrower to achieve.

White-hot flames burst out of the vampires' bulletwounds and raced up their torsos, igniting their clothing with a loud *whumph*. Their screams were swallowed up in an impressive fireball as the Mustang exploded, flipping over as its fuel tank ignited and blew the chassis apart. Large chunks of debris rained down all over the parking lot, littering the asphalt with flaming junk.

Blade landed gracefully a few paces away from the blazing wreckage.

Rule two of the chase? Get them before they get you.

As rules went, it was a good one.

Blade spun on the spot, aiming and firing in one smooth movement as the Eagle Talon and the two motorbikes peeled out of the parking lot behind him, their tires laying smoking track marks as they roared out onto the street beyond.

Then they were gone, swallowed up by the night.

Blade kept firing until he was out of bullets, the adrenaline pumping through his system keeping his finger tight on the trigger. A human would've died several times over by now, but then Blade wasn't human.

At least, not entirely.

As the last of his spent shells clattered to the ground, Blade sensed a presence behind him. He froze, his ears ringing from the din of the gunfire.

"No more bullets, Blade?"

Blade slowly turned to see four tall, shadowy figures move forwards to form a semicircle around him. They were vampires, and they were obviously pissed.

"Guess it's time for you to fall down and go boom." The vampire who spoke was called Ellingson. He ran this show, and he had heard a lot about Blade. Certainly enough to want to kill him. And especially now the sonofabitch had set a torch to his business, single-handedly slaughtering two-thirds of his staff.

Ellingson's eyes flashed like quicksilver and one his hands trembled in pain as his singed flesh slowly cracked in the cold of the night. He glanced around as his gang of heavies closed in on Blade and smiled grimly. It was time for this freak to die.

Blade took in the speaker's smoking clothes and general air of inexperience, and relaxed. Holstering his pistols, he idly turned his head from side to side, popping the taut muscles in his neck. Then he brushed a hand over the wicked-looking chain knife strapped to his leather-clad thigh and allowed himself the merest hint of a smile.

Taking this as an insult, Ellingson snarled and rushed at Blade, fangs bared.

Blade whipped out his knife and clicked down one of the buttons built into its base. *Zzz-zing!* The knife-blade ejected from the hilt and shot out at high speed towards the charging vampire, six feet of razor-edged chain snaking out behind it. The solid silver blade sunk into Ellingson's chest with a sound like a mallet going through fresh butter. The vampire gasped as a mini-geyser of fire belched out of the impact site. A wave of superheated flames quickly spread outward and upwards, ripping through his body like wildfire, engulfing him in seconds.

With a shriek, Ellingson exploded. The flesh flew off his bones in a grisly shower of carbonized matter, leaving behind a burning skeleton that flailed around angrily for a few moments before disarticulating and dropping to the ground.

Before the charred remains had finished disinte-grating, Blade hit the second button on his knife. The weapon rapidly retracted as the spring-loaded chain whirred back into the hilt. Then Blade spun around and triggered the first button again.

Behind him, one of Ellingson's vampire flunkies tried to duck as the knife sped towards him, but he wasn't quite quick enough. The sharpened chain wrapped itself around his throat like a whip and tight-ened, snapping taut. Blade gave the chain a casual tug, and the vampire's head detached as cleanly as if it had been removed by a surgeon. The stump glowed white hot, tendrils of fire racing downwards and set-ting the vampire's torso ablaze.

Without slowing, Blade kicked the twitching body over, sending bright orange sparks scattering across the parking lot. The vampire disintegrated in a cloud of fine white ash and was instantly whipped away by the wind. Then Blade triggered his knife again as the remaining two vampires advanced on him, one in front, one behind.

The knife hit the end of its chain and Blade jerked it upwards, whirling it over his head with a sound like a bullroarer. Blade swung the chain faster, eyeing up the two vampires. Then he suddenly dropped low on his haunches, whirling the chain downwards in a singing blur of silver.

The chain cut through the first vampire's legs, slicing through sinew and bone without so much as slowing. The hapless creature screamed as he tum-bled down onto the asphalt, his amputated legs imploding behind him in a burst of superheated ash. He reached out imploringly towards the other vampire, inadvertently betraying his position to Blade as he begged for help.

Before the second vampire could move, Blade whirled and thrust the silver knife backwards through the other vampire's abdomen, his movements fluid and unhurried. The creature didn't even have time to open his mouth to scream as the deadly white fire rushed through his body, chargrilling him from the inside out.

Blade retracted his knife with a flourish, straightened his leather duster and brushed some vampire ash off his sleeve. Third rule of the chase? Don't kid yourself that someone else will rescue you. Because usually, they won't, and then you'll look really stupid.

Not to mention dead.

Pausing only to decapitate the legless vampire with a casual swipe of his knife, Blade strode off to round up the other escapees.

Out on the main road, the surviving members of the vampire gang were several hundred yards away and accelerating fast. They cut across the traffic in a blare of horns, twisting the handle grips of their powerful motorbikes as they accelerated down an on-ramp onto the busy street below. The vampires didn't so much as glance back to see if their workmates had made it out alive. When it came to the crunch, it was every vampire for him- or herself. Only humans were stupid enough to go back and save their wounded, let alone stick together and try to fight.

Blade emerged from the car park entrance behind them, sprinting along the sidewalk in hot pursuit. Even on foot he moved at an incredible speed, faster than any human was able to run. He cut across a derelict gas station forecourt before charging out onto the concrete overpass, thundering along like a bull on steroids.

Through the darkened glass of his sunshades, Blade saw the vampires' bikes disappear out of sight as they left the main freeway. He gave a small grunt of annoyance, then touched a hand to the side of his head, where a tiny transparent receiver lay tucked behind his ear. He clicked it to transmit mode. "Whistler! I'm on the Stonebridge Overpass at Clemons."

The receiver cracked in response as the tinny voice of Whistler came over the earpiece. "Got it! Heading eastbound. I'm just beneath you..."

Blade leapt off the sidewalk and ran diagonally across the road. A passing car honked its horn and slewed wildly as Blade jumped onto the trunk, using the car as a moving springboard to launch himself up onto the safety rail of the overpass.

Crouching precariously on the narrow rail, Blade coolly scanned the traffic, apparently not bothered by the dizzying drop into three lanes of whizzing cars that lay before him. His eyes lit up as he saw a big-rig cab approaching, hauling a semi trailer behind it.

The cab thundered beneath the bridge, sounding its air-horn three times in rapid succession. Blade's mini-receiver crackled again. "*Go!*"

Without pause, Blade launched himself off the overpass.

Blade relaxed completely as he dropped, his long, leather coat streaming out behind him like great black wings. Time itself seemed to pause and he spread his arms slightly to steady his descent through the whistling wind.

Then the top of the moving trailer came sailing up to meet him in a rush of sound and color, and Blade expertly flipped his body over in the air, forcing himself to relax the muscles in his legs to avoid dislocating his knees on impact. He landed hard atop the semi, throwing out his arms to stabilize himself.

But despite his many years of training, Blade had misjudged the jump by a fraction of a second. He found himself tumbling forwards as the truck's momentum grabbed onto him like a giant hand, dragging him off his feet and sending him rolling over the edge of the rig.

Sheer instinct caused one of Blade's hands to snap upwards and snag one of the steel safety cables strung around the outside of the trailer roof. He jerked to a halt, hanging one-handed off the edge of the trailer. He dangled from the cable, breathing hard, and glanced fitfully down at the road flashing by beneath him. That could've been messy, he thought. Not for the first time that day, Blade was glad of the protection offered by his thick-cut leather gloves. The safety cable was strong, but it was also thin, and for the moment it was taking his entire bodyweight plus three dozen pounds of weaponry.

For one heart-hammering moment, Blade felt himself slipping as the strain of holding onto the thin wire made his hand cramp. He lunged upwards just in time and seized hold of the cable with his other hand, spreading his weight. Then he began swinging his body back and forth like a pendulum, ignoring the alarmed stares of passing motorists as he built up momentum. After the third swing, he tensed his heavily muscled arm and swung himself around the edge of the rig, right into the open back of the trailer.

Then he let go, vanishing inside.

A few seconds later there was a flash of flame in the darkness. The blast of an exhaust sounded from within its shadowy depths, followed a moment later by the roaring thunderclap of a high-performance engine turning over.

A midnight-black 1969 Dodge Charger rocketed out of the back of the trailer, sailing straight over the roof of a car full of aging boy racers who had been tail-gating the semi for the last few miles. The Charger landed hard in a spray of sparks, bounced once, and then accelerated, heading into three lanes of oncoming traffic at high speed. A cacophony of horns instantly blared out as the oncoming cars slewed and spun away, their drivers screaming abuse and making obscene gestures through their windows.

Inside the air-conditioned cool of the Charger, Blade calmly ramped down through the gears and hit the brakes, sending the battle-scarred car into a spin. He held on tightly as the car was buffeted around in a series of bone-jarring cracks and thumps, rebounding off cars in the surrounding lanes as they sped past him.

Now facing in the right direction, Blade touched the brake. Ignoring the frantic horn-blasts all around him, he glanced into the rear-view mirror to check his hair, and then put the pedal to the metal once more.

He had vampires to catch.

The Charger accelerated at breakneck speed, its dashboard-mounted tachometer redlining as Blade swiftly pulled alongside the big-rig. Up in the cab, a gray-bearded man with a weather-beaten face grinned down at him and tooted the horn, giving Blade a cheery little salute as he passed by.

Behind his sunshades, Blade's eyes creased briefly in amusement. He may be smiling now, but Whistler was going to kill him when he got a proper look at what he had just done to his car.

Shrugging, Blade reached between the seats. After only the briefest of pauses he activated the newly installed nitrous-oxide fuel-injection system.

Blade's trusty Charger had put up with a lot from him over the years, but even he had to admit that he was pushing his luck with this new gadget. Installing it had meant ripping out the ancient car's guts and replacing them with a fuel-delivery system that would make NASA green with envy, and easily get him banned from driving on every continent on Earth.

That was, if they could catch him.

The Charger shot forward with an ear-splitting whine as the nitrous injection system kicked in, boosting the car's engine by an extra three hundred horsepower. Flames belched from the exhaust pipe, quickly leaving Whistler and the enraged auto owners far behind him. In less than thirty seconds, Blade caught up with the vampire escapees and their modified motorbikes.

Stone and Campbell took one look at Blade's black Charger bearing down on them like an angel of death and drew their TEC-9 pistols. They opened fire, causing surrounding traffic to veer away in panic. Their bullets raked and sparked across the Charger, chewing up the bodywork and gouging long streaks in the paintwork. But the bulletproof windshield held, as did the Kevlar body panels protecting the fuel tank and engine.

Blade breathed a secret sigh of relief. Whistler had done yet another grand job.

He gave his car another jolt of nitrous fuel, homing in on the kill.

The Charger surged forward at breakneck speed, swiftly overtaking Stone and Campbell. The vampires immediately fell back, veering onto opposite sides of the lane in an attempt to split the target they presented. Their bikes growled in protest at the high-speed maneuver, forcing them to use every ounce of their superhuman strength and reflexes to keep the heavy bikes from flipping over and spinning off the road.

Blade had perhaps two seconds to decide on a course of action before the bikes were too far apart to catch. Timing was everything, especially where catching vampires was concerned. So he checked their position in the rearview mirror, and then slammed his booted foot onto the turbo-brakes.

The Charger bucked and skidded like a wild bronco as its speed dropped from a hundred miles per hour to less than fifty in a heartbeat. Blade casually crossed his arms over the padded steering wheel, narrowly avoiding smashing his face on the wheel as the momentum kicked his head forwards. Somehow, he kept in lane. A second later, the Charger rocked with the bone-shattering impact of two heavy-duty motorbikes rear-ending it. Glass and metal sprayed across the road as the riders were unceremoniously ejected over the handlebars of their bikes like crash-test dummies.

The appropriately named Stone flew through the air and smashed through Blade's back windshield, pulling the window frame into the car with him as he flew through like an unguided rocket, plunging headfirst into the front seat well. Campbell didn't fare much better, bouncing over Blade's roof and sliding down his front windshield in a rain of blood and glass. As he slid across the Charger's hood, he made a desperate grab for one of the windshield wipers, jerking himself to a spread-eagled halt across the front of the car.

Inside the Charger, Blade tightened his grip on the wheel and heaved a small, put-upon sigh. This was turning out to be a bitch of a day. Not only had he trashed his newly refitted auto in less than a minute, but now he had two new problems. One of them was currently wedged upside down in the front seat, howling for vengeance, and the other was stuck to his hood like a giant road kill, obscuring his vision and twisting one of his wipers into a completely unusable shape.

To make life even jollier, now he'd got windshield glass in his lap.

Trust him to wear his new leather pants today, of all days.

Blade instinctively ducked as one of Stone's steel-booted feet whistled over his head, then growled as a shard of glass dug painfully into his inner thigh. He glared at Stone as the vampire struggled to right himself, kicking and clawing in his frantic efforts to get free. This was no good. Blade locked one hand on the wheel, holding the speeding car steady as he reached quickly between the seats behind him. His fingers closed on the cold metal barrel of his twelve-gauge shotgun and he flipped the muzzle up towards the vampire, not really bothering to aim as he pulled the trigger.

The shot was deafening in the confined space, but it did the job. Stone shrieked and jerked in the seat as the silver-coated shotgun pellets penetrated his ribcage. His body ignited in a flash of blue and white fire and began to combust violently inside the car, the flames scorching the glass of the side window.

Shit. Blade thumped his hand on the wheel. Nice one.

Before Stone's body could turn into a cloud of interior-ruining ash, Blade hit the door auto-release button on the dash. The passenger door swung open, spilling the dying vampire out onto the road, right into the path of an oncoming bus. The bus jolted once, and Stone's remains were instantly pulverized, ground to dust beneath its wheels.

Back in the Charger, Blade slammed the door shut.

One down, one to go.

Blade turned his gaze back to Campbell, who had managed to pull himself up high enough to hook a hand under the air ducts at the top of the hood. The vampire began hammering away at the reinforced windshield with his other fist, trying to get into the car. Despite its toughness, the windshield was slowly developing spider-web cracks under the onslaught.

Speeding up, Blade swerved the car from side to side, trying to shake the crazed creature off, but it was no good. The vampire was holding onto the car as though superglued in place, like an ugly, bloody hood ornament.

There was a sudden burst of glass inside the car and a hole appeared in the windshield. Rearing backwards, Campbell punched his clawed hand further through and groped blindly for the steering wheel, smearing the inside of the glass with dark blood. Without missing a beat, Blade swung his shotgun up and shoved it back through the cracked glass, ramming the end into Campbell's snarling mouth.

Muttering an oath to the god of road safety, Blade pulled the trigger.

There was a loud *boom*, and the vampire's carbonized remains hit the windshield in a billowing black cloud, completely obscuring Blade's view.

Automatically, Blade hit the wipers. No good. The broken wiper flopped around uselessly, its servos wining as though in pain. Unable to see, Blade activated the washer jets and hopefully sprayed on some window cleaner. The vampire's remains instantly turned to a sticky black sludge, making his view even worse.

Blade swore.

Up ahead, the Eagle racer containing Gedge and his vampire buddy accelerated down the highway, weaving in and out of traffic. The driver thumped the wheel, whooping with the adrenaline rush of their getaway. Gedge sat back in his seat and fidgeted, glancing over his shoulder from time to time. He had heard enough about Blade to know that despite appearances, they weren't out of trouble yet.

In fact, they were probably driving deeper into it.

The hairs rose on the back of Gedge's neck as he saw the characteristic blunt-nosed shape of Blade's Charger edging through the traffic behind them. The car was badly damaged and covered in what looked like thick black mud, but it was accelerating fast, heading right for them.

Gedge cried out in alarm, alerting the driver, who leaned out of the Eagle's window and sighted his automatic pistol on the Charger. Aiming at Blade's cracked front windshield, he squeezed off a couple of rounds. The slugs tore into Blade's car, completely shattering the weakened front windshield, which exploded inwards in a burst of safety-glass nuggets.

Blade ducked down as the glass flew into the car around him, embedding itself into the worn leather of the seats. He straightened and reached out for the dash, hitting a blue button marked "UV." There was a whirring sound as a bank of high-powered ultraviolet spotlights folded out of the top of the Charger's roof. Swiveling in their mounts, they hummed for a moment, warming up. Then they clicked on, bathing the car ahead and its vampire driver with a lethal wash of ultraviolet light.

The Eagle's driver was caught by the full force of Blade's UV Day Lights. He screamed and threw an arm across his face in a frantic attempt to shield himself, but he was too late. His exposed skin stiffened and cracked apart like sun-dried leather, and his clothing caught light as flames belched out of the bone-deep cracks in his flesh. The fire burned furiously for a moment, then snuffed out as his entire body froze into a statue of solidified ash.

An instant later the car jolted over a pothole, jarring the vampire driver's charred carcass. It fell forwards and burst apart, showering messily across the seats. Driverless, the Eagle slewed to one side, out of control.

Gritting his teeth, Gedge scrambled over into the drivers seat and grabbed the wheel, wincing as hot vampire embers cracked and popped like bubble-wrap on the seat beneath him. The air in the car reeked of burnt cat hair and sulfur. Gedge wrinkled his nose in disgust. He grabbed at the steering wheel in panic as the Eagle rocked with a bruising side impact.

He glanced out of his side window in panic. The Daywalker was ramming his car! Was he insane? He would kill them both at this speed!

Over in the Charger, Blade adjusted his mirror, then rammed the Eagle again. The two cars ground together in a blaze of sparks, before disengaging once more. Unrelenting, Blade twisted his steering wheel a third time, giving the Eagle another bone-jarring slam, trying to force it off the road.

That did the trick. The Eagle lurched sideways as Gedge lost control of the vehicle. The steering wheel ripped itself from his hands as the car's wheels locked hard to the right, sideswiping several parked cars before running up a builder's ramp and launching itself off the top of a cement parking barrier. The ruined car flew through the night air, engine revving as its wheels spun in empty space. It came back down to earth with a thunderous crunch, smacking down hard on its roof and riding halfway up onto the busy sidewalk.

Its weight and momentum carried it along the sidewalk for several dozen yards, smashing through telegraph poles and newspaper vending machines as it went. Tourists out enjoying the night air dived for cover as the car headed on towards a sidewalk market. Tables piled high with cheap goods went flying as the Eagle skidded onwards, rolling over onto its side as it went.

Finally, its mangled front end hit an iron streetlight, bringing it to an abrupt and noisy halt. The streetlamp creaked alarmingly and crashed down across the wreck with an air of finality.

As the dust settled, the street slowly came back to life. Bystanders emerged from their hiding places and gathered around the smoking wreck, murmuring amongst themselves in shock and concern. At the bus stop, someone dialed 911. The bystanders respectfully kept their distance, fearing the worst.

Then a collective gasp went up as the Eagle's door slowly opened, now facing skyward. Gedge winced as he dragged himself from the tangled remains of the street racer, ignoring the bystanders. He was bloodied and bruised, but alive.

Using the car as support, he pulled himself to his feet and stood swaying for a moment, then reached back determinedly into the wreck. With some difficulty, he opened the upended glove compartment and pulled out a silver pistol. He clicked off the safety catch and threw a hunted glance over his shoulder, then limped away down the street. The crowd parted around him like the Red Sea.

Blade's Charger pulled up to the curb ahead of him and creaked to a halt, its engine making plinking noises from the heat of the chase. As one, the gathered crowd's eyes turned to the tall, dark figure as he stepped out of the semi-destroyed car, shotgun in hand.

The bystanders put two and two together and started to fall back; a mother screamed as she picked up her toddler and ran for safety. Blade ignored them completely. What was about to happen would make no sense to any of them, even if they saw it happen right under their noses: he would chase and shoot the vampire, who would explode into dust and vanish, leaving no trace of his existence behind.

It was handy, that. Blade had seen it happen a thousand times, and never failed to appreciate the convenience.

Then, after he had gone and the initial shock had worn off, people would decide that they had seen a practical joke, maybe an elaborate prank set up by some trashy live TV show. Within the space of a day, they would've forgotten about it.

Blade smiled grimly to himself as he strode towards the fleeing figure of Gedge. Humans would always see what they wanted to see, and no amount of logic or plain old-fashioned common sense could persuade them otherwise, including the evidence of their own eyes. It was regrettable that he had an audience, but it was his duty to finish the job. If so much as a single vampire escaped today's carnage, he might warn the others who were next on his hit list, blowing his hard-won advantage.

Blade lifted his shotgun, revealing a new modification—a rapid-fire stake launcher welded to the underside of the barrel. It was one of Whistler's latest experiments and Blade was keen to test it. Before anyone in the crowd could draw breath to scream he had sighted on the battered figure of Gedge and squeezed the trigger.

A silver stake shot from the launcher in a jet of CO_2 gas and struck the fleeing figure in the back, knocking him sprawling onto the street. Gedge's pistol flew out of his hand, spinning off into the gutter. The bystanders screamed and began to fall back, diving for cover as Blade strode towards the prone figure lying in the dust.

In the distance, there was the sound of wailing police sirens, but Blade paid them no heed. He would be gone before they got close enough to see him.

Right now, he had a job to finish.

Gedge stared up at the dark figure of Blade looming above him, and was suddenly very still. Of all the ways Gedge had pictured himself dying over the years, this wasn't among them. He'd always wanted to go out in the heat of the battle, surrounded by beautiful vampire babes dressed in skin-hugging black PVC, all of whom would gladly devote the rest of their lives to avenging his noble death.

But at the same time, Gedge found a small amount of comfort in the fact that his death wouldn't be completely meaningless. After all, he was making the ultimate sacrifice, dying so that others might live, and so bringing the long journey of his life full circle.

It was just a shame that the guy who was about to kill him was wearing leather pants.

Blade looked down at Gedge, puzzled. The vampire was still alive. And what's more, he was laughing. Why?

Gedge flashed his fangs at Blade in a token gesture of defiance, and choked back a bout of hysterical laughter as his lungs began to fill with blood.

Blade crouched before Gedge, staring down at him in the manor of a cat watching a toad. "I staked you with silver. Why aren't you ash?"

Gedge began coughing violently, blood welling from his mouth as he struggled to speak around his ruptured insides. "Why aren't you smarter?" he hissed. He reached into his mouth and tugged at his fangs.

They came away in his hand. They were fake, prosthetic.

"Not a vampire, dumbshit... Set your sorry ass up." Gedge looked up past Blade and flashed an insane grin at something behind him. Then his eyes widened and he slumped backwards, letting out his last breath in a rattling wheeze.

A feeling of uneasiness stole over Blade. Unwillingly, he turned and peered upwards into the darkness. A large residential block lay behind him, its front crisscrossed with iron walkways. The roof was easily accessible and offered a perfect view of the whole scene.

Blade saw a dark figure perched there, female, hungry-looking.

Watching him.

As the figure felt Blade's eyes on her, she unhurriedly stepped backwards and vanished into the shadows.

A sudden blare of sirens drew Blade's attention away from the mysterious figure, away from the dead human at his feet and the fleeing crowds, to the end of the street. The road was jammed with a solid wall of police cars advancing up the road towards him. The authorities had arrived in full force, and, for once, they were going to have some hard evidence to play with.

Blade rose to his feet like a ghost and pelted across the sidewalk to where the wreck of his Charger sat waiting. Jumping in, he gunned the engine and pulled out with a screech of tires. As the police cars closed in on him, he engaged the nitrous drive and accelerated off down the street into the darkness, desperate to get away from the mess he had made.

For the first time in his life, Blade found he hadn't a clue what to do next.

An hour later, in the high-rise comfort of the Phoenix Towers, Danica closed the door behind her and slipped a digital videotape into her slimline silver player. Sitting back onto her velvet-clad haunches, she pressed the play button on the machine.

A grainy image of Blade confronting Gedge flickered up onto the screen, filmed from a high angle. Danica's lips curved upwards into a smile as she watched the ensuing chaos unfold on screen.

Perfect.

She had the Daywalking freak now.

TWO

It was bitterly cold down at the docks. The wind whipped through Grimwood's close-cropped hair as he stood there, hands on hips, watching his vampire crew unload Danica's precious cargo from the belly of the ship. Heavy chains clanked and rattled across the wooden decking as winches were set up, double-tested and locked down into place. The night air rang with the crew's shouts as they manhandled the heavy steel box into position, slipping and sliding on the wet metal of the cargo hold.

Grimwood raised his cigarette to his lips, pulling the hot smoke deep into his lungs. He felt a warm rush as the smoke heated his cold insides. When he had been a human, Grimwood had been a thirty-a-day smoker. Now he was a vampire, he could easily smoke that many in an hour.

Asher materialized beside Grimwood, his colorless eyes narrowing with worry as he surveyed the scene before him. "Is he secure?"

"In that thing?" Grimwood gave a humorless snort. "About as secure as my dick. Just listen to him."

Asher was trying very hard not to listen. A restless growling came from within the six foot-high box, punctuated by a periodic hissing and clicking. Every few minutes there would be the sound of movement from within, a very definite scrape of claws as the box's inmate shifted around, moving restlessly from one corner of the crate to the other.

Asher watched warily as the vampire crew guided the chains down from a nearby winch truck and fastened them onto the giant hooks welded to all four corners of the crate. With an electronic whirr, the winch took up the slack, hoisting the steel box high up into the air on the end of its crane arm. Asher held his breath as the box lifted up out of the hold and swung slowly towards the dockside, where a large army truck lay waiting, surrounded by half a dozen human dockworkers. A mistake now would cost them all dearly, especially since Danica had entrusted the transportation of their living cargo to him. If he managed to screw this little job up, his fate when he returned home didn't bear thinking about.

Grimwood gave a hacking cough and Asher glanced at him in irritation. Thin streams of smoke were seeping through the big vampire's armored combat top, as though he were a giant colander. Asher grimaced and waved the smoke away from his face like an irked diner at a restaurant. "Can't you get that looked at?"

"Way ahead of you." Grimwood lifted up his armor, exposing his muscular tattooed stomach. A neat line of stitches covered by silver duct-tape strips bisected his midriff, which was covered in bone-deep bloody gouges. "I think I'm allergic to this stuff." He scratched helplessly, causing a fresh burst of pressurized smoke to vent from beneath one of the duct-tape strips.

"So don't scratch." Asher impatiently turned his attention back to the swinging box, ignoring Grimwood's grumblings. He still couldn't believe that they were actually going through with this screwball mission. He studied the box carefully, hoping that it was strong enough. The giant metal crate was almost featureless, save a small trapdoor set into the side. The trapdoor was about two feet square and had a small viewing slot at the top, about the size and shape of a letterbox. Three-inch-thick bars were welded over the top of the trapdoor, sealing it shut.

Asher stared up through the bars, but nothing was visible on the other side.

In fact, their captive had gone very quiet.

Asher listened carefully. Even with his superb vampire hearing, he couldn't make out any sounds over the rush of the sea and the mechanical whirring of the winch. He plunged his hands into his pockets and rocked back onto his heels, praying that this would all be over with as soon as possible. That thing in the box gave him the creeps.

"Where's Dan got to?" he asked, trying to keep the irritation out of his voice.

"She's gone home. Said she wanted to take a shower, wash all that blood off." Grimwood sniggered. "Damn waste, if you ask me..." He licked his lips, eyes glinting with mirth.

Asher swung around and gave Grimwood a hard stare. The big vampire returned his gaze impassively, puffing on his cigarette, the sodium deck spotlights glinting off his stainless steel incisors. Grimwood had lost his fangs two years ago while defending Danica against armed intruders, and he had been insufferable ever since. This latest victory was only going to make him worse.

Asher stepped closer to Grimwood. "Listen, you Neanderthal..." he began, then paused.

Grimwood bristled. "What the fuck are you—"

"Shhh!" Asher silenced him, listening. Seeing the expression on his face, the big vampire glowered and fell silent.

After a moment, they both heard the noise. A muffled, metallic scrape drifted through the night air, almost like someone sharpening a knife on flint.

It was coming from inside the crate.

As one, they turned and stared at the giant metal box as it slowly moved towards the edge of the cargo hold. Was it their imagination, or was it tilting slightly to one side...?

Clang! The box suddenly jerked forwards so hard it was as though an invisible tanker had rammed it from behind. As the vampire crew sprang to their feet, shouting, the box jumped again, so violently this time that it flipped up fully ninety degrees into the air. Its chains coiled around it as it swung upwards, then pitched back down again with a groan as gravity reclaimed it. One of the winch chains snapped under the sudden weight and the box pulled heavily to one side, swinging like a seesaw.

"What the hell?" Asher ran forwards, followed by Grimwood. Down below, the winch truck driver yelled as his vehicle spun around out of control, tipped up onto its front wheels by the violently shifting weight.

"Help him!" Asher shoved Grimwood towards the crane.

Grimwood didn't need to be told twice. He ran up behind the stricken vehicle and leaped upwards, grabbing hold of the back of the cab. Grunting with effort, he flexed his enormous muscles and slowly pulled the truck's spinning back wheels down onto the ground, the whole rig creaking under the strain. Keeping the truck secure with one hand, Grimwood ripped a length of tow chain out of the back of the vehicle and secured it to a cast iron anchor post nearby.

Sweating, he wiped the oil off his hands and turned to Asher, who was barking orders into a slimline walkie-talkie. They both watched as the vampire crew swarmed across the boarding walkway and began throwing ropes over the box from the shore, guiding it over the gap. Down below, the water boiled and foamed in the ten-foot space between the cargo ship and the asphalt of the dock.

What had Danica said about crossing running water? Grimwood cast his mind back guiltily over the weeks that had preceded their expedition. There had been a lot of research and training to prepare for this mission, mainly organized by Danica. He hadn't taken in half the stuff she'd told him, purely because he thought she'd been joking.

There was a furious screech from inside the box as it swung across the last few feet of water. Chains rattled as the crate was pounded back and forth from within, ripping the guide ropes from the vampires' hands, sending several of the crew tumbling into the ocean. Grimwood gave a shout of alarm as a second chain snapped. One end of the crate plunged downwards, scraping sparks as it smacked down onto the metal-edged platform of the docking bay.

Up above, the winch cable squealed with the strain of supporting the unevenly distributed load. The crate hung at forty-five degrees from its last two chains, the lowest corner buried in the soft metal of the platform. Smoke poured from the winch truck's motor as it revved frantically, trying to pull the crate back up into the air. But the edge of the crate was solidly embedded in the platform, and wouldn't budge.

The box jolted again and again as its enraged occupant tried to smash through the steel trapdoor, plowing the crate deeper and deeper into the lip of the dock. The air rang with a flurry of metallic-sounding blows as giant welts and cracks appeared in the wall of the crate. A moment later, the crew jumped back as a sudden explosion of flying bolts and rivets ran along the edge of the dock like aerial dominos. The cheap metal that lined the edge of the platform was beginning to give way under the weight of the crate. As the vampires watched helplessly, the entire front of the platform separated from the dock and began to tip forwards into the sea, taking the crate with it.

Without hesitation, Grimwood ran towards the winch truck. Bodily dragging the driver out, Grimwood jumped into the cab and disengaged the towline. Then he slammed the whole rig into reverse. The vehicle's tires skidded on the wet asphalt as they fought to get a grip, the arm of the crane creaking alarmingly under the strain.

Inch by painful inch, the crane moved backwards, dragging the crate up onto the platform.

When the whole thing was safely back on solid ground, Grimwood shut off the engine of the winch truck and jumped down from the cab. He watched as the vampire crew descended on the box, hurriedly climbing on top of it to detach the hoist chains.

Asher jogged up to him, looking even paler than usual. "Well," he said, "that was entertaining."

Grimwood glowered at him, and then turned to cast a wary gaze over the upended crate. A wrathful growl came from within, pitched somewhere between that of a yowling big cat and the deep bass snarl of a bear.

"I think he's pissed at us." Asher's voice sounded very small.

"Really? You think?" Grimwood dismissed Asher with a glare and stalked over to help the crew secure the crate and check it for damage. Thankfully, the steel walls were intact.

Grimwood ran a hand over the damp metal of the crate. Wouldn't like to be here if that thing got out, he thought. He scratched idly at his wounds, reaching up under his flak jacket to peel the itching strips of silver tape from his skin. His bout of exertion had made him tear all his stitches and blood was running down his stomach and soaking into the top of his jeans.

As he tried to mop it up, there was a shrill scream from behind him. Grimwood spun around to see one of the vampire crew thrashing around on top of the box, clutching at his leg. A muscular arm was sticking out through the barred viewing slot, its clawed hand clamped immovably around the ankle of the vampire.

"You gotta be kidding me!" Grimwood stared up at the arm. It was covered in what looked like scales and spurs, like a lizard.

As Grimwood watched, the arm's owner tightened its grip. The crack of bone breaking was audible even above the shrieks of the crew member, who blanched and began frantically tugging at the hand. Even with all his preternatural strength, the vampire couldn't pull himself free.

Grimwood began backing away as the thing in the crate pushed a second hand up through the slot and began yanking on it, working the welded trapdoor back and forth with animal savagery. The hinges gave way with a shriek of tortured metal and the whole thing vanished into the darkness of the box, leaving just the bars behind. The crew member paled as he looked down at what lay beneath him and renewed his frantic efforts to break free.

The rest of the crew dropped their ropes and began edging away. They weren't being paid enough to deal with this kind of crap. Grimwood shouted at them but, one by one, they turned tail and ran for the safety of the dockyard.

Grimwood turned to Asher who was cowering behind one of the anchor posts. He gave a mock bow and swept a hand up towards the struggling crew member. "Your call, Nancy boy."

Asher stared at Grimwood for a moment, then gave a small growl in the back of his throat and vaulted up onto the top of the crate. Why did everything have to be a competition with Grimwood? He'd show him.

Asher began striding across the metal towards where the thrashing vampire lay.

As he approached, he saw the scaled hand come up through the bars and grab hold of the crew member's other foot. Before the vampire could draw breath to yell, the creature yanked him downwards, hard.

Asher flinched backwards as a spray of blood flew through the air. The sheer force of the creature's tug had pulled the crew member down into the crate, the bars slicing him in two from groin to shoulder, like a stalk of celery being pulled through a kitchen slicer.

There was a clang as the vampire's head jammed between the two bars. An impatient noise came from down below and the diced body was pushed up slightly through the bars, olny to be yanked downwards again, tearing the head off and sending it tumbling off the edge of the crate. It rolled towards the edge of the docks and dropped into the water with a small, sad splash.

Wincing, Asher backed off and looked down at Grimwood, who was puffing away on another of his evil cigarettes, a look of infinite satisfaction on his face. He blew a puff of smoke out in Asher's direction, raising a sarcastic eyebrow. "Don't tell me. You forgot to feed him?"

Asher wiped the vampire's blood from his own face and jumped down off the edge of the crate, trying not to listen to the hungry, wet noises coming from within. He walked stiffly over to join Grimwood, too sickened to think of a reply. Together, the two vampires leaned back against the dock wall and stared at the crate.

"Do you really think it's him?" Asher was the first to break the long silence.

Grimwood snorted. "Let's hope so. Because if it's not, he's sleeping in your room tonight."

Asher gave a ghost of a smile. Then he turned and gazed up thoughtfully at the crate. He drew in a deep breath, steeling himself for the ordeal that lay ahead. He only hoped Danica knew what she was doing...

Twelve hours later, Danica moved soundlessly down the corridor of the high-rise Phoenix Towers, her heels clicking lightly on the marble tiling. Her eyes were set straight ahead, her jaw clenched with determination. It was dark in the hallway, but Danica had no need for lighting.

The hallway she walked along was of a high-tech, ultra-modern design, lined with glass and sanded steel. Its metal arcs and intertwined stone support columns screamed with architectural cleverness, as the architect himself had done when his vampire clients found they had no further use for him. There were no windows, no way of telling whether it was day or night. The only lighting came from bowl-shaped chromed lights that hung from woven steel cables overhead, creating intermittent pools of light and dark along the hallway.

As Danica walked, a cloud of delicate perfume trailed out behind her like a luxurious silk scarf. She had spent a good hour beforehand in her luxurious bathroom, styling her glossy black hair and applying subtle touches of make-up to her perfectly sculpted cheekbones to create a look of radiant professionalism.

She was in a position of great power—the ambassador for her entire race—and it was only fitting that she was thoroughly prepared. It was just a shame that she had burnt herself on her last cigarette, her trembling fingers betraying her as she had a quick smoke on the balcony beforehand to calm her nerves.

Danica smoothed down her tailored clothing as she walked, trying to project her trademark air of self-assurance and arrogance. She smiled slightly at her own fears. This should be no different to the dozens of interviews she conducted on a daily basis. It was a perfectly straightforward procedure. She had her agenda, and her prison... no, her interviewee had theirs. It was Danica's job to make sure that their two points of view coincided.

But deep down she knew that this was a meeting of an altogether different kind, and despite her usually rigid self-control, Danica was sweating.

Reaching the end of the corridor, Danica nodded to the imposing-looking soldiers who stood on guard nearby, clutching automatic rifles. A few feet away, Asher, Grimwood and a young female vampire named Virago were silently gathered by the colossal titanium vault door, waiting for her.

As far as it was possible for vampires to look nervous, they did.

Danica joined the trio with the briefest of nods, and turned to study a large video monitor that showed a thermal view of the interior of the vault. The enormous, lead-lined room was in total darkness. Through the optically enhanced camera, it was just possible to make out a shadowy figure sitting hunched in the corner of the room. Danica licked her suddenly dry lips and turned to Asher, fixing her brother with a sharp look. "What's he been doing?"

"Nothing." Asher spoke without looking up, his dark eyes glued to the screen. "Just been sitting there since we bought him in."

Virago cleared her throat and spoke up. "Do you think we've got enough security?" The pretty young vampire couldn't keep the tremor out of her voice. She lapsed back into an uncomfortable silence.

Danica didn't take her eyes off the monitor. "Virago, if he wanted out of there, there isn't an army in the world that could keep us safe." She turned up the contrast on the monitor, sharpening the image. "We didn't capture him. He allowed us to take him in." She took a deep breath, letting her words sink in. "You understand?"

There was no reply. The air around them seemed to get a little colder.

Danica nodded to the door, steeling herself. "Now open up."

The other three vampires stared at her. They hadn't thought that Danica would actually go through with this. Asher glanced at his sister, a worried frown on his face. She seemed perfectly relaxed. He had suggested to her earlier that perhaps Grimwood should be the first one to make contact with their guest. Obviously, she hadn't listened to a word he'd said.

But then, that was nothing new.

After the briefest of pauses, Danica calmly reached out and placed her manicured hand on the biometric scanner located nearby. After sharing a nervous look with the others, Virago stepped up to the computer console and quickly keyed in a series of commands.

There was the whirring of hidden machinery as the vault doors opened with a hum, revealing a darkened airlock-style vestibule that wouldn't have looked out of place on a spaceship.

Danica stepped inside. Virago hit a second button on the keypad, and the vault doors slid shut behind her with a hollow metallic boom.

Inside the vestibule, Danica's apparent composure vanished. She stared quickly down at the floor and took a shaky breath to steady her nerves. A series of air-blowers hummed into action around her, cycling the air in the lock and sending a cold draft down the back of her neck. She listened to the sound of dead-locks clunking into place behind her, and a chill stole over her that had nothing to do with the air conditioning. This was the moment she had been dreaming of—and having nightmares about—for the last three years. All her planning and dreaming had finally come together.

Now that the moment of truth had finally arrived, she found herself wishing desperately that it hadn't. One of Danica's hands clenched into a tight ball and she dug a freshly painted fingernail into the flesh of her palm, drawing blood as the second set of airlock doors slid smoothly aside into darkness.

Inside the vault there was no light. Nothing broke the deathly blackness. Danica could see very well in the dark, but in here, there wasn't even a glimmer of light for her eyes to work with. Closing her eyes was exactly the same as having them open.

It was unnerving.

Danica shook herself, trying to remain calm.

The silence was oppressive, and Danica's stress-induced breathing echoed loudly in her ears as she blinked rapidly in the darkness, trying to adjust. She found herself wishing desperately for shadows, just to give her eyes something to hold on to. She could cope with shadows. Here, there was just blackness. As far as she knew, she could be dead already and not know it.

"Why have you woken me?"

Danica jumped as a voice rang out like a shot in the night. The voice was a deep bass, low and rumbling, laced through with an ominous gravity.

Danica froze, fighting the sudden instinct to turn and run. Instead, she cleared her throat, willing her voice to remain steady. "Your people need you, sir."

Even to her own ears, her voice sounded weak and insubstantial, and she hated herself for it. Screwing up her nerves, she took a couple of steps forward, moving towards the sound of the voice, then carefully knelt down on the floor and bowed her head in the time-honored vampire posture of subservience. She knew that the others would tease her for this later if she survived, but knew that it was necessary.

After all, this was business.

Of a kind.

"My people?" This time, the voice was mocking. Danica flinched. There was a pause as the speaker mulled this over. "You think I'm your messiah? Your savior?"

There was a rustling sound in the darkness and Danica's survival instincts forced her to look up, although the rest of her remained rooted to the spot. A pair of red eyes opened above her and pierced the gloom, glowing with an internal phosphorescence. Their hellish glow illuminated the chamber and lit up the thing that stood before her.

Danica swallowed, fighting the urge to run. The half-light made what she saw all the more terrifying.

The creature sneered, its claws clacking on the steel tiles as it moved towards Danica's cowering form. "And what makes you think that I wanted to be brought back?"

An armored hand emerged from the darkness and reached downwards, spot-lit by the dim, red glow of the thing's eyes. It took all Danica's years of combat training to keep her from leaping to her feet, running across the chamber and scrabbling hopelessly at the reinforced door, screaming like a banshee. She forced herself not to flinch as a taloned finger reached out and brushed lightly against her throat. She stared straight ahead, chin up. "Times have changed. Science has made great strides—"

The thing above her made a dismissive sound, but Danica carried on, her voice growing stronger, more resolute. There was no going back now. "Your blood—the sacrament you provide... It can set us free now."

"I see." The tone of silence made it painfully clear that the speaker did not. "And the ones I killed earlier? They were vampire?"

Danica nodded, trying to burn the memories from her mind.

The creature made a rumbling sound that may or may not have been an attempt at laughter. "You must forgive me. It has been centuries since I last fed."

Danica drew another deep breath, clenching her fists. "I understand."

The creature's finger traced a pattern over the skin of Danica's throat and then brushed upwards to hook under her chin and tilt her head up. Danica was sure she felt scales on the underside of the bony digit. She shivered.

There was a movement in the blackness above her and the creature tightened its grip on Danica's chin. "Then offer yourself to me, child, and let me quench my thirst again."

Outside the reinforced door, Asher was growing restless. Danica had been inside for over ten minutes now and showed no sign of emerging. The monitor was on, but Danica hadn't moved from the doorway, which was right underneath the thermal security camera. The creature had gone over to meet her, and now neither of them was visible.

Asher found that he was pacing as his mind went into overdrive. He couldn't believe that he'd let his own sister go in there with that thing.

But then that was just typical of her. Danica had always been the reckless one in their family, despite all of his attempts to teach her otherwise. While he was content to simply sit back and let things happen, in their own time and at their own pace, Danica would always be the one rushing in there, guns blazing, trying to outdo everyone else before someone else stole the chance to be a hero from her.

That was how this whole thing had started. Not content with the power and prestige she already enjoyed, she had decided to go one further, by bringing him back.

Just because she could.

She said that she wanted to save their race, but Asher knew her better than that. She was doing it because there was no longer anyone around to stop her.

When the state council of the Vampire Nation had been destroyed by the bastard Daywalker three years ago, Danica had been waiting in the shadows, ready to seize power from the few remaining Purebloods left alive. The half-breed daughter of one of the vampire guards, she had long awaited the opportunity to rise above her lowly status and exact revenge on the stuffy, institutionalized joke that the Vampire Nation had become.

The Daywalker's attack had given her that chance. Asher remembered how his sister had rallied the guards in the aftermath of the attack and thrown the few surviving council members out onto the street. She had taken over what remained of the building, including all their assets and employees. Her discovery of the charred remains of the Book of Erebus—the vampire bible—down in the burned-out basement had been completely irrelevant to her, until Asher had deciphered one of the scraps out of curiosity.

Danica had immediately seized on the information it contained and ordered him to decode every last fragment left unburned. For here was a chance for her to thumb her nose at everything the council had stood for—keeping the Old Ways going and staying hidden, away from the prying eyes of the lowly humans. What good had this ever done the vampire race, apart from keeping them alive, one miserable day at a time?

This wasn't good enough for Danica. As well as staying alive, she had wanted to live. She dreamed of walking out into the sunlight, surrounded by cheering parades of worshipful subjects, finally freed from their night-dwelling curse.

And so her obsession had begun with unraveling the secrets of the origin of the vampire race, with the end goal of restoring them to their former glory. This fixation of hers had dragged them all to the four corners of the globe, from America to Africa, down through Europe and Asia and back again. Their three-year mission had finally ended in the Iraqi desert, in blood and death, and the discovery of that thing that now sat in the vault.

Asher shivered. This time, Danica truly had gone too far. Disturbing the tomb of one of the Ancients was sacrilege, even by a vampire's standards, and they didn't come much older than this.

He cast a nervous glance towards the vault door. If that monster in there was their salvation, he wanted nothing more to do with it. He had half a mind to lock the doors and leave the two of them in there to fight it out between them. Danica was hopelessly out of her depth and she was too stubborn to admit it.

Asher tried not to imagine what he'd have to do if anything had happened to her...

The vault doors slid smoothly open and Danica stumbled out, all but falling into her brother's arms. Her skin was bone white and there were fresh bite marks on her throat and shoulders, the blood staining her silk top in red rivers.

"Danica!" Asher tightened his arms around her as his sister's legs gave way. "Are you alright?" He knew this had been a bad idea. He reached for his gun, but Danica put her hand on his, shaking, struggling to recompose herself.

"Let him out. He wants to see what's become of his world."

THREE

THREE

Bently Tittle, the famous talk-show host, was having a good day. Not only had his third wife finally come through with the divorce papers three minutes before he was due to go on the air, but his producer had once again struck gold in his quest for the most ridiculous discussion topics America could produce.

Bently and his producer had been working on the show together for over eight years now, and had long since tired of the old TV mantra of informing, educating and entertaining with their material. Now, they picked their guests based on a sliding points scale, chosen purely to generate the greatest in-house amusement value for the least amount of cash.

Today, they were both in for a treat. Bently had a little bet with the lighting director that meant that if these guys came through, he could be looking at an extra couple of days in the sun this Christmas.

He rubbed his hands together while jacking up his trademark extra-wide TV smile. The darkened studio around him bustled with activity as the crew prepared to run the first take, checking equipment and switching on monitors. The darkened space in front of him was filled with a din of shouting voices and the clank of heavy machinery being dragged into place. Down in the pit, a power cable shorted out in a fizz of blue sparks as one of the camera guys ran their tracks over it. In the background, there was a strangled scream followed by a thumping sound, which indicated that the studio manager was well into the second phase of his daily nervous breakdown.

Bently sniffed, fixing the cowering cameraman with a look of faint contempt. They were like ants, the lot of them, running around doing a fat lot of nothing to pretend they were actually earning their salaries. When one of them dropped out, babbling a load of nonsense about exhaustion, another would swiftly pop up in their place like a dandelion, quietly taking over as though they had never existed in the first place. Bently had long ago stopped trying to learn anyone's name. He and the producer were obviously the only ones who ever pulled their weight around here.

Bently yawned and ran a manicured hand through his perfect hair. Then he glanced over to where the new intern girl was crouched down behind the Steadicam operator, gazing up at him with a rapt look that combined hero worship with professional hunger. Her name was Suzi, or possibly Sally... Ah, what did it matter?

He eyed her for a moment, then pulled a sheaf of interview notes off the table, toying with the paper-clip that held them together. Whatever her name was, the girl was a real stunner. He'd heard that her father owned almost as much prime real estate as a certain well-known hamburger chain. It was clearly a short-term partnership made in heaven.

Bently beamed benignly down at Suzi, mentally working out the fiendishly difficult logistics that would allow him to finish this show in record time and have her up against the wall of his trailer before they'd finished rolling the credits. It would be tricky getting her past security, but hell, what else was there to do in this dump?

Bently sighed, his mind awash with a mental three-reeler of private porno images. He was so engrossed in his fantasy that he barely noticed the young Mexican guy to his right counting him in.

Then the lights hit him and Bently cleared his throat, blinking the fog from his eyes. He beamed at the camera, trying to project the warmth and cloying sincerity that had landed him the job in the first place. Ten years ago he had embraced his work wholeheartedly, swimming through show after show driven by a genuine enjoyment of his job and an urge to entertain the world, making it a better place in some small way.

Now, the mere act of smiling at the camera made him want to smash his head against the cheap Plexi-glas tables before whipping out his mini Glock pistol to gun down the entire sound crew in a blaze of crackling flames, laughing like a maniac as the whole studio burned to the ground around him...

Bently swallowed, his throat suddenly dry. The effects of his prescription-only pills must be wearing off. But before he could reach into his pocket for another dose, the show's title music boomed over the studio PA.

He was on.

Bently picked up his papers and ruffled them in what he hoped was an earnest fashion, a huge glassy smile plastered across his face. "Tonight, we interview Doctor Edgar Vance, forensic psychiatrist and author of the New York bestseller *Human Health: The Whole-Being Breakthrough.*"

Ignoring the muffled snigger from one of the lighting crew—and making a mental note to get him fired at the earliest opportunity—Bently smoothly turned to the second camera and went on. "Also joining us tonight is Martin Vreede, Chief of Police. They're here for an hour and they'll take your calls— next on Bently Tittle Live."

Bently sat back in his leather upholstered executive chair and beamed at the man sitting opposite him. Edgar Vance was in his early forties, with the kind of well-scrubbed good looks that only a six-figure salary and regular visits from a female colonic irrigationist could achieve.

Edgar smiled back, almost matching Bently's oral wattage, mentally hearing the soft rustle of dollar bills cascading into his bank account. He had agreed to do this show on the condition that he received sole merchandising rights to this episode. He had a six-man team printing up the video dust jackets at that moment.

He hoped that his mother was watching this. If not, he would sell her a copy at the first opportunity.

Bently steepled his fingers as the music faded out into a burst of canned applause. "Doctor Vance—

you're a psychiatrist and a biochemist, isn't that right?"

Vance nodded. "That's correct." He shifted in his chair, trying to ensure the lighting hit his face consistently, without creating any ugly shadows. "I've long believed that in order to achieve true health, we have to reconcile the body and the mind." He paused, directing his magnetic gaze straight into the camera. "Of course, that also requires letting go of a lot of old notions and superstitions, which is what my work is all about."

Bently nodded smoothly, his mind still preoccupied with an onslaught of sensual images involving young Suzi and a very large jar of chocolate spread. "Let's talk about that. How do you account for the fascination with things that go bump in the night? Movies, books, videogames—seems like we can't get enough of our bogeymen."

Vance untwined his fingers and leaned forward, skillfully playing to the cameras. "Monsters provide a means for us to transfer our darker and more primal urges onto something external." He looked up as the camera zoomed on his face, warming to his subject. "In the case of vampires, you're dealing with taboo issues like predatory rage and sexual sadism. These are scary subjects for people to own up to."

"So we pass the buck to someone else?"

"Exactly. Historically, people suffering from medical conditions have always been our psychological scapegoats. In the middle ages, schizophrenia was often attributed to demonic possession."

"And vampires?"

"Well, there's a hereditary blood disease known as porphyria that has symptoms remarkably similar to the classic vampiric traits. People suffering from this disease are anemic. They become sensitive to sunlight, they can't tolerate garlic—"

"Which is too bad, since my doctor tells me that it's good for the heart." Bently gave a little stage laugh, then coughed his way into silence. Ignoring Edgar's look of intense annoyance, Bently turned to the video-screens above them. A red light blinked on as Chief Martin Vreede flashed up onto the giant plasma screen TV, joining them via a remote feed. "Chief Vreede? What's your take on all the recent rumors we've been hearing about vampires?"

Chief Vreede chuckled. Although square-jawed, the man was a little less good looking than Vance, which was probably why he hadn't been invited onto the show. He was in his late forties and buzzed with a nervous energy that was one double-strength espresso away from mania. He shrugged and gave a rugged smile. "The only vampires I'm worried about are the ones passing the bar exam."

Bently's eyes flicked to the side, where his producer was making frantic little "Cut!" motions with his hand. Bently decided to ignore him, hoping that the sponsors hadn't picked up on that one. That was always the problem with live feeds, but he felt that it added a bit of much-needed spice to the show, if only from a career point of view.

Up on the screen, Chief Vreede was getting into the swing of things. "Seriously folks, if vampires existed, don't you think we'd be onto them by now?" He smiled winningly. "The truth is, our streets have never been safer. Homicides, assaults and violent crime is down across the board."

He paused to let his little police plug go down for a minute and then wagged a finger at the camera. "If people want to be concerned, they should focus on criminals like Blade."

Bently sat up in his chair, grateful for the change of subject. "Now, who's this? Tell me about him."

Chief Vreede took a deep breath. "He's a sociopath we've been pursuing—"

"Blade is a very disturbed individual," Doctor Vance cut in smoothly. Ignoring Vreede's look of irritation, he went on. "Even the name he has chosen for himself is troubling. According to reports, he operates under the belief that a vast conspiracy of vampires live amongst us."

Vance tried to hold back a smile, but failed. He crossed his legs and turned in his chair, staring straight into the camera. "You have to look at the psychiatric underpinnings here. What does a person like Blade really want? Odds are, he's really trying to work out some kind of inner trauma. He thinks he's slaying monsters, but he's really trying to murder aspects of himself."

Bently raised an eyebrow. He wondered if he could bribe someone to get hold of a copy of this guy's book. He could use it as kindling when he eventually got around to burning down this blasted studio, preferably with the last three seasons of interview guests still inside.

He gave a small sigh of pleasure at the image. As Vance went on, Bently let his mind drift away into the warm arms of an involved scenario involving himself,

Suzi and the entire Canadian all-female mud-wrestling team.

Damn, he loved this job.

Fifteen miles away at the regional headquarters of the FBI, Agent Ray Cumberland clicked off the set and stared at it for a moment, digesting Dr Vance's words. It was an interesting take on the whole mystery of Blade, and he made a mental note to get one of his men to contact the doctor at the earliest opportunity.

Cumberland glanced at a note written in smudged blue biro on the inside of his wrist and hurriedly turned the set back on, flicking through the channels in search of the twenty-four hour news channel. He had stayed behind at work for nearly five hours this evening in order to tape this broadcast, which had been heavily advertised on the primetime network since the police reports had started coming in earlier in the evening.

Staying late at work was nothing unusual for Cumberland. It was his job to be one step ahead of everyone else, and he was proud of it. Even his wife had stopped complaining and had started communicating with him via Post-it notes stuck to the inside of his briefcase.

But this evening, he had even outstayed the cleaners. The main offices of the FBI regional headquarters were empty, the silence broken only by the crackle of the sickly overhead strip lighting.

For something big had happened.

Cumberland leaned forward in his office swivel chair as the promised news feed finally came on, trying to control his excitement. The feed started with a tight close-up of a woman's face, slowly zooming in as she got more and more distraught. "It was horrible," she blubbered. "The one car crashed, then the guy in the coat was shooting the other guy..."

The camera turned back to the stern-looking reporter. "That was just a taste of the mayhem that occurred during tonight's brazen shootout that left at least four people dead. It appears that an anonymous citizen captured the whole event on video."

Cumberland clattered away on a computer keyboard placed next to the TV. His computer whirred into action and began recording the footage as a series of still captures, which flashed up on the screen as a high-speed slide show. The images were slightly grainy, shot from a high angle through a night-vision camcorder, but he could clearly see what was going on. Cumberland studied the images carefully as they strobed past in front of him, excitement beating in his chest like butterflies on steroids. If these reports were correct, his career would be made.

As the tape rolled, the detective's eye left the screen and traveled around his cramped, cluttered office, untouched by any personal effects or attempts at cleanliness. Reams of computer printouts spilled from the dozens of cardboard boxes shoved into every spare nook and cranny, and a dozen unwashed coffee mugs were piled precariously on the edge of his desk, fighting for space with stacks of unread mail from his overflowing "In" tray. On the cupboards above, handmade tracking charts plotted his weekly progress in bold florescent hues. A wall-mounted bulletin board was nearly completely obscured by surveillance photos and news clippings of his suspects.

Cumberland felt a jolt of hope go through him. Most of the photos were blurred and indistinct, like snaps taken of Bigfoot, but this time, he had struck gold.

Finally, he had something real to work with.

The news feed, like everything around him, was dedicated to his current case, one that had baffled and defeated every agent in the building. It was a case that Cumberland had devoted a great many years of his professional life to following. Although he would never admit it, capturing the dangerous criminals Blade and Whistler had become something of an obsession. He knew that this had made him something of an in-joke around the office, but he didn't care.

It would be all the sweeter when he finally came up with the goods.

"Ray! Heard we've got a lead!"

Cumberland rubbed his hand over his eyes as Wilson Hale rushed into the office, bubbling over with excitement. The young Hale had been assigned to his case less than three months ago, but he had already outstayed his welcome.

As Cumberland watched, Hale ran over to his notice board and ripped down a blurry street webcam picture of Whistler, dislodging several important printouts, which fluttered downwards and immersed themselves in a cold cup of double-strength coffee abandoned on the edge of the detective's desk.

Cumberland closed his eyes for a second, made a silent wish, then opened them again. To his disappointment, Hale was still standing there. If he had a tail, he would be wagging it.

Switching off his computer, Cumberland got to his feet, resigned to his fate. "Book us a cab, Hale. Time to take these cowboys down."

A chill breeze rippled across the water as Blade's battle-scarred Charger pulled up beside a decaying boathouse by the river. It was late at night and the moon was full in the sky, painting the exposed landscape with a wash of ghostly color. A cricket chirped out a warning in the bushes as Blade killed the engine and climbed out, closing the door quietly behind him.

Blade stood on the grassy bank for a moment, savoring the stillness of the night. The evening air was alive with the sound of nature going about its business, in a thousand tiny but important ways. Beneath him, the wind whipped the black water into a foamy froth, building small islands of trash up against the moldering reed beds.

Blade put his hand on the warm metal of the Charger's hood and inhaled, breathing in the faint, sharp smell of saltwater blowing in from the sea. The wind ruffled through his close-cropped dark hair, and Blade closed his eyes against it for a moment, steeling himself for what was to come.

Then he turned and looked up at the boathouse.

The place was in darkness, but Blade's extra-keen senses picked up the smell of a cigarette stub smoldering gently in the grassy scrub nearby, its tip glowing orange like a tiny beacon in the night. Peering closer, he spotted several small chinks of yellow light peeping out from the boarded-up doorway on the ground floor.

Blade made a mental note to get Whistler to collect some paint-on tar from the builder's yard tomorrow. It wouldn't do to have their cover blown by nosy passers-by, or worse, the police.

Not that Whistler would be in the mood to listen to him after tonight's little performance...

With a haunted look up at one of the darkened windows, Blade pulled his leather jacket more tightly around himself. He then walked slowly up the muddy path towards the back door.

The interior of the boathouse was cluttered and brightly lit by powerful UV spot lamps, in stark contrast to the darkness and desolation outside. Blade removed his jacket and hung it up on the improvised metal coat rack by the entrance.

Blade swept his gaze around the room, searching for signs of life. The room was cold and smelled strongly of oil. Banks of industrial-style machinery were lined up around its walls, interspersed with a strange combination of high-tech tool boards and old-fashioned gun racks. A dartboard hung over the doorway and the floor had been resurfaced with a mixture of cheap scrap boarding and chipboard, the gaps filled in with ground-down rubble. An eighties-style boom box sat on one of the benches, surrounded by a pile of scratched CDs.

The place was a mess, but at the moment, it was the closest thing Blade had to a home.

With a furtive glance around him, Blade walked over to one of the worktables and began methodically stripping off his Kevlar body armor. The lab appeared to be deserted and Blade fervently hoped that Whistler had decided to go on one of his nighttime walks to the local 7-Eleven. He could really, really use a mug of strong coffee and a long sit-down before dealing with—

"What the fuck happened tonight?"

Blade mentally flinched. He continued removing his armor, piece by piece, staring straight ahead as he worked. He chose his words carefully, trying to appear unconcerned. "How should I know? He was human."

Whistler stepped through the doorway behind Blade and regarded his young protégé with a silent scowl, the wrinkles on his weathered face deepening. He pursed his lips and watched as Blade undid the buckles holding his body armor in place, sending shards of broken windscreen glass clattering to the ground.

Blade felt Whistler's steely gaze burning into his back. He began casually reloading his bandolier with silver stakes, concentrating on the job in hand in the hope that Whistler would let it go. An argument was the last thing he needed right now. Blade realized that Whistler hadn't yet mentioned the damage he'd done to the Charger and felt a chill go through him. The old man must be really pissed, and he was the one person in the whole world who could really make that matter to Blade.

Silence hung in the air between them like knives.

Whistler fumed. What the fuck did Blade think he was playing at? He was acting like this was no big deal, as though he had no choice but to carry out a vampire execution in full view of the public.

Arrogant son of a bitch.

Whistler's long grey hair flew around him as he strode across the room with a clomp of motorbike boots, angrily unzipping his flak jacket as he walked.

The wiry, muscled physique revealed beneath was a tribute to the twenty long years of vampire hunting that had kept him in shape, at the expense of so many other things.

Whistler pulled out his sawed-off shotgun and dropped it down onto the metal workbench, noting with a small stab of satisfaction that the noise made Blade jump. Then he turned his back on Blade and loosened the straps on the jointed metal brace that encased his right leg. Damn thing seemed to be getting heavier by the day.

Opening a small bottle of malt whisky, Whistler took a gulp, grimacing as the amber liquid burned his empty stomach. Then he tilted the bottle towards the light and gazed down at the label. It was a good vintage. He wished that he had more of it.

"You've been getting careless, Blade," he said gruffly. "You kill a vampire, they're ash, don't leave any proof of their existence." He rubbed a hand through the gray stubble on his chin. "But something like this, a human corpse—it's messy."

There was a metallic *thunk* as Blade removed his weapons belt and dumped it down on the bench. Pulling out a box of refill clips, he started reloading one of his Mach pistols, taking his time about it.

Whistler watched him for a moment, then shook his head in exasperation. If he couldn't get through to him, no one could. Trouble was, Blade had been playing this game for so long that he thought he was invincible.

Well, Whistler knew a thing or two about pride and what usually came after it, but try telling that to a guy who could bench-press a police riot van...

He shook his head. "You better hope to hell that nobody IDed you."

Blade shrugged carelessly and said nothing.

Sighing, Whistler dug into his canvas backpack and pulled out a new gadget. He wordlessly handed it to Blade, who took it automatically and turned it over in his big hands. "What's this?"

"A new delivery system for your serum. It's an effervescent inhaler. Works faster. Should be less painful."

Blade examined the gadget closely, an expression of surprise on his face. The serum was his lifeline, a complex cocktail of allicin and various retroviral compounds that kept his particular "condition" under control. Whistler had toiled for years trying to get the formula just right, but even he admitted that it wasn't perfect. For one thing, Blade's body was constantly building up a resistance to it. When he had first started taking the serum, Blade only needed a couple of milligrams for it to take effect. Now, nearly twenty years later, he was up to over fifty milligrams, a near-lethal dose. And the method of delivery—an injection in the neck from a horse-sized pressurized injector—was far from comfortable.

"Just bite down on the mouth guard. Delivery's automatic."

Blade looked up at Whistler, an unspoken question on his lips.

"Some friends of mine made it." Whistler spoke without looking up.

"Friends?" Blade asked.

"Yeah." Whistler paused for a beat. "Remember those?"

FOUR

In the city outside the FBI building, it was rush hour. The grimy streets were choked with traffic, the sidewalks jammed with pedestrians fighting their way home at the end of another long working day.

In daylight hours there were dozens of little market stalls set up along the sidewalks of this street, selling cheap fruit, silver jewelry and brightly colored knock-off clothing—the staples of the tourist industry. But by night the tone of the place changed, became darker, more sinister. Now, the pretty displays were gone, replaced by large mounds of leaking rubbish bags and boxes of squishy out-of-date fruit discarded by the daytime vendors. Sushi carts sprouted like carbuncles on a corpse, and the back streets became a living throng of casual-looking businessmen who slipped weasel-like from door to tasseled door in search of the latest fully exchangeable wipe-clean porn flick. Every kind of humanity could be found here, in the cultural melting pot of the evening, from giggling pre-teens dressed like hookers to elderly hobos rooting through trash bins for discarded fast-food.

Living in the city wasn't always glamorous, but it had its advantages.

Convenience being one of them.

A trio of young vampires dressed in skate-punk clothing sat atop a grimy office building, scanning the crowds below them in the way a starving man might peruse an all-you-can-eat buffet. Their faces were gaunt and angular, lit by the multi-colored wash of flickering lights from the streets below.

Their leader, a skinny vampire known as Squid, flipped his chromed banana-seat bike up through a series of daring maneuvers, enjoying the night air rushing over his face. After a couple of spins and jumps he scooted over to his friends with a rattle of wheels. They had been sitting there for well over five minutes, which in Squid's mind was five minutes too long. He crouched down beside them and peered over the grimy concrete edge, squinting against the bright glare of the neon sign hanging below.

He pointed at random, trying to hurry them up. "How about that one?"

The gang sniggered. "No fatties. They taste like Cheetos."

Flip, the youngest of the gang, suddenly jumped up in excitement. "How about that shrunken-headed bee-yatch-o-saurus over there?"

Squid looked where he was pointing, and his mouth twitched in disgust. No way! The bitch was wearing so much make-up that it would take them a week of shoveling to unearth a vein. "Fucking blow me, man!"

The trio exploded with laughter, the neon lamplight glinting off their various piercings. They were in their mid-teens and sported all the latest tattoos and MTV-inspired hairstyles. In their own small ways, they had been vampires all their lives.

Dingo, a wiry loner in a ratty *Lost Boys* movie T-shirt, spoke up, irritation sparking in his voice. "C'mon. Just pick one."

"Got it! Baby on board!"

As one, the gang turned and gazed downwards to see a mousy-looking woman walking past below, lugging a newborn in a baby carrier strapped to her chest. She was laden down with groceries and walked in a slow, tired way. She looked exhausted.

As the vampires watched, the woman hoisted the baby a little higher on her body, then turned off the sidewalk and disappeared into the elevated rail station entrance.

Easy pickings.

Dingo nodded and smiled approvingly, giving Flip the thumbs-up. "Looks like we got ourselves a combo-meal."

"Once you buy a prize, it's yours and yours to keep." Dingo glanced sideways at the lanky figure of Proof, who grinned back at him insanely, dancing a little jig of excitement. Dingo shook his head. Either the freak had been on the meths again, or he'd been dining on junkies. If he'd told him once, he'd told him a thousand times...

Down in the subway, the young woman pulled her bulky coat a little tighter around herself as she made her way downwards into the station. Her name was

Abigail and she was on her way home. She picked up her pace as she neared the platform, glad to be coming to the end of another long, hard day.

The platform down below her was of the depressing, badly lit urban variety. Swirls of Manga-style graffiti covered the wall-mounted timetables, and litter clogged the track like snow. The place stank of ammonia. Above the digitized station clock, a dead pigeon hung from the wire-covered ceiling, hopelessly entangled in the mesh, its sunken black eye sockets staring downwards accusingly.

Abigail shivered as she found herself a spot to wait on the drafty concourse. The station was deserted, which meant either that she was early, or that she had just missed her train.

Typical.

Abigail glanced around her, hefting her heavy grocery bags. Spotting an bench, she carried her bags over to it and sat down to wait. It was freezing and the cold metal of the tramp-resistant seating beneath her seemed to leech the warmth from her body even faster. She couldn't wait to get home.

She was starving, besides anything else. Abigail's mind tracked back over the events of the day. Work had been tough, but she had managed to pick up a couple of pounds of cheap over-ripe tomatoes from the market stalls on her way home, which would go nicely into some kind of hot, rich, bubbling stew. The tomatoes would last her for days, and would be well worth the backache of carrying them the eight blocks to the station.

Abigail's stomach rumbled as she licked her dry lips, mulling over her options. Perhaps she could chop the tomatoes, along with some mushrooms and onions, and whip up a big bowl of Mediterranean pasta like her mother used to make. The leftovers could be made into a nice thick soup for tomorrow, which would keep well in the fridge if she didn't manage to eat it all in one go.

Afterwards, she would have a warm shower to get the smell of the city out of her hair, and then have an early night to recover from the stresses and strains of the last week. She would need to get up bright and early tomorrow, ready for—

Abigail was jolted from her thoughts by a loud rustling noise and she glanced up sharply.

There was nobody there.

Abigail leaned forward in her seat, peering round the edge of the pillars guarding the entrance to the station. The concourse was completely deserted. She shivered slightly, digging her thumbnails underneath the nylon straps of her baby carrier and moving it higher up on her lap. The elasticized waistband was killing her. Where the hell was her train?

She glanced up at the digital platform clock, but it was stuck at twelve past midnight, the orange neon seconds jittering spastically back and forth. She sighed.

Then she jumped as a dark shadow flitted across her peripheral vision. She swung her head to try and follow it, but the shadow vanished as quickly as it appeared.

Abigail's heart began beating faster, and she got swiftly to her feet, cradling her baby carrier protectively. She could've sworn that someone had just ducked behind the concrete pillar underneath the clock. She backed up a few steps, keeping a wary eye on the station entrance as she glanced behind the pillar.

There was no one there.

Abigail tried to control her breathing. There was no sense in getting herself all worked up over nothing. It could've been a pigeon. They sometimes got into the stations to roost. But she hadn't heard the sound of wing beats. Maybe she was imagining it.

Or maybe not.

Abigail let out a gasp at the sound of rapid footfalls behind her. She spun round, but once again she found herself alone. The foul-smelling wind blew through the tunnel, sending piles of trash bumping and skittering over the line.

Silence.

Thoroughly unnerved by now, Abigail scooped up her grocery bags and turned to go...

Blam! She walked straight into the open arms of Dingo and Proof, who were standing right behind her. She gasped in fright, staring up at them. They didn't look like they were there to help her carry her shopping.

"Hey, pretty lady."

"Sophisticated mama."

Dingo and Proof smiled widely at her. Abigail took one look at their sharpened fangs and screamed.

Backpedaling frantically, she spun around and made a break for the exit. But Flick and Squid had ducked out from behind their pillar and smoothly moved into position behind her, blocking her way.

The two young vampires laughed as she cannoned into them. Then in one quick move they were upon her, ripping the baby carrier from her chest and shoving her backwards towards their fellow gang-members. Dingo grabbed Abigail by the hair and kicked her legs out from beneath her, hurling the screaming woman to the floor. He and Proof started tearing away at her clothing, laughing uproariously. They hadn't had this much fun in days and intended to make the most of it.

Dingo grabbed a fistful of Abigail's shirt and ripped it clean down the middle. "Scream if this hurts, chica!"

Standing a few feet away, Flick made a hungry noise as he removed the baby from its carrier, drooling in anticipation.

Lunchtime.

But Flick was so engrossed in watching the spectacle in front of him that it took him a moment to realize that something was wrong. The baby in his arms was curiously light, and it wasn't moving. Flick looked down at it, incomprehension creasing his face.

Hang on a moment. This wasn't a baby.

It was a goddamn plastic doll!

Holding it up to the light, Flick saw it had the words FUCK YOU! scrawled in black ink across its chest.

What the...?!

Flick was confused for about two and a half seconds, then the "baby" exploded violently, spewing out a cloud of concentrated, noxious-smelling gas that enveloped the vampire's gaping face in a toxic swirl.

Flick recoiled, retching. "Aghhk... it's fucking garlic!" He hurled the doll to the ground and started wiping frantically at his burning face.

From ground level, Dingo and Proof paused in their attack and glanced up at him, bemused.

Beneath them, Abigail ceased her struggles and silently twisted on the floor, pulling one of her knees back up against her chest. There was a tiny click and a barbed silver spike slid smoothly out of the toe of her boot. Glancing at her wristwatch, Abigail braced her back against the floor. Then she kicked upwards with all her strength, driving the spike up through the underside of Proof's chin.

With a shocked screech, the vampire burst into flames, the silver entering his bloodstream through a thousand tiny capillaries and rapidly spreading through his system, trailing blue fire in its wake. Proof frantically grabbed at Abigail's boot with blazing hands, trying to pull the deadly hooked blade from his jaw.

But it was too late. Proof sagged as the chemical reaction roared through his body, obliterating his internal organs and fusing the joints of his bones together. Proof's body literally dissolved, his skin flaying off in clumps as the underlying flesh turned to charcoal, the silver effectively cooking him from the inside out. His glowing skeleton burst into ash, showering across the stained concrete of the platform.

Dingo just stared, dumbfounded. Before he had a chance to react, Abigail wrapped her legs around the tattooed vampire's calves and yanked for all she was worth.

Dingo fell over backwards, landing heavily on his backside. He stared up at Abigail in shock, his surprise growing as she sprang to her feet, shedding her heavy coat and hat in the process. Long tresses of glossy hair tumbled downwards and spilled around her shoulders, coiling into bouncy ringlets.

Dingo's jaw dropped. The woman wasn't mousy at all.

In fact, she was gorgeous.

Abigail took a pace backwards, staring at the floored vampire with ill-concealed contempt.

Despite himself, Dingo's gaze automatically flicked downwards. The sight of the veritable arsenal of weapons strapped to Abigail's lithe, muscled body was worrying, but it was the look in her eyes that was the biggest shock. Despite the fact that he was already dead, Dingo felt a cold hand wrap around his heart and begin to squeeze.

He then caught sight of the others staring at him, and shook himself. It was only some bitch. She'd got lucky, that was all. He could take her down in a second.

With a defiant snarl, Dingo began to climb to his feet.

Without seeming to draw breath, Abigail whipped a booted foot up and kicked him full in the face with her metal-tipped heel, smashing his nose. As Dingo yelped and clutched at his shattered face, Abigail kicked him a second time, snapping his head back, then followed up with a barrage of lightning-fast punches that spattered the station floor with blood.

As Dingo slumped backwards onto the floor, Flick and Squid recovered from their initial surprise. They charged towards Abigail, whooping, fangs bared. Squid attacked first, grabbing Abigail from behind in an iron chokehold. He tightened his grip and wrenched her backward, intending to snap her neck like so much dry kindling. But Abigail anticipated the move and leaned hard to the side, breaking the vampire's grip and using his own momentum to flip him up and over, using her shoulder as a pivot.

Squid spun upwards, performing a full three-sixty-degree turn in the air before landing with a winded yelp at her feet. Abigail gazed down at him, then remembered what he and his friends had done to her shirt and took the opportunity to kick him nastily in the groin.

As Squid curled up into a fetal position, groaning, Abigail quickly turned to ward off an incoming attack by Flick by driving her elbow into his throat, breaking his charge and nearly snapping his neck. Then she spun around and cracked her forearm downwards like a whip, ejecting a silver katar dagger from the spring-loaded dispenser strapped to the inside of her wrist.

Squid saw what Abigail was holding and gave a very small, very unmanly whimper. A heartbeat later, and he was nothing more than a vampire-shaped pile of ash illegally littering the platform.

Barely pausing to acknowledge her grisly handiwork, Abigail reached back and pulled a crescent-shaped device from the leather docking-sheath strapped to her back. Flick prowled towards her, his eyes flashing, growling low in his throat. Abigail completely ignored him. Holding the device in the middle, she carefully pointed the curved ends away from her and twisted a dial set into the center.

Clink! The device sprung open, telescoping outwards on either side to form a three-foot arc of springy steel. A powerful ray of UV laser light buzzed between the two curving ends, making a sound like a swarm of angry killer bees.

As Flick hurled himself towards her, Abigail turned up the voltage on the device, waiting for him. Before Flick could halt his charge, Abigail lashed out and casually lopped off one of the vampire's arms, like a forester pruning a tree. The severed limb didn't even have time to fall to the ground before she had struck again with deadly accuracy, shoving the device through Flick's mid-section like a cheese-cutter.

Flick literally fell apart, his upper torso sliding cleanly off his trunk, his face registering total shock as his upper torso swiftly turned to flaming ash and cascaded down onto the concrete platform. A second later, his disarticulated lower half joined it. The wind blew across the merrily blazing corpse, creating a whirling maelstrom of glowing sparks.

Abigail stared into the flames for a moment, the flickering light casting jumping shadows across her face.

Then she turned to face Dingo, who took the opportunity to run for his life.

Retracting her UV cutter, Abigail unhurriedly slotted it into its case on her back. Then she pulled out a strange-looking gun with a flared barrel. Taking careful aim, she fired it at the fleeing figure of Dingo.

A high-pressure jet of anti-personnel foam sprayed across the platform, spattering across the backs of Dingo's legs. The foam hardened instantly on contact and Dingo pitched forwards, his legs suddenly glued together. Panicking, Dingo reached around and clawed at his legs, frantically trying to scrape off the gunk and free himself. The only thing he succeeded in doing was getting both of his hands stuck to the hardening mess.

Dingo whimpered. He was stuck.

Abigail calmly approached him, taking her time. She watched the little thug's eyes widen with fear as she stared down at him, not even bothering to conceal her indifference to his suffering. Holstering her dripping foam gun, she reached down and withdrew a silver stake from the pack of eight strapped to her thigh.

She raised it high above her head.

"Scream if this hurts, Chico."

As Dingo turned into a pile of screaming, thrashing embers, Abigail brushed her hands off and slowly straightened to survey the mess she has made. The ashes of the vampire gang were strewn across the station, popping and cracking like campfire cinders in the aftermath of the intense heat.

Abigail glanced at the digital chronometer set into her wristwatch. Thirty-seven seconds had elapsed since the vampires had first jumped her.

She pulled a face. Not bad, but still not approaching her personal best.

Shrugging to herself, Abigail collected up the two silver stakes lying amid the ashes on the platform, then turned and picked her discarded coat off the ground. Shaking the vampire dust out of the lining, she pulled it on, then tucked her hair beneath her hat and picked up her groceries from the nearby bench.

As she did so, a gust of stale wind blew down the tunnel. Her train had finally arrived, pulling up to the station with the hiss and clunk of hydraulic brakes. Abigail stood patiently behind the safety line as the doors chugged open and a stream of passengers flooded out onto the platform. The crowd headed towards the exit, trampling over the cooling ashes of the vampires without so much as a downward glance, completely oblivious to the carnage that had just taken place.

Abigail watched them go, smoothing an errant curl of hair behind her ear as she considered her options. Perhaps she would pick up a couple of bags of rice from the 7-Eleven on her way home. That would mean that she could save the tomatoes for tomorrow, when she would have more time to make a big dish of risotto. It would last a lot longer than the pasta, and better still, it would have only half the calories.

Yes, that would be the best plan.

Pleased with herself, Abigail pushed her way through the crowd, fighting against the flow of shoving commuters. She boarded the train just as the doors were closing, the lone passenger in the now-empty carriage. The train sped off into the tunnel, disappearing into the darkness.

It was the end of just another day's work for Abigail Whistler.

FIVE

FIVE

Closing time was fast approaching as Whistler waited patiently by the checkout desk of the local 7-Eleven. Behind the desk, the young cashier hunted on the shelves for a pack of nicotine patches, rummaging behind security-tagged bottles of vodka and rum.

Whistler glanced around the store while he waited, humming tunelessly under his breath. The store smelled of fried food and lemon floor cleaner. Every inch of free wall space was filled with garish technicolor displays and tatty out-of-date sale posters. Over by the end wall, a soda machine blinked on and off as the humid atmosphere slowly rotted away at its internal wiring.

Whistler had been almost pleased to find that he was running low on his patches—it had given him the perfect excuse to get out of the boathouse for a while and gather his thoughts. God knows, he needed a break, especially after the events of today. He couldn't even think about it without getting mad at Blade, and he knew that wasn't what either of them needed right now.

"Sajne pluvos." He spoke to the cashier in Esperanto, trying to make conversation. Looks like rain.

The cashier nodded absently in reply and continued to bumble around, pulling out boxes and examining packets in a casual yet increasingly desperate way. Whistler smiled wryly to himself. The young man had only been working here for two weeks, and hadn't quite got the lay of the store yet.

Whistler remembered what it was like to work in a place like this. He himself had worked briefly in a local store when he was younger. He knew it was hard trying to make ends meet while keeping some modicum of self-respect. It wasn't so much selling out as allowing oneself to be temporarily bought, he had told himself at the time, and he had believed it.

After all, it was only for a short while, until something better came up...

Whistler remembered telling himself this for almost eight months, until a late-night disagreement with a drunken, heavily-armed Hell's Angel over the price of a bottle of scotch had forced him to reconsider his career options, not to mention making the management rethink its interior decoration scheme. For an inner-city liquor store, it was decided, it was somewhat foolish to outfit the counter area with light-colored flooring.

It was always like that, thought Whistler. Most people would quite happily put up with the fact that their life sucked, so long as they believed that their situation was only temporary. Indeed, some people could live their entire lives looking forward to the future, while their real life—their day to day life— played out unnoticed around them in small sad minutes, which soon turned into hours, then days, then years...

Whistler shook his head, rooting through his pocket for change. The cashier handed him the slim carton of patches and he dropped them into his inside pocket, which was heavy with leftover bolts and greasy engine parts.

Whistler believed very much in making his own luck—quite literally—and he made sure he took pleasure in what he did, on a day-to-day basis wherever possible. These nightly walks to the store were one of the few indulgences he allowed himself, a brief visit to the world of normality before returning to his own life of vampires and violence. To the average passerby, he was just a normal man who had popped out for a nighttime stroll. Whistler liked that, more than he dared admit.

While he knew that secrecy was of the utmost importance to their mission, he enjoyed his little ritual too much to give it up. The long walk up the lane and fifteen minutes of browsing the shelves would calm him and give him time to think. By the time he returned home with his bag of supplies, he would be ready to face the world again.

Whistler shook his head sadly, then turned and started walking towards the door.

He wished that Blade would come out with him just once. Instead he chose to stay at home, sharpening that damn sword of his and brooding.

That was Blade's problem, Whistler thought. The guy didn't know how to relax. Blade shared many characteristics with the human race, but being a hybrid only seemed to serve to reverse the symptoms. Blade dreamed of a better tomorrow—a world without vampires—but refused to allow himself to enjoy today, even though he was painfully aware of how precious every second was.

Something caught Whistler's attention. He paused, opposite the magazine racks, then backtracked to the revolving wire display stand that held today's newspapers.

Ah, crap.

Most of the newspapers were running the same headline—the usual electoral chaos—but the splash heading on one tabloid inescapably caught Whistler's eye.

The cover story featured an artist's impression of Blade.

The likeness was inescapable, and a chill ran down Whistler's spine. Next to the sketch was the headline "Gun-Toting Psychopath Captured on Film!"

Well, that was one for the scrapbooks.

Next to the drawing was a grainy photo of Blade's recent melee with the vampires, apparently taken as a still capture from a video camera. Whistler picked up the tabloid, studying it minutely but being careful to appear casual. "Looks like a bit more than rain," he muttered under his breath.

Dammit. He had known that this was going to happen one day. Even he had noticed that Blade had been taking more and more risks recently, maybe figuring that the more he put at stake, as it were, the bigger the results would be. Whistler knew that Blade was getting tired of fighting—they both were—but this wasn't the way of solving things.

There would be no global solution to the problem of vampires. Blade knew it as well as Whistler did, but refused to accept it. When the two of them died, the war would rage on, maybe for a generation, maybe for a hundred generations. There was no way of knowing. All they could do was fight, and try to enjoy their small daily successes. A life saved here, a gang taken down there—it all added up, and made the world a better place.

It was just when they looked to the long term that despair started to creep in.

Whistler shook himself. The cashier was staring at him.

"That it?" he asked, in Esperanto.

Whistler nodded absently and handed over a fistful of oil-stained coins, waving the newspaper like it was an afterthought. "I'll take this, too."

The cashier gestured to the headline on the paper as he rung up the purchase. "That guy needs a new hobby," he smiled.

"Let's hope not," replied Whistler, gazing down at the picture.

He left the store in a blur, perusing the tabloid as he walked.

The old man was so engrossed in reading his paper that that he didn't notice a shadow move on a nearby rooftop. Up in the darkness, an FBI surveillance agent crouched atop a gallery walkway, his digital camera's high-speed drive whirring as he snapped shot after shot of Whistler, his face obscured behind his giant telephoto lens.

As the old man moved away out of his sights, the agent lifted up his lapel and spoke quietly into the two-way radio clipped to the lining of his jacket. "Subject is heading west."

In the civilian car parked nearby, Agent Cumberland ducked down behind the wheel, peering up out of his side window, scarcely daring to hope. Up ahead of him, a scruffy looking man strode out of the store and began pottering down the sidewalk, his eyes glued to the tabloid paper he held in his hands.

In his mind, Cumberland heard the Hallelujah Chorus.

The man looked like he was in his early sixties and he walked with a slight limp. He had to pause for breath before crossing the road, barely bothering to check for cars before hobbling over to the opposite sidewalk, his nose buried in his newspaper.

He didn't look in the least bit dangerous, but Cumberland had worked in this job for long enough to know better than to judge people by their appearance. The man's long, graying hair was unkempt and his clothes were ragged, but to Cumberland, it was like catching a glimpse of the Holy Grail.

Abraham Whistler.

At last.

Whistler was Blade's partner in crime and one of the most wanted criminals on the FBI's monthly suspect list. Although seemingly old and fragile, the guy had a rap sheet longer than even Blade's. Cumberland remembered when he'd seen it for the first time. Unbelieving, he had requested a copy to take home with him to read, but the office printer had run out of ink several pages before the end. Arson, aggravated burglary, kidnapping, attempted murder, resisting arrest... You name it, Whistler had been seen doing it at some point over the years.

But he had never been caught.

Cumberland smiled for what felt like the first time in weeks. He lifted the police radio to his lips, keeping his eyes firmly fixed on Whistler. If he looked away, he had the feeling that the old man would vanish like dust in the wind. He clicked the transmit button on his radio. "Got him."

Finally.

His pulse racing with excitement, Cumberland started the car and began creeping down the road, lights out, tailing Whistler.

"Congratulations. You're famous. Just what we needed."

Whistler slapped the newspaper down on the workbench. Blade stared down at it, his face blank. His eyes scanned the headline with interest, and then moved down to study the picture.

It really was quite a good likeness. Only his chin was a bit more sculpted than that, and the picture didn't really do justice to his hair...

Whistler banged his hand down across the picture, making Blade jump. "Blade. Somebody screwed us. Your face is all over the papers, the television." Whistler's brows drew together like two angry gray caterpillars and he waved a hand wildly in the air. "The media's eating it up."

Blade snorted. "Like I care?"

"You should." Whistler's voice was hard. "Something like this," he gestured to the tabloid, "taking out a human, even one working for the vampires—as far as the rest of the world's concerned, you're public enemy number one."

Blade gave Whistler a sidelong look. "Didn't realize this was a popularity contest."

Whistler's jaw clenched as he struggled to control his anger. "Dammit, Blade, don't you see what's happening?" He picked up the paper and shook it at his protégé, littering the floor with a colorful snowstorm of pullout adverts. "The fuckers are finally getting smart. They're waging a goddamn PR campaign." He threw the newspaper down on the workbench. "Now it's not just the vampires we have to worry about, we're gonna have to take on the rest of the world, too."

Whistler turned away from Blade and stared around at the converted boathouse, his mind racing. The vampires had taken everything from them, and now they wanted more. They were already living like rats, sacrificing all comfort and sanity in order to save lives, and now it looked like they may have to give up the few scraps they had left.

It really was too much.

Whistler's cobalt-blue eyes swept fiercely over the workroom, taking in the cobbled-together fixtures and fittings. He'd done his best with what they had salvaged from their previous headquarters, but the vampires had smashed most of it beyond repair. The few remaining tools and pieces of equipment he now owned were mostly "borrowed" from the big medi-lab on the outskirts of the city. The other furniture had been there when they moved in, left behind by the farm workers who used to live here.

It had taken him weeks to get the smell of goat out of the mattresses.

Whistler turned back to Blade, fighting to keep his voice steady. "They've got us on the run. These last few months we've barely been staying ahead of the curve..."

Blade put his hand on Whistler's shoulder and squeezed it. "You worry too much, old man."

Whistler's eyes blazed with anger and he wheeled around, knocking Blade's hand away. "I've been doing this since before you were born, Blade. The moment you stop worrying, you're dead."

Whistler held Blade's clear gaze for a moment, their faces inches apart. Then the old man's face softened. "Since the day I found you, you've been like a son to me. I taught you everything I know." Whistler took a wheezing breath and let it out in a long sigh. "But I'm tired. You understand?"

With that, Whistler turned on his heel and walked away.

In his sparsely furnished room, Whistler sat on his cot in the dark, staring at the tarnished wedding ring he wore. He slowly spun it around his calloused finger, a meditative look on his face.

Across the hall, Blade sat before a small Zen shrine, his eyes closed. Incense smoke coiled upwards from a tarnished silver burner placed on the floor behind him, filling the room with a sweet, slightly gritty scent. Nearby, Blade's namesake weapon rested on a ceremonial stand, its acid-etched titanium length glinting in the moonlight. Beneath it lay his sun-shades and leather jacket, the sleeves of which were still damp with spatters of vampire blood. The silence of the room was punctuated only by the intermittent swell of the ocean outside and the quiet sounds of the wind gusting through the cracks in the window frame.

Blade concentrated on the sound of the sea, willing it to drown out the ugly noises in his head. Screams and echoing gunshots ran on an endless loop inside his tired brain, underpinned by the relentless growl of his Charger's engine. Again and again he saw the look on Gedge's face as he had died, the triumph lurking like a rattlesnake behind the fear and the pain. The man had thought that his death meant something. As if he was making some kind of a sacrifice.

Blade was in trouble, he knew that much. He had killed a human, in public, and he would have to pay for it.

But he and Whistler would be okay. They were always okay. He just had to get the sounds of death out of his head, and then he would look at the problem from every conceivable angle and figure a way out of it.

It was what he always did.

Blade had spent his whole life fighting the vampire menace, from the time he was cut from his dying mother's stomach, through the dark years of pain and suffering that had lasted right up until the day he met Whistler.

He was a survivor. He'd had to be.

For he was one of them.

The vampire that claimed his mother's life all those years ago had also irreversibly affected Blade, in the deepest sense possible. When the vampire had bitten her, the parasitic virus in the creature's saliva had passed to him through the placenta, infecting his bloodstream while he curled up and screamed soundlessly in his mother's womb.

Before he was even born, Blade had been forcibly changed into something he didn't want to be, not quite human, not quite vampire. He never had the chance to save himself, to protect himself and his mother from the monster who ripped her throat out and left her to die on the streets of the city.

Blade had spent every day of his adult life killing vampires in the hope that somehow, it would make things right again. Each one he killed gave him back a tiny piece of himself, although he knew in his heart that he could never truly be whole again.

In some ways, Blade knew he was lucky. He had all the strengths of the vampire race that had spawned him, but none of their weaknesses. Immune to the destructive effects of garlic, silver and sunlight, Blade had the advantage when it came to fighting vampires, and exploited it to the max.

The Daywalker, they called him.

Behind his back, they called him other things.

Instead of being a full-blooded vampire, Blade was a living, breathing human being, but also something far more. The virus had given him great power, increasing his blood pressure and metabolism exponentially, while eliminating all the risks normally associated with this process. His body had been optimized far beyond any other human's, so that it could instantly convert stored blood sugar into energy and utilize the oxygen in his blood with almost a hundred percent efficiency.

Whistler's initial research had also indicated that Blade's adrenal glands had been rebuilt by the virus. His tests showed that the adrenaline they produced was perhaps ten times more potent than any normal human's, and was released in a constant stream rather than just in emergencies. It was all this, and various other biological tweaks and restructurings, that had made Blade so superhumanly fast and strong, and able to heal so quickly.

He was grateful for it, in his own way. It helped him do his job.

But there had been a price to pay for all of this. For he also had the vampire's thirst for human blood.

Blade's formative years had been spent fighting the urge to kill, as the vampire parasite bound tightly to his every cell cried out to be fed. Blade had survived his youth by living rough, feeding on hobos and tramps, hating himself for doing so but unable to do anything about it. The thirst had kicked in when he hit puberty, turning the occasional craving for a blood-rare steak into a fully-fledged urge to kill. Blade had run away from his foster parents and spent the next few years living on the streets, trying to stay alive and avoid the authorities who constantly chased him, seeking to put him behind bars for good.

Whistler had changed all that: taken him in, looked after him at considerable risk to his own life and sanity. Pain had taken on a whole new meaning as the old man had patiently taught him to take control of what he was, rather than to rage against it. Whistler had taught Blade to fight rather than hunt, to give chase rather than to run, to hate the vampires rather than hate himself.

The old man had taught him the weaknesses of the vampire race—sunlight, garlic and silver—and had spent years of his life coming up with new and technologically inventive ways to utilize them as weapons. Whistler's previous life as a gunsmith was forgotten the day the vampires massacred his family, and he intended to put his training to the only use it could now have.

As part of Blade's rehabilitation, Whistler had also created the serum-based vaccine, a drug that could be injected directly into the bloodstream to stave off the worst effects of the vampiric thirst constantly raging within him.

And in doing so, he had done the unthinkable. Whistler had given Blade back his life.

Now, twenty-odd years on, the unlikely duo were still going strong, fighting the creatures of darkness that constantly threatened humanity. Unpaid and definitely unappreciated, they were the unsung heroes of the city.

Until now.

Blade came back to the present with a nasty bump. The screaming in his head instantly died away, to be replaced by a ringing, urgent silence. Blade's eyes snapped open in the darkness, all of his attention focused on the tiny noise nagging at the edge of his hearing.

Something was wrong.

Blade was on his feet instantly, his tiredness shattering like plate glass. Lifting his sword from its cradle, he ghosted through the door into the big, deserted workroom outside. Moving over to one of the side windows, he lifted one of the slats of the huge wooden blind with the tip of his sword, listening intently. Outside, the moon was bright over the water and the smell of the sea drifted in through the cracked window.

All was still.

Too still.

There was a small sound behind him. Blade half-turned to see Whistler slide into the shadows behind him, fully dressed, clutching a Browning nine-millimeter pistol.

"What is it?" Whistler's voice was a dry whisper.

Blade turned to face the ocean again, taking a step back from the window and raising his sword. He swallowed, trying to fight down the sick feeling that rose in his throat like dark bile. "What you've been worrying about."

They both stood there together, motionless, listening to the rise and fall of the ocean swell.

The waves came in, then went back out again.

In, then out.

In—

The window in front of them shattered, blowing back into the room in a shower of spinning glass. Blade and Whistler ducked for cover behind a workbench as two heavily armored SWAT team members crashed through the window shutter and lowered themselves into the room, hanging from black rappelling lines. Two more agents burst through the banks of windows on either side of the boathouse, swinging in towards Blade and Whistler. They fired cans of tear gas in their wake, pouring out a wall of thick gray smoke, filling the lab from door to door.

The authorities had found them.

Blade rushed forward to engage them, shouting at Whistler to fall back.

As the old man disappeared into the relative safety of the armory, the reinforced front door exploded inwards, hitting the floor with a metallic *crump*. A dark tide of armed agents streamed into the workroom like rats into a grain hold. They wore full body armor and gas masks, and were armed with Heckler and Koch MP-5 assault rifles.

One of them threw a stun grenade. Blade closed his eyes before the flash went off, but didn't cover his ears fast enough, hampered by the sword in his hand. He grunted in pain as his hypersensitive hearing was swamped by the explosion.

As the echoes of the stun grenade faded away, a series of explosions came from outside. Blade watched through the shattered window in disbelief as the chained barricade protecting the waterside entrance to their refuge was flattened by the explosion, splashing heavily into the water below. An inflatable military-issue Zodiac boat nosed its way through and flew up the wooden ramp outside, docking alongside the boathouse. It was packed to the brim with more agents, dressed in black body armor and equipped with searchlights and guns. They jumped ashore and began fanning out around the boathouse, deploying rapidly, establishing a perimeter.

Blade ducked down behind a pillar, his heart racing. This was all his fault. He had been careless, and now he was going to have to pay the price.

Blade swore heatedly under his breath as he watched the agents tear through the workshop, knocking over trays of delicate equipment in their mad stampede. Blade flinched at the sound of glass breaking. There would be nothing of the place by the time the cops had finished with it. He knew from long experience that the police were worse than the vampires when it came to breaking stuff.

He only hoped that Whistler had taken out insurance on this place...

In the dark depths of the armory, Whistler pounded across the room and wrenched open his wooden munitions cabinet, blinking in the semi-darkness. He knew he had seconds before the agents came looking for him. But he couldn't use his pistol on the human SWAT team. If nothing else, it would only encourage them to shoot back. The last thing they needed was a multiple police body count to add to the media's interest in Blade.

He had to find something a bit less lethal with which to defend himself.

He spun around as a black-clad agent burst into the open-plan armory behind him, aiming his pistol at Whistler. "On the floor! On the floor!"

Whistler dived to the side and fired off a warning double-tap round in reply, aiming at the ground beside the agent. Then he made a run for it.

Other agents stepped in behind the first and swiftly returned fire, forcing Whistler to duck behind a concrete pillar as a volley of slugs tore through the room, blasting a line of shrapnel into the air. Whistler retaliated with a sweeping round of fire, driving the agents back out of the room. Without waiting to see if he had hit anything, Whistler gave a fearsome shout and charged across the room towards the computer bay.

The agents started in after him, but their leader held up a hand, motioning for them to keep back. He pulled a tear gas canister out of his backpack and removed the pin with his teeth and tossed it through the door after Whistler.

They would smoke the crazy old guy out.

Together, the SWAT team waited, guns at the ready.

Outside, a large convoy of police Cruisers and SWAT trucks swept down the dirt track, converging on the boathouse with their sirens wailing. The doors slid open and a second wave of FBI agents and police leapt out, unloading assault rifles and shouting at one another through loudhailers. Over by the dock, Agents Cumberland and Hale emerged from an unmarked car, wearing bulletproof vests and brandishing firearms.

They were taking no chances with these freaks.

Cumberland pulled out a police radio. "Lock it down! Keep them contained!"

More police boats chugged into the docks, clogging the river from bank to bank. Up above them on the rooftop, a score of SWAT snipers took up position, waiting for the suspects to emerge.

Inside the boathouse, Blade was on his feet, urgently trying to fight his way back through the surging mob of police to get to Whistler. He knew that the old man could look after himself, but he realized that he would probably try to stay and fight. Blade knew from a glance outside that this was no longer an option. Their new headquarters was already lost—they had to abandon the building. There were too many invaders to fight and they couldn't kill any of them without risking severe repercussions.

Blade had faced greater odds than this before, but this was different.

These were humans. Innocent ones.

Even one human death was too many, and the fact that he now had over a hundred eyewitnesses watching his every move would only guarantee that if he were caught, he would never see the light of day again.

Blade scanned the surging crowd with a practiced eye. Then he lowered his shoulder and charged through a wall of half a dozen agents, sending them flying in all directions. Unwilling to use his sword, Blade grabbed the first agent he could get his hands on and head-butted him to oblivion, breaking the man's nose and sending blood spattering across the walls. Lifting the man's limp body into the air, Blade sent him flying into the path of two others who were trying to rush him from the side. Then he reached behind him to grab the clothing of a third agent and tossed him out through the window at the rear. There was a satisfying splash as the man ended up in the river, but four other agents immediately took his place, blocking Blade's path.

Blade growled with impatience. There were too many people in his way! He had to get through to find Whistler, but he couldn't keep fighting like this without causing major bloodshed.

Blade began to fall back, slapping and shoving at the agents to clear a path for himself. He had caused this mess and it was up to him to fix it. He only hoped the old man would have the sense to stay down, out of harm's way.

Next door in the computer bay, Whistler quickly located the main workstations and booted them up, moved with increasing urgency as the room filled with seeping teargas. Coughing and half blind, Whistler hurried over to a bank of old-fashioned computers, typing in a series of commands with clumsy fingers. The half-dozen computer monitors on the benches around him blinked into life as the workstations synched up with the servers, all showing the same protocol message:

-- Server 1 Protection ENABLED
-- Server 2 Protection ENABLED
> Data Protection Routine Enabled Y/N?

Whistler hit the "Y" key, and ducked behind a workbench.

There was a brief whirring sound, oscillating in pitch as the computer's hard drives performed a final remote backup of last night's data. A red light flashed at the front of the network storage unit, shining with a steady light.

A moment later, a pack of Semtex taped to the side of the unit glowed deep orange and exploded impressively. After a brief pause, the second networked server on the other side of the room blew up too, showering the room with charred wires and sparking debris.

Whistler surveyed the destruction with a look of deep regret. Then he wrapped an oily rag over his nose and mouth and plunged onwards through the smoke.

Outside by the police cruisers, Cumberland ducked behind the hood in panic as a third explosion lit up the interior of the boathouse. Smoke mushroomed out of the windows, coiling downwards and filling the parking bays below with choking fumes. Frantic with worry, Cumberland clicked on his police radio. "What's going on in there?" he barked.

An agent's voice crackled over the radio. "It's some kind of self-destruct program. They're fragging their hard drives."

Cumberland bit his lip anxiously as he switched the radio off. Criminals with computers? This was even worse than he thought.

Inside the boathouse, Whistler was starting to tire. The smoke was getting thicker. The agents had fired a second canister in through the door behind him, trying to drive him out into the open. He had managed to smash a window before the canister had exploded, letting some of the smoke out, but it was still nearly impenetrable.

Whistler could barely see his own hand in front of his face, but he kept moving, operating the computers by touch. He knew that the smoke was doing serious damage to his lungs, but he didn't care. A lifetime of smoking fifty a day had already done most of the groundwork.

Whatever happened, he couldn't let the police get their hands on his databases. The video footage of

Blade killing the human had been incriminating enough. But if the cops got their greasy paws on his spreadsheets, which detailed everything from local bank vault schematics to records of Blade's daily vampire kill ratio... well, he wouldn't like to be the one who had to rescue Blade from the city's one and only public hanging.

Whistler was so engrossed in his work that he didn't notice an agent rising silently out of the smoke behind him.

The agent saw he had a clear shot, and took it.

Whistler half-turned at the rustle of clothing, but it was too late. The bullet struck him in the chest, dead center.

"Whistler!" Next door, Blade heard his mentor cry out in pain, but he was cut off from the old man, swamped by too many agents to fight. Bellowing like a bull, Blade plunged back through the hostile crowd towards the armory, plowing his way through the forest of punching fists and jabbing rifle butts without bothering to defend himself.

One agent cleared enough space to swing his rifle up and aim at Blade, but frantic to get to Whistler, the Daywalker would not be slowed. He slammed a heavy punch into the side of the agent's head, throwing him aside before he had the chance to open fire.

In the next room, Whistler staggered from the impact of the blast but kept moving, his mouth set in a grim line of determination. Blood flooded through his clothing, and he grimaced and pressed the heel of his hand against the wound to try and prevent too much blood loss.

Whistler knew that he was hurt bad, but he had to keep going. The sons of bitches would have to put a bullet through his head before he gave up. He had to protect their secrecy, and this was the only way to do it. He might not make it, but he would be damned if he would let them take Blade down too.

Fighting against the blackness closing in on the edge of his vision, Whistler staggered over to another bank of workstations and triggered the emergency protocol, entering the self-destruct codes. Colorful data-loss warnings flashed up on the screens as their memory banks purged themselves at high speed before exploding, one after another.

Then a second agent cautiously poked his head around the door. He got a bead on Whistler and fired a round into his thigh, trying to stop his progress.

Despite himself, Whistler screamed.

At the sound of a second shot, Blade threw off the pile of agents that had jumped on him, his face twisting in anguish. His hands, elbows, knees and feet blurred around him with impossible speed and bone-crunching power as he tried to fight his way clear, desperate to get to Whistler. Limbs snapped and blood spurted in his wake, but Blade didn't care.

He couldn't let Whistler die.

But the police weren't about to give up yet. As Blade neared the armory, a pair of agents launched themselves at Blade in a joint attack, their rifle butts catching him in the chest and ribs. Such was their speed and determination that Blade was knocked off-balance, staggering under the double impact. His boot caught against a heavy bundle of cables and he

fell backwards, seizing the agents' tunics and dragging them down with him.

Before he could halt his fall, the computer workstation on the bench next to him exploded, launching
Blade and the two agents into the air. The trio flew
backwards through the main door in a spray of glass
and splinters, and landed hard atop a pile of broken
timber outside the boathouse.

As the dust settled, Agent Cumberland sprang into
action, brandishing a requisitioned loudhailer and
waving frantically at the assembled police. "Take him
down!"

One of the waiting FBI agents raised a Coda net gun
and fired at Blade. Four dagger-like projectiles
streaked out of the barrel and buried themselves into
the ground behind Blade. The steel netting strung
between them sprang taut, wrapping itself around the
stricken Daywalker and tangling his limbs as he
fought to free himself. Blade was immediately
obscured by flying bodies as a small army of agents
leapt from their cars and dived on top of him, pum-
meling away, trying to beat him into submission. A
nervous-looking medic climbed out of a black army
van nearby, holding a large syringe of tranquilizer.

Over by the squad car, Agent Cumberland punched
his fist into the air and danced a triumphant jig of joy.

Back in the shattered remains of the boathouse,
Whistler was not yet dead. But he knew he would be,
very soon. Every cell in his body told him so, and for
once, he didn't argue. He knew what was coming, and
he wasn't afraid.

It was worth the price.

Blade's life for his.

It was a cost he'd always known he'd have to pay, one day. But as the time approached, Whistler couldn't help wishing that he could put this one on credit.

Dragging his bullet-riddled body across the floor, Whistler wrapped a sticky hand around a piece of heavy machinery and hauled himself up into a sitting position. Grunting with effort, he propped himself up against the machine. Blood streamed from a multitude of blown-open wounds in his chest and leg, pooling in black puddles on the sawdust-strewn floor beneath him.

Whistler's eyes narrowed in frustration as he gazed through the smoke-obscured doorway. There was one more server left next door, but he knew that he would never reach it in time. He could feel his body shutting down further with each second that ticked past, and realized that he may not have long left.

A sudden burst of shouting came from the river-bank outside, interspersed with loud grunts and cracks and the sound of Blade swearing furiously.

The corner of Whistler's mouth twitched up in a painful smile.

So that was that. Blade was clear of the building.

There was only one more thing left to do.

Whistler spat more blood onto the floor, then wiped his lips and waited.

After a moment, the ghostly shapes of a dozen FBI agents emerged through the smoke and warily closed in around him, guns at the ready. They had never seen anything like this. The old geezer should've been dead about three rounds ago, and yet he still hung on, clinging to life with his teeth. As if a criminal like him could have anything worth living for at this point.

One of the agents pressed a switch on his gasmask to address him. "Move a finger and you're dead."

The corner of Whistler's month twitched, his breath coming in great wheezing gasps. He flicked the middle finger of his free hand towards the agents in a derisory salute. "How 'bout this one?"

Then he let his other hand uncurl to reveal the small black shape of a remote control device. All eyes locked in on it, taking in the large digital timer counting down...

00:04. 00:03. 00:02....

There was a collective intake of breath.

One of the slower agents, a middle-aged man known as Spud, reached out and pointed accusingly. "Hey, he's got something in his—"

A series of massive explosions rocked the workshop as three barrels of kerosene heating fuel exploded, setting off the two dozen claymore mines packed into the wall cavities.

The boathouse, with Whistler in it, was blown sky high.

Outside, police and agents ran for cover as the whole face of the building exploded outwards in an eruption of glass and fire. Clouds of black smoke and flaming debris mushroomed skywards, rolling up into the night while the shockwave of the blast swept the watching crowds off their feet.

In the midst of the conflagration, Blade briefly managed to tear free from his captors, shouting his mentor's name. He clawed at the thick steel netting imprisoning him, trying to tear through it with his bare fingers.

But it was too late.

As Blade watched helplessly, the explosion in the armory set off a chain reaction that ripped through the building, triggering mine after mine like a trail of breadcrumbs. The lab blew up, followed by the workshop, igniting the spare canisters of nitrous oxide stored in the outside shed. A wall of light and fire rushed outwards from the boathouse, sweeping up everything in its path.

And then it was over. Debris rained down onto the ground, pattering down all around them.

Blade stared into the raging inferno that was all that was left of his home, and with it, his life. The world swam, and he threw out a hand to catch himself. He was dimly aware of an army of officers surrounding him, slowly inching closer, wary of this blood-covered man who had taken down half of their force, single-handedly.

Almost single-handedly...

A muscle twitched in Blade's jaw. Abruptly, he dropped to his knees and laid his sword almost tenderly down on the ground in front of him, bowing his head in tribute.

Whistler was dead. Nothing mattered any more.

Then the uniformed agents rushed him, seizing hold of his clothing, Blade felt a sharp needle pierce the skin of his arm, and mournfully turned his face up towards the sky. He watched with dimming eyes

as a police helicopter descended slowly towards him
with a thump of rotors, its searchlight washing over
him as his world faded out to a blinding white.

SIX

In the darkness, something moved.

Blade frowned, his eyes flickering beneath their closed lids. He was cold and overwhelmingly drowsy, but he knew that it was vitally important for him to stay awake.

He waited, listening. An age seemed to go by; every second was an eternity, and it seemed that there was no end in sight.

Then, after what seemed like forever, there it was again. A tiny movement in the infinite blackness, so small and quick that it was over in a heartbeat.

Blade opened his eyes and turned towards the movement, his ears suddenly ringing with the echo of a noise just on the periphery of his hearing. Frowning, he climbed to his feet and began cautiously stepping forwards in the darkness, his nerves twanging and alert. His legs were rubbery and there was no sensation of his feet touching the ground, but Blade knew he had to move quickly. There wasn't much time, and it was desperately important that he got back home before whatever was making the noise caught up with him.

He began walking, his footsteps ringing in the night.

A snatch of noise came from behind him, like a single frame cut from the soundtrack of an old movie. Blade swung around, dropping down into an en-guarde position, but there was only blackness behind him.

Blade's eyes ticked left, then right. A dull, dragging stillness descended, pouring over him like glue. Blade held his breath and listened, hearing his own heart pulsing steadily in his ears, overlaid with the high pitched ringing of amplified silence.

Then he turned back to his path with renewed urgency.

Blade picked up his pace, jogging lightly through the darkness, his senses greatly heightened as he concentrated on staying alert for the tiniest of sounds.

A flash of blinding light suddenly cut across his vision. Blade reeled, falling backwards and spinning towards the ground in slow motion. He landed with a bruising thump and clawed at his eyes, gasping. Burned into his brain was the after image of a sword—his sword?—slashing down towards his face, the diamond-ground edge striking sparks off his optic nerve as it cut through his skull like a guillotine.

Blade lifted his head and looked frantically down at his fingers, expecting to see blood.

There was nothing there. His hands were perfectly clean.

A long, low howl sounded in the darkness. It came from far away, but the echoes were unnaturally close, raising strange vibrations in his bones. Blade felt his hackles go up, the hairs rising on the back of his neck as a shiver of warning swept through him. He took a steadying breath, feeling his body flood with heat and adrenalin, ready for battle. His gums smarted as his canines began to lengthen, growing into jagged points that stung the inside of his mouth.

The howl died away, leaving behind an urgent silence. Cautiously, Blade climbed to his feet and stood swaying in the cold night air. The atmosphere around him crackled with menace, almost like a malignant presence. As Blade watched, the velvet darkness that was stretched out in front of him moved, a brisk wind whipping up like a storm on a black ocean.

Blade stood still, breathing deeply, strongly. His arms dangled loosely by his sides, ready to whip out a stake or a dagger and turn whatever the hell was making that noise into bleeding, screaming dust. He had never been here before, but somehow he knew what was coming, with the blind inevitability of fate. There was something out there, something bad, and he had to get to it before it found him. If he didn't catch it unawares, he would never be able to beat it.

He strained his senses, trying to pinpoint where the sound was coming from.

As he listened, something cold dripped onto his chin. Blade lifted a hand and wiped at it distractedly. Could it be raining? No. This fluid was black and slightly sticky. Blade sniffed at it. It wasn't blood. The liquid smelt tangy and sharp, almost like the smell of ammonia, but sweeter and less pungent. Weird.

The wind intensified, blowing up into a stiff breeze around him. Blade looked up, his clothing streaming out behind him. The air was cold, and brought with it the strong scent of the sea. He must be by the river somewhere, but where, exactly? He didn't recognize the landscape at all.

Then Blade coughed. He felt something almost like bile rising in his throat and he coughed again, sharply, to clear it. When he looked down, his hand was spattered with black liquid. Blade stared at his hand in horror as more of the fluid welled out of his nose and eyes, streaking down his cheeks like freezing black tears. He wiped at it in revulsion, but more seeped out in its place.

Spooked, Blade whirled and began to run. He had to get out of here. Whatever this was, it wasn't something he could fight. He knew instinctively that the longer he stayed here the harder it was going to be to leave, and he wanted to leave very badly indeed.

Footsteps pounded behind him as he hurtled through the darkness. At first there was only one pair of feet running after him. Then others joined the first pair, until soon, the night was ringing with the sound of pursuit. They had found him.

Without looking back, Blade doubled his pace, drawing on his reserves of preternatural stamina. The footsteps easily kept pace with him. He could hear shouting now, and the baying of dogs. The light of blazing torches flared in his peripheral vision, and Blade's flight took on a more urgent pace as he realized that he wasn't simply being chased; he was being hunted.

He flew across the ground, legs pumping as he sought to escape from his pursuers. But after a while he realized that not only were they keeping up with him, they were gaining on him with frightening speed.

Blade suddenly found to his horror that he was slowing down, the black fluid seeping down inside him and filling his limbs with a creeping numbness. What the hell was that stuff? Blade gave a growl of frustration as he felt his leg muscles flood with the deadly liquid, the cold burrowing into his nerve fibers and shutting them down almost instantly. He stumbled and almost fell, but caught himself at the last moment and carried on, gritting his teeth as he dragged himself along.

The shouting voices were very close now. Blade fought to keep his body moving, but even breathing was becoming difficult. Waves of weakness poured through him, and black-tinged sweat flooded out of his brow as he labored onwards, fighting against the steadily rising wind.

Before long, Blade realized that he couldn't go on. The wind was getting frighteningly strong now, and the tiredness in his muscles was overwhelming. He had to save his strength to fight the crowd that was chasing him.

Snarling, Blade bared his teeth in readiness and whirled to face his pursuers.

The space behind him was empty.

An instant later, he was knocked sprawling as a wave of bodies poured over him from behind. Blade felt hands seize his limbs and press them into the dry earth beneath him. Other hands ripped at his clothes, tearing his shirt off and exposing his chest to the coldness of the night. Faces loomed above him, leering, mocking him, faces with sharp teeth and yellow eyes.

Vampires.

Blade fought to break free.

But these were unlike any vampires he had ever seen. Blade stared as the lead vampire approached him, growling under its breath. The creature sported an impressive set of inch-long teeth, and had a small wave of bony spines running up the centre of its forehead, almost like a crest. The vampire cocked his head like a bird of prey and leaned over Blade, reaching out curiously to touch his face...

Blade broke free with a bellow, wrenching his body to the side and rolling to his feet. Then he put his head down and charged through the forest of jeering figures surrounding him, using his remaining strength like a battering ram to clear a path to freedom...

Crack! His head struck an immovable object. Dazed, Blade shook his head and looked up to see Whistler standing in front of him, his long gray hair and beard whipping in the wind. The old man was leaning back quite casually on the crumbling mud walls of what looked for all the world like a massive pyramid.

Blade rose to his feet, unsure. He was fairly certain that the pyramid hadn't been there a moment ago. But that was the least of his worries. He glanced back over his shoulder to see the vampires behind him surge forwards, darting towards Whistler with their fangs bared. Blade opened his mouth to shout a warning to his mentor, to tell him to run before it was too late.

Before he could speak, Whistler was suddenly, impossibly, standing beside him. Blade spun round in surprise as the old man reached behind Blade and drew the sword from Blade's back scabbard with a soft hiss of metal.

But wait a minute. This wasn't his sword.

The weapon welded by Whistler was ancient looking, made of pitted and blackened metal. As Blade stared at it in confusion, Whistler reached up and put a hand on Blade's shoulder, his eyes lit from within by a soft smile.

Then he drove the sword through the center of Blade's chest, burying it up to the hilt.

Blade gasped. He reached out and clutched Whistler by the shoulders as hot blood seeped through his torn shirt. He stared into his mentor's face in shock. The old man's expression hadn't changed, but then his smile widened to reveal a set of sharp curved canines.

Blade knew then that he was lost.

His knees buckled and he collapsed onto the ground. The blackness took form around him, swirling down from the unseen sky in a torrent. As Blade writhed around on the ground, thrashing and choking, it formed into a single, cyclonic spiral, sucking up everything that it touched. As it reached the pyramid, a heavy cracking sound rent the night air. Blade watched, unable to move, as blackened fissures tore through the pyramid behind the vampires, running from ground to sky like a negative lightening bolt.

Seemingly oblivious to the wholesale destruction going on behind them, the vampires crowded around Blade, pushing and jostling. One by one, they pulled out wooden stakes. Blade tried to cry out but his voice was whipped away by the wind. The next thing he knew the vampires were upon him, pushing him down flat onto his back and driving their stakes through his wrists, his shoulders, his ankles. Blade felt no pain, only a heavy sense of pressure that increased as more and more stakes were driven through his body.

He watched helplessly as Whistler stepped forwards and stood over him, holding out the ancient sword. Slowly, the whites of the old man's eyes began to bleed out an oily black fluid. Whistler took a step forward and laid the tip of the sword on Blade's bare chest. He began to cut a pattern into his flesh, the metal hissing and squealing as if it were red-hot.

Blade gritted his teeth. The pain was intense, but it was nothing compared to the anguish he felt at the loss of Whistler. Above the sound of the rising gale, he was dimly aware of the great mud blocks that made up the pyramid shifting in the wind, crumbling and cracking and filling the air with flying debris. A deep bass rumble shook the earth as though the ground itself was seeking to cave in and bury the lot of them in its dark depths.

Above him, Whistler finished off his pattern and withdrew his sword, tilting his head and frowning slightly as he surveyed his handiwork. It was a small gesture, but it was so familiar to Blade that he almost wept. Looking down at his own chest, Blade saw that a large, primitive-looking vampire glyph had been carved there, outlined in torn flesh and red blood.

At the sight of the glyph, an overwhelming sense of dread rose through Blade in a screaming tide. He had been here before, and now he remembered what was to come. He tried to pull free of the stakes, but he no longer had the strength. All he could do was watch as Whistler raised the sword over his head, watching him with those awful black eyes of his. Behind him, the gale rose to hurricane force, dragging the air into shrieking vortexes and sending the other vampires flying away into the sky like autumn leaves.

With an almighty crunch, the pyramid was ripped apart by the storm, its walls flying outwards and upwards as though blown out by an explosion. A yawning black void was revealed at its heart. Writhing black shadows spilled from the void, spreading out along the earth in a dark wave, hissing and shrieking until the sound seemed to fill the whole world, drowning out the sounds of the hurricane.

As Blade lay in the dirt and screamed soundlessly, Whistler smiled again and stepped forwards. The ancient sword flashed downwards, driving with unstoppable speed towards Blade's heart...

Blade's body jerked in his sleep, his eyes flickering wildly beneath his closed lids. Then his breathing steadied and his body twitched as he began to wake, swimming up through the black tides of sleep towards the surface.

As his consciousness started to return, Blade gradually became aware of his body. His limbs felt curiously heavy. There was an odd sensation in his chest, dull and tingling, as though he had recently been struck by an ice pick.

Blade frowned beneath his closed eyelids and tried to let himself drift off, but it was no good. Something was pulling his mind back to the land of the living, something gleeful and mean that whispered in his ear that whatever he saw upon awakening, it would only cause him more pain.

"Rise and shine, sleepyhead."

Blade groaned, trying to hang onto that precious moment of gray oblivion that separated sleeping and waking. He felt weak, exhausted. His whole body ached, and he felt like his head was full of small, angry mosquitoes trying to chew their way out of his skull.

Blade squeezed his eyes tight shut, trying to sink back down into the merciful nothingness of sleep, but a small voice in the back of his mind screamed at him. He ignored the voice. It screamed louder. Blade tried to lift a hand to rub his head. His wrists were manacled together.

Shit.

It was no good.

With a sigh, he slowly opened his eyes.

He was in a small, rectangular room, with no windows and yellow, buzzing strip lighting. Two very pissed-looking middle-aged men were glowering at him from across a long metal table. One was tall and stern looking, whereas the other was much shorter, with an unfortunate toupee stuck to his head like molting road kill. They were both dressed in casual clothing, which they wore as though it was some kind of uniform. Behind them was a one-way mirrored window, and in the corner of the room, a CCTV camera whirred and clicked as it zoomed in on him, its red recording light on.

Blade groaned. This did not look promising. He ran his tongue around the inside of his mouth and tried to lift his head, which felt as heavy as a cannonball. "Who..."

The older and less charming of the two men glowered back at him. "Special Agents Ray Cumberland and Wilson Hale, FBI. We've been tracking you for a long time."

Despite his disorientation, Blade was impressed at how well the man could pronounce the capital letters in his own title. He must've practiced that one in front of a mirror for ages.

Memory hit Blade like a hammer-blow to the temple. He jerked upright in his seat, suddenly wide-awake. He took a deep breath, afraid to say the name that had just slammed into his concussion-fogged brain. "Whistler..."

Cumberland shook his head, his eyes full of cold loathing. "Dead. Just like all of your victims."

Blade squeezed his eyes tight shut.

This couldn't be real, it couldn't be.

Cumberland stood up behind the table. "How many people have you killed? Thirty? Forty? Fifty?" The detective's voice was carefully controlled but Blade could detect the anger simmering behind it, along with a dangerous dose of self-importance.

"One hundred and eighty-seven," Blade growled, ignoring Hale's sharp intake of breath and mentally adding "...this year." He tried to sit up straighter in his chair, looking the detective in the eye. "But those were familiars—people who worked for them."

"And by 'them' you mean vampires, right?" Cumberland sat back down again, gripping the edge of the table tightly. "I suppose next you'll be telling us that Bigfoot's in on the conspiracy too?"

The detective gave a tight-lipped smirk as Blade glowered at him. "So what kills these bloodsuckers, tough guy? Maybe you can give us some pointers." Cumberland started ticking off points on his fingers. "You can stake 'em, right? Then there's sunlight— what about crosses, Wilson? Do those still work?"

"I don't know, Ray. What if a vampire's Jewish?"

"That's a good point." Cumberland gave a smile that stopped just short of his eyes. "And does garlic work on a Hindu vampire? Or do you need saffron or something?"

Hale sniggered.

Cumberland shook his head, his smile fading. "You can keep doing your song and dance as long as you want, Blade, but it's not going to play. You're a stone-cold killer. And you're as sick as fuck."

"Let's leave the diagnosis to the professionals, eh, Ray?"

Cumberland turned in his seat to see the tall, graceful figure of Doctor Edgar Vance standing in the doorway, watching them. Vance nodded to Cumberland in greeting, and then strode across the room to join them. He set his black leather case on the table and took a seat by Blade, who stared at him with instant dislike.

Vance turned his chair towards Blade, his face the very picture of professional concern. "Hello, Blade.

My name is Doctor Vance. I'm with the Department of Mental Health. I've been charged with conducting a psychiatric evaluation of you."

Vance turned to the two detectives. "Gentlemen, would you mind giving us a few moments alone?"

Hale looked at Cumberland, who blew out his cheeks in exasperation. Eventually, he nodded. The detectives rose with a scrape of chairs and exited the room, leaving Blade alone with Vance. The door slammed behind them.

Vance smiled at Blade, trying to project an air of non-judgmental sympathy. He held out his hands and spoke to Blade in the careful, earnest manner of someone addressing a mentally challenged puppy. "I imagine this must be very frightening for you. But I want you to know that I'm here to help. In order to do that, I need to ask you some questions." Vance repositioned his chair. "Now, can you tell me what day it is?"

Blade just stared at Vance, not even bothering to reply. He could smell the blood racing through the man's veins, and knew that he was not as cool and collected as he made himself out to be. Above them, the clock ticked away, accentuating the silence.

A full twenty seconds passed. To Blade, they felt like an eternity.

Whistler was dead...

"What about the president?" Vance continued smoothly. "Do you know who's in the White House at the moment?"

"An asshole." Blade couldn't stop himself.

Vance sighed, mentally ticking a box in his head. So Blade was one of those.

"Alright then. Let's talk about vampires. What can you tell me about them?"

"There's nothing to tell. They exist." Blade's voice was flat, emotionless. He was acutely aware of Cumberland and Vale watching him from their little booth on the other side of the one-way mirror. There was someone else in there with them too. Blade blew out his nostrils in a sharp blast and inhaled surreptitiously. Whoever was in there smelled of fear and, bizarrely, bacon and egg sandwiches.

Blade's nose twitched in disgust. It was not a good combination.

"And are you one of them?" Vance sat forward in his chair, moving closer to Blade. He waited another five seconds. "What about blood? When you drink it, do you find yourself sexually aroused?"

Blade gave Vance a stony glare, hoping that the arrogant bastard would burst into flames. Behind his back, he began flexing his wrists, trying to find a weak point in his cuffs. At full strength, he would be able to snap his bonds like cotton. As he was, he could barely muster the energy to form his hands into fists. He hadn't taken his serum in over forty-eight hours now, and without it, he was in much the same condition as a vampire who hadn't fed in a month.

As Vance droned on, Blade's stomach growled. He began breathing heavily, trying to control the gnawing fire that rose in a flood through his body. He was painfully aware of the presence of food nearby—food that pulsed warmly through the body of the human... the man... standing next to him...

Blade gritted his teeth, fighting for control.

Vance carried on blithely, unaware of the danger he was now putting himself in. "You see, it strikes me that this business of vampirism has strong connotations of sexual confusion. Bodily fluids being exchanged, that sort of thing." Vance glanced down at his manicured fingernails, and then buffed them on his jacket. "You have to ask where that comes from. I'm wondering, for instance, what your relationship was like with your mother. Were the two of you close?"

Blade's eyes narrowed.

The minute he got free, he was going to have to kill this guy.

Ten minutes later, Dr Vance joined the two detectives and the newcomer—Police Chief Vreede—in the observation room. He closed the door behind him carefully and locked it, looking grim.

Chief Vreede stepped forward anxiously. "What's your assessment, doctor?"

Vance shook his head sadly, motioning back through the mirror towards Blade. "He's psychotic, with paranoid features, possessing dangerous levels of sociopathy." The doctor pulled out his notepad and glanced at it. "He's also exhibiting disorganized behavior. He obviously doesn't have a properly formed conscience." Vance snapped his notebook shut and tucked it into his back pocket, then spread his hands in a gesture of sincerity. "For his safety and the public's, I'm recommending that he be transferred to the County Psychiatric for further treatment."

Cumberland gasped. His mouth opened and closed several times, like a landed fish. "That's unacceptable," he spluttered. "This man's wanted in connection with a laundry list of federal crimes." He stepped up to Doctor Vance, looking him squarely in the eye. "I need him on a plane to the Detention Center in Washington tonight."

"Agent Cumberland, that man is in no condition to undergo prosecution."

Cumberland and Hale stared at Vreede in disbelief.

Hale cleared his throat. "chief, we've got a federal arrest warrant here that clearly supersedes—"

"I don't care about your warrant." Police Chief Vreede stepped across the room and stood beside Dr Vance, backing him up. "We're in my jurisdiction now. You've got an issue with that, you take it up with the local magistrate."

Dr Vance shrugged apologetically at the detectives. "I'm sorry, gentlemen, but the call has already been made. A team from the hospital should be here momentarily to oversee the transfer."

Downstairs, Danica stepped boldly through the marble-stepped entrance at the front of the police station, dressed in a gleaming white lab coat. Asher and Grimwood followed, buttoning up their requisitioned hospital gowns as they walked. Four vampire flunkies dressed as hospital orderlies tailed them, carrying a reinforced straightjacket, a bag packed with various evil-looking metal restraints, and a collapsible transport gurney.

Danica walked up to the front desk, her heels clicking on the tiled floor, and flashed a hospital ID badge at the sergeant, giving him her biggest, warmest smile. "Hi. We're here to transfer a patient to County General?"

SEVEN

Vance walked across the floor of the interrogation room towards Blade, humming a cheerful little ditty under his breath. With the briefest of glances at the CCTV camera, he flipped open the locks of the leather case which lay on the table. He removed a large plastic syringe and a glass ampule of colorless liquid and held it up to the light, swirling it around to check for sediment. He spoke softly to Blade as he filled the syringe with the fluid. "Just a little something to keep you compliant."

Blade glared up at Vance, hate filling his eyes. There was something not right about this guy. He was way too slick. His voice was soothing but he moved in a flowing, reptilian way, like an alligator creeping through the long grass towards prey.

The guy didn't smell like a vampire, but he sure as hell was acting like one.

Vance tapped the syringe with a fingernail, making sure there were no air bubbles in the fluid. His mouth curved upwards at the corners. "The normal dose is two, maybe three hundred milligrams. But for a strapping young hybrid like yourself...' Vance glanced at Blade, his eyes narrowing as he calculated body mass. "I think we'll kick it up to a couple thousand."

Blade stared at Vance, his mind a whirl of confusion.

Then Vance hefted the syringe and reached for Blade's arm. Blade pulled away sharply and tried to kick out at him, but his legs were completely numb and moved as though they were made of concrete. Sweat broke out on Blade's forehead as he concentrated on them, willing them to move.

It was no good. Either he had already been drugged, or he had been sitting here unconscious for one hell of a long time.

Adrenaline flooded through him, flooding his muscles with a jolt of energy that inflamed his growing hunger and honed his senses to a razor edge. His belly felt like it was filled with molten lava and the scent of Vance's blood called to him with a siren song of dark sweetness. Blade closed his eyes briefly, fighting against the increasingly powerful urge to feed.

While Blade struggled with himself, Vance grabbed the Daywalker's upper arm and swiftly plunged his needle into one of the big veins running down the inside of his elbow. Blade growled in pain and yanked his arm away, but it was done. He glared up at Vance, sweat trickling down his forehead.

Vance smiled condescendingly. "There. That wasn't so bad, was it?" He tipped his head to one side and studied Blade coldly. "You're weak, aren't you? In need of your serum, no doubt." He put his syringe away and snapped his leather case shut. "Who would've guessed a mere human like me could over-power you?"

Blade stopped struggling as realization dawned. His mouth fell open. "You're with them... A familiar..."

"Going on five years now." There was a touch of pride in Vance's voice. He held out his own arm, and pulled back his shirt cuff a little to reveal a thumb-nail-sized glyph tattooed in dark ink on the underside of his wrist. Vance pulled his cuff back down and smiled at Blade, who gaped at him, lost for words as the implications of this hit home. "It's the end-game, Blade. All their plans are finally coming to fruition. So just sit back and enjoy the show."

Adrenaline kick-started Blade's system and he turned to the one-way mirror, suddenly frantic. "He's one of them! Dammit, he's working for them!"

Vance looked straight into the two-way mirror as Blade ranted, cocking an eyebrow and shrugging in an exaggerated fashion for the benefit of the video cameras. He had given the man one tiny sedative injection and he had gone mad.

The fellow was quite clearly deranged.

Ignoring Blade's increasingly urgent cries, Vance stood up and walked next door to join the detectives. All four of them gazed back through the glass as Blade raged away, shouting and struggling against his bonds like a lunatic.

Vance held out his hand to Chief Vreede, who reached out to take it. As they shook hands, the police chief's shirt cuff briefly rose up, revealing a similar glyph tattooed on his arm.

They smiled at one another and then left the room, leaving Cumberland and Hale staring mutely after them.

Long minutes passed. On the other side of the mirror, Blade stared at his own refection, slowly slipping down in the chair. Why was he so blurry? He couldn't seem to focus at all. Hunger stabbed deep within him like a white-hot poker, dimming to a dull drowsing sensation as the drug crawled through his veins, relaxing his body. He knew that the drug's effects probably wouldn't last long, but in his weakened state, he couldn't muster the energy to fight them.

His body convulsed as a wave of shivers drove through him. Blade's breath hissed out through his teeth as he rallied his flagging resources to do battle with his own primal urges. He focused all his remaining energy into his breathing, slowing it down until he was taking a bare handful of breaths a minute. He felt his heartbeat slow in unison and the pain in his blood diminished as his body dropped into a state of torpor.

Ignoring the languid pull of his deepening hunger, Blade focused on his breathing, feeling his lungs expand, then contract, pulling cooling air into the boiling pit of fire housed within his body. This was a trick Whistler had taught him, honed over the years, to enable him to regain control over himself when the Thirst struck. He had to use this as a reflex action to his hunger before Whistler had finished refining his serum, back in the days when a single dose would last barely six hours. The old man sometime didn't get to him in time before the Thirst kicked in, and some of Whistler's more interesting scars bore tribute to his sheer determination in house-training the young Daywalker.

Blade's eyelids flickered closed, then sprung open again as his body slowed down. He had to stay alert. When the time came for escape, he had to be ready.

Out in the hallway, the elevator's steel doors slid open to reveal Danica, Asher, Grimwood and the four vampire orderlies, who were wheeling the hospital gurney ahead of them. As they stepped out into the long, brightly-lit corridor, they passed detectives Cumberland and Hale, who were in the process of chasing down Chief Vreede as he strode off towards the front exit. Vreede increased his pace, pretending that he couldn't hear the detectives shouting at him.

Cumberland was nearly apoplectic with rage. That Vance character had no right to just step in and take away Blade before he even had a chance to question him. How dare he! This was his case, and Blade was his responsibility. With Whistler dead, Blade was his only link to a hundred unsolved crimes the length and breadth of the state. He would be dammed if he was going to lose his prime suspect after all this time.

Seeing Vreede's medical escort approaching, Cumberland put out an arm across the corridor to stop them. "Just hold it right there."

To his surprise, the nurse leading the party shoved him aside and kept going, completely ignoring the detective.

Cumberland looked at Hale, warning bells sounding in his head.

Something wasn't right here.

He started running after Vreede, tailed by the faithful figure of Hale.

Back in the interrogation room, Blade struggled to free himself from his restraints before Vance came back. He was firmly in the grip of the drug now, the room blurring and spinning with each movement of his head. His belly burned with a dull ache as the Thirst built within him, growing stronger by the minute as his own iron-clad control slipped, weakened by the drug stealing through his veins. Blade fought to keep his eyes open as he did battle with the drug. If he let them close, it would all be over for him, and quite possibly everybody else within a hundred yard radius.

Trying to ignore the seventies-style special effects hampering his vision, Blade concentrated on wrestling with his handcuffs. For ordinary metal, they seemed extraordinarily tough. Beads of sweat ran down into Blade's eyes as he tensed the muscles in his arms, trying to snap the links of the chain that held the cuffs together.

As he struggled, the door opened and five figures entered the room. Blade blinked, trying to focus on them, and frowned as the figures divided and swam back together, leaving glowing movement-trails behind them. The musky, snake-like smell of vampire was unmistakable and Blade growled low in his throat, trying to rise.

The first figure, a woman, planted her metal-tipped heel against his chest and shoved him back down into the chair. "Easy, lover. You're not going anywhere."

Danica moved closer to Blade, gazing down at him hungrily. It was a little unreal being this close to the

fabled Daywalker after years of long-distance surveillance work. Danica took a deep breath, savoring the
moment. It was truly wonderful seeing Blade like
this, drugged and incapacitated, unable to fight back.
She only wished that Gedge was here to see what his
sacrifice had achieved. She hadn't particularly liked
the guy, but for a human, he'd had such ambition...

Danica smiled impishly, unable to resist the temp-
tation to brag. She hoped that Blade could still hear
her through his drug-induced lethargy. "We moved
the humans around like pawns, Blade. Used them to
flush you out."

Despite his disorientated condition, a primitive
reflex clicked on in Blade's brain as the meaning of
her words hit home.

This woman was responsible for Whistler's death.

Blade's eyes snapped into focus and he snarled at
her, then dragged his feet under him and tried to
lunge from the chair, his cuffs pulling taut as he tried
to break free. Grimwood immediately stepped up to
Danica's side and cracked Blade across the jaw with
his fist, a solid punch that snapped the Daywalker's
head to one side and knocked him back into his
chair.

Blade sagged, all the fight going out of him.

Grimwood grinned, exposing his surgical steel
fangs. "Don't worry, sunshine. Soon as we get you out
of here, you'll get a chance to play."

Danica motioned to the two vampire orderlies.
They nodded and stepped forwards, unshackling
Blade. One of them pinioned Blade's arms with a
vice-like grip while the other pulled the metal-
reinforced straightjacket onto him.

Blade started thrashing around, albeit weakly, in an attempt to break their grip on him. The first orderly scowled, straining to fasten the metal clamps around the back as Blade pulled them apart time and time again. It was like watching a teacher trying to put a winter coat on a reluctant two year-old. Grimwood laughed, enjoying the show.

Danica stepped forwards, adopting a patronizing tone. "Don't make this any harder than it has to be." She moved in closer, her eyes locking with Blade's as he fought against her assistants. "You're all alone, Blade. No one can help you now—"

Boom! With impeccable timing, the one-way mirror above them shattered, exploding outwards in a shower of silvered glass fragments, carrying with it the body of one of the vampire mental health flunkies. The corpse sparked and flamed as it sailed into the room, landing in a cloud of ash in the middle of the table.

As Asher and Grimwood jumped up in shock, a man vaulted through the blown-out window, simultaneously drawing two high-tech electronic pistols. He landed solidly on the table, glass crunching beneath his boots, and straightened up to face the cowering vampires. Slapped onto his black jacket was a "Hello, my name is..." hospital sticker. In place of a name, the words "FUCK YOU!" had been scrawled in what looked like red felt pen.

The stranger shot a slight bow towards Blade and then turned to face the trio of vampires, grinning insanely. "Tell me, why don't vampires have any friends?"

Asher stared at him, enraged at the intrusion.

The newcomer clicked a fresh round into his pistol without waiting for a reply. "Because they're a pain in the neck."

Danica snarled, recognizing the intruder instantly. "King!"

Then the lights went out.

Green emergency lights immediately flashed on above the exits, followed by a shrieking cacophony of fire alarms. In the confusion that followed, King took the opportunity to fire both of his pistols at Asher. The vampire dropped to the floor just in time and dived behind a pile of stacked metal chairs. The bullets whistled over his head and struck the unfortunate vampire orderly standing behind him, lodging in his chest and exploding in an intense burst of blue UV light. The vampire instantly disintegrated as the light chewed up his insides. Within seconds, he was little more than an empty carbon shell.

King whipped around in a low crouch and fired a second round at Danica, who dived for cover behind the heavy metal table. She upended it single-handedly, using it as a shield. King kept on firing, bullets sparking off the table, hoping his UV rounds would punch through the tabletop and hit Danica. King's pistols clicked on empty and Danica flung the table at him as though it weighed little more than styrofoam, then turned and pelted out of the room.

As the battle raged around him, Blade decided that this was as good a time as any to leave. Forcing himself to concentrate, he fought against the effects of the drug. Focusing intently, he managed to wrench himself to one side, tipping his chair over and sprawling full-length onto the floor.

The noise of his fall immediately caught Grimwood's attention. The big vampire made to grab Blade, but the Daywalker kicked up and out, his heavily booted foot connecting solidly with the hulking vampire's mid-section, sending him flying backwards. Grimwood hit the thin partition wall and ploughed his way through it, vanishing into the adjacent room in a cloud of plaster dust and flying wood fragments.

King ran over to Blade and grabbed the Daywalker's forearm, pulling him to his feet with an effort. He reloaded and whipped around, aiming another sweep of blue fire at the cowering Asher, sending the vamp scurrying out of his hiding place like a rat from a bonfire.

King turned back to Blade. "Let's fly, kemosabe!"

King half-carried, half-dragged Blade towards the door and out into the darkened corridor of the police station.

At the other end of the hallway, Cumberland and Hale ran towards the sound of the commotion, their faces pale with worry. Someone had activated both the fire and the intruder alarms, and as far as Cumberland could see, there was no fire. But he knew in his bones that the alarms were connected with Blade, somehow.

Cumberland skidded to a halt at the end of the corridor. As though in a dream, he saw his worst fears played out in front of his eyes as he watched Blade stumble out of the interrogation room in a cloud of smoke, being dragged to safety by a tall, well-muscled young man. Blade moved unsteadily, reeling as though he was drunk. Nevertheless, his accomplice looked more than strong enough to carry the both of them, if need be.

And more to the point, he was armed.

Cumberland reached for his pistol. "He's getting away!"

King fired a last couple of shots through the doorway into the room behind him, making sure the vampire imposters were contained. Then he pulled a grenade from his bandolier and tossed it back in through the doorway. The grenade exploded in a massive blast of flying debris, knocking the two detectives off their feet. A long red tongue of fire licked outwards at the ceiling, filling the corridor with choking black smoke.

Blade collapsed against the wall, shaking, close to passing out. The hunger was so strong in him now that it was almost unbearable, and it took every last ounce of his self-control to stop him from turning and sinking his teeth into the throat of the young man who had just rescued him. He groaned under his breath.

"Don't die on me, you undead motherfucker!" King grabbed Blade under the arms and hauled him upwards, dragging him back upright.

With a grunt, Blade staggered to his feet and lurched off down the corridor, leaning heavily on King.

Twenty yards away, a half-dozen uniformed officers were engaged in hand-to-hand combat with a second intruder, an athletic-looking young woman clad in military-green combat pants and a skin-tight modern biker's jacket. Three officers were already down, snoozing peacefully into the acrylic pile, blissfully oblivious of their broken noses and bruised skulls. Within seconds, the deadly beauty had finished off two of the other three.

King rounded the corner and called out to the woman. "Whistler! We need that serum NOW!"

Blade's head jerked up, hope flaring in his bloodshot eyes. Whistler? Surely, he had misheard?

Abigail Whistler executed a graceful spin, slamming a booted heel into the temple of the last police officer. He bounced against the wall with a dull *thud* and crumpled to the floor. Abigail reached into her backpack and withdrew an effervescent inhaler device. She tossed it to King, who gently placed it in Blade's shaking hands.

Realizing what it was, Blade quickly lifted it to his mouth. He bit down on the mouthpiece and pulled a tab on the side of the device, ignoring the flashing lights that danced in front of his eyes at the movement. The device hissed and the serum flowed into his lungs and through his system in a cool, clear torrent, dampening down the screaming of the starving vampire virus and restoring his own natural strength and vitality. He sagged in relief, breathing deeply as he willed his body back to normalcy.

Within moments, he looked up at King, clear-eyed. His superhuman strength renewed, he easily snapped his restraints apart.

King grinned at him, pleased. "Hey, Blacula. You ready to shake and bake?"

Blade responded with a swift uppercut to King's jaw. King staggered back, staring at Blade in shock.

Blade's face might as well have been carved from stone. "Call me that again, and I'll give you fucking brain damage."

King massaged his jaw for a moment, then shrugged and tossed Blade one of his pistols.

Tough crowd.

Cumberland and Hale ran around the corner towards them, shouting and holding up their FBI badges. Making a snap decision, King leapt forwards and punched Hale full in the face, knocking the detective down. At the same time, Blade kicked Cumberland in the chest, sending him hurtling backwards through the door of the men's room. He struck the bathroom mirror with a crunch and fell to the floor. He didn't get up again.

There was a sound like stampeding cattle as Grimwood came charging round the corner, followed by the three surviving vampire orderlies. Grimwood's hair was smoking, and there was a large burn mark across his barrel-like chest.

Blade fumbled with King's pistol for a moment, before figuring out that it was an automatic. He rose to his feet, squaring his shoulders. Then he poured round after round of explosive bullets into the corridor. The bullets smacked into the walls and floor as the vampires dived for cover, exploding in blinding bursts of UV light. Grimwood and his two vampire cronies were forced to fall back under the onslaught.

Blade and King ran up the corridor to join Abigail, coughing as gunpowder smoke filled the air of the police station. The emergency lighting seemed to be dimming, and it was getting increasingly hard to see.

Up ahead, a group of police officers spilled out from a stairwell. They were heavily armed and clad in bulky bulletproof vests. One of them was still frantically chewing his last mouthful of cucumber sandwich, having being wrenched cruelly from his lunch-break.

Seeing Blade and King, the police troop immediately opened fire.

Blade and the others ducked back into an alcove as bullets thudded into the walls around them. They pressed themselves back against the plaster as shot after shot blasted over their heads, the muzzle flashes lighting up the smoke-filled darkness.

King ducked as a bullet zinged past his ear. "We're pinned down!" He turned to Blade in frustration, willing him to do something about it. This guy was supposed to be a superhero, and he was just standing there like a big leather-clad lemon. "Can't you do something?"

Blade flourished his pistol helplessly. "I can't shoot around corners!"

"I can."

They both turned to Abigail. They saw the look in her eye.

As one, they stepped out into the corridor and laid down a barrage of covering fire. As the police fell back, withdrawing into a covered stairwell, Abigail slipped out behind them and withdrew a strangely shaped device from a pouch on her back. She gave a flick of her wrist and the device sprung open with a snap, unfolding into the shape of a compound bow. The weapon was crafted in blackened aluminum, its limbs fitted with vibration dampening modules embedded in key positions along its sleek length, giving it the look of being covered in metallic spines. Blade had never seen anything quite like it.

Abigail withdrew a silver arrow with a studded base from her quiver. Nocking it against her bow, she took careful aim at a fire extinguisher mounted on the wall at the end of the corridor. Her target was barely visible in the smoke-shrouded gloom, but it would have to do.

In one smooth motion, she pulled back the string and released it.

Abigail's arrow struck the fire extinguisher with a clang, ricocheting off down the corridor. A split second later, it embedded itself in the shoulder of one of the advancing vampire orderlies, who yelped and instinctively tore the arrow from its body. It looked down stupidly at the bolt clutched in its bloodied hand, panting with relief.

Close one.

Then there was a click and a whirr as the tiny egg-timer-like device on the end of the arrow spun around, activated by the impact. Two white notches on its surface lined up, and a red LED came on. The vampire peered down at it stupidly, reaching out a curious finger to touch the pretty red light...

The arrowhead exploded with a blast of intense blue UV light, catching all three vampires in the fallout. Despite his size, Grimwood was surprisingly quick at ducking away from the explosion as two of the vampire orderlies turned to flaming ash, their bodies shielding him from the full force of the blast.

The single surviving vampire orderly tried to duck into an office to take refuge, slamming the door behind him. Abigail swiftly fired another arrow, which punched straight through the door and into the smoking body of the cowering vampire. A blast of dirty orange light spilled under the door as it exploded.

Then it was Blade's turn to move. He pounded off down the corridor towards the cowering police squad, followed by Abigail and King. As they reached the stairwell, Blade grabbed hold of the steel door guarding it and ripped it clean off its hinges. He hurled it back down the stairwell at the squadron of police reinforcements, who were once again charging up the stairs. The cops went down like ten-pins, leaving the way clear.

Finally, they had an opening.

But as they charged down the cleared stairwell, Blade suddenly froze and yelled "Wait!"

King and Abigail pulled up in mid-stride, looking around at Blade in panic.

Blade twisted his hands together. "My sword. They still have it."

King stared at Blade. "Are you insane? We're practically home free! We can't go hunting for your fucking butter-knife now!"

But Blade was already heading back up the way they had come, head down, resolute in his mission. King turned and yelled after him. "Hey. Hey! Come back here! This is supposed to be a rescue!"

Abigail grabbed King's shoulder and pulled him back down the stairs. "Forget it, King. Let's move."

A racket of blaring police sirens greeted the pair as they hared through the front door of the police station. The metal station gates were locked down, and cop cars were surging through the opening in the gate, heading straight for them. It looked like reinforcements had arrived.

Once again, they were trapped.

The pair quickly pulled back, moving towards the relative shelter of the police station. Before they reached the door, there was an almighty crash from above them. A window on the third floor of the station exploded outwards, and Blade dropped the three stories to the ground, landing in front of Abigail and King in a cat-like crouch. He made it look so easy.

King stared at Blade, aghast.

The sonofabitch had his sword in his hand.

Blade grinned at King and flicked a middle finger up at him. "Now we can go."

King nudged Abigail, unbelieving. "Is he epic or what?"

The police scrambled out of their Cruisers and ran towards them, aiming pistols and shouting. For once, Abigail and King seemed to be unconcerned, gazing expectantly past the assembled hordes of police towards the gate. Blade stared at them, then switched his gaze to the road outside.

Powerful headlights washed over the front of the station as a beefed-up, seventies-style Land Cruiser screamed up the street towards them. The Cruiser jumped onto the sidewalk, scattering the small crowd of watching pedestrians in all directions, and smashed right through the gated wall to the police station, the reinforced bull-bars on the front taking the brunt of the impact. It screeched to a stop between Blade and the police cars. A compact, gruff-looking man leaned out of the window of the driver's seat and gave a cheery little wave to Blade as the rear doors of the Cruiser popped open. "My name is Dex. And I'll be saving your ass this evening."

Blade and his two new companions quickly scrambled into the back of the Land Cruiser, ignoring the increasingly urgent shouts of the police behind them. Dex slammed the Cruiser into reverse and floored the gas, bumping out backwards over the rubble of the wall. The police opened fire, but their bullets sparked harmlessly off the armored sides of the Cruiser. Cops scattered as the vehicle screeched across the front lot in a smoking one-eighty, then accelerated off down the street, heading for freedom.

Abigail peered back through the Cruiser's rear windshield as they hurtled through the nighttime streets. They had maybe ten seconds lead, which should be enough to guarantee their escape. She strained her eyes through the gloom, on the lookout for signs of pursuit.

But instead of the expected police Cruisers, she saw something chilling—the lone figure of Grimwood was coming after them, his small beady eyes fixed on the back of their Cruiser like a pit bull chasing the postman.

And what was more, the big bloodsucker was actually gaining on them.

Picking up her compound bow, Abigail quickly leaned out of the rear window. She nocked a UV arrow into the bow and pointed the device at Grimwood, aiming at his head. Bracing her body against the side of the car, she let the arrow fly.

Thunk! The arrow crossed the distance between them in a split second and buried itself deeply in

Grimwood's right eye. Grimwood yelped and went down like a stone, his speed causing him to somersault across the asphalt in a tangle of flailing limbs. They quickly left his prone form behind as Dex accelerated, picking up speed.

The four of them finally relaxed, basking in the adrenaline rush of a battle well fought. The engine purred beneath them as they headed out onto the Interstate. In the ensuing silence, Dex's cell phone rang. He picked it up and listened for a moment. "We have him. We'll be there soon."

Clicking the phone off, he casually turned to Blade. "So my entrance back there—what do you think? Too flashy? Right on the money?"

In the back seat, King unbuckled his combat harness and removed it with a wince, revealing a bulletproof vest beneath it. The front of the vest was riddled with slugs. King rubbed his ribs and gave a sigh of relief, glad to be able to breathe again. He was going to have some really interesting bruises in the morning.

King looked up to find Blade watching him. As far as it was possible to make out an expression on Blade's deadpan face, King could've sworn that the Daywalker looked faintly impressed. He picked up King's ruined harness and examined it. "Who are you people?"

King swelled with immediate pride. "The name's Hannibal King. I'm a hunter, like you." He gestured towards Abigail. "And this little hellion is Abigail."

Abigail stared silently towards Blade. She'd heard so much about the Daywalker that she felt like she already knew him, inside and out. She'd wanted to meet him for years, although her father had forbidden it.

But now that he was here, she felt strangely afraid of him.

That feeling pissed her off, and she pulled herself together quickly, slamming down her defenses like iron shutters.

Blade returned Abigail's gaze, his head cocked slightly to one side as he tried to place her. As he watched, she narrowed her eyes sharply and tossed her head slightly, as though daring him to pick a fight with her. It was a tiny movement, but one that sent a flood of memories through Blade's brain. He'd seen that gesture before a million times.

"You're Whistler's daughter, aren't you?" Blade spoke his thoughts aloud before he could check himself.

King smiled, seeing Blade's expression become a little more frozen, if such a thing was possible. He was learning to read the guy already. "That's right, Blade." He sat back in the warm leather of his seat as the Cruiser rocked and bumped its way down the highway, heading out towards the coast. "You see, Abby, Dex, myself... we're all part of Whistler's contingency plan."

King reached into his pocket and pulled out a pack of gum. He chose a stick for himself, and then offered the pack to Blade. "Juicy Fruit?"

Blade just stared at him. King popped the gum stick into his mouth and began to chew, settling back into his seat with a shrug.

This was going to be a long ride.

EIGHT

As night fell, the Land Cruiser containing Blade, Abigail, Dex and King rolled across an abandoned shipyard towards the weed-choked ruins of an abandoned drydock. Blade gazed thoughtfully out of the tinted rear window as the Cruiser crept past the skeletal remains of old fishing rollers, broken-down forklifts and various other rusted remnants of a once-bustling shipyard. The place was a mess. If Blade didn't know any better, he would've thought that this was nothing more than a junk-yard.

The Land Cruiser bumped its way up a rubble-strewn concrete track and turned in towards a large, covered work area surrounded by stacked shipping containers and concrete outbuildings. It was deserted, and the night wind whistled across the canisters and rattled the joists as though to empha-size the bleakness of it all.

The cruiser entered the loading bay and Dex killed the engine.

In the ensuing silence Blade could hear nothing but the noise of tarpaulin flapping in the wind and the distant rush of the sea. King and Abigail unbuckled their seatbelts and dismounted. Blade followed suit.

The covered work area was dark and cavernous, smelling strongly of sea salt and engine oil. A lamp flared in the darkness as Dex turned on the main power switch by the gate. Peering through the gloom, Blade could dimly see half a dozen vehicles in the process of being retrofitted with armored panels and weaponry. There was a small legion of HOG softail cruisers in various stages of repair, plus a handful of Buell sports bikes lined up against the walls. High-tech tools and machine lathes filled the rest of the space, throwing creepy shadows over the floor.

A tiny humming sound drew Blade's attention. He looked up to see a bank of surveillance cameras mounted on a rack above him, whirring and clicking as they tracked his progress across the room.

Blade felt a chill go down his spine. This whole set-up was so familiar. He peered around the place and held his breath, half-hoping to see a familiar gray-bearded figure duck out from under a bonnet, wiping his hands on an oily rag before starting to scold him about his latest mishap.

Whatever this place was, it had the old man's name written all over it.

Without turning, Blade motioned to King. "I thought the vampires murdered Whistler's family," he said softly.

Abigail stepped up behind him. "They did. I was born later, out of wedlock." Abigail stood beside Blade, gazing around at the machinery and equipment. "After the murders happened, he kept me hidden. He wanted me safe. Away from all of this." She gestured towards the deserted workshop. "But I guess hunting just runs in our blood."

King motioned Blade forwards, and led him towards a stairway set back in the work area. The steps were slippery with mud and algae and led downwards towards the ancient drydock.

Blade walked down them feeling unreal. Less than seventy-two hours ago he had been enjoying a pre-battle chat with Whistler over a cup of coffee, engaged in a lively debate over whether Batman or Wolverine would make a better vampire hunter. Now Whistler was dead and his life was quite literally in ruins, to be replaced by this strange alternate reality. How could he have kept all this a secret from him? It seemed that despite everything, the old man was still full of surprises, even after his death.

A tiny noise drew Blade's attention. Squinting upwards, he caught sight of a little girl, around five years-old, peering down at him intently from atop one of the bulky shipping containers. Seeing that she had been spotted, the girl immediately ducked down, mouse-quiet, and hid in one of the shadows.

Blade shook his head.

More secrets.

He moved on downwards towards the bottom of the stairway.

As they reached the last step, Blade tensed as a small but significant bank of automated guns dropped down from the ceiling and swung smoothly around to track them, moving on a multi-jointed robotic arm. Blade and the others were spotlighted in a crisscross of infrared targeting beams. Blade froze as the glowing beams played across his forehead, hoping like hell that whoever was controlling these things was paying attention and had his or her fingers a safe distance from the firing button.

Abigail dismissed the guns with a tilt of her head, raising a hand in greeting towards the camera mounted on the chipboard ceiling. The red beams tracked onto her and ran swiftly over her face, then a small light set near the door blinked to green and the guns retracted as the auto-recognition system deactivated.

Abigail casually turned back to Blade, continuing her story. "When I came of age, I tracked my dad down, told him I wanted in." She shrugged matter-of-factly. "Been doing it ever since."

They reached the end of the walkway which led down to the stone steps of the drydock. There was an enormous, heavily-armored barge resting on struts, clearly in the process of repair. Abigail waved again at the camera and the steel door of the barge hummed open, letting them in.

On the other side of the door, Blade found himself in a surprisingly spacious room. The steel hull of the huge barge housed the interconnected shells of a mechanics shop, a laboratory and a miniature firing range.

Blade liked the place at once.

The barge was much more up-market than his boathouse had been, but still betrayed the fact that the occupants probably weren't listed in the phone book. Its interior was a hodge-podge of the old and the new, with a small mountain of rusting parts from the shipyard stacked by the door, fighting for space with an arsenal of high-tech weaponry and medical equipment. Old industrial gear and damaged shipping crates poked out from behind microfuges and DNA sequencers, and there was a huge mildewed fishing net stuffed into a crate behind a cutting-edge electroporater.

The overall effect was that of a garage sale at the Pentagon.

King smiled and threw his hands out expansively. "Welcome to the honeycomb hideout."

Despite his intense curiosity, Blade carefully kept his face blank. He didn't want to give these people anything they could use against him. He was thankful to them for rescuing him, but he had a sneaking suspicion about where this little tour was heading. He was sure they wouldn't go to all this trouble just to bring him back here for ice cream and cookies. King in particular had been watching him all the way home, as though trying to make up his mind about him.

No, these people wanted something from him, and Blade was more than willing to bet he knew what it was.

That much said, there was some serious gear in this place. Blade gave a low whistle as he studied the machinery stacked around him. He freely admitted that he hadn't a clue what half of Whistler's equipment did, but he was well aware of what it all cost. He'd paid for most of Whistler's gadgetry over the years by pawning items requisitioned from dead vampires and familiars—a wallet here, a diamond necklace there—it all added up, and helped them to survive for one more day.

But this place was at least four times the size of their old operation and twice as well stocked. He turned to King, curious. "How do you bankroll this place?"

"Internet porn." King's face was as blank as Blade's. "See," he elaborated, "we're using cocksuckers to pay for the bloodsuckers."

Blade looked at him, his face expressionless.

King cracked an ingratiating smile and slapped Blade on the back. "Joke."

Blade kept on looking.

King's smile got even wider. "Come on, man. This isn't some piddly little hoopty-ass operation, Blade. We take our jobs very seriously."

Up ahead, two new people paused in their work as they saw Blade arrive. They put down their tools, watching him with interest. King waved to and made a round of introductions. "You met Dex. This is Hedges and Sommerfield."

Hedges was a young man in his mid-twenties. He was wearing a scruffy Buell biker T-shirt, and had the far-away look of one whose mind was far more at home wrestling with the intricacies of wires and voltages than of tackling the day-to-day problems of living. Behind him on his workbench sat an entire legion of empty take-away containers. Blade guessed he was an engineer of some kind.

Sommerfield was a pretty young woman in her late twenties. King told Blade that she was a geneticist, one of the best in the state. She was the one who had built Blade's new serum inhaler. Sommerfield was also completely blind, operating her computers via a top-of-the-range voice recognition program. Everything around her was labeled in Braille, including her computer keyboard. She wore trendy dark glasses and a cheerful smile.

King waved a hand toward the door, keen to move on. "The runt you saw earlier is Sommerfield's daughter, Zoe." He smiled at his fellow team-members, pausing dramatically. "We call ourselves the Nightstalkers."

Blade snorted. "You sound like rejects from a Saturday morning cartoon."

King grinned. "We were gonna call ourselves the Care Bears, but that was taken."

Abigail entered the room, casually greeting the others. Approaching a bench, she started to rid herself of weaponry. Blade's eyes widened behind his shades as Abigail pulled an impossible number of stakes and knives out of a dozen unlikely places all over her body, like Doctor Who at an airport check-in gate. She finished off the pile with her bow and a large black quiver of arrows.

Stretching lightly and avoiding Blade's stunned gaze, she picked up her compound bow and handed it to Hedges. "Tiller needs adjustment."

In her mind, Abigail saw Grimwood going down with her arrow lodged in his right eye. She shook her head, mentally scolding herself.

She'd been aiming for his left one.

Hedges nodded. "I'll run it through the bow press."

Moving away from King, Blade prowled around the workshop, examining some of the equipment, trying to get an idea of the scale of the operation. "How many of you are there in total?"

"Enough." King nodded at the others. "We operate in sleeper cells. When one goes down, a new cell activates to pick up the slack." He looked up at Blade and smiled warmly. "Consider us your reinforcements."

Blade peered closely at a weapon that looked like a tiny rocket-launcher powered by two AA-size batteries. He had been waiting for that line.

So much for the ice cream and cookies...

He snorted, feeling his anger rise. "Let me get this straight—you amateurs are supposed to help me?"

Blade carefully put down the weapon. Then he stepped up to King. Whipping off his dark glasses for the first time since his arrival, he gave King a bone-chilling stare. "You're kids." He waved a hand at King's clothing. "Look at how you're dressed—you call that tactical?" He peered closely at King's nametag from the hospital. "And what the fuck is this? You think this is all a joke? Some kind of fucking sitcom?"

King frowned, offended. "Excuse me, but didn't we just save your ass back there?"

Abigail stepped forwards. She'd been prepared for this. "Look, Blade. My father meant for us to help you. Like it or not, we're all you've got."

Sommerfield spoke up. "When Whistler died, he activated an emergency protocol." She gestured around her at the packed workshop. "All his knowledge was transferred to our servers here."

Blade's eyes hadn't left King's. He stared at him coldly, his voice soft. "And what makes you think you know so much about killing vampires?"

King stepped forwards, into the light. Reaching for his collar, he pulled the neck of his jacket down to reveal a mass of pale scar tissue in the telltale shape of a deep vampire bite-mark. For the first time since they had met, King's smile faded. "Well, for starters, I used to be one." King looked up to Blade, his face in deep shadow. "Do I pass the audition?"

"Fucking Hannibal King!"

Up in the luxurious penthouse of the Phoenix Towers, Danica slammed her bare fist into the wall, punching a hole in the solid cinderbrick. Cracks appeared in the wall above and below the hole as she wrenched her fist back out again with a yell. Her hand wasn't so much as bruised.

What remained of the room around her was impressively furnished, the décor speaking of power, money, and a certain perverse aesthetic. It certainly wasn't the kind of place you'd want to house a vampire having a temper tantrum.

But Danica owned the place, and didn't give a damn.

The vampiress punched a second hole beside the first, beside herself with fury. That cretin! How dare he show up like that? Months of careful planning and scheming down the tube, and now they had less than they started with. And worse! Now that Blade had seen their faces, it would only be a matter of time before he decided to come and hunt them down.

Danica remembered the look on the Daywalker's face when she told him what she had done, and practically heard his unspoken accusation: she'd killed

Whistler. Blade would make sure that she paid for the old man's death.

And with King at his side, the Daywalker would be as good as unstoppable.

Danica spun around in a shower of plaster dust, enraged. Behind her, Asher and Grimwood sat stiffly on plush velvet cushions, having their wounds attended to by a medic. Grimwood was trying not to flinch as the medic attempted to ease the arrow out of his swollen and blackened eye socket.

The sight of the pair of them only served to further infuriate Danica. She looked around for some more expensive things to break. There was practically nothing left of the enormous room, but she managed to find a couple of shattered china vases lying on the carpet. She stamped on them, breaking them up into even smaller pieces.

A trio of vampire guards standing by the entrance of the door flinched at each act of violence, nervously trying to lean as far away from Danica as possible without actually moving from the spot. An enormous Rottweiler sat at their heels, watching attentively. Beside the Rotweiller stood a small Pomeranian dog, which yapped and wagged its tail with canine glee every time Danica broke something, as though egging her on.

Danica ran her hands through her wildly tangled hair, and then grabbed an exquisitely leather-bound book from the mantelpiece above the fireplace and hurled it through the remains of the window with all her might. There was a faraway smashing sound as it shattered the top floor window of the skyscraper office block opposite. She shouted out of the window after it. "We had Blade! We had him! I should have ripped his bleeding heart out when I had the chance!" Danica swung round and pointed an accusing finger at her brother. "And don't you dare tell me 'I told you so!'"

Asher raised a hand silently, clearly not wanting to infuriate his sister any further. With a cry of disgust, Danica continued her tantrum, smashing a priceless marble statue into very expensive rubble before sending it spinning across the room, shattering a heavy glass tabletop.

Finally Danica subsided, collapsing into a chair.

Asher raised an eyebrow. "You through remodeling?"

"Blow me."

Danica slumped down in the chair. The Rottweiler uncoiled itself from the shadows and ambled over to her, its muscles moving under its sleek black coat like snakes writhing in oil. It sat down in front of Danica and propped its heavy head on her knee, gazing up at her with mournful eyes.

Undeterred, Asher continued. "Face it, Dan. We got caught with our pants down. We underestimated the Nightstalkers."

"Pants down?" Grimwood broke in. "They practically fucking ass-raped us. OW!" He yelped in pain as the arrow was finally removed from his head, leaving behind a gory hole.

There was a ringing silence, and then Asher said, "Has he been told yet?"

"About your failure?"

The vampires jumped to their feet and stood in a frozen little tableau as a dark-haired man entered the room. Although not especially tall, the stranger had a commanding presence, and his voice radiated power and charisma. In appearance, he looked as though he was in his mid-thirties, although his eyes told a different story. The guards snapped to attention and even the Rotweiller whimpered and backed off into a corner, its ears flattened back against its skull in fright

The stranger's cold eyes roved around the penthouse suite. Danica glanced around at the mess she had made of the room, and seemed to shrink a little inside herself.

"Yes, I have been told." The man walked over to Danica and placed his hand on her shoulder. His touch was light, but it chilled Danica to the core of her being. She glanced away, unable to look him in the face.

The man either didn't notice Danica's discomfort, or didn't care. He turned his attention to the city skyline, the lights twinkling through the smashed window.

"Perhaps it is time I entered the fray."

Back at the Nightstalkers' headquarters, King was slowly buttoning up his collar, watched closely by Blade and Abigail.

"You know the kind of woman that just screams trouble?" King stared at the floor as he spoke, seemingly wrestling with himself. "You see her and every warning bell in your brain starts going off but you still ask for her number? Well, that's all I ever hook up with." King paused, remembering. He lowered his voice and gave Blade a conspirital glance. "But this

Betty blew 'em all away in the shit-storm sweep-stakes."

King walked over to the nearest computer and pulled out his electronic pistol. He pressed a button on the side and ejected a small silver mini-disk from the handle of the gun. Then he placed it inside the external disk reader attached to the computer and tapped in a password on the keyboard, calling up a piece of digital footage recorded by his gun-cam during their recent fracas at the hospital.

Despite his misgivings, Blade was secretly impressed.

Despite the poor quality of the digitized footage, the faces of Asher, Danica and Grimwood were clearly recognizable. King clicked the mouse, slowing the footage so that it moved in slow motion, advancing frame by frame. He tapped a finger against the face of the woman on the screen. "Her name's Danica Talos. You met her earlier. The man on the left is Asher, her brother." King clicked the digital magnifier, and the image zoomed in. "The knuckle-dragging Hershey-squirt behind them is Jarko Grimwood."

King clicked the mouse again and the image froze, showing an enlarged, pixelated shot of Danica's face. He gestured at the screen. "I picked her up in a bar, had a one night stand with her and then spent the next five years playing step-and-fetch-it as her little vampire cabana boy."

King stared at the screen as though hypnotized. Danica truly was beautiful, but the hate he felt for her was so all consuming that it took him all his self-con-trol not to smash the screen, just to be rid of her image. Painful images poured through his head like a wave of shining razor-blades and he shook himself, trying to crush the feeling. Revenge would come later, once they had found out what she was up to.

Beckoning Blade over, King flipped open his belt buckle and lowered his pants slightly. Blade stared at him, but King merely gestured at the telltale black mark of a vampire glyph tattooed at the top of his pelvis. It was Danica's name written in vampire script.

King paused while he let his little revelation sink in. Then he buckled up his pants and turned back to Blade. "Eventually, Abigail found me. Sommerfield here managed to treat me with a cure. Now I kill them."

King took a deep breath, struggling with himself, and gave a weak smile. "That's called turning a frown upside down."

Abigail swiftly stepped in to cover for him. "We need to pool our resources, Blade."

Blade's eyes were still riveted on King. "Why?"

"Because he's come back." Abigail tossed a *Tomb of Dracula* comic book across the table to Blade. The Daywalker took one look at the cover and stared up at Abigail.

"You gotta be kidding me."

"He's real, Blade." King spread his hands. "Dig beneath all the movies and myths. All the layers of bullshit that've cluttered our culture for the last five hundred years, and eventually you'll strike the truth."

Blade wasn't convinced. "So the movies are true?"

King shook his head. "The movies are just a comforting fairytale compared to the real deal. There's no happy ending with this guy. Peter Cushing isn't going to run in at the last second and save the day with a cross and some holy water." King gestured at the lurid cover of the comic book. "See, good old Bram Stoker, he wrote a nice yarn. But the events he described in 1897 were only a tiny piece of the mosaic. The real Dracula's origin goes back much further than that."

"How much further?"

Abigail spoke up. "Try six or seven thousand years."

NINE

In the corridor adjacent to the now ruined penthouse suite of the Phoenix Towers, the dark-haired man stood by the open window, gazing out at the city. Far below, neon signs flickered and flared for miles in all directions, lining the perfectly straight roads. The bright lights of cars and offices shone upwards, tinting the night sky with an acidic yellow glare. The moon and stars were invisible, burned out of the sky by the artificial glare of the city. Even the distant mountains seemed overshadowed by the concrete landscape spread out in all directions around them.

He found it both beautiful and repellant.

It had been three hundred years since he had gone to sleep. The female, Danica, had told him as much. In the space of little more than a day, she had filled him in on nearly three hundred years of human history. It had been a lot to take in, even for one such as himself, made more so by the incessant interruptions of the woman's pet rodents. What had they called themselves? Grimwood and Asher, that was it.

Degenerates, the pair of them.

They had told him that he could no longer use his old name—that it was too well known. It had been gratifying to know he had not been forgotten.

For he was Draculea—or "Dracula" as the apes in the apartment behind him had insisted on pronouncing it. He had been a prince and a warrior, a butcher and a conqueror, a god amongst so many lesser creatures. Why should men have forgotten the name of one such as he, whether he had slept for three centuries or thirty?

But Danica had insisted that he adopt a new name for this new age, one that would not attract unwanted attention to himself. It was irrelevant to him of course. He had used so many names in his long life that he could not remember all of them. But it seemed to matter to them, so he let the woman choose a new name for him.

She had suggested Drake, a shortened version of his old name.

The one called Grimwood had snorted at the suggestion, but that only sealed it. Drake had accepted his new name and had then turned his gaze on Grimwood, daring him to say anything more. Naturally, the other had paled and looked away.

Drake smiled. The creature had not been born who could meet his gaze if he did not wish it to. A petty half-breed like Grimwood was no exception.

Drake returned his thoughts to the view beyond the window in front of him, tuning out the petty bickering of Danica and the others in the chamber next door, and listening instead to a new sound—the heart-beat of the living, breathing city.

It was the sound of eleven million people living in a giant artificial habitat they had built for themselves, severing their few remaining links with the land itself. From Drake's vantage point, it would be a simple thing to believe that the city was some kind of paradise of light, a final triumph of civilization over the wilderness.

But Danica had told him that crime was rife in this place, with murder and rape and fear lurking in the city's grimy backstreets, on a scale and in a way that had not existed in any previous century.

For all its apparent "advancements," this civilization was just as brutal in its own way as any other in history, more so perhaps. For in centuries past, the only men one had to fear were those who were strong and skilled with fists and sword. Yet Danica had told him that in this new world, technology had reached a point where a decrepit old hag with a gun could kill you just as easily as a young man in his prime.

As a result, everyone had become afraid of everyone else.

Not that this would apply to Drake of course. It was beyond the ability of any mortal to kill him, regard-less of whatever dangerous technologies they might come armed with.

Drake stepped closer to the window and stroked a finger down the glass, captivated by its smooth per-fection. Humans had made this. They were inventive creatures, but only in the way that ants building their colonies were. They built their wonders in order to survive, for they knew that they were weak. They had no natural weapons to protect themselves with—no claws or horns, meager strength and weak, blunt teeth. Although spectacular, their great cities were there to protect them from nature, in all its forms. Even he could see this.

Drake swept a mocking glance down the length of the darkened corridor, at the soft, uniform flooring, the humming air conditioning and the water fountain set into the wall. There was more to this than just survival. To the humans, nature represented uncertainty, the uncontrolled, the wild.

That, he mused, was what scared humans the most.

And that was why they had sent their hunters after him. Drake represented all those things that terrified humanity so deeply, and more. For this reason the humans had tried to destroy him more times than he could count.

And each time, they had failed.

Drake gazed out at the urban sprawl and allowed his mind to wander back through the millennia, thoughts threading through his synapses like an oiled black spider web. He cast back through the seven thousand years of his existence, remembering how things used to be...

He remembered the fertile banks of the River Euphrates and the people who had first settled there. His people, whom history had named the Ubaidis. Men and women who learned to till the land and herd cattle while the majority of the world's population still lived as hunter-gatherers. He remembered the dawn of the civilization, because he had been there. He was one its founders.

He remembered how he, above and before any other man or woman, had been chosen for greatness. For immortality.

Drake never knew how he came to be, but he knew that from day one he was different.

Truly, horribly, tragically different.

Once he had killed his mother, his father, and every family member who had run screaming out into the wilds to try and escape from him, he had been faced with the prospect of growing up in a world in which he was truly unique.

In those early days the Thirst had been strong in him, too strong for him to control, and he hunted his own people through the days and the nights, through the years and the decades, until they scattered and were forgotten.

The centuries passed and new peoples came and went. Drake had preyed on them all, irrespective of race, rank or class. Yet as the years rolled by, his control over his hunger grew, until a new people settled beside the Euphrates, a people who would build the first great nation upon its banks. They cultivated the land and made it their own. They gave it a name, Sumer, and upon its fertile soil they built their towns and made laws.

It was then that Drake had realized what his purpose was. He was not destined simply to prey upon the humanity that he himself had left behind.

His purpose was to rule them.

For was he not stronger and wiser than any of them? Had he not already lived for longer than any other being, and seen more than any other? He resolved that these Sumerians would be his subjects as well as his cattle.

And so he subjugated the people of Sumer and set them to build a city where he would rule them as their king. And they gave him a new name to replace the one he had so long forgotten.

Gilgamesh.

His name and his accomplishments throughout the following years would resound down the millennia, forming the foundations of the first recorded legend.

But nothing lasts forever, and he was no exception.

The rulers of other cities grew jealous of the seemingly immortal king, and they grew to covet his city and its prosperity. Drake remembered the first time an army was raised to march against him, but with his nation at his back he had scattered his enemies to the four winds. But more came, and more, and though Drake had finally learned how to pass on his immortality and a modicum of his strength, it had not been enough to save his city from destruction, nor keep a crown upon his brow.

Even with the first of his vampiric offspring fighting at his side, Drake's armies were finally crushed by the man whom history recalled as King Etana, the uniter of Sumeria.

Drake remembered the last days of that war. He remembered how his warriors had fallen around him until only he remained, beyond the clutches of death and unbeatable by any mere mortal. Yet so many were the enemies ranged against him, and so absolute was the destruction they had brought against his city and his subjects, Drake knew that he had nothing more to gain from the conflict. He had quit the field of that battle, leaving piles of the dead and dying in his wake, and swore to himself that he would have his vengeance.

Drake remembered his resolution after that battle: if the humans, in their jealousy, refused to accept his rule over them, then he would be their ruler from below.

If they would always seek to bring war against the seat of his power, then he would make that seat within their hearts. If they would not respect and fear him as he ruled them in the sunlight, then they would respect and fear him as he hunted them through the night. If they would not acknowledge him for the god he was, nor worship at the foot of his throne, then he would make them fear him for the monster he would become, and beg in the dust at his feet.

As King Gilgamesh, Drake vanished from the eyes of history. For long centuries he roamed all the settled lands of humanity, and wherever he went he made sure to leave tales of horror and destruction behind him.

When the armies of King Sargon of Akkad moved against the lands of Sumer, Drake joined with him, fighting under a white-hot sun against the people who had overthrown his own reign. But in time, and as was his wont, Drake turned against the Akkadians as well, becoming a demon remembered in the religions of the region for centuries afterwards.

Drake went on to cut a bloody swathe through history, undying, unrelenting, drawn to any war or battle as he slaughtered his way through seven millennia of humanity. He fought against the Assyrians and the Hyksos, the Egyptians and the Cushites, the Babylonians, the Canaanites, the Israelites, the Persians, the Greeks and so many countless others throughout human history. There wasn't a nation or a people whom he had not preyed upon, hunted and butchered. By some he was remembered as a terrible warlord or mercenary, by others a savage and merciless demon of folktale.

From China to India, to Africa, Norway and Siberia and through all the lands that lay in between, the history books were full of Drake's conquests and infamies, most of them unnamed, all of them unchallenged. He had been with humanity since the beginning, watching as the human race multiplied and diversified beyond all recognition, and like the original serpent in the Garden of Eden, he did his best to destroy humanity's hope for salvation, turning all that stumbled into his path into the purest of evil.

Most profoundly of all, he had single-handedly spawned a new race, his own species: hominus nocturna.

The vampire.

But as time went by, their glory had faded. Drake had felt it in his bones. Whereas he had been born into strength and immortality perfect, like a Great White shark at the pinnacle of its evolutionary ladder, his children had changed.

Across the millennia he had watched as the others of his kind grew weak through their contact with the accursed humans, until they reached the point where some of them became so interbred that they were unable to walk in the daylight, as even a passing touch of the sun's rays would catch them alight and burn them instantly. The wretched weakness had spread so far and so fast that not even he knew its full extent.

Danica had explained to him the experimentations done by the Vampire Nation over the centuries since he had vanished. She had told him that there was a specific wavelength of the sun's rays—something she called ultraviolet light—that caused the damage. The light's particular frequency could easily penetrate a vampire's hyper-sensitized cells, igniting the phosphorus that was stored at high concentrations within. This would trigger an unstoppable chain reaction within a vampire's body, causing it to immediately burn to death.

This was all very well, but Drake knew the truth of it. These lesser vampires were being punished by and for their pettiness, their arrogance and their carelessness.

Drake remembered when this weakness had first started to manifest itself amongst the baser of his kind—desperate half-breeds who fed upon, and in their carelessness spread vampirism to, the derelicts whom even their fellow humans had rejected, be they the insane, the plague-ridden or diseased, and the narcotic-addicted.

All this served to turn the blessing Drake had bestowed so freely to the first of his kind into a warped and diluted thing. Added to this, millennia of incestuous inbreeding amongst many had made their blood weak and flawed. In some vampires, Drake's original bloodline had become so contaminated that the vampires infected with it were almost an entirely different species.

As the years had gone by, more and more vampires succumbed to this inherited disorder, until eventually Drake's most distant and degenerate offspring turned on him and the few thousand or so of his surviving Pureblooded children. Envying their fearsome strength and resistance to sunlight, the lesser—and yet more populous—vampires began hunting the Purebloods down, killing them wherever they could.

Drake had sickened of them. He hated the half-breeds for their disrespect and misplaced arrogance, and he grew to despise the Purebloods for their obvious and growing fear of the lesser vampires who hunted them.

So he left them. All of them.

Towards the end of the eighteenth century he returned to the land of his birth, making sure to avoid any settlement of humans or vampires and went underground, quite literally. He hoped that when he finally awoke from his indefinite slumber, his offspring would have cured themselves of their stupidities and their weaknesses, or else wiped themselves out completely. Drake intended to have no further dealings with his degenerate kind until such a day.

As things had turned out, he had slept for a mere three centuries before Danica and her baboons had found him and dragged him, kicking and screaming, into the twenty-first century.

Once he had calmed his hunger enough to take on a fully human appearance, Drake had asked Danica to take him to the Purebloods, if any still lived in this era. But she had told him although some of them still lived, their main enclave in the region had been destroyed by a vampire/human crossbreed, a renegade known as the Daywalker.

In fact, she said, this Daywalker had become the bane of all vampires, be they Purebloods or half-breeds, butchering them all with equal contempt, and, it would seem, the greatest of ease.

Drake brought himself back to the present, and gave a ghost of a smile.

He would like to meet this Daywalker. He was curious to meet the vampire-man who could walk in the sunshine, like all Drake's children should be able to, but who despised his own kind with such a passion that he sought to destroy them as a species.

To a certain degree Drake found himself in some sympathy with the Daywalker.

From the scant information Danica had offered him, vampire numbers were unbelievably low, a mere fraction of that of the human population. Apparently, most humans did not even believe they existed at all. "Modern" vampires, as far as Drake could gather, seemed to prefer to stay underground, organizing themselves into exclusive cliques and societies. Their meeting places and affiliates were recognizable only by the widespread use of the vampire glyphs, ugly shorthand symbols derived from the few surviving ancient Sumerian texts in existence.

A frown darkened Drake's exquisitely handsome face. This trend had started many, many centuries ago. He didn't like it then, and he didn't like it now. Vampires had begun to hide themselves from humanity for almost as long as their line had been degenerating. Invariably, they did not "hide" in the sense that Drake himself did—traveling from nation to nation, adopting new names and guises, with the purpose of instilling within all races an inherent fear and horror, making the petty humans realize that there were still things out there that were greater than them, things that could catch and break them, regardless of their wealth, their power or their stature.

No, the vampires of this day and age seemed as petty and weak as any, hiding away from humanity because they were frightened of discovery and persecution. But at least they showed Drake the respect that was due him. They also seemed to have found the beginnings of a technological means to shake off their inherited weaknesses and become once more the living gods he had intended them to be.

Perhaps there was hope for them yet. For even if the common populace of humanity did not believe in vampires, they at least remembered him—albeit by his former name. That was a good sign, if it was true.

But he could not rely on the sycophancy of Danica and the others.

Turning away from the window, Drake walked down the corridor behind him, and disappeared down the stairwell at the end of it.

He would search for the signs of his great legacy by himself.

TEN

A dark figure walked through the grime-choked streets of the city's downtown commercial district. Car horns blared and chilidog vendors shouted as Drake walked down the boulevard, weaving in and out of the surging crowd. Clad in casual modern attire, Drake blended seamlessly with the throngs of humanity that choked the sidewalk on this warm, dark evening.

Drake gazed around him, wondering at the sheer pace and intensity of modern life. Such movement! Such noise! The brash neon lights washed over him in an overlapping sea of flashing electric color, cool blues and glowing reds painting his face with highlights of fire and shadow. Pedestrians brushed past him without the slightest hint of fear, and Drake's nostrils flared at the scent of fresh blood surging beneath the surface of their skin, just detectable beneath the foul stench of diesel fumes that hung in the air like the smoke from a bonfire.

The steady drone of the inner-city traffic receded into the background as Drake concentrated intently, focused in on the sounds which mattered most—the thousand-and-one individual heartbeats of the humans surrounding him. For here was the true lifeblood of the city, the animate corpuscles building and rebuilding the immortal body of civilization, one dollar at a time.

Here was a little girl, riding piggyback on her father's shoulders, laughing delightedly at the lights and noise and at the joy of being up past bedtime. Drake listened closely as he passed by. The youngster's heart was beating strongly, untainted by the ravages of time. She had her entire life ahead of her, unlike her father, who, judging by the laboring of his cholesterol-choked heart, would be lucky if he survived to see his daughter's fifteenth birthday.

There was a junkie, sprawled in a nearby doorway, a sickly youth in his mid-twenties. He had pale, clammy skin and a pulse like a burnt-out racehorse. As Drake watched, the boy fumbled in his pocket, got his hand stuck in his clothing and threw back his head, laughing hysterically up at the night sky before turning and vomiting noisily in the corner. The boy would be dead before the year was through, not from the drugs, but from the tiny irregularity in his left ventricle, poised like a plague-rat to pounce on any blood clot bigger than a sand grain and strangle his heart with it.

Drake regarded him for a moment, his black eyes untainted by pity. If what he had heard of modern medicine was true, this child could be saved. But who would take notice of yet another opiate addict shaking in a dark corner?

Drake moved on.

Ah—here. This was what he had been looking for.

Culture.

The tenement buildings gave way to store fronts, and Drake strode over to them, intensely curious to see what lay within. A large, colorful shop window drew him over and Drake paused outside, studying the goods on display with intense interest. This was clearly the shop of some kind of carnival or masquerade costumier, although one of below-average skill judging by the number of crudely constructed masks on display. They leered down at him, a luridly painted plastic mass of bloodshot eyes and bared teeth. Every manner of beast was represented, from zombies to werewolves to...

Drake paused, studying one of the masks, a caricatured carving of a pale man with slicked-back dark hair and elongated canines. The man was depicted as laughing wildly, a thin trickle of red blood running from the corner of his month.

Drake raised an eyebrow, surprised.

So the humans did know of the existence of vampires. And, looking at the name written on the packaging above the mask, they remembered him.

Dracula.

Drake flinched at the common mis-spelling of his old name, then studied the mask again. It was a caricature, almost comical, and was most certainly not a fitting tribute to the being it parodied so crassly. Drake's lips pulled back into a sneer.

He moved along the window. Next to the mask was a packaged set of plastic fangs and an exceedingly foppish black cape lined with faux red-velvet. There were more vampire representations beneath, laid out neatly in rows, all supposedly depicting him. All of them were travesties, his name and a grotesquely caricatured face gracing key-chains, lunchboxes, T-shirts and pencil cases. There was even a stuffed child's doll in "his" image, a hideous affair decorated with silver buttons and ridiculous gold clothing. A button below the doll was labeled with the legend, "Press me and hear me scream!"

Drake straightened, his graceful, well-tailored silhouette a stark contrast to the mass-marketed crap before him.

What had they done to his once proud name? Just how far had he fallen in the eyes of humanity? For the first time he could remember in his millennia-spanning existence, Drake felt a creeping sensation of doubt start to grow within him.

A bell on a spring tinkled cheerfully as Drake entered the store. It was a far cry from the frantic warning gongs and war horns that usually marked his approach and Drake paused on the doorstep, frowning.

His eyes flitted around the store, quickly adjusting to the light. Although it was lit by more than a dozen flaming lamps, the room gave the illusion of being even darker inside than it was out. The store was humid and untidy, packed to bursting with a tacky array of low-end goods, cheap novelties and printed T-shirts. Fake wood bookshelves lined the far wall, bearing a selection of comic-books, role-playing games and horror movies. Burned-down wax candles and painted plaster skulls were strategically arranged along the shelves, and in the back corner stood a metal rail bearing a selection of black lace clothing and PVC underwear.

Drake stepped forward, scanning the murky interior of the store through narrowed eyes, not quite believing what he was seeing

Behind the counter sat a pallid young boy with multiple piercings, dressed in torn black clothing fastened together with metal rivets. Drake noticed the word "Goth" tattooed across the knuckles of the boy's left hand. He was wafer-thin and was shoveling food into his mouth from a yellow polystyrene container with the letter "M" engraved on it. Nearby, a cartoon blared from the battered store TV. The set was draped with fake spider webs, and had what looked like a bloody severed arm wrapped around the aerial.

Behind him stood a sultry female dressed in similar attire, but with her arms folded, looking bored.

Drake strode over to the counter. The boy didn't so much as glance up, his eyes riveted to the animated antics of the cartoon character, a cavorting cartoon vampire with the captioned name of "Little Bit." Suppressing his rising anger, Drake cleared his throat. "In the window—you sell vampire merchandise?"

The Goth boy looked up for a second, faintly irritated, wiping at his mouth with a napkin. Clearly, Drake was intruding on his dinner break. "Uh, yeah— look around, we might have a few things."

He and the girl shared a snigger at Drake's expense, dismissing him with a glance. If the big freak couldn't see all the vamp gear stacked around him, there was nothing more that could be done for him.

Then the girl remembered the newly installed CCTV camera and stood up, scowling. Some days the fat schmuck who owned this dive remembered to hit "record" on the security tape, some days he didn't. It was just the luck of the draw what day this was. She waved a hand over to the nearest display case, trying to seem a little more helpful. "We've got Dracula lunch boxes," she drawled. "Did you see those?"

Drake gritted his teeth at her mispronunciation of his name. He looked at the items on display in front of him, his lip curling in disgust.

Then he transferred his gaze to the girl, a far more pleasant view than the refuse on sale throughout the shop. Her skin was ivory white, made whiter still by the contrast of her over-tight black clothing and her studded silver dog collar. Her eyes were accentuated by thick black eyeliner, which was running slightly in the damp heat of the store.

Drake's eyes slowly tracked over her body like a hand running over soft velvet. Although maybe ten pounds overweight, the girl wore it well, mainly upfront, and had a curve to her hips to set any man's blood pumping. Beneath her lacy top, the plump full-ness of her breasts strained enticingly against the dark material that enclosed them. Drake felt the hunger rise within him once more, intensified by the memory of his centuries-long fast. The blood of the vampires he had taken earlier had been filling, but not satisfying. Vampire blood had no spark in it, no life. It burned the tongue like a piquant spice, but was otherwise thin and empty. Unless a vampire had fed very recently, their blood wasn't worth bothering with.

Unlike the blood of humans.

Especially young female humans...

The girl blithely carried on chattering away in a monotone, unaware of the fact that she was currently facing the greatest physical danger of her life. "We've got bobbleheads, PEZ dispensers. We've got just about anything you can think of."

Something in the back of the girl's brain poked her as her one remaining survival instinct kicked in. Not quite knowing why, the Goth girl looked up at Drake, registering him as a person for the first time. She got all kinds coming in here, true, but she got the distinct impression that this guy wasn't after trading cards. He was well-dressed in nicely tailored clothing that gave more than a casual impression of what lay beneath, and he seemed to loom rather than stand.

Obviously the guy had money. Maybe power too, if there was a difference between them in this day and age.

In fact, he wasn't bad looking, in a creepy kinda way.

The Goth girl smiled cheekily, then reached round behind her and pulled something out of the display case as she continued her sales pitch, suddenly feeling playful. "We've even got vampire vibrators."

Drake stared at her for a long moment, trying to decipher the meaning behind her words, and then dismissed her with a snort. There was nothing for him here. The entire shop was a travesty, its contents good for a pyre and nothing more.

Drake directed his icy gaze across the store towards the unkempt boy, who was still chomping away on his take-out meal, his back turned. Drake sniffed the air, and then blew out his nostrils in disgust at the nauseating smell of fatty fried meat. There was no fear there. The boy couldn't care less about his presence. A deep fury began to rise within Drake and his hunger pains faded into a dull throb.

Drake's sparkling eyes flicked back to the suddenly less-attractive girl. To his disgust, she was now gazing up at him like an infatuated sow, still trying to sell him some kind of fertility item cast in the shape of one of his own effigies!

If these children would not show the respect or the fear that was due him, then who would?

Drake looked around him, a muscle in his jaw twitching as he ground his teeth together. Everything he saw only fanned his escalating rage. They even had vampire Christmas ornaments! Did they not know the true history of the event? And what were those printed pictures up there? *Nosferatu, Lugosi, The Little Vampire* and *Love at First Bite*. They had vampire plays now?

No. These were all abominations. They were using his image to sell fictions and to tell false stories. None of the vampires portrayed were him.

Drake stepped away from the posters on the wall, shutting his eyes against their garish contempt of his memory. The world had forgotten the truth. They had forgotten all that he had done, and all that he had stood for.

The world had truly forgotten him.

"Here, check this out." The girl smiled up at Drake, trying to be friendly in the hope that the creepy rich guy would buy something, or even better, ask her out. She reached under the counter and pulled out a can of soft drink. The label read "DRA-COLA," and featured a stylized vampire biting into the brand banner.

The girl gave it a shake. "Makes you wanna cry, doesn't it?"

Drake stared at the can, his mind retreating back through the safety of the centuries from the sheer horror of it. Seven thousand years of life, of slaughter and greatness, of being a god amongst so many insects, and this was all that was left of his great reign? He couldn't believe that in under three short centuries the world had moved on so far. Both vampires and humans had left him behind.

And this was how he was to be punished for his crimes.

They had made him into a joke.

"Hey, guy, she's talking to you."

Drake's head snapped up, his black eyes burning with hatred as the goth guy started pouring himself a bowl of Count Chocula.

Passers-by ducked for cover as the screaming figure of the goth boy crashed through the display window of the store at terrific speed. His trajectory described a perfect parabolic arc as he sped clean across the road and smashed head first through a plate-glass storefront on the opposite side of the street.

Inside the store, the girl shrieked at the top of her lungs as Drake advanced on her, his eyes black with righteous fury. Before she could draw breath for a second scream, Drake's arm lashed out like a viper and he grabbed a handful of her hair, and dragged her backwards across the counter. His jaws clamped around the smoothness of her throat, blood spraying as his now hideously extended canines punched through her pale skin. A thick stream of warm blood ran across his tongue and poured down his throat and Drake fed hungrily, lapping in time with the rapid beating of the girl's heart. He could feel the life filling him, even as it left her. His pale skin flushed with color as the stolen hemoglobin started to take effect, rejuvenating him at a cellular level

The counter glass beneath the girl's twitching body started to crack. Drake tore his mouth away from her throat with an effort, trailing a glistening string of blood across the whiteness of her skin like a knife-slash. He lifted his bloodstained face blindly upwards, the bones beneath his skin seeming to shift and writhe and hint at another, more sinister shape lurking beneath the surface of his flesh, like a crocodile in a swamp. It was a shape that mankind had not seen for hundreds of years, but one which still periodically re-emerged in its nightmares and dreams of death.

It was the shape that lurked beneath the beds of children, eyes flaming red as it waited to grab and devour...

The shape that followed young teens down the street at night, always staying just beyond the reach of the streetlights...

The shape that made grown men awaken screaming and clawing their sheets at three in the morning, striking out at shadows as the witching hour dissolved into dawn...

And now, finally, the nightmare had been let out.

Into the real world...

Drake flung the broken, blood-drenched corpse of the girl aside, sending it crashing through the over-loaded racks of toys and magazines. As the body ploughed to a halt halfway through a Buffy-themed display cabinet, Drake turned and unleashed an ear-splitting roar of rage towards the black-painted ceiling.

The unearthly sound echoed through the concrete canyons of Downtown, to be answered by a chorus of melancholy howls from the canine population as the strays screamed in the streets.

The message was quite clear.

The humans would pay dearly for this.

As dawn broke, Blade and King were joined by the others in the armory of the Nightstalker's headquarters.

The pair had talked through the night. Blade was wide awake, wired with the adrenaline-rush of discovery. King was rubbing his eyes and yawning. The skylights above them had been flung open and white-hot bars of sunlight fell across the room, striping their shoulders with its warmth.

Together, they sat in reflective silence, watching the steam rise from a brewing pot of black coffee.

Blade was bemused by what King had told him. They'd discussed the events of the last twenty-four hours from every single point of view and he was still no closer to understanding what the vampires were up to. He leaned back against the scarred workbench, stretching his powerful arms over his head as he turned the whole thing around in his mind: the heightened vampire activity over the past three months, the existence of Dracula and his subsequent resurrection, the vampire gang's attempt to frame him.

It all had to be connected, somehow.

Blade tapped his fingers on the bench, drumming out a Morse code tale of indecision. "So why wake him up now?"

Abigail combed a hand through Zoe's hair as she looked around at the cluttered lab, her expression distant. "That's what we've been trying to figure out."

King turned to Blade thoughtfully. "When I was under the fang, there used to be talk of some kind of vampire Final Solution." King rubbed at the back of his neck, musing to himself. "But I could never figure out why they'd want to destroy their food source." He looked up at Blade. "I mean, seems stupid, right? They've always had plans for the human race. Seems like whatever they're cooking up, Dracula's return is a part of it."

Blade nodded pensively.

King leaned back on the workbench next to Blade, and gazed up at the sunlight streaming in through the windows. "Let's face it, Blade—we're fighting a losing battle. So we kill a few hundred of them a year? Big deal. There are thousands of them out there. Maybe tens of thousands. We need a new tactic."

Blade shrugged, unimpressed. "Like what?"

Kings leant forwards, his eyes glinting. "A biological weapon."

Sommerfield moved over to her Braille keyboard and tapped in a key code. She smiled, her back turned to them. "For you sighted people—here's a little show and tell."

Blade and King gathered around as a nearby flatscreen monitor sprung into life, offering them a real-time magnified view of a virus replicating itself. As they watched, the virus divided over and over again at an incredible rate, quickly filling the screen with an evil-looking mass of black cellular junk.

Sommerfield tapped a key, zooming in on one of the squirming cells of the virus. It was dividing so quickly that it was almost a blur. "For the last year, I've been working with synthesized DNA in order to create an artificial virus targeted specifically at vampires. We're calling it DayStar."

King stood up excitedly. "Think about it, Blade. We could wipe them all out in a single move."

Blade was unconvinced. "So what's been holding you back?"

Sommerfield sighed. "We've tried it on number of captive subjects. We've got the disease vector worked out fine—it's easily transmittable. But the lethality in vampires is still spotty."

Abigail stood up. "Bottom line is, we need a better DNA sample to work with." She turned and gazed pensively out of the nearby window. "We need Dracula's blood."

Blade stared at her.

Sommerfield switched off the computer. "Vampire DNA is a hodge-podge of different genes, mixed in with all sorts of useless junk DNA." She gestured at a chart on the wall. "Because Dracula's the progenitor of the vampire race, his DNA is still pure. It hasn't been diluted by a hundred generations of selective mutation. It still has all the necessary cellular compounds for the virus to code to." She paused. "We get his blood; we can boost DayStar's viral efficiency to a hundred per cent."

King turned to Blade, watching this sink in. The Daywalker's face was unreadable as he mulled this new information over, but King could safely guess at what he was thinking. He could almost hear the cogs turning inside Blade's head.

Blade tried to ignore King's eager gaze as he mulled this new information over. A virus that could wipe out vampires—and not just the vampires here in the city, but the whole world over.

This was huge. Really, really huge.

It would mean an end to his lifelong struggle against the evil bloodsuckers, a victory that would ultimately benefit the whole of humanity. It would mean hundreds of thousands of lives saved, a whole future generation growing up without knowing the pain of a mysterious death or disappearance in the family.

And more than that, it would bring him salvation, a cessation of the daily violence and killing that was slowly eating away at his dwindling stockpile of sanity, tarnishing his soul with a gloss of dried blood as his body count mounted, day by day.

King nudged Blade, his face bright and eager. "So. You want to join our club? Can we sign you up for a Nightstalkers secret decoder ring?"

ELEVEN

Drake sat in his darkened antechamber in the Phoenix Towers. He had returned home around dawn and had been sitting in his room ever since. No one had dared enter to check on him, fearful of his wrath. Already he had seriously wounded two vampire guards who dared suggest that he take the elevator instead of the stairs. It would seem that Drake was not best pleased with the modern world.

The vampire king brooded in silence, his thoughts lost in the murky depths of history. Shadows draped over his body like ropes of darkness, binding him to the present. The only source of lighting in the room was a series of small, slatted skylights in the ceiling, from which shone clear shafts of blinding white light, knifing the gloom with their brilliance.

Drake appeared to reach the end of his chain of thought, and gave a great sigh that came from the very depths of his being. Then he turned his face upwards towards the daytime sky and allowed the light from the beams to wash across his face, as though cleansing him of his worries. His eyes closed as he blissfully soaked up the sunshine, letting its golden light warm his cold flesh.

Soft footsteps sounded in the darkness, tentative-sounding, hesitant. They approached the doorway and stopped outside. After a moment they restarted, moving away quickly down the outer corridor.

Then they stopped again, and after a pause headed back resolutely towards Drake's chamber.

Drake opened his eyes to see Danica step cautiously through the doorway. She hovered in the darkness, standing a cautious distance from the pool of light that bathed him. She looked for all the world like a small dog that had chewed its master's slippers in his absence, and was now waiting for either punishment or absolution. Her gaze flitted nervously over Drake's face, searching for some crumb of emotion that would betray her fate.

Drake wearily rubbed a hand across his eyes, motioning for her to approach. There was no sense in hiding what he thought of her world. He had hoped to find a thriving community of Pureblood vampires. Instead, he had found nothing but sickly, light-hating half-breeds, living on the streets like rats.

Could this be the case across the whole world? He had to find out.

Turning his back on Danica, Drake spoke without looking up. "This world sickens me. The humans have soiled it with their filth."

Danica hung back in the shadows. "We can raze their cities to the ground. We can bring the old world back." Her voice was insistent, compelling.

And over-eager to please.

Drake turned his head sharply, staring at Danica through narrowed eyes. He didn't like the way this one spoke to him. Respect, he could take—he expected it—but Danica's puppy-dog devotion was getting on his nerves.

But there was something else in her demeanor as well, something that Drake did like.

Danica was afraid of him.

More to the point, she was afraid of what he represented.

Drake remembered the way the half-breeds had looked at him before the so-called Vampire Nation had descended into its internecine warring, back in the sixteenth century. All of his council at the time had been Purebloods, distant descendents of his children and his grandchildren, but he had employed a handful of the more expendable half-breeds as guards, to defend his council members from attack, and occasionally from each other.

Yet despite the fact that these guards were twenty times more powerful than the strongest human being, able to lift the bodyweight of a horse without so much as breaking into a sweat, they were nothing compared to the Purebloods, and they knew it.

Drake could see it in their eyes every time he looked at them.

Over the centuries, jealousy had turned to fear among the half-breeds, which had soon led to fighting and bloodshed. Though Drake knew he could have crushed every last one of them, he had soon tired of their petty bickering; indeed, he had despaired of all his children, whether they were his by birth or by proxy.

Shortly before he went underground, the half-breeds—those who had been 'turned' from human to vampire rather than born as one—outnumbered the Pureblood vampires by more than a hundred to one. Drake had despised the half-breeds for their effrontery, but he had also grown to despise his Pureblood offspring for their seeming inability to keep their subjects under control.

So Drake turned his back on them all, returning in secret to the land of his birth so many millennia before, hoping that when he finally chose to re-emerge, the "Vampire Nation" would have found its heart and spine once more, or else destroyed itself altogether.

Now it looked like the latter was to be the case.

Drake turned his eyes skyward once more and then flicked his gaze over to the young vampire cowering in the shadows. "Come closer."

Danica gestured up at the sunlight helplessly. "I can't."

Drake sat back in his chair, a frown darkening his brow. "And do you know why?"

Silence. Danica's cheeks flamed in the darkness, and although she had no idea why, she suddenly felt ashamed.

Drake sighed, settling back into his chair with a creak. He steepled his fingertips and rested his chin on them. "Once, my kind could brave the day. We were true predators. The world was ours." He gave Danica a sidelong glance. "And then, somewhere along the way, the purity of our bloodline became diluted. Polluted by the blood of the humans."

Danica shook her head vehemently. "That's impossible."

"Is it?" Drake got to his feet, and was suddenly standing beside Danica. She blinked—she hadn't even seen him move. Her eyes darted towards the door but she stood her ground.

Drake stared thoughtfully at Danica for a couple of seconds, feeling the fear roll off her in waves. Then he reached a clawed hand into the shadows and gripped her wrist. "You are bastard children. No longer as pure as you pride yourself on being."

With that, Drake pulled Danica towards the pool of sunlight.

To her credit, Danica didn't so much as flinch. She continued staring at Drake, willing him not to do this. He was their salvation. This had to be a test.

Drake drew her hand to the very edge of the sunlight, to the border where darkness became light.

And there he stopped.

As they both watched, stray UV radiation spilling from the beam of sunlight began attacking the skin of Danica's hand, scorching the very tips of her fingers. Danica couldn't stop herself from wincing as the light chewed on her flesh. As the scent of burning skin filled the chamber, she looked up to see Drake's eyes locked on hers, coldly watching her suffer.

After a few seconds, Drake released her hand. Danica unthinkingly pulled it away from him and cradled it against her chest, blinking back tears of pain. She dropped her gaze to the floor, ashamed of her weakness.

Drake watched her for a moment, then reached out and brushed a tear from Danica's cheek. "My people. How far you have fallen."

Then he turned and walked away, passing through the alternating shafts of light and darkness before vanishing into the shadows at the end of the chamber.

Blade watched as his newfound companions raided the makeshift armory, pulling out enough weapons to start a minor war. The heavy wooden workbenches at the center of the room had been pushed together and now groaned under the weight of a vast assortment of weaponry and ammunition.

Blade was impressed. He'd only asked for an ammo refill for his new pistol and the Nightstalkers had jumped at the chance to show him how many technological advances they had made. If Blade wasn't mistaken, it was more a chance for them to show off rather than to find anything useful, but he relished the opportunity to see how far anti-vampire weaponry could be taken. Over the years, the vampires had found a way around every weapon he and Whistler had invented, from ceramic armor plates to ward off stakes, to fully insulated body suits to protect themselves from his UV torches. It was good to be given some fresh ideas.

Perhaps these Nightstalkers could be of some use to him, after all.

Hedges stood over the table, his eyes gleaming, unable to hide his pride. "We've got a wide assortment of ass-kickery for your viewing pleasure." He reached into the growing pile and hefted a strange-looking pistol with blocky rubber grips, holding it out for Blade to examine. "Electronic pistol. Comes with a built-in fingerprint security system. Fires a three-shot burst in one five-hundredths of a second. Bullets can also be triggered remotely." King ejected the clip and tossed Blade one of the bullets.

Blade caught it one handed and held the round up to the light, studying it carefully. There were seams running in a crisscross pattern around the bullet, as though it had been through several different stages of casting. Its tip was transparent, crafted out of sturdy glass. Blade understood what it was immediately. Whistler had been working on something similar just before he died. He waved the bullet at King. "Explosive rounds?"

King nodded. "But with a concentrated burst of UV light instead of your standard hollow-points. I call 'em Sundogs."

He turned and pointed to an impressive-looking weapon laid out at the opposite end of the table. "Hedges—super-size me, baby!"

Hedges tossed King an enormous, four-barreled firearm. King hefted the colossal weapon with practiced ease, buffing the casing to a gleaming finish with a corner of his T-shirt. Blade saw that there was an irreverent decal of the mud-flap girl silhouette stenciled onto the gun's stock, making the weapon look almost cartoon-like.

King stroked it lovingly. "This little peashooter—it's a modified version of the Army's Objective Individual Combat Weapon. Pick your poison: stakes, Sundogs, heat-seeking mini-rockets... Whatever gets you hard, this puppy will pump out." He gestured to Blade's sword sarcastically. "Of course, it doesn't have the range of a sword, but..."

Blade gave the grinning King a blank stare, and pretended to examine his fingernails, studying the

weapon out of the corner of his eye. Already, he
wanted it. Now, if he could just create some kind of a
distraction...

Then Blade's eyes widened as he homed in on a different toy wielded by Hedges, a lethal-looking
crescent-shaped device.

Blade didn't know what it was, but he immediately
wanted it, too.

For a moment he hesitated, torn between the two
weapons. His fingers itched to reach out and flip up
the bench, grabbing what he could before making a
bolt for the door so he could jump in his Charger
and...

Hang on a moment. Wasn't his Charger back at the
Boathouse?

Blade sagged. Small gap in the plan there.

He watched sulkily as Hedges polished the chrome
sides of the silver crescent on his tattered sleeve. He
held out the device at arm's length and gave the two
halves a gentle twist. "We call this the UV Arc."

The device shot out a curving metal telescopic array
from each end. A concentrated blue-white laser
flashed between the two anodized ends like the string
on a catapult, making a humming, buzzing sound
that made the inside of Blade's brain itch.

Blade shook his head like a dog to clear it, and then
gazed at the weapon longingly. It was such a simple
concept, but already he could picture all the fun he
would have using such a device in battle. In fact, he
could think of one or two vampires he would like to
test it on straight away...

Hedges gave a little smile of professional pride as he
saw the look on Blade's face, and began to

demonstrate the device as though extolling its virtues on the Home Shopping channel. "You hold the arc in the center, curved away from you. Connecting the two tips is a powerful UV laser beam. Because of its high focus, the laser cuts through vampire flesh like a knife through butter."

King nodded approvingly and leaned back on the workbench next to Blade. He saw that the Day-walker's gaze had flicked thoughtfully towards the Tomb of Dracula comic book on the workbench and he tried to pick up the threads of their earlier conversation. "We're still trying to sort out fact from fiction when it comes to Dracula. Turning into mist? Kinda doubt it. But general shape-shifting? Maybe."

Blade raised an eyebrow. He had never heard of such a thing, except for of course in the movies. As far as he knew, there was no way known to science that a body could change into something else.

In fact, if he were here, Whistler himself would probably have a thing or two to say about the scientific probability of shape-shifting. Blade remembered sitting around watching ex-rental DVDs with the old man, who would take every monster movie apart at the seams as a matter of course, relishing the challenge of unpicking the logic of the film with his annoyingly practical brain. "That would never happen," the old man would scoff, letting exactly five and a half seconds go past before wagging a finger and adding, "And I'll tell you why..." He would then spend the next ten minutes listing the mind-bogglingly dull scientific reasons why they wouldn't, until Blade developed a headache and had to turn it off.

As a result, Blade would usually wait until Whistler was in bed before watching any new releases, only to be scuppered by the old man's incredibly penetrating voice calling down the stairs, "Spiders shoot their webs from their asses, not their wrists. Damn fool scriptwriters..."

King saw the wistful look on Blade's face and interpreted it as a look of doubt. "He couldn't change into a bat or a wolf or anything like that. But another human, someone with the same approximate body mass—given enough practice, it might be possible."

Blade considered this, and then asked the million-dollar question. "How?"

Hedges retracted the UV Arc with a clunk, rejoining the conversation. "Drake wouldn't have a traditional skeletal structure. Probably something more like a snake, with thousands of tiny bones in the place of a normal array." He looked at Blade shyly, warming to his topic. "Commensurate with this would be an exquisite control of electrical potential across his tissues, resulting in an ability to effectively change shape at will—"

King raised a hand to stop him as Blade stared in nostalgic admiration. "Question. Have you ever been laid, Hedges?"

An hour later, Blade, King and Abigail were fully suited up for their mission. They had donned full body armor: Kevlar vests, strap-on joint braces, steel-capped boots, the works. There was no knowing who—or what—they might run into tonight.

Blade pulled on his long, leather duster and tightened a Velcro body-strap around his chest, to which was fastened an assortment of weaponry.

Then he strode through the door and joined King and Abigail by a new Land Cruiser, which stood gleaming in the muted sunlight washing down from the skylights. Dex pottered out to meet them, waving a hand proudly towards the vehicle. "Got you some new wheels."

Blade reached the driver's door a fraction of a second before King did. They made eye contact for a moment. Blade smiled toothily and King quickly stepped aside to allow him to board, then walked around the front of the vehicle and climbed grumpily into the passenger's seat.

Pushy son of a bitch.

Blade reached around and hefted his back-holstered barrelgun a little higher up around his body, allowing him to buckle up his seatbelt. "Time to apply some pressure." He tilted the rear view mirror so that he could see Abigail. "The weak link in the vampire chain of command has always been their familiars. Vampires can't go out in the day, so they get humans to do their dirty work for them. Blood-running, safe-house maintenance, whatever." He slammed the Cruiser's door shut behind him. "We bleed the wanna-be vampires, they'll lead us to the real thing."

He started the engine with a jangle of keys and glanced over to check on Abigail, who had chosen to sit in the back. She hadn't said a word in quite a while. Blade saw that she had a laptop on her knees and was frowning down at it intently. What was this? Some kind of tactical extrapolator, perhaps?

Blade raised his eyebrows. He would never admit it out loud, but these Nightstalkers were clever sons of bitches. Not as clever as him and Whistler, of course, but hell, everybody had to start somewhere.

King saw Blade's interest and motioned him to lean in closer so as not to disturb Abigail. "She's making playlists. Likes to listen to MP3s when she hunts. Her own internal soundtrack, you know." He glanced at Abigail with affection. "Dark-core, trip-hop, whatever kids these days are listening to." He smiled. "Me? I'm more of a Kenny G fan."

They both watched as Abigail tapped the touchpad of her laptop and slipped a pair of silver ear buds into her ears, downloading the playlist to the whirring hard-drive of her portable MP3 player. She smiled approvingly as the smoking baseline to Jurassic 5's "A Day at the Races" kicked in inside her head.

This was the stuff.

Blade fired up the Cruiser's engine with a roar and peeled out of the warehouse, heading for the sunlit streets of the city.

They pulled up outside a scuzzy bar, well outside the comfort zone of downtown. The big Cruiser jumped the curb and rocked to a halt in front of the entrance.

Abigail and King pried their whitened fingers from the seat rests in front of them, staring at Blade as smoke drifted up lazily from the tires.

Now they knew why the Daywalker's own auto had looked the way it did.

Blade ignored them both, nodding towards a vampire glyph scrawled on the wall of the bar amidst the creative swirl of graffiti and band flyers. These archaic symbols spelt out vampire slogans chosen by the owner of the place, marking their territory in much the same way as their human familiars were branded.

As far as Blade could make out, the glyphs were based on passages taken from the revered vampire bible, an ancient text named the *Book of Erebus*, written in Akkadian on parchment made from human skin. Blade had found and destroyed the oldest version of the so-called bible several years back, but there was a rumor that some fragments of it still remained. Thinking back, Blade found himself wishing he'd taken a look before setting it alight. Might have said something useful about the enemy they now faced.

Blade shrugged to himself. Pulling his sword out from between the seats, he jumped out of the Cruiser and strode confidently towards the front door of the bar.

Inside, the muggy atmosphere clung like smoke to the bar's various seedy inhabitants. Remixed jazz-trance music played over the PA, adding to the general air of gloom, made worse by the blacked-out windows. Above the bar, a red neon sign flickered and flared, advertising various beverages, some of them legal, some of them not.

A man dressed like a dockyard worker sat on the high stool by the corner of the bar, drinking alone. He swirled his drink around the bottom of his glass, staring moodily into its murky depths. He'd ordered a Bacardi and coke. This tasted more like lighter fluid cut with sugar, which, knowing the barman, was probably a conservative guess.

But he'd paid for it, dammit, and he was going to drink it.

The man's name was Jack Hoop. He came to this bar every weekday, regular as clockwork, partly to relax and unwind after his nightshift down at the docks, but mostly to put off going home to his wife, Sally-Anne.

He supposed some people might regard Sally as a good woman. But this "goodness" manifested itself in very disagreeable ways, the main one being her drive for cleanliness and order, which drove Hoop to distraction on the best of days.

It wasn't good enough his hands being clean, they had to be hygienic, as should be his face, boots and whatever portions of his anatomy she could reach with her sanitized scrubbing brush. When he came home from work he couldn't just come in and sit down on the couch, for he may still have evil outdoor germs on his clothing, spreading disease and general nastiness around the house.

Worst of all, her intense desire for cleanliness carried itself over into their bedroom, where Sally refused to do anything remotely carnal with Hoop unless they had both washed, brushed teeth, scrubbed fingernails and washed again, until Hoop was forced into the emasculating position where he was usually sound asleep before Sally finally emerged from the bathroom. After six years of marriage, they still had no children.

Lately, Hoop was finding himself irresistibly drawn to the girl who worked behind the bar here. She wore week-old stockings, chewed fried-bean nachos with her mouth open and wouldn't know what dental floss was if she was garroted with an entire packet of the stuff.

Hoop stared at her now, watching wide-eyed as she poured the contents of the beer slop tray into a glass by the sink, stole a quick peek over her shoulder to ensure that no one was watching her, then took a hasty gulp from the glass, wiping her dripping chin with a wet bar towel.

Hoop sighed, gazing at her lustily.

One day, she would be his...

Hoop was jolted from his dirty little fantasy as the bar door was kicked open with a bang. Three strangers walked in. Hoop ignored the two men—a big mean-looking black guy in a long leather duster and sunshades, and a white dude in a scuffed jacket. His roving eye immediately settled on the woman accompanying them. Hoop felt an instant shock of lust go through him.

Man, this chick was hot.

Hoop ran an appreciative gaze over her, from the tips of her metal-studded boots to her tousled blonde hair. The babe was cut like an Amazon, with sharply defined cheekbones and features like the finest porcelain he had ever seen. She was wearing combat pants, leather gloves and a cool biker's jacket with red front panels. Her outfit was covered in a light coating of road-dust, as though she had just been driving with the windows open.

Hoop drooled, wondering with a stab of delicious guilt whether she took off her make-up before getting into bed at night.

As though feeling the heat of his gaze on her, the beauty's eyes suddenly swiveled in their sockets and locked with his. Hoop's goofy smile froze to his face as the woman's eyes bored into him like a laser scalpel in his brain.

She knew.

Hoop felt the certainty of it in one heart stopping instant. Before his brain could kick in, his legs had done his thinking for him, pulling his sozzled carcass to its feet and taking off at high speed towards the back door. He didn't know why he was running, but he knew he had to get out of here, fast.

As he sped past the bar, he saw the big black guy vault over the counter like a gymnast and begin rummaging in the refrigerator under the counter. Oh, shit. The shelves were packed full of packages of refrigerated blood, labeled with tags from the inner-city blood bank.

Hoop felt the world receding from him. This bar was just a front, like so many others all over the city. In the back Hoop knew that there were dozens of high-tech coffin-like beds where the vampires could safely sleep through the day unmolested.

The stranger's presence here could only mean one thing.

They'd been found out.

Hoop gave a little unconscious gibber of fear at the thought and streaked past the bathrooms, crashing through the double doors at the rear of the bar. The warm, fetid smell of the dumpsters in the back street hit his nostrils, and then he was out into the morning sunlight and open air.

Hoop gave a sob of relief to have escaped and then shrieked like a girl as he ran flat-out into the Amazon woman from the bar.

She'd been waiting for him.

Hoop spun on a dime and started to run back the way he'd come, then found his feet vanishing from beneath him as the woman tripped him up, catching him in mid-fall with an arm hooked around his throat. Hoop felt small but strong hands close on his flailing wrist, twisting one of his arms so far up behind his back that he squealed.

The woman supported his weight on her bent knee and pulled his collar down, as though examining lettuces at the supermarket. She calmly checked over the back of his neck, taking in the vampire glyph crudely tattooed there in dark blue ink.

Then she smiled.

Two hours later, the rooftops of the city echoed with frantic screaming. Cheerfully oblivious to his captive's squeals, Blade stepped up to the parapet of the multi-story car park, holding the quivering, bruised form of Hoop tightly in his gloved grip. Out of the dozen or so familiars they had captured and interrogated over the last couple of hours, Hoop was the only one who had refused to spill the beans.

Blade knew that this could mean one of two things. Either Hoop was hiding something, or he was very, very foolish.

The Daywalker stepped closer to the parapet and peered over the edge, tutting loudly at the sight of the vertiginous, dizzying drop to the ground.

Then he tossed the skinny familiar off the roof.

It was a six-story drop. Hoop screamed at the top of his lungs as the concrete sidewalk below flew up to meet him.

Then his head whiplashed around as he was jerked to a bone jarring halt, ten feet above the ground. Hoop dangled helplessly while the world span around him, still screaming although there was no more air left in his lungs, and wished heartily that he had never been born. The thick rope tied around his ankles creaked alarmingly, tightening like a vice, but it held.

For now.

Blade stood on the rooftop above, the other end of the rope casually looped around his shoulders. Effortlessly, he winched the man back up, foot by painstaking foot, stopping with just a few yards to go. King and Abigail stood behind Blade, staring at him.

Hoop hung upside down below them, spinning on the end of the rope, his entire being concentrated on the drop beneath him.

Blade had never seen someone go truly green before.

At least, not a human.

"Want another spin, asshole?" Blade grinned, enjoying himself immensely. Whistler had been right about one thing—it was the little things in life that were the most satisfying. He let go of the rope with one hand to wave at Hoop, engendering a fresh volley of shrieks from the upside down familiar. "Eventually, your head's gonna pop off."

Hoop scrabbled at the side of the building with bleeding hands, frantically trying to get a grip on the bare brickwork. "Shit! Oh Jesus, please..."

"Who's your handler?" Blade toyed with a loose thread in the rope, idly fraying the end.

"I don't know his name, I swear..."

Wrong answer. Blade prepared to drop the man again.

***

On the circular exit ramp below, a family station wagon wound its way slowly downwards. The two young boys in the back seat scrambled from window to window in excitement as they watched the funny man bounce up and down on the end of his rope. This was great stuff. They had spent the last three hours trudging around shoe shops with their mother, and getting to see this had made it all worthwhile.

Up above them, Hoop closed his eyes and screamed in anticipation of a third and final drop. As he did so, a cell phone rang in his pocket. Hoop's eyes reopened, flicking from side to side as he realized he hadn't been dropped. Then they opened wider and he began kicking frantically, trying to reach for the ringing phone. Oh, this was not good...

Curious, Blade hauled the man up to the lip of the ledge. Holding the rope between his knees, Blade ripped Hoop's jacket open with one hand and used the other to fish around inside for the familiar's cell phone. Locating the device, he flipped it open and read the caller ID. The display listed the caller as being one Edgar Vance, and gave the number of a pager.

Blade smiled.

Jackpot.

He dialed the number and listened intently for a moment. Then he snapped the phone shut and looked down at Hoop, who gave him a sickly smile, desperation and guilt written all over his ashen face.

Blade smiled back, a glint in his eye.

Then he let Hoop drop.

The screaming familiar plunged five stories to the ground, and jerked to a spinning halt just ten feet above the concrete. Above him, Blade tied the end of the rope to the metal barrier and walked off, whistling.

At the bottom of the exit ramp, the family station wagon finally passed by Hoop. The two young boys in the back seat stared intently at the dangling man in silent appreciation. They hoped that he'd be here again next week, when their mother did her grocery shopping.

Up above them, Blade and the Nightstalkers made their way back across the parking lot. King hurried to keep up with the Daywalker, chattering away amiably. "You might want to think about doing some inner work. Sitting down with someone, having a little share time. Getting in touch with your inner child..."

The silence coming from Blade was almost deafening.

Unfazed, King carried on regardless. "I know we just met, but I care about you. I just don't want to see you drop into a shame spiral." He gazed up at Blade. "Also, maybe think about blinking once in a while... It's just a thought."

Blade gave King a sidelong glare.

King finally got the message. "Sorry. I've eaten a lot of sugar lately."

The three of them walked off towards the elevator at the top of the exit ramp.

Time to go Edgar hunting.

TWELVE

The Edgar Vance Institute for Whole Being was a crowded office complex situated towards the expensive end of town. It was perfectly located on a popular tree-lined street, surrounded by meticulously groomed grounds. Streams of people swarmed in and out of the revolving doors set into the front of the building, its clients ranging from college graduates to high-flying city businessmen clad in black Armani suits. A looming aluminum sign with a "VANCE INSTITUTE" logo dominated the front yard, casting a shadow over the front of the building.

Blade strode confidently up the paved front path, not bothering to hide his approach. He was tailed at a small distance by King and Abigail, who were trying to look as unarmed and inconspicuous as possible and failing dismally on both counts.

Abigail noticed a surveillance camera on a pole tracking them as they closed in on the building. A shiver ran through her at the thought of what they were about to do. Blade's approach was a lot less subtle than the Nightstalker's usual method of attack, which generally involved a lot of waiting around and calculating risk factors, followed by a small but perfectly planned raid. They had to research the situation meticulously, for if the single vampire they went out to kill turned out to be a dozen vampires, the mistake could cost them their lives.

But Blade seemed to think nothing of bulldozing right into the thick of things as soon as he had enough info to point him in the right general direction. Abigail wondered what his vampire/human kill ratio was—how many humans Blade had killed by mistake over the course of his twenty-year career. She hoped for his sake that it was as low as Whistler had promised her.

As they passed the staff parking lot, King nudged Abigail and pointed out a blue Jaguar parked in front, complete with personalized vanity plate reading "VANCE-1."

King arched an eyebrow at the plate, and Abigail shared his unspoken thought.

This guy had class.

It was just a shame that it was of the remedial kind.

King trotted forward and hurried to catch up with Blade, trying to hide his nerves. This place gave him the creeps already. There was a distinct air of foreboding hanging over the grounds, and he didn't have much confidence in Blade's plan of smash-and-grab. He dug through his internal stock of vampire jokes for something appropriate to lighten the atmosphere. "Hey, Blade—why didn't the vampire bite Keith Richards?"

Blade gave him a pained look. He was not sure how much longer he could take this. If being a vampire for five years couldn't daunt King's spirit, he had the feeling that nothing could.

King waited for a moment, hoping for a reply. One day, the big motherfucker would surprise him by growing a sense of humor. There had to be something else aside from brooding and killing in that big noggin of his.

Spreading his arms, King delivered the punch line. "Because you can't get blood from a Stone."

Blade walked off, shaking his head.

King watched him go. "Hey! They can't all be gems!"

Ignoring him, Blade stepped up to the front of the Institute and pushed his way through the heavy revolving door. Inside lay an airy, neat, clinically scrubbed reception area outfitted with water coolers and leafy green pot plants. The lighting was low and the walls were painted in varying calming shades of hospital green. On the wall hung a dozen framed black and white signed prints, as various B-list celebrities gave their glowing—and financially rewarding—endorsements to the Vance program.

The clients gathered by the front desk turned and watched the tough-looking trio enter and started to whisper amongst themselves.

Blade's gaze passed over them without interest, his eyes scanning the reception area for some clue as to Vance's whereabouts. They paused on a glossy cardboard cutout featuring Vance's grinning face. Beneath it a line of embossed gold text read:

EDGAR VANCE, MD
PRESIDENT, VANCE INSTITUTE for
WHOLE BEING

Nearby, a bank of video monitors showed a beautiful young couple basking in the light of a golden sunrise. Blade watched them cavort in the waves as a solemn voice intoned, "Regain control of your life. Wake to a new dawn. At the Edgar Vance Institute for Whole Being, we believe in an integrated approach to Human Health."

The image onscreen cut to a shot of Vance himself, flatteringly lit and poised casually on the edge of his desk. He leaned forwards towards the camera, as though addressing the viewer exclusively. "I'm Doctor Vance. Welcome to our facility." His voice was sonorous and educated. "As a member of the medical profession, I want to assure you that I will do everything in my power to provide you with the care and compassion that you deserve."

Snorting, Blade motioned to the others to follow him. Care and compassion was one thing. Sticking him full of needles and handing him over to his enemies had been another. And don't even get him started on all that crap about sexual repression...

They strode towards the elevators where two more video screens hung showing the same PR feed tape. King and Abigail tugged their jackets more closely around themselves, feeling the effects of the blasting air-conditioners positioned every few yards in the ceiling.

As they approached, two uniformed security guards moved swiftly to intercept them. "Excuse me, can I help y—" The guard's patronizing smile turned to a painful grimace as Blade grabbed him by the front of his jacket and hoisted him into the air. Grabbing the second guard, Blade casually tossed the pair of them aside, sending them crashing through the nearest bank of video monitors.

The trio continued on their way, moving quickly before they were recognized. A white-jacketed doctor stepped out of a doorway at the commotion, and Blade punched him full in the face. As the doctor went down, Blade was already moving, loping off around the corner where he nearly collided with two more security guards coming in the opposite direction. Seeing their fallen comrade groaning on the floor, they pulled out their nightsticks and advanced. They swung their weapons at Blade, one going for the side of his head, the other for one of his knees.

Blade ducked and spun away from their blows, then retaliated with a rapid-fire barrage of uppercuts and weighted jabs aimed at the vulnerable parts of their bodies, intended to stun and injure rather than kill. The corridors rang with the dull thuds of skin striking skin and the surprised grunts and yelps of the guards. Even so, the men were worryingly well trained and Blade had to stop himself from inflicting more serious harm on them, as their blows came within inches of his body.

Vance's face beamed down from a large plasma-screen TV hung on the wall as they fought. "What does it mean to be human?" Vance intoned gravely as Blade flew past him, sending one of the security guards spinning through the air with a sweeping roundhouse kick. "Since the dawn of creation our ancestors have asked themselves that question. The modern world today is filled with countless challenges..."

The first guard feinted a kick at Blade's groin, then at the last moment changed his target to Blade's stomach. His foot glanced off Blade's sculpted Kevlar body armor and the guard howled, staggering away. Blade easily knocked him to the floor and rapped him on the temple with his steel-capped biker boot, bouncing his head off the tiles and sending him spinning into the arms of oblivion. Blade immediately turned to engage the second guard, who leapt at him, reaching for his gun.

Vance's PR video carried on playing above them, the doctor's voice as soothing as any hypnosis video. "We think we're healthy, but the truth is, our immune systems are engaged in a life or death struggle to maintain our well-being..."

As the second guard dropped to the floor clutching his broken wrist, Blade spun around and swung a well-judged kick at the screen, knocking it off the wall and sending it tumbling to the ground. It impacted in a shower of flaring plasma sparks, turning the cutting-edge monitor into little more than a very expensive picture frame.

Blade led the Nightstalkers along the darkened corridor to a large, official-looking door located at the end of the hallway. He gestured to the others to stand back, and drew his gun. Abigail cleared her throat primly, and Blade hesitated for a moment before obligingly trying the door handle.

The door was unlocked.

Blade burst into the office.

Before he had a chance to take a step inside, an immaculately dressed executive assistant moved smoothly forward to intercept him. "I'm sorry, but you can't..." His eyes flicked downward as the Nightstalkers opened their jackets, revealing a scary looking array of concealed weaponry.

In the split-second before his eyes moved back up again, Abigail stepped forwards and kicked the suited man in the kneecap while simultaneously chopping her hand into his windpipe.

The man dropped to the ground, quietly gagging.

Blade scanned the area, quickly locating the main office by the brass nameplate on the wall next to the door. While Abigail's back was turned, he withdrew his shotgun from the folds of his leather duster and screwed a silencer onto the end. Chambering a round, he fired once into the keycard scanner. The unit flared up, littering the carpet with sparks, then disengaged the lock with an affronted electronic whine. Blade gave the door a hefty kick, bursting it open and stepped through into Dr Vance's office.

Blade got a quick, distracted impression of the size and opulence of the room before zeroing in on the man sitting in front of him.

Finally. Doctor Vance.

The Doctor jumped up hurriedly from behind his desk, startled, wiping at his mouth with a napkin. He was dressed strangely, not at all like the doctor he proclaimed himself to be. Although well tailored, his clothes seemed fractionally too big for him, like a child dressing up in his father's work clothes.

He looked the intruders up and down, outrage vying with bewilderment on his face. "What—"

"Payback, Vance."

Blade aimed his shotgun at the doctor's head and clicked off the safety catch, watching for Vance's reaction.

To his surprise, Vance merely smiled.

Sensing that something was wrong, Abigail held up a hand to Blade and warily circled around the other side of Vance's desk to check that he was unarmed.

She froze, not quite believing what she was seeing.

The body of a man dressed in a doctor's uniform lay behind the desk. His throat had been ripped out. He was lying in a pool of fresh blood, an expression of shock frozen onto his face.

Abigail gasped. The man's face was identical to that of Doctor Vance.

King put two and two together first. Backing away, he reached frantically into his jacket for a silver stake. "Jesus, it's him! It's Dracula!"

All eyes went back to the man standing behind the desk. He then smiled, jumped onto the tabletop from a standing start and swatted the muzzle of Blade's shotgun aside as it went off, shattering the office window. Snarling like an animal, Vance's double snapped a powerful kick into Blade's chest, sending him flying across the office. The Daywalker struck a display cabinet in a blaze of glass and fell to the ground, the ruined cabinet crashing down all around him.

King pulled a silver stake from the harness at his belt and ran forwards to back Blade up. Then he stopped and stared as the bones in the doctor's face twisted around under the surface of his skin with a sickly cracking sound, writhing like eels in jelly.

Despite himself, King began backing away as the mutating "doctor" advanced on him. This was some freaky shit. He knew he should've brought his exorcism kit with him...

Before King could decide on a course of action, the now unrecognizable doctor leapt forward so quickly that he became a blur, knocking King off his feet and slamming him down onto the desk. Grabbing King's wrist, he twisted the stake from his hand. In one easy motion he flipped the stake around and hammered it down through King's ribcage, nailing him to the wooden desktop.

As King's screams reverberated around the room, the imposter turned to face Abigail, the last of Vance's features melting away to reveal Drake's snarling visage.

Abigail reached for her crossbow but before she could bring it to bear Drake had crossed the short distance between them and knocked her back across the room with a tooth-jarring backhand. Abigail slammed into the blood-covered desk next to King's writhing body, striking her head as she did so. She slumped to the carpet, dazed.

Then Drake was off, sprinting across the room towards the shattered window. He leaped through it without so much as a glance backward.

Rolling to his feet, Blade shook off the clinging remains of the wooden cabinet and ran across the room to the window. He slammed his hands onto the ledge and looked down to see Drake land safely on the ground, three stories below. The vampire king glanced back up at Blade, baring his teeth in an expression that could just as easily have been one of amusement as one of defiance. Then he pelted off around the side of the building, heading towards the back entrance.

There was only one thing left to do. Gritting his teeth, Blade climbed through the window after Drake and leapt downwards, his black jacket billowing out behind him as he fell. He landed in a low crouch on the pathway below, like a sprinter on the starting blocks, and coiled his muscles in preparation.

Then he launched himself off to intercept Drake.

Outside the Vance Institute, Drake tore through the milling crowds of clients with inhuman speed. Finding the back gate locked, he scaled the high chain-link fence in a single bound then barreled straight through the wooden traffic barricade on the other side without so much as slowing, smashing it to firewood. He tore off down the back alleyway and headed for freedom.

Blade pounded after Drake, rounding the corner just as the ancient vampire leapt with impossible grace over the large dumpster at the other end of the alley, a hundred yards from him.

Blade gave chase.

Drake turned briefly at the sound, his gaze penetrating the shadows of the alley as his ears picked up Blade's rapid footfalls, slowed down by his fierce concentration.

The Daywalker was following him. How predictable.

Drake set off at high speed through a crowded urban market that was taking place in the square behind the Vance Institute. His trajectory described a perfectly straight line across the square, smashing aside stalls like a wrecking ball and knocking down pedestrians. Blade followed in his wake a couple of seconds later, trampling over merchandise that had been strewn across the street by Drake.

Bursting through the rickety fence on the other side of the market, Drake found himself on the sidewalk of a busy street. His escape was cut off by four lanes of whizzing traffic. Undaunted, Drake immediately ran into the road and leapt onto the hood of an oncoming car, balancing easily as it blared its horn and spun across the road in a squeal of smoking brakes. As the car rocked to a halt, Drake leapt off its hood onto a second moving car, then a third.

But the first car's spin had lost him vital seconds. On the other side of the road, Blade crashed through the hole in the fence. Taking in the situation at a glance, he followed Drake in a likewise fashion across the busy road, ignoring the honking cars. The pair of them raced across the flowing traffic, using the hoods and roofs of the cars like moving steppingstones.

Leaping off the trunk of the last vehicle, an out of control pizza delivery van, Drake ran towards a dark alley on the other side of the road. He heard the rumble of tires just in time and hurled himself backwards as a garbage truck thundered past him out of the alley, blaring its horn.

Cut off from Drake by the truck, Blade was forced to wait for it to pull out before he could continue the chase, losing precious time. On the other side, Drake tore across the sidewalk and ran into the first building he came to: an old apartment block.

Mounting the front steps five at a time, he burst through the main entrance and ran through the foyer, taking off up the spiral staircase like a rocket.

The Daywalker followed him in hot pursuit, arriving at the top of the stairway just in time to see Drake disappearing around the end of a corridor. In his path lay a chaotic tangle of furniture and laundry. A dog darted out of an open door, barking at him and halfway down the corridor an elderly Jamaican man lay on the floor, muttering obscenities under his breath. He struggled to reach for his Zimmer frame, which Drake had knocked over in his mad dash.

Blade instinctively moved forwards to help him up, then froze at the muted tinkle of glass breaking. A woman's voice screamed, "My baby!"

Blade's head snapped up. He leapt over the prone form of the old man and hared off down the corridor. Moments later, he burst into the flat at the unlocked end of the hallway.

Drake was nowhere in sight.

Blade took in the hysterical mother staring at her up ended crib and ran swiftly across the flat, towards the open window curtain. Without hesitation he launched himself through it, tucking his body into a compact ball to avoid the jagged edges of the glass and landed with a clang on the black metal fire escape outside.

Glancing up, he caught a flash-frame glimpse of Drake moving away from him overhead, climbing up towards the roof at superhuman speed. Growling under his breath, Blade threw himself onto the rickety metal ladder, his hands moving in a blur as he pulled himself upwards, rung after rung.

After the third floor, Blade found himself beginning to slow. Despite his superhuman endurance, the after-effects of the sudden chase were beginning to catch up with him. His hands felt like lead as he pulled himself up higher and higher and a muscle in his thigh cramped, threatening to throw his whole leg into spasm. Blade's strength and stamina were far beyond that of any normal human, but despite all of this, he was still human. Mostly.

His senses twanged, and he reflexively swung himself out sideways to avoid the large planter that came hurtling down the ladder towards him, clearly intended to knock him off and send him plunging to his death. He felt the rush of air on his face as it flew past him, and his stomach lurched at the sight of the dizzying drop beneath him.

Blade dangled one-handed from the ladder for a moment, grimly willing it not to break, then quickly swung himself back onto the rungs and resumed his pace in double-quick time. He couldn't let Drake get away. Who knew what diabolical plans the vampires might be hatching for him, right at this very moment? He had to be stopped, and quickly.

Blade shinned up two more levels before finally reaching the top of the fire escape, disturbing a cloud of roosting pigeons which took flight all around him, blinding him with their panicky flapping. Shooing the creatures away, Blade made a giant leap for the roof of the building twelve feet above him, catching the tiled edge and swinging himself upwards like an acrobat.

Flipping himself over in mid-air, Blade landed on his feet, drawing his sword with a scrape of metal. He quickly scanned the area, panting.

There was no one in sight.

"So you're the hunter they all fear."

Blade spun around.

Drake was standing on the very edge of the rooftop, cradling a baby in his arms. The sight of the baby was the only thing that halted Blade's charge, so ready was he to fling himself at Drake and send him spinning over the edge of the roof. The yellow afternoon sun glared in the sky behind Drake, surrounding the ancient vampire with a blinding halo of light.

Drake kept his eyes fixed on Blade as he inclined his head, nodding towards the infant held in the crook of his arm. "Just so we understand each other, Daywalker."

With his free hand, he reached up and massaged his jaw. Blade heard a popping sound as the last few pieces of cartilage in Drake's chin settled back into place after his transformation.

Blade let the air out of his lungs in a careful breath, trying to regain control of his breathing. It wouldn't do to let Drake see him betray any kind of weakness. Sweat trickled down his forehead into his eyes, and he wiped at his brow, trying to make the motion appear casual.

Hunter and predator stood on the rooftop, sizing each other up.

Blade was the first to speak. "Why did you kill Vance?"

Drake shrugged. "He'd outlived his purpose. Become a liability." Drake seemed irritated by the topic. He looked Blade over with interest, changing the subject. "Your sword—I've seen that hilt before. Eight or nine centuries ago." He glanced up at Blade, impressed. "The hunter who carried it was an accomplished fighter." Drake tucked the infant closer to his body, gesturing towards Blade's sword. "He was honorable, in his own way. He died a good death."

Blade wasn't buying it. "I wouldn't know about that."

"You lie." Drake said the phrase without rancor, merely stating it as fact. "You are part of a grand tradition, Blade. You hunters have plagued my people since the day we first walked the earth." He rubbed his jaw again. "And I have vanquished them. One by one."

Turning away from Blade dismissively, Drake gazed down at the baby and chucked it under the chin. It waved its pink, chubby arms at him, reaching out blindly as it sought something edible to grasp. Drake smiled, not unkindly. Humans were such fragile things, yet they acted as though they were indestructible. It was mankind's greatest folly, yet also, perversely, its greatest strength.

Out of the corner of his eye he watched Blade hover, agonizing over the choice he had to make. He could practically hear Blade's thoughts. Here was his big chance. The king of the vampires, alone, unarmed, and trapped on a rooftop. But what about the baby? Should he rush Drake, sending the three of them plummeting to the ground, or should he try to save the little one first?

Drake chuckled softly to himself and transferred the baby to his other arm, moving slowly backwards towards the seven-story drop. The fall wouldn't kill him, but he was guessing that it would do serious damage to the so-called Daywalker. If he survived the drop, the death of the baby would make him just that little bit more predictable in his quest for vengeance, putting him right where the vampires wanted him.

Blade moved with Drake, his eyes flicking down to the child, frantically casting about in his mind for something to stall the vampire with. He said the first thing that came into his head. "How can you exist in the daylight?"

Drake smiled proudly. "I've always been able to. Haven't you read Mr Stoker's fable? I was the first of the vampires. I am unique."

A light finally dawned inside Blade's head. The words were out of his mouth before he could stop himself. "That's why they brought you back."

Drake nodded. There was no harm in letting the Daywalker in on his little plan. It would only serve to make things more interesting when he finally came to kill him. "Yes," he said. "My children seek to isolate the properties in my blood that make me immune to sunlight." He gazed down at the baby in his arms. "Through me, they believe they can all become Day-walkers."

Shouts came from below. Drake glanced down at the street beneath them where a surprisingly large crowd of onlookers had gathered, pointing up at him and milling around in excitement.

Some of them were even taking pictures.

"The world's changed much since I went to sleep," Drake mused. "How crowded it's become." He glanced at Blade and nodded at the throng down below. "Look at them down there. Lives brief as fire-flies. Do you think they can ever grasp what it means to be immortal, like us?"

Blade fixed Drake with a look of contempt. Was the evil bloodsucker actually trying to compare the two of them? His lip curled in anger. "You're not immortal. I must've heard a hundred of you people make that claim. And every one of them has seen the end of my sword."

Blade shifted his weight onto the balls of his feet and bent fractionally at the knees, preparing to tackle Drake. He had to get to that baby.

Drake smiled despite himself. He'd heard those words so many times over that he'd stopped counting. Still, there was no loss in humoring the young hunter. "Perhaps I will as well, then," he said, taking two steps backwards. "But I think it's more likely that you will fall before mine."

As Blade tensed, ready to strike, Drake's smile faded. "Catch."

He tossed the baby at Blade.

Without thinking, Blade performed an impressive dive forwards, twisting in mid-air to catch the falling infant as it dropped towards the concrete, its white shawl streaming upwards.

Blade landed on his back and rolled to his feet in one quick motion, hugging the child to his broad chest. Turning, he glared back at the empty space where Drake had been.

"Shit!"

Three blocks away at the Vance Institute, Abigail braced her knees against the desk and wrapped her hands around the end of the silver stake protruding from King's ribcage. She looked down at her comrade's white face, her eyebrows raised in an unspoken question.

King nodded fractionally at her, staring fixedly out of the broken window.

Before he could change his mind, Abigail wrenched the stake from King's chest. It came out with a gory *gloop,* trailing a thin string of blood behind it. King cried out in pain and clutched at his chest. Abigail caught him as he slumped downwards, close to passing out.

Lifting his limp form, she carefully lowered him to the ground and propped him up against the wall by the window. King clutched at the gaping wound in his side, in terrible pain. Blood ran between his fingers and soaked into his clothing, making a small pool on the floor beside him.

"Jesus, it hurts." King wiped a trembling hand across his brow and squeezed his eyes tight shut, trying to keep himself from going into shock. "I wanna be a vampire again—fuck!" He pointed weakly to the window above him, hyperventilating. "Did you see that guy? We're gonna lose, man. We're gonna fucking lose."

He subsided, groaning.

Abigail studiously ignored him and began cutting open his shirt with her pocketknife. From the look on her face, it was not the first time she had done this. She removed a small aerosol canister from her belt.

"What's that?" King asked, instantly wary.

"Fibrin sealant foam. It's an elastic protein." She motioned to King's ribcage. "Help me spread the wound open. The foam should seal the hemorrhaging in your body cavity from within."

Ignoring King's look of alarm, Abigail placed a hand on the wound and pulled the bleeding edges apart.

King started breathing hard, fighting back the pain.

"Hey..." King nudged Abigail, struggling for breath. "What'd the one lesbian vampire say to the other?"

Abigail shook the sealant can. "Shut up, King."

King smiled weakly. "See you in twenty-eight days..."

His voice trailed off as he passed out cold.

THIRTEEN

Several hours later, back at the Nightstalker's head-quarters, Abigail stood naked in front of the cracked mirror in the shower room. She gazed at her reflection without expression, her thoughts distant. She looked exactly how she felt—exhausted and beaten, and covered in someone else's blood. The cut on her cheek where Drake had struck her was swelling up nicely, turning an interesting shade of blue. She had a matching bruise on her thigh where she had struck the desk on the way down.

She put a dab of antiseptic ointment on the cut, hoping that it wouldn't scar. That would be the last thing she needed at the moment.

Shivering, Abigail opened the door to the shower stall and quickly stepped inside. She turned the heater dial and stood beneath the showerhead as the water cut in, closing her eyes in anticipation. The water sluiced down her body and drenched her blood-matted hair, turning it a soft honey color and enveloping her in a heavenly cloud of steam.

Abigail turned her face up into the warm spray with a groan of relief, beads of water clinging to her long lashes. She felt the water start to wash the crusted blood from her skin, tracing long crimson lines down the length of her body. King's blood had soaked through her cotton T-shirt when she had lifted him, and was now dried in dark red-brown patches all over her stomach and hands. It was going to take a while to remove the stains.

Abigail picked up the soap and scrubbed at it methodically, washing pink soapsuds and dark red flakes of blood down the drain. She watched it swirl around and around before vanishing through the grate at her feet, and shivered despite the heat of the water. Her hands painted bloody fingerprints along the white china tiles as she fumbled with the shower dial, turning up the temperature as far as it could go.

Maybe if the water was hot enough, it would make her feel warm again.

Or indeed, feel anything at all.

But the stinging little drops bounced off the surface of her skin, the heat evaporating before the warmth could penetrate inside.

The soap smelled like lavender. Abigail's hands began to shake as she slid the bar over her aching limbs, running her soapy fingers up and down the smooth length of her calves in an attempt to bring some kind of feeling back into them. Then she put both hands on the wall in front of her and tipped her head downwards, letting the water trickle down into her eyes. If only she could wash them, too, scour out all the horrors she had seen and done until nothing remained but clean, white bone.

She would never say it out loud, but some days she envied Sommerfield, not having to look at herself in the mirror or see the evils that went on in the world, despite all the efforts and sacrifices she had made to stop them.

Abigail watched with a strange detachment as bloody soap suds ran down her legs and swirled down the drain, and wondered how much longer she could keep this up.

It had been her choice to join the Nightstalkers, so she had no right to complain. The other guys—they hadn't chosen. That was what set her apart from them.

She saw how they looked at her sometimes—with affection, but without the unspoken respect and understanding they had for one another. She had been fighting alongside them since the beginning, but it was as though an invisible barrier separated her from the others, through no fault of her own. They fought because the vampires had stolen someone dear from them: family, friends, precious loved ones. She fought the vampires because she had chosen to, because she wanted to help her father.

Although the other Nightstalkers loved her, she knew that she would never be anything more to them than the proverbial boss's daughter, both in their minds and in their hearts.

But now that her father was dead, things were suddenly and inescapably harder. Abigail had always known that his job was high-risk, and had reacted to the news of his death with a kind of numb acceptance that had earned her worried looks from the other Nightstalkers. Rather than making things even between her and the team, it seemed that Whistler's death had only served to drive them further apart

Abigail knew that it wasn't her fault. Deep down inside, a part of her had already come to terms with the idea that one day, her father's job would kill him. He took far too many risks for it not to. Although it deeply distressed her, she had allowed him to continue fighting the vampires because she knew that it wasn't just a job for him. It was what he needed to do to make peace with himself.

When the vampires had butchered Whistler's family—his darling wife and their two beautiful teenage girls—they had beaten him so badly that he had barely escaped with his life. The leg brace he had worn right up until his death had been a daily reminder of his loss. For after watching his family being torn apart in front of his eyes, one by one, he had kept on fighting till the vampires threw him from the top story window.

He had survived the fall, and went on to hunt vampires. It was a simple as that.

Abigail, on the other hand, had never suffered such a loss. She had grieved alongside her father for his first family, but she felt only anger and the righteous drive for revenge, rather than personal suffering. When she had joined the Nightstalkers, it was because she wanted to make a difference to the world, and spare others the pain her father had gone through.

She had never known that pain herself, but she liked to think she understood it. She knew it was why King sometimes went out in the middle of the night

and came home at 5am covered in blood, why Sommerfield fell asleep at her Braille keyboard every
evening, plotting brain-numbingly complex disease
vectors for the Plague virus, why Dex pushed the
needle in just that little bit deeper when taking blood
samples from captured vampires.

They weren't just doing it for humanity. They were
doing it for themselves.

And now Abigail had a real reason to fight. But to
her surprise, she didn't feel any different. It was as
though nothing had changed. She had expected to
react to the news of her father's death—when it finally
came—with a burning fury that would fire her up and
send her out onto the streets, slashing and hacking at
marauding gangs of vampires until the streets ran red
with their blood.

As it was, she just felt tired.

Whistler was dead, but the world went on. There
were still plans to make, weapons to reload, dirty coffee
cups to wash. She had gone to the little ceremony
Hedges had held for her father and tried to cry for him,
but the tears just wouldn't come. She had felt like an
intruder there, standing dry-eyed by the river with the
little pot of ashes that King had scraped from the blackened floor of the boathouse. King himself had admitted
that they were very probably the ashes of Whistler's
toaster, but she had appreciated the thought and scattered them into the river anyway. Then she had quietly
gone back home and got on with her laundry.

Since then, she had been waiting for her life to
change, but it hadn't. In a way, she was almost glad
that they had found Blade, if only to give her a sense
that things were different. She hadn't even seen her

father's body. Looking at Blade was the closest she was going to get to accepting the reality of his death.

As was Dracula.

In the shower, Abigail put down the soap. Some bloodstains still remained, but she suddenly found she didn't have the strength to remove them. Goosebumps raced across her skin despite the heat of the scalding shower and she began to tremble violently as the enormity of what had just happened began to sink in.

They had found Dracula. The key to the vampire's plans, as well as their own. With just a few drops of his blood they could've put an end to all this, saving thousands of lives the length and breadth of the planet and sparing countless others the agony of losing a loved one.

And they had let him get away.

Even catching the vampire king off-guard hadn't been enough to give them the advantage. He had beaten them as thoroughly and as surely as if he had planned their visit all along.

And even worse, he had seen their faces.

Abigail ran an unsteady hand through her soaking hair, fighting to control the shaking of her body. Then she switched off the water, taking a deep breath as steam clouded the air, beading across her bare skin. She reached for a towel and wrapped it tightly around herself, hugging the rough cotton against her skin.

She ended most nights like this, in the shower, washing off blood. But tonight, things really were different.

Now, the clock was ticking.

* * *

Next door in the infirmary, Blade gazed down at King as he drowsed on his cot, drifting in and out of consciousness. King's shirt was off and a white clinical bandage covered half of his chest, which was covered in a sheen of sweat. His skin was pale. Dex had dosed him up with a cocktail of strong painkillers and left him to sweat it out, which he seemed to be doing just fine.

A muscle twitched in Blade's jaw as he regarded King's semi-conscious form. His every instinct told him to leave, to get out now while the Nightstalkers were regrouping. He needed time alone to think things through and decide on a course of action.

Drake must be eliminated, he knew that much. If what the vampire king had said was true, the vampires could already be in the process of developing their vaccine to make them immune to sunlight. Even one Daywalking vampire out there on the loose was one too many, and if that one vampire was somehow able to spread the Daywalking gene to its victims—well, he might as well turn in his sword right now and go buy himself a condo on the moon, because that was the only place that would be safe if the vampires got their way.

Blade looked around him at the gleaming racks of polished equipment lining the infirmary. He sniffed. Okay, he'd admit it—at the end of the day, these people weren't doing too badly. Determination and guts counted for a lot in this job, and the fact the Nightstalkers had made it this far was a testament to that.

Blade sat down on the edge of the bed and gazed thoughtfully down at King, watching as fresh blood slowly seeped through his bandages. Despite all their training and equipment, the Nightstalkers weren't like him. Not by a long shot. They were just humans, which meant they were fallible, and they could be hurt.

That didn't mean that they shouldn't be fighting, but at the same time Blade felt a small stab of frustration at their weakness. Even the smallest vampire was easily as strong as the lot of them put together.

Blade removed his sunglasses and rubbed his eyes. He had always known that other vampire hunters existed. But somehow, he'd always pictured them as small groups of ragged-looking men hiding out in underground shelters. In his mind, Blade saw them clutching wooden stakes and kitchen knives, images drawn from the comic books of his youth. He knew that these images were unrealistic, even petty, but if he was honest with himself, he didn't care.

It wasn't that he had no interest in these people. It was just that he had put so much effort into keeping himself and Whistler alive, that he simply didn't have the time to be interested, let alone to actively seek them out.

Blade gazed down at King, wondering how long the Nightstalkers had known of the existence of Dracula, and why they hadn't passed that information on to Whistler. Blade felt a stab of anger at the thought. Had they deliberately chosen to withhold what they knew, or simply thought it was not worth mentioning? Had they thought that they could deal with it on their own, that his and Whistler's operation was somehow inferior to theirs?

Blade looked around him at the gleaming cleanliness of the med lab, at the organized stock charts on the wall and the color-coded nametags on the medical supply lockers, and sighed.

He and Whistler hadn't been inferior—they were the best damn fighters in the country—but they sure as hell couldn't compete with all of this. He was the Daywalker, but so what? Did he know how to electroplate a dagger, or how to decarbunkle a cofragulater or whatever the hell they called that silver thing in the corner?

No, of course he didn't. He'd thought of himself and Whistler being high-tech, but compared to these people they were amateurs, more brawn than brain. Did King spend four hours every evening melting down stolen silver jewelry in order to hand-cast silver bullets, squeezing them out of the rusty old press one slug at a time?

What King had told him earlier had given him great cause for concern. The increased vampire activity around the drug factories had previously led him to believe that the bloodsuckers were up to something, perhaps plotting some kind of a chemical attack on the human population of the city. Now, it would seem that they had gone one better, attempting to rejuvenate the vampire race by effectively starting from scratch, replacing their corrupted genetic junk with Drake's pure DNA.

Blade's heart quickened at the thought. If all vampires became Daywalkers, what was there to prevent them from taking up positions of power across the cities, blending seamlessly with the humans, able to manipulate events from above rather than below?

He couldn't let it come to that.

Blade got to his feet. On his own, he was quicker and less vulnerable to attack. But now he was getting to know these people, he found that something terrible had happened to him.

He had got himself involved.

And worse, he felt responsible for them.

Blade glanced down at the sleeping figure of King and one corner of his mouth twitched. The guy was a pain in the ass, sure, but at least he was fighting back against the creatures who took five years of his life. You had to hand it to the guy for trying.

Perhaps he should stay here, find out whether the Nightstalkers really did have this "anti-vampire" plague virus. Who knows, maybe they would even be able to pull this thing off.

There was a polite cough. Blade blinked and refocused on King, who was now awake, regarding Blade with a steady gaze.

Blade cleared his throat and started to turn away, hoping that King hadn't been able to read his expression, but King put a weak hand on the Daywalker's arm to stop him. As Blade cast through his meager supply of small talk for a comment about the weather, Abigail saved him by walking in through the door, freshly showered and dressed in a light T-shirt and combat pants.

King waved a groggy greeting to her, then cleared his throat, seeming to read Blade's mind. "Hey, Blade, say we were successful. Say we wipe the vampires out. What happens then? You ever ask yourself that?"

Blade considered this, and found he had no answer. He looked back down at King, shrugging. King coughed. "Somehow I don't picture you parked on a porch with a jigsaw puzzle."

Blade arched an eyebrow and walked out the door.

King turned to Abigail, picking at his sheet. "He hates me, doesn't he?"

Abigail just smiled as King slid back into unconsciousness.

Up in the Phoenix Towers, the moonlight washed over two pale, naked figures, moving slowly together, casting a ghostly reflection on the mirrored windows of the penthouse.

Danica held tight onto Drake's hand and gasped as he moved inside her, finding a deep, primal rhythm that matched her unnaturally powerful heartbeat. She looked up at Drake, moving above her in the moonlight, his face upturned and covered in a faint sheen of sweat. She thought she'd felt desire before, but it had been a dim echo compared to this. Her eyes glazed as she felt Drake's orgasm roar through him, followed a moment later by her own.

A minute later, Drake rolled over, studying Danica through heavy-lidded eyes. She was naked save for the slim chain she wore around her neck. A tiny steel crucifix hung upon it, resting lightly in the hollow of her throat.

Drake reached out a cool finger and nudged the crucifix. "Why do you wear that... symbol?"

Danica reached up and closed her hand around the cross defensively. "Old habits." She found to her surprise that she was shivering. She sat up, draping a sheet around her. She looked up at Drake, her brown eyes appearing black and liquid in the moonlight. "I was a good Catholic schoolgirl. Once."

Drake nodded, his thoughts seemingly distant. Recognizing the look on his face, Danica lay back on the soft pillow, waiting for him to speak. Drake did that, sometimes, retreating to a place so far inside himself that to touch him would be to break the spell. The guy was thousands of years old, and his memories seemed to take a little time to come back to the surface.

She gazed down at Drake's sculpted, muscled form while she waited, noting with interest a mass of old scar tissue on his chest. A primitive vampire glyph had been carved into his flesh, with what looked like a very blunt instrument. Danica raised an eyebrow, but said nothing.

When Drake finally did speak, his voice was measured, brimming with darkness. He pointed to the cross around Danica's throat. "I was there when they crucified him. He died for their sins, not mine."

Danica looked coyly up at him, not sure whether to believe him. She traced a cryptic pattern on the bare skin of his throat. "And what are your sins? Would you care to confess them?"

Drake made a dismissive gesture, pushing her hand away irritably. "Too many to confess." He nodded towards the crucifix, the spell broken. "Take it off."

"Why?"

Drake drew her gently in towards him. "I'll make you a better one."

Stroking Danica's sweat-drenched hair away from her throat, he leaned in close, brushing his nose against her skin to locate a vein. Then he tilted her chin away from him and slid his fangs through her bare skin. After a few moments he pulled his head back. They both watched as two dark rivulets of blood trickled from the fresh wounds.

Drake reached for the sheet, pulling it from Danica's unresisting hands. He dipped his fingertips into the trickle of blood and painted a long streak of it down between her breasts. Then he drew a second line horizontally across them. He stroked Danica's cheek softly, gazing into her eyes. "There's an old saying. Kill one man, you're a murderer. Kill a million, you're a king." Drake smiled dreamily, licking his fingertips. "Kill them all—a god."

As the moon rose, Drake slept.

Within his time-ravaged subconscious, the centuries melted away and once again he was standing at the head of the storm-blown cliff top, somewhere near the Adriatic. It was a recurring dream, one that had often enlivened his nights shortly before he had gone underground. Drake's battle with the Daywalker had unlocked a flood of long-buried memories, and now they swept through the slumbering vampire in a tide...

The vampire hunter stood on the sandy hillock opposite Drake, watching him in much the same way that Blade had done earlier, up on the rooftops. They stared one another out, Drake resplendent in his black polished battle armor, the hunter trembling as the night wind whipped at his torn clothing, exposing a number of bloody wounds in his torso.

The hunter had been tracking Drake for a number of months and had finally caught up with him in the town, far from home. He had called on his people, driving Drake out of the tavern in which he was resting, and the pair had engaged in a prolonged street battle that had ended with the two of them up here on this cliff top, standing mere yards from the great drop onto the jagged rocks below.

Drake saw how the hunter's eyes gleamed as he drew his sword, anticipating victory, even though it was plain to even a casual observer that he was hopelessly outmatched. Blood dripped from the hunter's many wounds, splashing onto the muddy grass at his feet, while Drake didn't have a scratch on him.

It was an ancient game. Cat and Mouse. Hide and Seek.

A game with a billion different variables, yet it always ended the same way.

The man raised his sword, his eyes alight with determination and something like religious zeal as he faced this monster in human form, the creature whose death had obsessed him for so long.

Drake watched the man with curiosity, marveling at his tenacity. He had done comparatively little to this one, yet the hunter had pursued Drake across half a continent with a single-minded ferocity that not even the armies of old had matched. Drake could see that the man's strength was now on the wane, dripping out of him in liquid rivers, but still he refused to admit defeat, even to himself.

Drake spent a few moments pondering the eternal mystery of the human spirit.

Then he shrugged, pulled out his own sword, and charged.

Despite his wounds, the hunter was strong, driven by the internal fire of vengeance. He held Drake off for an impressively long time. Their shouts and the clash of their weapons echoed off the wild landscape around them, drowning out the crash and swirl of the sea below.

But the hunter was only human and Drake took great pleasure in wearing him down until the man was exhausted. Drake could see it in his eyes as their swords met with each quivering blow, the almost imperceptible change as the man's thoughts turned from attack to defense, from hunter to hunted, from killer to prey.

Then, the hunter made one tiny mistake.

He paused for breath.

Just the once.

Drake seized on that split second's respite to duck in under the hunter's reach, inside his guard. He grasped the point of the hunter's sword in his powerful metal-gloved grip and brought his other hand up, lightning fast, to slap the hunter's wrists from below, knocking his sword into the air.

The sword spun around in a complete circle and Drake snatched up the pommel as it whirred towards him. Gripping the sword at either end, he lunged towards the hunter, burying the blade up to the hilt in its owner's chest.

Drake saw the look of shock on the hunter's face as he felt the air hiss out of his body, followed by the faint patter of his own lifeblood spilling onto the rocks in the moment of silence that followed. He gazed at the man's face in eager anticipation. For of all the things he had seen and done over the course of his unnaturally long life, death was the one experience Drake could never participate in. Deep down inside him, a small voice whispered that with each mangled corpse he left cooling at his feet, he took a tiny step closer to knowing what death was.

And just maybe, one day, he could experience it for himself.

Drake stepped forwards and drove the sword in deeper, keen to watch the man's death. He felt the flame-hardened iron slide through muscle and sinew, cleaving bone apart as through slicing through rotten wood. He gazed hungrily into the man's eyes and watched the life fade from them, the brilliant spark of righteousness draining away to be replaced by a distant, unfocussed gaze. The man's pupils dilated in death, locking wide open as if to burn the image of his killer onto his retina.

Everyone has to die sometime, Drake thought. So why act so surprised when it finally happens to you?

Back in the moonlit room, Danica was still awake. She rolled over in bed, watching Drake while he slept, and envied him his ability to do so. As a race, vampires were genetically bound to sleep in the daytime, although it was more a kind of semi-hibernation than true sleep. Danica hadn't slept at night for as long as she could remember.

As she watched, one of Drake's hands twitched slightly, as though he was dreaming. She studied his face, wondering what he was seeing beneath his closed eyelids. Although Drake was thousands of years old, he looked almost like a child in sleep, his smooth face untroubled by the faint lines that eventually formed on the faces of even the youngest of vampires.

Danica reached out and stroked a hand softly over the pale scarring on Drake's chest. She couldn't believe that he was finally here. His flesh was warm beneath her touch and seemed to hum with a faint electricity, as though his skin itself was alive. She could smell the blood pulsing in his veins, cut through with the unique smell of his skin, musky and cool like the sickly-sweet scent of dead roses.

What was it like to live for seven thousand years? Danica tried to imagine it. She herself had been alive for a mere hundred-odd years, but that in itself was already starting to take its toll on her mind. Every thought, every memory, every stupid mistake was locked up inside her head, the pressure increasing as the years sped by, until sometimes she thought she could barely stand to live through another day.

The human mind was never designed to tolerate eternity and Danica was already starting to pay the price. She wished sometimes that she could press a button and erase it all, to start again with a clean slate, but knew that it was never to be.

Danica looked down at Drake's slumbering form, fancying that she could see every century that he had lived through, pressing down on him like a great weight. Danica couldn't begin to imagine the things Drake had seen in his life, she wondered how he'd got through it with his sanity intact.

Then she remembered the history books of her childhood and realized that he hadn't.

In a way, she had done Drake a favor by bringing him back, even though he had been displeased with her for doing so. This would be the closest he could ever get to a fresh start, a new beginning for his race and a shining new life here in the twenty-first century. With her by his side, there would be nothing that they couldn't achieve together.

Drake rolled over in his sleep and Danica recoiled from him, jumping backwards with a start. She stared down at him. An unbidden chill ran through her, despite the heat of the night, and a picture slammed into her head of Drake as she had first seen him.

She suddenly remembered how she had felt at the sight of him. Terror hadn't been the word for it. Even now, the memory was like icy needles in her brain. Drake looked like a man now, but back there, in the darkness of the tomb, he had been something else.

A shudder slid down Danica's spine at the thought. She remembered how she had berated herself throughout their long journey home from Iraq, trying to come to terms with what she had done. She had betrayed the Elders and broken every rule in the vampire book, and for what? To dig up the creature from the black lagoon?

The vampire king was not at all what she had expected. The vampire bible had told of his nobility and wisdom, the creature in the hold was still growling and snapping and trying to chew through the solid metal of its crate even after being shot with a dozen rounds of elephant tranquilizer. Danica had been appalled. She had gone in search of a shining prince, and returned with a monster.

But now, things were beginning to look up. The monster wasn't really that bad, once you got to know him, and now Danica was now getting to know him very well indeed.

She wiped absent-mindedly at the twin puncture wounds in her throat, noting with alarm that they still hadn't healed. She would have to get those looked at in the morning, preferably by a medic who was expendable. It wouldn't do to let any rumors get out, especially not with Asher hanging around, watching her like a disapproving hawk.

Wrapping the silk sheet around herself, Danica slipped off the edge of the bed and stood up, ignoring her light-headedness and the shaking in her legs. Soon it would be sunrise and this great room would be filled with light. The moon was bright in the sky outside and she could feel it tingling faintly where it touched her skin, giving her the vampire equivalent of sunburn.

Leaving Drake snoozing in the big bed, Danica padded to the door as quickly as she could and vanished into the darkness of the hallway, leaving bloody footprints on the floor behind her.

FOURTEEN

Blade sat on the edge of his bed, back straight, hands on his knees, waiting for the sun to rise. Despite the lateness of the hour he was still fully clothed, clad in his black pants and body armor. His sword lay across his lap, glinting faintly in the blue moonlight.

The others were in bed next door, sleeping off their aches and pains. Blade's body was tired, but he would not allow himself to succumb to sleep. He needed to stay alert.

Blade stared at the patch of moonlight on the wall in front of him, letting it soak through his retinas and fill his senses with crisp light. In the background, his subconscious hummed with white noise, processing and sorting the information he had learned during the day and cross-referencing it with what he already knew of the vampire's plans. There were so many holes in the picture and Blade hoped that the missing piece would come to light with enough analysis.

He blanked his mind of all conscious thought, giving his subconscious free reign to sort out the tangle of new facts. It was a form of meditation that Whistler had taught him when he was younger and used to lie awake, unable to sleep, paralyzed by nightmares of blood and death. Usually it worked well, and in the morning, he would arise as refreshed as if he'd had a full night's sleep.

Unfortunately, all that he had succeeded in doing this time was giving himself a headache.

There was too much he didn't know. He needed to find out more.

Blade blinked, and the static of his subconscious died away to be replaced by the warm glow of his conscious mind. He blinked again and looked around him, licking his dry lips. There was the faint sound of activity coming from next door, the clink of coffee cups and the splash of running water, followed by the muted sound of voices raised in greeting. It looked like Blade wasn't the only one who couldn't sleep.

Blade put his sword down on the bed, then got to his feet and stretched mightily.

It was time to go and find that missing piece.

As the clock ticked towards three in the morning, Abigail poured Blade another cup of hot black coffee as he sat on the workbench, listening intently to Sommerfield run through the technical details of their new plan. In the hour since he had joined them, the Daywalker had questioned her intently, finding out things that not even Abigail herself had known. Blade's thoroughness was impressive, and also a little scary.

Abigail watched Blade out of the corner of her eye. Her father had told her so many things about Blade over the years. She almost felt like she knew him from the tales she had heard of his bravery and strength.

But being here with him in the flesh was something else altogether. It was one thing being told that Blade was a vampire hybrid. It was another thing sitting right next to him, feeling the warmth of his skin from less than a foot away. Blade seemed to radiate heat, and with it came an aura of tension and suppressed energy that spilled off him by the bucket load.

He was physically strong, yes, but there was more to it than that. Even when he was sitting still, he was never relaxed. Blade was like a giant coiled spring, just waiting for an opportunity to unwind with devastating force and fury. Abigail knew that the Daywalker would never intentionally hurt her, or indeed any of them, but at the same time, she couldn't help but feel threatened by him. Her guard had been up ever since they had met, and now she finally realized why.

Blade wasn't human. Abigail was shocked by the realization. He looked like one, but he was as far removed from the human race as a shark was from a tadpole. Abigail could feel it in her bones, an instinctive nagging feeling that warned her to stay as far away from him as possible. She could imagine lion tamers feeling this way as they entered the cage, knowing that although the creatures in front of them appeared docile, at any minute and for any reason, they might choose not to be.

Abigail glanced at Blade as he chatted with Sommerfield. Blade didn't look like a vampire, despite his impressive physical stature. Nor did he smell like a vampire, that faintly musky scent of death and decay that stuck to the back of your throat like smoke from a funeral pyre. Abigail inhaled surreptitiously. Nope, nothing even remotely unpleasant there. Blade smelled like leather and unscented soap, clean scents tinged with the faint tang of charcoal and gunpowder, where his clothes had absorbed the smells of his trade.

She looked at Blade again, more carefully this time. Despite everything, it was only his rare smile that gave him away, the slightly pronounced canines that were made to seem longer and sharper by the expression that came into his eyes whenever he grinned.

But there was more to it than looks, as anyone who dealt with vampires on a regular basis soon came to realize. It was all in the details.

Abigail watched as Blade stirred his coffee with the end of a teaspoon. Blade always asked for coffee, but she never actually saw him drink it. Abigail wondered whether she should be offering him pig's blood or something equally gross. Whistler had never been too specific about the vagaries of Blade's diet, and she could never quite bring herself to ask.

Beyond the practicalities, Abigail realized that, more than anything else, it was Blade's attitude that really got to her. The Daywalker didn't seem to want to engage with any of them. He kept his sunshades on even when he was indoors, and on the rare occasions when he removed them, it was as though he still wore them. His gaze was guarded, as though calculating the exact amount of risk he was taking by interacting with them and letting them live.

Abigail got the impression that Blade didn't really like interacting with anyone...

Abigail jumped as Hedges put a warm hand on her shoulder. He smiled down at her, a questioning look on his face. Abigail realized that she had been stripping splinters off the workbench with her penknife as she pondered, and now a large pile of them lay in front of her. She smiled apologetically at Hedges and swept them off the bench into an empty polystyrene cup. She tried to focus on what he was saying.

The engineer was in the process of wrapping up his long monologue. He turned back to Blade. "So basically, we're in an arms race. They're using Drake's DNA to build themselves a better vampire."

"And we need his blood to kill them." Blade thought for a moment, then touched Sommerfield's arm. "How's this weapon of yours coming along?"

"We're almost there." Sommerfield gestured to a series of ampule-shaped prototypes lying in neat stack on the nearest workbench. "The virus is harmless to humans. So we decided to go after the vampire's food source." She ran a fond hand over the smooth glass of one of the prototypes. "The one thing we know for sure about vampires is that they have to drink blood. If we manage to pull this off, we'll be able to contaminate every blood source on the planet. They won't have anyone left to feed on."

Abigail stood up, pacing restlessly. She had heard all this before. "That doesn't do us any good if we don't have time to finish it." She didn't turn around, but Blade knew she was talking directly to him. "We can't just sit here. We need to take the battle to them."

Sommerfield nodded unhappily. She rubbed her chin, thinking. "If the vampires are trying to isolate the hereditary factor in Drake that makes him immune to sunlight, they'll require certain kinds of laboratory equipment and provisions. For instance, there's an enzyme called Taq polymerase they'll need, and there's only a limited number of suppliers." She paused, realizing that she had been thinking out loud. "Give me a few hours. I'll see if I can't hunt us up some leads."

As the others joked and clattered around next door, Blade stole into the deserted armory and sat down on a bench in the darkness. Pulling his serum inhaler out of his jacket pocket, he bit down on the mouthpiece and pulled the steel trigger. There was a brief hiss as the serum blasted into his lungs.

Blade tensed slightly, feeling the liquid seeping through his cell walls into his bloodstream, hot and cold at the same time. He gave a sigh of relief as he felt it burn away the hunger that had been growing inside him all night. This stuff really worked.

He dropped the inhaler onto the table beside him and tried to relax.

The serum was Whistler's most precious legacy to him. As far as Blade could understand, it contained a human hemoglobin substitute, combined with a strong antiviral formula that temporarily disabled the vampire virus inside him, preventing it from replicating. For it was only when the virus tried to breed inside the human host that it needed to be fed, driving the host to kill again and again until the virus had enough fresh food available in which to propagate.

Blade was lucky. After performing many tests on him, Whistler had discovered that his body contained a stable version of the vampire virus, one that worked with his body rather than against it. Blade remembered asking Whistler why this was, only for the old man to launch into a long-winded scientific explanation that left Blade with his mouth hanging open and a very large mental Post-It note slapped over the subject, reading "Do Not Ask About This Again."

As far as Blade could understand, vampirism couldn't be caught by simply being bitten, Whistler had been very clear about that. His tests had shown that the virus was so alien to a healthy human body that in most cases, it would be caught by the immune system and destroyed.

Whistler had hypothesized that the only way a human could be turned into a vampire was by forcibly infusing some infected blood into the victim's body, allowing the vampire's infected red blood cells to agglutinate—or stick to—the cells of its new host. It was this process that allowed the virus to bypass the body's defenses, injecting itself straight from the vampire's "donated" cells into those of the victim, before their immune system had the chance to do anything about it.

Blade shifted on the edge of the workshop bench, seeing again in his mind's eye the writhing red cells replicating under the microscope at an incredible rate, mutating and dividing. Whistler had shown him this process many times during the course of his treatment, and seeing it happen right under his nose had never failed to give Blade the creeps. Seeing the virus up close, he had always felt a terrible urge to sweep the microscope right off the edge of the table and to stamp on it until all the freaky little bugs were dead.

The vampire virus was very clever, Whistler had explained. Once contracted, the fully blown version would carry on replicating and corrupting its host's DNA until his or her genes were almost unrecognizable. The host's body would then "die," usually from system-wide shock or blood loss, and the brain would go into a state of induced hibernation while the virus built itself up sufficient numbers to kick-start the body once more. The brain would then come out of hibernation and the newly hijacked body would begin "life" anew, as a dedicated virus-spreading machine.

This process usually took as little as two hours to complete.

Blade's brow furrowed in the half-light, staring down at his own arms and legs. The demon was in every cell, wasn't it? It had to be, to keep the body of the vampire moving. It commandeered muscle, blood and bone, and sat there gloating like a spoilt child while the soul rotted away beneath, helpless to fight back. Serum or garlic burned it out for a while, but it always came back, like a black tide of cockroaches into a dead man's house.

Blade had been lucky in that respect. Despite the virus living and breathing inside him, he had retained his humanity, his free will. Most others never had that chance. Blade knew that most newly turned vampires were little more than pack animals, devoid of anything but the drive to feed.

They would gather in small underground gangs, devoting the first few years of their new "lives" to eating, fighting, and having sex with anything that moved, or in most cases didn't move. They were sloppy and undisciplined and their foolhardy bravado made them relatively easy to kill. Blade had killed thousands of them over the years.

It was the ancients, the so-called Purebloods, who were the hardest to kill. Blade felt a chill go through him at the very thought of them. Rumored to be descended directly from Dracula himself, these ancient creatures were born vampires, and in turn were able to bear their own children. Modern or "turned" vampires were usually sterile, relying purely on the strength of the derivative vampire virus to replicate themselves.

Blade knew that the Purebloods' had one main advantage: they could tolerate sunlight. They could go out in the daytime so long as they applied heavy sun block containing octyl salicylate and powdered white lead, a trick stolen from the sun-hating Elizabethan aristocracy. There were even reports of a growing trend amongst the Moderns to use this long-lost capability to their own advantage. According to insider information, the vampires would fast for a week, then go out and capture an Ancient in order to kill them and consume their blood. Drinking "pure" vampire blood would give Modern vampires the ability to walk outside in the daylight for a day, provided they took the same precautions as the Ancients.

Blade clenched his jaw, anger rising inside him. Deacon Frost, the vampire who had attacked and killed his mother, was rumored to have regularly used this trick to get about during the day. In fact, the first time he and Blade had met, Frost had been wearing the white sun block mixture, confirming his suspicions.

Whistler had a theory about Frost, directly relating to Blade's hybridism. He believed that the sheer quantity of Ancient vampire blood Frost had consumed over the years had lead to a mutation of the modern-day vampire virus within him, making it regress to an earlier stage in its evolution. It was through this process, Whistler had assured Blade, that the virus had been able to infect his mother, and therefore himself, in the first place. A minute quantity of Frost's blood or cellular matter had entered his mother's bloodstream, presumably through her neck wound, which had then passed straight through her into him.

Whistler hypothesized that it was this one-in-a-million coupling that caused the vampire gene to be absorbed into Blade's genetic makeup, peacefully integrating with it rather than overriding it completely. This precarious coexistence had made Blade what he was, a hybrid rather than a fully fledged vampire or human, neither one thing nor the other.

Over the years, Blade had made sure that any vampires who found out the circumstances of his "miracle" birth were found and killed. There was a good reason for this. Most vampires knew of him, if only as a myth, but there were many who sought to discover the concrete facts of his birth and replicate them, usually with fatal results. From what Blade had managed to beat out of the vampire perpetrators before killing them, there were two usual outcomes of these experiments. Either the experiment wouldn't work at all, and the newly turned mother would try to eat her human baby as soon as it was born, or the gene would switch on immediately in the unborn child, causing it to become rabidly vampiric and start consuming its mother from within, with spectacularly messy results.

Blade gazed out through the barred window of the workshop, listening to the sounds of the sea lapping at the quayside. He really had been fortunate. Frost's blood should have either killed him or turned him into a fully-fledged vampire. But, perhaps due to Frost's predilection for drinking the blood of the Ancients, it hadn't.

But the virus inside Blade still cried out to be fed on a regular basis, dousing his body with adrenaline and sending powerful chemical messages to his brain and stomach. Blade would be crippled by the almost rabid urge to feed, unable to fight the overwhelming cravings.

That was, until Whistler had invented his vaccine.

In the beginning, taking the prototype vaccine had been a terrifying ordeal for Blade. The virus inside his body would rally his hyper-accelerated immune system against the synthetic antibodies of the vaccine, tying his body into convulsing knots of pain as the two compounds fought a silent war inside him. Over the years, his system had learned to adapt, but the side effects were still just as strong. Even recently, Whistler had to literally chain him to a chair to prevent him from damaging himself as a serum-induced fit kicked in.

Now, it would seem, the Nightstalkers had had finally succeeded in engineering an upgraded version of the serum. Sommerfield had explained how she had taken Whistler's basic formula and stripped it of several key proteins that had been binding to Blade's nerves as well as to the virus. Now, the formula went down as smoothly as an iced glass of cream liqueur.

"Why do you do that?"

Blade snapped back to full alertness and peered into the shadows to see little Zoe crouching on top of an old shipping crate, watching him.

Always watching, that girl. Nothing got past her.

Considering the fact that her mother was blind, that could only be a good thing. Blade grunted non-committally, trying to keep his voice steady as the vaccine burned through his veins. "There's something bad inside of me. This keeps it from getting out."

Zoe looked at the gleaming inhaler on the table beside Blade, her eyes huge. "Couldn't you just be nice?"

Blade followed her gaze, and rubbed unconsciously at his neck. "Good question."

Zoe continued staring at him.

Feeling uncomfortable, Blade abruptly stood up and walked out of the room, joining the rest of the Nightstalkers as they gathered in the lab next door.

Sommerfield stood in front of her bank of computers, reading a tactile Braille display. The atmosphere was tense with expectation. King was absent from the group, although Abigail was looking much better. The cut on her face was healing well.

The results of Sommerfield's research came up on the display with a beep and she tapped it triumphantly. "I think I've got a lead. Biomedica Enterprises. They've been buying up all sorts of supplies: Taq polymerase, bone marrow growth supplement, genetic sequencing enzymes..."

Blade hefted his shotgun, which had now been modified to take UV rounds. "Let's check it out."

FIFTEEN

The skinny female vampire known as Virago sat at a computer workstation deep in the heart of the Bio-medica compound, conferring with Police Chief Vreede. The building was quiet. The only sounds audible were the soft hum of the fan inside her computer and the scratching of Vreede's pen as he took notes from the screen.

Virago popped a red pill into her mouth and chewed distractedly. The pill was a compound of pure Ecstasy mixed with dehydrated red blood cells. It delivered an instant high, one that Virago found she increasingly needed to get through the mind-numbing tedium of the night watch. It was a dull job and besides, it wasn't as though what they were watching could just get up and walk out.

Sniffing, she typed up a few more statistics, then turned and watched Vreede plot them onto the chart laid out in front of him. Under the acid-yellow strip lights, the chief's face looked drawn, strung out, a patchwork mosaic of highlight and shadow. Above them, the hand of the industrial punching-off clock ticked towards four in the morning.

A loud rap at the reinforced metal door echoed around the room, making them both start. Vreede looked at Virago, who scratched his head and shrugged.

They weren't expecting anyone at this hour. Who could it be?

Virago got up from her lab stool and moved soundlessly towards the door, checking the small security monitor set into the wall panel beside it.

The corridor outside was empty.

Strange.

She shrugged and turned back to Vreede.

She went flying across the room as the door was smashed inwards, exploding out of its frame as though yanked out by a giant invisible hand. The heavy wooden door plummeted downwards, crashing down on top of Virago. As the dust settled, dark fingers of blood reached out from underneath the fallen door, trickling across the ribbed metal floor towards Chief Vreede's boots.

Vreede jumped backwards in horror as Blade stepped through the smoking hole, drawing his gun. Taking in the layout of the place at a glance, Blade reached down and pulled the battered form of Virago out from underneath the fallen door. The vampire was badly bruised, but still alive.

Chief Vreede swore and began backing away, reaching into his jacket for his gun. As he did so, there was the unmistakable click of a safety catch being removed. Vreede swallowed as he came face to face with the barrel of Abigail's gun. He froze, and slowly removed his hands from inside his jacket.

Blade's face was like stone under the glare of the strip light. "Doing some moonlighting, chief?"

Blade nodded to Abigail, who reached into Vreede's jacket to disarm him. Then he tightened his grip on the groaning Virago, and whispered, "C'mere. We need to talk."

Virago leaned in expectantly towards Blade. The Daywalker beckoned her in closer, raising his eyebrows encouragingly, then punched her full in the face. Virago sagged, momentarily stunned.

"Now spill it, bite-girl." Blade growled.

Virago staggered to her feet, shaking off Blade's grip. She wiped reproachfully at her bloody nose. "You know what we're doing. Drake has come back to us." She glared at Blade. "Soon, we'll all be Daywalkers. And when that day comes, the world will truly be ours."

The vampire's voice had more than a trace of dementia in it, possibly due in part to all the drugs she'd taken that night. All that was missing from her little proclamation was a bout of hysterical, evil-genius laughter.

Blade and Abigail exchanged a look. The girl was quite clearly a loon.

Blade nodded towards the back of the lab, where another door—a very secure-looking door—was located. "What's back there?" he asked lightly.

They both saw Virago and Vreede share a panicked glance.

Bingo.

After a moment of stillness Virago flew towards Blade with a snarl, attacking him in a savage whirl-wind of fangs and fists...

There was a loud bang and Virago vanished, to be replaced by a mushrooming cloud of white ash. The flaming embers of the vampire fluttered down and settled on the floor in carbonized drifts.

Blade opened his eyes, checking that all of his limbs were still attached. He brushed a big heap of Virago-ash from his coat collar and shot Abigail a reproachful look as she reholstered her UV pistol. "Thanks," he said dryly.

Abigail shrugged. She'd helped, hadn't she?

Aside from the copious cinders, all that remained of Virago were her glasses and the singed remains of her keycard. Blade reached down and gingerly plucked the plastic card from the smoldering heap. He glanced over his shoulder at Vreede, who was cowering in a corner, staring in shock at the big pile of ash on the floor that just a moment ago had been Virago. Judging from the expression on the chief's face, Blade guessed that he had never seen a vampire die before. He hoped that he would remember this when considering his future career options.

Blade snapped his fingers to get Vreede's attention, and then pointed to the big door behind him. "So, what's behind door number one?" he thought, flexing the keycard between his thumb and forefinger.

Vreede shook his head frantically, waving his hands. "They'll kill me."

Blade gave one of his rare grins. "So will I. But I'll enjoy it more."

Vreede thought this over, then climbed miserably to his feet and flipped open a card-swiping device by the door. Blade slid the security card through the electronic swiper unit. The door LED changed from red to green with a chirpy *bink* noise.

The reinforced door slid open, revealing a cavernous room.

Abigail gasped, and even Blade's mouth fell open. "God in heaven..."

The room revealed was vast, football pitch wide, and was lined with hundreds and hundreds of gleaming glass capsules. The pods were filled with bright red plasma, with thick industrial pipes at top and bottom that chugged mechanically as they circulated the fluids in the tank. The pods were all linked by thick cables to a central control unit, almost like the inside of an electricity station.

Inside each capsule was a human body.

As though in a dream, Abigail stepped forwards and walked towards them, unable to believe what she was seeing. The bodies were naked and suspended on wires like nightmarish marionettes, hooked up to an elaborate system of biosensor feeds. Each one was plumbed into an IV drip that slowly drained into their bloodstreams, feeding them vital nutrients.

Blade was drawn forwards almost against his will, his footsteps ghosting on the wet floor, sickened and shocked in equal measures. There were so many of them. He couldn't tear his eyes from the bodies. He'd seen something like this before, but not on this scale.

"What is this place?" Blade's voice was little more than a whisper.

Vreede shifted from foot to foot, looking acutely uncomfortable. "It's a blood-farming facility." He gazed up at the banks of jacked-in humans, bobbing weightlessly like long-dead specimens in laboratory jars. "They decided that hunting humans on a piece-meal basis was too inefficient. Why kill your prey when you can keep them alive, productive.' He gave a nervous titter, glancing fitfully towards the door. "Under optimal conditions a donor can generate any-where from fifty to a hundred pints of blood a year."

Abigail felt like she was going to throw up. Shaking herself, she forced herself to ask the question that was burning in her mind. "But where did you get all these people?"

Vreede shuffled, dropping his eyes to the ground. "They pull them in off the streets. They've got pro-cessing centers in every major city. In any given year you've got two to three million homeless people wan-dering around America." He shrugged. "No-one cares about them. We're doing the country a service, really." His voice tailed off as he saw Abigail's expres-sion.

Blade shook his head slowly, disgusted at the hor-rible efficiency. "The vampire Final Solution."

He moved towards one of the pods, gingerly stroking his hand across the glass as he studied the comatose person inside. The pod's occupant was a woman, well into her early fifties. Her long gray hair was wrapped around her face, half obscuring her weathered features. Her eyes were closed, her body motionless.

Waves of anger swept through Blade, but he con-trolled them, burying them deeply inside where they compressed, diamond hard, into the stockpile of hate he had been building since birth.

There would be time enough for vengeance later.

"Are they aware? Do they feel anything?" Blade's voice was light, but it had a core of steel within it that told Vreede to choose his words very, very carefully.

Vreede shook his head, his heart pounding. "They're in a chemical-induced coma. They're brain-dead. Vegetables."

Blade stared at him, fighting for control as the memories rose through his mind in a choking tide. Three years ago, Whistler had been kidnapped by Deacon Frost and his henchmen. Blade had eventually found him after an epic search, imprisoned in a giant capsule device, presumably a prototype of the ones he now saw before him. The old man had been living in a fully conscious, nightmarish suspended animation while the wounds they had inflicted on him healed.

It had taken Blade over a year to find him.

Blade hadn't even known that his mentor was still alive. For the last time Blade had seen him before the kidnap, Whistler had been dying. Blade had left the old man alone in his workshop for just half an hour, and they had found him.

Questioned him.

Ripped him to pieces.

A lifetime of friendship destroyed in less than thirty tiny minutes and they hadn't even had the decency to let him die with dignity. Blade had returned home to find his mentor dying, clinging to life by a thread. He had seen the bone-deep bite-marks covering Whistler's body, and had known what he had to do.

Blade had handed the old man one of his own Mach pistols, and had walked away with the sound of a single gunshot ringing in his ears.

But when he had returned later that night, Whistler's body had gone.

Luckily for Whistler—if such a thing could be said—his subsequent year in the tank had prevented the vampire virus from taking hold properly. Blade had managed to work an effective cure on him by pumping the old man full of a home-made cocktail of his own serum and allicin, in the last-ditch hope that the two combined would burn the vampire garbage out of his system rather than kill him outright.

Either fate was better than the alternative.

Now, looking around him now at the hundreds of preserved bodies, Blade felt a cold steel fist close around his heart. It looked like the vampires had finally perfected their sick little process, by letting the captive human's brains die while keeping their bodies alive.

For all these people, there was no coming back.

Without warning, Blade grabbed Vreede and shoved him face-first against one of the pods. "Look at this! Is this the future you want? You think there's a place for you in their world?"

Vreede started crying, blubbering like a baby. "We don't have a choice! They're going to win, don't you see that? He's come back! There's nothing stopping them now."

Blade pulled Vreede back so that they were nose-to-nose. Vreede stared into Blade's burning eyes, and became very still.

Blade let a beat tick by, then said simply, "There's me."

He released Vreede, who fell forwards, gibbering with fear. Blade jerked his head towards the open door. "Go. You've got thirty seconds."

Sobbing with relief, Vreede turned tail and stumbled towards the main door.

Blade watched him run then turned and gazed out at the human farm in front of him. So many people...

After a moment he unholstered his Mach pistol. Without even looking round, Blade tracked the sound of Vreede's footsteps and squeezed off a single shot. There was a sound like a sack of wet sand hitting the floor as the police chief dropped, center-punched by the .22 slug.

His eyes still fixed on the rows of bodies, Blade reholstered his pistol.

He strode over to the central control panel, which beeped and whirred as it regulated the heartbeats and body temperatures of nearly a thousand lost souls. Locating the master control switch, Blade gripped it and slowly, almost tenderly, flipped it over into the "off" position. Immediately, a warning message appeared on the console:

WARNING:
All life support systems have been terminated

Emergency beacons flared into life overhead as the interlinked bio-support systems ground to a standstill. Food pipes shut off with a gurgle and a thousand oxygen pumps slowed and stopped. One by one, the vital signs and EKGs on each pod flatlined. Their warning tones rose together into a collective, piercing wail, oscillating like the screams of the dead.

Blade turned to Abigail, his shoulders sagging. There was no more he could do here. "Let's go."

Back home, Sommerfield worked quietly through the remainder of the night as she waited for Abigail and Blade to return. Zoe sat nearby in front of the lab's security monitors, watching Dex and Hedges play basketball next door in the storage area, burning off their nightly caffeine quota.

The lights in the lab were off; Sommerfield didn't need them on in order to work. She was rather proud of this tiny detail, looking on it as her bit to help the environment. She frequently surprised people who came blundering into the darkened room and bumped into her sitting there, working away at her bench.

Sommerfield activated her computer's text-to-speech engine in the dim light and sat back to listen as the computer read out various statistics to her about the newly modified DayStar plague virus. "Cytogenetics audit data from August fifteenth. Amniotic fluids, input delay; zero. Abnormal samples; two. Banding quality; seven point two."

The computer's light, synthesized voice carried on, but Sommerfield's attention drifted as she worried about where Blade and Abigail had got to. They had been gone for ages. She hoped they hadn't got herself into any trouble.

After a minute of dithering, she pulled out a colorful paperback from amongst her scattered Braille printouts. Zoe looked up with glee as she saw her mother pick up the book and clapped her hands together in delight. Her patience had been rewarded: it was storytime.

Sommerfield took off her dark glasses, the dim glow from the computer screen flickering over her pale, cataract-clouded eyes. She flipped the book open at a marker, skimming her fingers quickly over the large Braille text.

The book was *The Emerald City of Oz*, one of Zoe's favorites.

Sommerfield began to read. "The reason most people are bad is because they do not try to be good. Now, the Gnome King had never tried to be good, so he was very bad indeed."

Sommerfield flipped the page and went on as little Zoe gazed up at her adoringly. She had heard this story a thousand times, but she still loved to hear it read out loud.

Her mother continued the tale. "Having decided to conquer the Land of Oz and to destroy the Emerald City and enslave all its people, King Roquat the Red kept planning ways to do this dreadful thing, and the more he planned the more he believed he would be able to accomplish it..."

Behind them both, a bank of black and white surveillance monitors showed a view of every room in the place. They were all empty; some of them black where the lights had been shut off.

All except for one.

The corner monitor showed a view of the main storage area. The main door was open, the fluorescent strip-lighting spilling out into the large covered work area, providing an improvised spotlight for Dex and Hedges' basketball game. This was nothing unusual. The pair had a match every Thursday night to work off the tensions of the week. You could almost set your watch by them.

But as Sommerfield read on, a shadow moved behind the two men. Moments later, a dark figure peered out from behind the parked Land Cruiser. As soon as the two Nightstalker's backs were turned, the figure stepped out from behind the vehicle and looked around to get its bearings. Then it started moving quietly towards the door, walking with a slight limp.

In the background, Dex and Hedges carried on with their basketball game. They were so engrossed that they didn't notice the figure slip around the side of the building and walk quickly towards the main entrance to their living quarters. As the figure stepped in front of the security camera, light spilled briefly across him, revealing a wizened, bearded man in torn clothes.

The automatic surveillance system immediately sprang to life, throwing flickering green beams over the man as it scanned his face. Then it deactivated with a beep of recognition, unlocking the main gate for him.

Pushing through the unguarded steel doors, Abraham Whistler entered the Nightstalker's head-quarters and headed for the stairs.

King was snoozing on his cot, sleeping off the last of the tranquilizer pills when the infirmary door slid open, rebounding gently off the metal doorstoppers.

King's eyes flickered open at the sound. He looked up to see a dark figure standing silhouetted in the doorway, unmoving as it gazed into the room.

King squinted blearily into the light, yawning. About time, too. He ran his tongue around his parched mouth, wondering how long he had been asleep. He was so hungry that he felt like his stomach could get up and crawl to the supermarket by itself. He waved the figure over eagerly. "You get me those Fruit Roll-Ups like I asked..?"

The figure stepped forward into the light.

It was a very familiar figure.

King's mouth fell open. He shaded his eyes against the light, unbelieving. "Dude. Aren't you dead?"

The gray-bearded man didn't reply.

King shuffled forward on the bed and tried to sit up to get a better look at the old guy standing before him. What was that stuff Dex had shot him up with? He had to get himself some more of that. This couldn't be real. He'd seen the boathouse, or rather what remained of it. All that was left of Blade and Whistler's hideout was a collapsed shell of blackened timbered and the twisted beams. The place had been so completely destroyed that they hadn't even found Whistler's body.

There was no way anything living could have survived that explosion.

King stared up at Whistler in puzzlement, and opened his mouth to speak. Instantly, the old man crossed the space between them in two great strides and clamped his weathered hand over King's mouth, shoving him back down onto the bed. King struggled, but the old man was impossibly strong. King fought and twisted beneath his iron grip, his eyes wide with confusion, tearing at the suffocating hand across his mouth as it clamped down still tighter...

Outside the storage area, Dex was winning the basketball game by a long shot. Although the shorter of the two men, his daily vampire fighting and weight training gave him something of an unfair advantage. Dex ducked and dodged, easily outstripping the panting Hedges as they raced across the rough chalk marks drawn on the dusty floor of the storage bay.

Dex scored another slam-dunk and bounced the ball with a whoop of victory, laughing at the expression on his teammate's face. In his opinion, Hedges spent way too much time indoors, tinkering around in that pokey little lab of his. Hell, the dude was so out of condition that if a vamp ever attacked him, he wouldn't have a clue what to do with himself.

Dex smiled, remembering. The one and only time they'd taken Hedges out on an operation, they'd given him the simple job of holding down a young child vampire while King hacked its head off. Hedges had screamed like a girl when it had exploded, and then thrown up heartily when the blast threw the creature's disintegrating intestines around his neck, like a scarf of sausages. Dex had laughed so much he had almost been sick himself. That one had kept him smiling for weeks.

Dex, on the other hand, made sure he kept himself in shape. He volunteered for anything and everything Abigail could throw at him, from stacking crates in the warehouse to assisting in her vampire interrogations, playing "bad cop" every time. He was the muscle behind the operation and he made sure that everyone knew it.

Years ago, he had been a bare-knuckle boxer, fighting for the big jackpot every Wednesday night in front of a baying crowd of hundreds. He had been undefeated until one fateful night in the late autumn when a disgruntled vampire punter had killed his fiancé as revenge for beating the local middleweight champ. Now Dex fought a different kind of battle, clawing his shattered life back an inch at a time with every bloodsucker he killed.

Dex heard the silent roar of the crowd in his ears as he easily stole the ball from Hedges and made a sneaky jump shot behind the engineer's back. The ball thudded through the hoop for the third time in as many minutes and Dex punched the air in celebration.

It was too easy. He was just gonna slay this guy tonight.

Behind him, a gray-bearded figure stepped out of the shadows.

Sommerfield was nearing the end of Zoe's story when she heard a strange sound coming from the storage bay. There was a muted thud, followed by a dull trickling noise, like the sound of a tap left running. Abruptly, the sounds of the one-on-one game stopped, to be replaced by a deathly silence.

Curious, Sommerfield swiveled her chair round and turned to face the open door to the storage area. Her computer carried on reading the data results to her in its calm, measured voice. "Blood input delay, zero. Abnormal samples, ten. Banding quality, eight-point-one—"

Sommerfield strained her hearing. The silence was unnerving.

She reached out a hand and paused her reading program. "Guys? You okay?"

As though in reply, a basketball came bouncing through the doorway. It rolled over to where she was sitting and rebounded gently off the legs of her chair, rolling away underneath a bench.

Sommerfield tracked the ball with her ears. Then she picked up her cane and got carefully to her feet, tapping her way over to it. She fished the ball out from under the bench with her cane and picked it up, her eyes creasing with amusement.

The guys must have overshot the hoop again. She'd told them to keep the door shut, hadn't she? Well, at least they hadn't hit anything expensive this ti...

She froze, her hands on the ball. There was something warm and sticky splashed across its surface. Sommerfield dipped a cautious finger into the goo, then rubbed it between her fingers for a moment, feeling its texture. She gingerly raised her hand to her nostrils.

Blood.

Sommerfield's heart started pounding wildly. The ball fell from her suddenly nerveless fingers and bounced away across the floor. "Zoe?" she called.

The little girl looked up obediently at her mother.

"Go find someplace to hide, sweetie."

Zoe hesitated, her eyes flicking from her mother to the upturned storybook.

Sommerfield lashed out with her cane, banging on a rack of equipment. "Damn it, go! Get out of here, Zoe!"

With a small cry of fear, Zoe scuttled away.

Moving as quickly and quietly as she could, Sommerfield tapped her way across the lab, moving cautiously towards the storage area. She located the gun cabinet on the wall beside the door and groped around inside for one of King's electronic pistols. Then she edged her way through the doorway into the storage area.

The interior of the bay was icy, kept cool by a series of ventilation fans up near the roof. Sommerfield's skin prickled with danger as she paused in the doorway, every nerve alert for the tiniest sound. Her own heartbeat thudded in her ears and She shook her head in frustration, betrayed by the workings of her own body.

She waited, every nerve jangling as she listened intently, but there was no further noise from the warehouse. She could sense a living presence in there, though, something to do with the way the air moved, the way the acoustics of the room had altered. She knew every foot of the dockyard off by heart and could feel the sense of wrongness hanging in the air like a pall of choking smoke.

Sommerfield quietly clicked the safety off King's gun. If Dex and Hedges were playing some kind of stupid practical joke on her, it would be their own darn fault if she killed them both.

But even as the thought went through her mind, Sommerfield knew that this wasn't the case. It was too still in there, too quiet, as though time itself had been frozen.

Sommerfield let a full minute tick by, breathing shallowly through her mouth to calm herself. She had to do this. There was no other way. Abigail and Blade were miles away on the other side of town and King was in bed upstairs, unconscious.

She had to protect Zoe, whatever the cost.

When the minute was up, Sommerfield took a cautious step forwards, out of the doorway and into the open, praying fervently that the intruder—if that's what it was—would have taken the opportunity to leave.

Sommerfield had no way of being able to see the horrific scene that lay before her, but she could smell the blood. The stench hit her in an overpowering gust, stirred up by the powerful ventilation fans as they cycled the air though the room. The concrete floor was slick with the stuff and Sommerfield fought back a small cry of horror as her cane slipped about in it.

She began walking across the floor, slowly, carefully, tapping her cane about in front of her as she walked. In her other hand she gripped the pistol tightly

After a couple of paces, Sommerfield's foot nudged against something heavy lying on the ground. She gave a little inadvertent scream as she felt it give against her skin, oozing wetness like a sodden sponge, soaking through her clothing in a flood of soggy warmth.

Sommerfield's heart was beating madly now. She backed away, holding up her cane in front of her as though to ward off demons. What did she think she was doing? She couldn't see, for the love of God! What chance did she think she had against whatever was in the room? She had to get away, lock down the doors on the barge and sit tight till Blade and Abigail returned.

Unless whatever had killed Dex and Hedges was already on the barge...

As the horrendous thought hit her, Sommerfield heard an indistinct cracking noise coming from the open doorway behind her, like the sound made by someone stepping on a pile of dried chicken bones. Fighting a rising feeling of dread, Sommerfield slowly turned towards the noise, raising her pistol with shaking fingers...

Three rooms away, Zoe tore down the corridor towards the bathroom, sobbing in fear as her mother's screams echoed through the barge. She rushed into the bathroom and ran around in a frenzy, pulling lockers open and throwing laundry around her in her frantic search for somewhere big enough to hide.

She spotted a metal heating grate near the floor behind the shower and ran over to it, weeping. She tugged at it, but it was stuck fast. She dropped to her knees on the wet floor and yanked with all her might, her little body shaking with the effort.

Fear lent her strength and on the second tug it came free. Tearing the dusty wire filter out with her bare fingers, Zoe pushed her head inside, frantically checking that it was big enough for her to fit into. Then she climbed into the duct feet first, pushing her legs before her, scooting inside as fast as she could go.

Inside, the heating duct extended a short way in front of her before making a ninety-degree turn upwards. Zoe pulled herself all the way in, scrabbling for a handhold on the slick metal sides. Then she reached back and pulled the grate closed behind her, sealing herself inside the duct.

Zoe waited in the darkness of the metal duct. It was hot and cramped and she felt claustrophobia set in immediately. Her ears rang in the silence and she imagined that whoever was outside could hear her thudding heartbeat echoing through the polished steel tubes, broadcasting her location in every room.

Her pulse raced faster at the thought. Zoe reached above her head and forced herself further backwards into the duct. After a minute of concentrated wriggling she managed to jam herself all the way back into the space below the ninety-degree bend, curling up into a near-fetal position against the back of the pipe.

She waited there in terror, her entire consciousness focused in on the tiny rectangle of light visible through the slatted grate. All she could see was the white tiled floor and a small portion of the open doorway, leading to the corridor outside.

Never lock the door behind you. Her mother had taught her that during their many games of hide-and-seek. These games were played for a reason, as well as for fun. Sommerfield wanted to be sure that if Zoe was ever threatened, she would know what to do. If she were chased by one of them, her mother had told her gravely, a locked door would only make them want to tear it open to see what was inside, like a starving man faced with a sealed can of beans.

Then they would get you.

Unlike most five year-olds, Zoe knew who "they" were. She had only been three when the vampire gang had burst into their house in the middle of one December night and ripped her daddy to pieces, but she remembered that, too.

It was the screaming that had been the worst. She hadn't known that a human being could made noises like that, especially not a big man like her daddy. Zoe hadn't known what death was either. But lying there that night in her pink-painted bed, amongst her dolls and teddies, she had pulled the blankets over her head and wept with fright. She remembered the strong smell of blood as her mother had grabbed her from her cot and fled through the house, tripping on toys and stumbling over furniture, until they had reached the safety of their lockable garage.

The vampires had followed them, laughing, and had tried to kick the door down. Zoe remembered being nearly deafened by the clanging as her mother had pressed her against the back wall, trying to shield her with her body. But the creatures had been unable to tear through the thick metal door.

The gang had eventually given up and gone away, leaving them both a little seasonal present: the shredded remains of her father, draped around the big Christmas tree outside the house. Zoe remembered vividly, in a way no five year-old should, how his insides had been twined around the tree with the lights like gory, bloody decorations.

It had been the one time in her life when Zoe had been glad that her mother was blind.

Since that day, a lot of things had changed. Sommerfield had made sure of it. This was why Zoe was currently wedged into a service pipe rather than hiding under a bed or in a locker.

The moonlight reflected on the tiles outside the black square of the grate. Zoe stared at it, mesmerized. The horrible sounds from outside had stopped. Zoe's imagination went into overdrive as she listened with every fiber in her being. She tried not to breathe, choking as her heaving lungs betrayed her.

Silence.

Then... footsteps.

Zoe bit back the urge to scream and forced herself further back into the pipe, squashing herself up against the back wall as hard as she could. Through the grate, she saw a pair of man's boots appear in the doorway outside and stop there.

Whoever they belonged to seemed to be listening, too.

Zoe put her hand over her own mouth in fright as the boots did a left turn and marched straight towards her, into the bathroom. At the last moment they veered to the left, towards the showers. The following sounds seemed ear-shatteringly loud as the man started wrenching open lockers and shower stalls, as though searching for something.

Searching for her.

Zoe watched, terrified, as the boots passed by the grate again, closer this time. They paused there for a moment that seemed to stretch into infinity, and Zoe squeezed her eyes tight shut. She couldn't stand it.

There would be no escape this time.

After what seemed like an age, she heard the boots scuff on the tiled floor and move away from her, towards the door. Relieved, Zoe let out the breath she had been holding, and opened her eyes.

A dark face was pressed up against the grate, staring at her.

Zoe screamed.

With a roar, the man ripped the grate off the wall. Pushing his head into the duct, he tried to force himself inside, wrenching his body from side to side like a shark in his efforts to get to Zoe. But his upper body was too big and got stuck fast in the square opening.

Pulling himself back out with a snarl of frustration, the man got down on his knees and reached into the duct with his right arm, stretching in as far as he could. His clawed hand lunged towards Zoe, who whimpered and tried to compress herself back an extra few inches, tears streaming down her face as she curled into an even tighter ball against the back of the pipe.

She watched helplessly as the man's fingers reached out towards her, blotting out the light as they closed in on her...

Then they stopped, grasping at the air a scant few inches away from her face.

He couldn't reach her.

Zoe let out her breath in a gasp. She had been given a reprieve.

Then there was the sound of popping cartilage. The man's hand changed shape as tiny bones shifted beneath his flesh, making it writhe about as though his skin was full of worms. As Zoe watched in uncomprehending terror, the man's fingers started to elongate. They reached out for Zoe's face, rapidly closing the distance between them.

Zoe closed her eyes and screamed again.

* * *

Outside, the black Land Cruiser glided slowly through the deserted shipyard. It turned in towards the docks and rolled to a halt with a crunch of grit beneath the covered work area. Blade climbed out of the Cruiser and slammed the door.

As Abigail climbed out he paused, keys still in the door, staring fixedly at the lock in front of him. A strange echo hung in the air, although no noise had preceded it. Blade frowned, then removed the car keys and hurried after Abigail as she walked down the steps towards the armored barge.

Inside, the place was in darkness. Blade's razor-sharp senses immediately pricked up and he put a hand on Abigail's arm to hold her back.

It was too quiet.

Something was wrong.

Abigail glanced at Blade, picking up on his uneasiness. Without saying a word, she reached out and flipped a nearby light switch.

Nothing happened. The power had been cut.

Instinctively they both drew their weapons, crouching low and moving to opposite sides of the room. What now? Abigail removed the safety catch from her gun and ghosted across the room into the hallway. Either Hedges had blown the power supply trying to make Pop-Tarts in the steam press again, or something, somewhere, had gone terribly wrong.

Abigail shut her mind to the possibilities, focusing instead on keeping up with Blade as he darted through the door ahead of her. Groping behind the lab door, Blade pulled a flashlight off a hook and fumbled with it for a moment before switching it on, flooding the chamber with a wash of yellow light.

Abigail gasped, her heart in her mouth. Sommerfield's entire lab had been destroyed. It was as though
a tornado had touched down inside the room. The
computer workstations had been dragged off their
benches and smashed on the floor, and even the
heaviest banks of equipment had been overturned.
Further on down the room, tables and chairs had
been overturned in a frenzy of indiscriminate
destruction that reached the length and breadth of
the lab.

Abigail put a hand on the lab bench to steady herself. She turned to Blade, the taste of fear like a bar of
cold metal in her mouth. "King..."

They rushed into to the infirmary area. King was
gone. The place had been trashed, medical equipment and supplies strewn across the floor. Moving as
though in a dream, the pair followed the trail of
destruction back through the lab into the storage
area.

As they opened the door, Abigail jumped backwards, clapping a hand to her mouth to stop herself
from screaming.

The concrete floor was swimming with blood. Bits
of Dex and Hedges lay scattered all over the place,
like so much discarded meat on an abattoir floor.

Abigail stared, feeling an icy wave of shock flood
over her.

This couldn't be happening.

She found her gaze drawn as if by a magnet over
the butchered remains of her workmates, her eye
moving over the glistening innards that lay draped all
over the floor. She knew that she shouldn't look, that
she would regret it on the thousand nights she would

have to spend alone in bed after tonight, but she couldn't help herself.

There was no way she could've ever prepared herself for this. It was as though someone had found out her worst nightmare and arranged to have it happen, down to the last detail, like some sick television stunt. She'd known in her gut that the day could come when the vampires would find them, but in her mind, it hadn't played out like this.

Never like this.

Blade stepped forward, lifting a hand to gently touch her on her shoulder, but Abigail jerked sharply away from him. If he touched her, she would be lost. She needed to see this, to give her the strength to destroy whoever—or whatever—was responsible.

Something crunched beneath her boot. Abigail looked down to see Hedge's watch floating in a pool of blood at her feet, yards away from the bloody stump of his severed wrist. Something inside her clenched tightly at the sight and she felt a blinding wave of rage rip through her. This went beyond the mere ending of life. This was carnage, plain and simple. Whatever had killed Dex and Hedges had enjoyed doing so. There was so much blood, more than two human bodies should possibly be able to hold...

Abigail stiffened, a thought cutting through her like a white-hot knife. "Zoe. Where's Zoe?"

With increasing urgency, Blade and Abigail searched the headquarters: the bathroom, the garage, every nook and cranny.

There was no sign of the little girl.

"Where is she?" Abigail felt the world receding from her as she pounded through the building, throwing open doors and closets as she shouted Zoe's name. A hundred nights she had lain on her cot and dreamed fitfully of this moment, only to wake to the sound of Hedges and Dex joking and teasing one another in the workshop, while Sommerfield typed up her nightly reports next door in the lab with a soothing clatter of keys. Life had seemed so normal, as though this was how things had always been, and always would be.

Abigail had always known at the back of her mind that the Nightstalker's operation was a fragile thing, by its very nature not meant to last, but somehow, routine had lulled her into a sense of invulnerability.

The edge had gone, and over time, they had all got careless.

And now, something had got them.

Abigail looked up at the sound of Blade's shout. Her stomach clenched into a cold ball and she rushed to join him, refusing to let herself think about what she was about to see.

She burst into the bathroom. Blade stood over by the washbasins, his shoulders bowed. Wordlessly, he gazed down at the thin stream of blood snaking its way across the damp shower tiles.

Abigail stared at it for a moment. Then her mouth set into a hard line. Taking the torch from Blade, she grimly followed the line of blood through into the showers, dreading what she might find.

The light from her torch washed across the white tiled wall, and Abigail shut her eyes with a gasp. But it was too late. The image was there, burned into the inside of her eyelids in stark detail.

Sommerfield's body.

Bled, broken, desecrated.

Propped up between the shower-pipes in mock-crucifixion style, blood spilling from her eyes and mouth in winding streams.

On the wall next to her was a message, written in thick daubs of her blood:

> "IMMORTALITY WILL COME TO SUCH
> AS ARE FIT FOR IT"

Sommerfield's dark glasses lay next to her on the floor, pointedly smashed into a thousand pieces.

Abigail made a small noise in her throat and rushed to Sommerfield's side. Blade stared at the message, then at the broken body of the young geneticist.

Slowly, his hands clenched into fists.

Drake.

Blade went to help Abigail. It was all that he could do.

Together, they lifted her down off the wall and Abigail cradled the body, rocking it in her arms, tears streaking her face.

Blade watched her from behind his dark glasses, his face emotionless. Then he put a hand on Abigail's shoulder. "Use it," he whimpered.

Abigail didn't respond. Her whole body was shaking.

Blade tightened his grip on her shoulder. "Use it."

Abigail slowly raised her head to meet his gaze. Her eyes were red-rimmed, filled with hatred.

Blade didn't move his hand. "Use it!"

Abigail lifted her head and let loose a tortured scream from the very pit of her soul.

Outside the Nightstalkers' headquarters, Drake listened, and smiled.

SIXTEEN

As consciousness slowly percolated into King's body, he became aware of three things.

Firstly, his head hurt.

That was nothing new. King had been knocked unconscious more times than he could count over the years. Name your evil, and it was a safe bet that King had been knocked out by it at some point in his life. As a result, his skull as slightly thicker than that of the average human, his brain slightly better protected. He usually woke from his concussions with a headache and a strange longing for beef jerky that not even Sommerfield's expert ministrations could cure.

Hell, nobody was perfect.

Secondly, his wrists hurt.

Again, that was not always bad. The bargirls up at the Dog House could be real devils after lights-out, in some cases, quite literally.

Thirdly, he had the strangest sensation that someone was stroking his cheek with a small piece of cold, wet sandpaper.

What the hell...?

King sighed under his breath. Put together, these things meant that either he'd had one heck of a night out last night, or that something had happened to him that was too horrible to even contemplate.

He shifted slightly, trying to get comfortable. The floor beneath him was very hard. His head throbbed with a dull ache that seemed to permeate his entire body, from the top of his head to the soles of his boots. Something unpleasant lurked just beneath the surface of his consciousness, like a used cigarette butt in a half-finished can of beer. He knew that if he gave it more than a moment's thought it would suddenly make its presence known in some horribly real way, and then he'd have to deal with it.

It was no good. He was going to have to wake up.

King gave a loud groan, in the manner of one who is determined to suffer as loudly and as annoyingly as possible.

Then he wearily opened one eye.

Vertigo hit him full force and spun his brain around as his eyes contradicted what his body was telling him. He wasn't lying down. In fact, he was sitting, and the concrete he'd thought was beneath him was actually supporting him. His hands were tied behind his back, and he was freezing, chilled to the bone by the over-enthusiastic air conditioning.

Where was his shirt? He was sure that he put a shirt on this morning. What in the blue blazes was going on?

Then King looked behind him, and got his answer.

Some fucker had stripped him half-naked and chained him to a pillar.

King looked around him, hoping against hope to see dancing girls, preferably similarly naked and covered in cherry-flavored whipped cream.

The anticipatory smile dripped off his face as he took in his surroundings. He was in a large, dimly lit room. Although luxurious, the place looked like a herd of buffalo had recently charged through it. The opulent carpet was torn in a multitude of places and paintings hung askew on the walls, which were similarly scarred by fist-sized holes in the masonry. One of the shuttered windows was smashed and a statue lay toppled across the remains of an expensive-looking glass table.

As King stared around him in confusion, something warm ran down his forehead. King watched, mesmerized, as a large drop of blood ran down the side of his nose and dripped onto his cheek.

Then a tiny pink tongue appeared out of nowhere and lapped the drop up.

King opened his other eye with a start. A small, fluffy-haired Pomeranian dog stood beside him on its hind legs, paws on his chest. The mutt was enthusiastically licking the blood off his face.

Spluttering, King tried to twist his head away. He was rewarded with a small but throaty growl. Raising an eyebrow, King squinted down at the canine ball of fluff as it resumed its snack. "Back off, pooch."

He was in no mood for niceties. He had to get the hell out of here and find Blade, to warn him about Whistler before he...

The Pomeranian growled again, louder this time. An instant later, there was a strange, organic ripping sound. A thin line of blood ran up the dog's chin, as though it had been cut open by an invisible knife. As King watched in horror, the cut grew, running rapidly up the dog's tiny, lion-like face like a statue cracking in an earthquake.

Without warning, the creature's muzzle suddenly split open down the middle. King jerked backwards in shock as its lower face twisted inside-out with a wet sucking sound. It folded back down the sides of the dog's head, like two halves of a banana skin. A hellish, barbed tongue-stalk shot out of its gaping maw, reaching out greedily towards King, who pressed himself back against the pillar with a yell. The Pomeranian planted its feet on the ground and roared at him, ready to bite off his head.

"Jesus Christ!"

Laughter exploded from all around him. The hulking form of Grimwood stepped through the door and yanked the mutant animal back on its leash, away from King. His tattooed muscles bulged with the strain as the tiny creature lunged and snapped in a frenzy, foaming at the mouth. Asher and Danica appeared from behind a pillar, giggling like school-girls.

"What the fuck! What the fuck!?" King gaped up at the trio of vampires, his heart hammering wildly against his ribcage.

Asher stepped forward smoothly. "His name's Pac Man. We've been experimenting with porting the vampire gene over into other species." As King stared, Asher bent down next to the snarling hell-dog and smoothed the fur on its head. At his touch, the creature retracted its insect-like tongue, then folded its muzzle closed, the pieces curling back into place like an intricate origami puzzle.

The Pomeranian looked up at Asher, its tongue lolling, panting happily,

King was beside himself. "You made a goddamn vampire dog?"

Grimwood sniggered. "Yeah. Cool, huh?"

King sagged, trying to get his breath back. He was as white as a sheet. "Depends who you ask, because clearly this dog had a bigger dick than you."

Grimwood growled. "And when the fuck have you seen my dick, fuckface?" Furious, he punched King in the head.

King reeled and pointed at Danica. "Ow! I was talking to her!"

Danica's smirk vanished and she stepped forwards, neatly kicking King in the face with her metal-tipped stiletto heel. Then she crouched down to examine the wound, a look of mock concern on her face. "Poor little King. You look so distraught." She wiped the blood from King's mouth as he glowered at her, then on impulse touched her bloody fingertips to her tongue. She smiled. "You're tasting a little bland, lover. Not getting enough fatty acids in your diet?"

King glared at her, not trusting himself to reply.

"Seriously," Danica said. "Have you tried mackerel? Lake trout?"

King looked up at her brightly. "How about you take a sugar-frosted fuck off the end of my dick?"

Danica frowned for a moment, and then laughed. "Oh, there'll be time to play doctor later, believe me."

She crouched down low, her eyes glittering as she cast an appreciative gaze over King's muscular upper body. "But for now, we need to have a little talk." Her gaze lingered on the bloody stake-wound in his chest for a moment, then she stroked his chin with her finger and the smile faded from her face. "Tell us about this bio-weapon you've been building."

King blinked a slimy mixture of blood and dog drool out of his eyes, surreptitiously testing the strength of the metal cuffs behind his back. "I can tell you two things. Diddly, and shit. And diddly just left the building."

Grimwood crossed the room in two great strides and slammed a hand around King's throat. "Spit it out, you fucking fruitcake!"

King's body jerked as he fought for air. Grimwood relented slightly.

"Okay, here's the deal with the weapon." King coughed. Danica and Asher leaned forwards, their lips parting in expectation.

King spat blood onto the floor and grinned. "It's a new flavor crystal formula. Twice the chocolaty goodness, half the calories. Plus, it helps prevent tooth decay—"

Grimwood moved to grab King by the throat again, but Danica held up a hand, stopping the big vampire in his tracks. She leaned in towards King, a soft smile on her full lips. "You're brave, King, I'll give you that." She moved closer, caressing his face. "But underneath all your swagger, I know what you really fear. What would hurt you more than anything else."

King's smile became fixed, the humor slowly draining out of his eyes.

Danica rubbed her cheek against King's stubble, purring like a cat. Her lips grazed his ear as she whispered, "You don't want to go back to being one of us, do you?"

The muscles in King's jaw twitched. Sweat mingled with the blood on his forehead as he tried to turn his head away, not wanting Danica to see the fear in his eyes.

Danica gripped his chin with her delicate hand, turning his face back towards hers. She smiled cruelly, whispering into his ear. "I'm going to bite you again, King. And then I'm going to leave you here while you turn." She tenderly pushed King's blood-soaked hair back out of his eyes. "I'm going to watch you, day after day, while the thirst keeps building and building. And then, when you can't stand it any more...' Danica nodded to a figure standing in the shadows. Drake stepped forwards into the room, Zoe held firmly in his arms. The little girl was gagged, terrified but alive.

Danica went on sweetly, "I'm going to bring the little girl in for you to feed on." She stroked a finger fondly along his jaw line. "Would you like that, King? Would you enjoy taking her life?"

King turned his head away and squeezed his eyes tight shut, sickened.

Danica smiled. "Now we're getting somewhere, my pet."

Abigail stood by the tool bench in the workshop of the Nightstalkers' headquarters, quietly restringing her bow.

It was nearly morning, and the tables around her were strewn with an assortment of equipment: a bow press, string jig, bow scales and various sizes of wrench sets. Her eyes burned with the need to sleep, but she grimly pressed on, making sure that everything was prepared. She concentrated intently on the job in hand, trying to close her mind to the events of the past few hours.

Of all the new techno-weapons Hedges had designed for her over the years, the bow was her favorite. The sheer amount of equipment in the workshop dedicated to maintaining it bore silent witness to that fact. There was even a whole room set aside for her to practice in. Across the hall, a half-open door revealed an improvised shooting range set up with a variety of targets, ranging from simple bullseye boards to army-style sniper targets.

Abigail had dedicated a large portion of her time with the Nightstalkers to mastering the bow. She had put the design to Hedges as a joke, and had been surprised and pleased when he had actually managed to pull it off.

Abigail looked down at it now as she tightened the tiny screws that held the whole thing together. It was different from a traditional bow, slightly lighter due to its titanium build, but far more powerful and responsive. The string was so delicately weighted that it only took a second's inattention to wind up with a crossbolt buried in your kneecap, so Abigail had trained hard to control her reflexes. She was the only one of the Nightstalkers who knew how to use the bow correctly. Dex had been too strong and prone to snapping the string and King was too impatient, much preferring his guns. He'd always said that he was a real point and shoot kinda guy...

Abigail quickly banished the thought of King from her mind. Right now, she needed to stay focused.

Abigail had always been good with the bow. When she had been younger, her father had sent her a toy bow and arrow in the post for her thirteenth birthday. It was only cheap one made of plastic with a nylon string, but Abigail had surprised and eventually irritated her mother by taking it with her wherever she went. Local cats soon learnt to avoid Abigail's house as she practiced endlessly, to the point where her step-dad had confiscated it to save their last few remaining houseplants and ornaments from destruction.

But no matter where he hid it, Abigail would always find it, digging through cupboards and climbing on top of wardrobes to get her favorite toy back. One day, her step-dad had tired of their little game and had thrown it in the trash. Abigail had been upset, but not as upset as her parents had been when, three days later, a real wooden bow had turned up on her doorstep, complete with a quiver of arrows and a human-shaped target wearing a wig the same color as her foster-dad's hair.

Like any father, Whistler had always wanted to keep his daughter safe, away from the horrors of the world. But at the same time, he must've realized that wrapping Abigail up in cotton wool wasn't the best way to do that. After the murders happened, Whistler had cut off all contact with her and her mother, fearing for their safety. For years, neither Abigail nor her mother knew where Whistler lived. They didn't even have his phone number.

But still, Abigail had the constant feeling that he was near, maybe even watching over her. She had practiced with her new bow day and night, desperately wanting to help her dad kill the monsters who had murdered his other family.

When she finally managed to track Whistler down after years of searching, he had forbidden her from going anywhere near a vampire, until he saw what she could do with her bow. After that, he became almost resigned to the idea.

But he had insisted that if she was so determined to help him, she must join the new team that he was putting together: the Nightstalkers. At the time, the team were a fairly rag tag band of outcasts, refugees from their own lives, united only by the collective drive to put an end to the creatures that had destroyed their happiness. Whistler had helped them find a base for their operations, then given them full access to his databases and taught them everything he knew about killing vampires.

The rest, he left up to them.

These people would look after her, he insisted. It was far too risky having his own daughter working with him. If ever she was captured by the vampires, Whistler had told her sternly, he knew without question that he would willingly give up his own life, and maybe even the life of Blade to save her. He couldn't have that kind of worry hanging over him.

Besides which, he'd confessed somewhat sheepishly, he just knew she wouldn't approve of their weekly horror movie and curry nights.

At least she would be safe with the Nightstalkers, and wouldn't have to spend all her time cleaning fossilized naan bread out from underneath the cushions. Together, their individual talents would unite to create a powerful secret weapon against the vampires, one that could carry on in his place should anything ever happen to him and Blade.

It was the closest thing to a living will he could manage.

Abigail gazed down at the bow in her hands, fighting down a sudden wash of fear. Goosebumps crawled over her skin and she put a hand on the table to steady herself. Her father had only been dead for two days, and already the Nightstalkers had been taken down in the most terrible way imaginable.

She had only gone out for an hour...

Abigail shook her head. She couldn't blame herself for this. She knew that if she had been there at the time, in all likelihood she would've been killed, too. It wasn't her fault.

So why did she feel so goddamn guilty?

Abigail pulled out a tiny screwdriver and worked on her bow with quiet precision, resetting the arrow rest and making minor adjustments to the center-shot position. Tears prickled in her eyes and she angrily wiped them away so that she could see what she was doing. If King was still alive, she was going to need every millimeter of accuracy she could get.

The darkness outside the workshop moved, and Blade appeared in the doorway, a shadow within a shadow. He watched Abigail work for a moment, uncertain of whether or not he was intruding. The girl had been fiddling with that bow for over an hour now. What was she doing that was taking so long?

Blade leaned back against the metal doorframe and watched Abigail as she worked. Her head was bent in concentration, her nimble fingers making minute adjustments to the electronic tension gauge.

After a moment, Blade cleared his throat. Abigail carried on working, turning her body slightly away from him as she picked up a lens cloth and carefully began cleaning the electronic range sights on her bow.

Blade frowned. Why was she ignoring him? Perhaps he was intruding, but she had barely said a word to him since they had found Sommerfield's body. Blade felt that he should say something before the silence between them stretched much further. Like it or not, the two of them were all that remained of their respective operations. It was important that they kept up regular communications.

He cleared his throat again, slightly louder this time. "You all right?" he said gruffly.

"I'll be fine." Abigail's reply was automatic, but her tone was sharper than she'd meant it to be. She coughed and stared fixedly down at the cloth in her hands to stop the tears from coming. Just go.

Blade nodded to himself. Abigail wanted to be left in peace, that much he got. He wasn't completely insensitive.

He turned to go, but hesitated in the doorway, wrestling with himself. He glanced back at Abigail as she recommenced cleaning her bow sights, head bowed. A memory sparked in his head and he gave a tiny, sad smile.

Like father, like daughter. He had only known Abigail for a short time, but already he was picking up on all the little traits she shared with her father. Whistler was just as stubborn when it came to expressing his own emotions. Many nights, Blade would return home from a job to find the old man sprawled in front of their tiny black and white television, a bottle of scotch in one hand and a fistful of faded snapshots in the other. He would stuff them under his cushion as soon as he heard the front door slam, but not before the Daywalker had seen the tears in the old man's eyes, always quickly wiped away with a sleeve or an old engine cloth.

He still grieved for his lost family, Blade knew that much. But Whistler kept his feelings under tight control, hiding behind habitual gruffness and macho bluster. He wanted Blade to see him as being strong, thinking that this would make Blade strong himself. But in practice, it had only made Blade just as hardened, making him ill equipped to deal with situations other than hunting, killing, and buying the occasional bag of groceries.

By its very nature, Blade's life was full of extreme emotions. But as the years went by, Blade had increasingly ignored them, allowing them to become just another part of his job. The way he saw things, it wasn't his job to clean up after the vampires. All he had to do was to kill them, and then let the rest of the world sort out the mess afterwards. He was a killer, not a counselor.

It wasn't that he didn't care. It was just that he didn't know how to express it. Blade's mind was like a well-oiled knife, full of practicalities and strategies, of countermeasures and attack plans. Kill the vamp. Rescue the girl. Get the kid to hospital. Torch the place. When it came to hunting vampires, Blade was the best there could be. But when it came down to dealing with emotional situations, Blade avoided them like the plague, passing dying victims on to hospital staff like living postal deliveries, his mind already on the next job as he sponged their blood off his clothing and took pills to get their screaming out of his head.

Situations like this one...

Blade watched as Abigail picked up a wrench and began quietly adjusting the tiller on her bow. His first and most powerful instinct was to leave her alone, to let someone else deal with her.

Blade paused in the doorway. Everybody else was dead.

Damn.

Blade thought for a moment, loitering uncomfortably. He scratched his head, then removed his dark shades and rubbed at his eyes. What would King say in a situation like this?

Finally he turned to Abigail and gave her the only piece of advice he could think of. "Don't let it turn inward," he said simply.

"It already has," Abigail spoke without looking up.

Blade raised his eyebrows. He hadn't been expecting a reply, and certainly not so quickly. It was almost as though Abigail had been wanting him to speak.

He watched as she put down her cloth. Still facing away from him, she leaned on the workbench and gazed out of the dark window.

"Since I can remember, I've had this knife of sadness in my heart." Abigail's voice was so soft that Blade had to strain to hear it. She picked up the cloth again and began to worry it, picking bits of invisible fluff off the edges. "As long as it stays there, I'm strong. I'm untouchable. But the moment I pull it out...' Abigail turned to face Blade, briefly raising her eyes to his, "I'll die."

Then she turned back to her work and carried on as though Blade wasn't there.

Blade waited for a minute, but Abigail simply continued with her labors, once again ignoring him.

Blade left as quietly as he had arrived.

Abigail waited till the Daywalker's footsteps had faded away. Then she stood up and moved quickly across the hallway into the firing range.

Strapping on her quiver, Abigail nocked an arrow in her bow and pulled the string back, feeling the muscles in her toned arm tense as she took the strain. She took careful aim at a three-dimensional human-shaped target strapped to a net at the end of the gallery. Time seemed to pause as she shifted her position minutely, lining up the crosshairs of her sights with the target while the bow hummed under the tension.

Then she released the arrow.

Whoosh! The arrow flew across the darkened chamber, sinking into the target's chest, right over the heart. Abigail glanced at the chronograph next to her, connected to a ballistic computer. The arrow's speed was two hundred and forty feet per second.

Not bad.

Abigail fired again. Two sixty-nine.

Better, but still not good enough.

Three hundred feet per second.

Three-fifteen.

Three-thirty...

The computer bleeped rhythmically as Abigail pulled her bowstring again and again, until she finally stopped, grasping at empty air. Her quiver was empty.

Abigail looked back down the room at the target, which now had a dozen arrows buried in the mathematical dead center of its chest, forming the shape of a cross.

That would do.

Outside, Blade stood at the open entrance to the docks, his every sense alert as he waited for Abigail. The night sea breeze was mild, but Blade found it uncomfortably cold and damp, as he was used to the dry heat of the inner city. He fidgeted, pulling his long leather jacket tighter around him and stamping his feet to warm them.

Abigail had made a phone call less than twenty minutes ago to a friend who said he had somewhere for them to stay. This guy was now apparently on his way over to collect them, and Blade wished that he would hurry up. The sooner they got out of this place, the better. The entire building smelt of blood, and Blade had found to his revulsion that it was making him feel hungry. If Abigail could see inside his head, she would probably put one of her arrows through his still-beating heart.

Blade glanced up at the night sky. They had to stay on the move from this point on. They couldn't remain in the old headquarters now that it had been breached. Vampires were like wasps, if you let one in, and very soon, more would follow. They would have to bunk down with Abigail's friend for the night, and

return the next day to start the long process of trans-
ferring all of the Nightstalker's equipment elsewhere.

Blade shivered, trying to pretend that he didn't
care. He was into unknown territory now. The only
reason he had stayed this long was to make sure Abigail was safe. It was what Whistler would've wanted.

He could leave any time he wanted to.

Abigail stepped out of the building and walked
towards him, carrying her bow and a slim sack of provisions. Blade stood up to greet her. She seemed
calmer, and taller, somehow. "I'm ready to go," she
said.

Together, they settled down to wait.

Shortly, headlights appeared in the distance as a
Land Cruiser approached, weaving through the
skeletal remains of the shipyard like a battleship
moving through nautical burial grounds. The vehicle
was newer than King's Cruiser, with a different paint
job and black-painted hubcaps. It was coated with a
thin layer of sand, as though it had been driven
through a desert recently.

Blade noticed with interest the crudely patched
bullet holes in the front and rear body panels. This
was one interesting "friend" that Abigail had.

The Land Cruiser pulled to a halt in front of them,
and the driver's window rolled down. A clean-shaven
man sat behind the wheel, slightly younger than Dex,
but no less good looking. He raised his hand in
greeting. "My name's Culder. And I'll be your driver
this evening."

Blade felt a chill go through him.

Minutes later, the Land Cruiser was gliding through
the darkness of the city nightscape. Blade sat back in

his seat and tried to meditate, gazing out of the side window. The city flashed by, a blur of sodium lights and neon glare. As they drove, there was a faint clinking sound as two vampire canines looped onto a piece of string rattled together, strung around the driver's mirror in a parody of the usual fluffy dice.

The corner of Blade's mouth twitched up.

Whistler would've appreciated that one.

A thought occurred to Blade, breaking his concentration, and he leaned forward to touch Culder on the shoulder. "Where are you taking us?"

"Another safehouse." Culder flicked his driver's mirror down so that he could keep an eye on Blade, and then turned his attention back to the wheel.

Blade grunted. He wanted more information, but the atmosphere in the Cruiser was not exactly conducive to in-depth conversation. This Culder guy didn't seem like much of a talker. Blade began unconsciously drumming a beat on his knee as he tried to remember what King had told him about the Nightstalkers. It all seemed so long ago now...

Abigail stirred in her seat, shooting Blade a sharp glance. Blade stopped his drumming instantly. Abigail tucked her supply pack beneath the seat in front of her, thinking. Then she turned back to Blade, answering his unspoken question. "We told you, Blade. We operate in sleeper cells. When one goes down, a new cell activates to pick up the slack."

Abigail said the words mechanically, trying to shut out the accompanying images in her head. Then she turned away and stared out of the window again, watching her breath condense and evaporate on the cool glass.

She knew that Blade was in no way personally responsible for the deaths of her friends. But just having him near her and knowing that he was part vampire was enough to make her feel uncomfortable, as though there were tiny, icy ants crawling beneath the surface of her skin. She wanted this journey to be over as soon as possible, so that she could have some time alone to regroup her thoughts.

She wondered about her father, about how he had dealt with Blade. As far as she could make out, Whistler hadn't seemed to give Blade's pedigree a second thought, blithely living, eating and sleeping under the same roof as the Daywalker as though he was some sort of goddamn pet. As far as Abigail knew, Blade had never once intentionally hurt her father, so Abigail couldn't understand why she was having such difficulty in accepting him.

But at the same time, her mind was filled with so many questions. How much control did Blade really have over himself? What would happen if he ever ran out of his serum? And how far could she trust him to work as part of a team?

Abigail shifted uncomfortably in her seat. Whistler had often complained to her about Blade's stubbornness and pig-headed autonomy. He'd told her about the time—and many others like it—when Blade had walked fifteen miles home on foot rather than get back into the car after an argument. This raised all kinds of questions for which Abigail didn't have answers. What if the Daywalker decided that working with her was too much of a risk?

Abigail suddenly realized something. Despite her own personal reservations, she really needed Blade to hang around. She would have to try and deal with her fears, for one very good reason. If King was...

Abigail's mind ran out of steam. She shifted in her seat and tried again.

If King was dea...

Still no good.

Abigail blinked fiercely, tightening her grip on her bow.

If something had happened to King, she was going to need all the muscle she could get. She had to stop Drake, even if it killed her. She couldn't let the blood-sucking bastard get away after what he had done to the rest of the Nightstalkers, and there was no way she could fight the vampire king on her own. Only Blade had the strength and the stamina to do that, which meant very simply that she was going to have to learn to live with him, whether she liked it or not. If nothing else, she would need his help to avenge King's dea...

Damn it!

Blade glanced at Abigail enquiringly. She stared out of the window, breathing lightly, pretending not to notice his gaze.

Trouble was, Blade needed her too, and from the unhappy look on his face, Abigail could see that he knew it. He had to stay with her. She was his only link to the Nightstalkers organization, and with it, all their tools and technological intelligence. With Whistler dead and his boathouse destroyed, Blade had no way of maintaining his weapons, let alone obtaining his vital serum.

Abigail was pretty sure that Blade didn't know the first thing about genetics, chemistry or pharmaceuticals, and if he did, she wouldn't like to be around when he came to test the potency of the resultant serum. Surely he could see that the benefits of staying with her and the remaining Nightstalkers far outweighed the risks?

Abigail glanced quickly at Blade. If her own face were a closed book, Blade's face was a book that was closed, superglued, wrapped in chains and buried at the bottom of the ocean. He had turned away from her and was staring moodily out through the side window, barely blinking, totally cut off from her and the outside world. Abigail opened her mouth to speak, and then thought better of it.

This was not the time. It was as though there was a physical gulf in the few feet separating the two of them, a rocky chasm filled with bodies and blood and a lifetime of pain and regret. She could see that pain etched into the harsh lines of Blade's face, turning the corners of his full lips down and accentuating the strong lines of his jaw.

Abigail tilted her head slightly and studied Blade out of the corner of her eye. It was an attractive face, really, one that might in a different reality be seen gracing magazine covers and fashion spreads, rather than the front page of FBI's Most Wanted. Abigail noticed for the first time the thick, tribal-style tattoos that ran up the back of the Daywalker's ebony neck, swirling gracefully along his hairline and blending with the angular, military-style patterns shaved there. She wondered where he had got them, and how far down they extended...

Sensing Abigail's eyes on him, Blade turned and deliberately met her gaze for a couple of seconds, his expression completely blank. Then he returned his eyes to the road unwinding in front of them, nodding his head curtly to himself as though he had made some kind of point.

Abigail felt the tiny hairs rising on the back of her neck. She turned away, wondering what the hell she was doing taking in this hybrid stray. He might be good-looking, but Blade truly was one scary son of a bitch. She hoped to God that Culder had enough of Blade's serum to get them through the next twenty-four hours, because if he didn't, she was outta here.

Culder pulled up in front of an aquarium supply store, which was set back off the main road down a small bumpy side street. They dismounted and Culder beckoned them over to the side entrance. The windows of the store were dark, but both Blade and Abigail knew from experience that this didn't mean it was deserted.

Inside, Culder pulled out a big set of keys and unlocked an accordion-style security gate. Opening the back door with a whisper of hinges, he ushered Blade and Abigail inside, leading them through the darkened aisles of the aquatic store.

Fish tanks loomed on either side as they walked through the store, aerators bubbling, aquatic animals of every kind swimming around in the artificial brightness. A giant koi carp watched them closely as they passed, swimming excitedly around a molded plaster skull in anticipation of being fed. Above them, a colorful fish mobile swung slowly in the draft, dangling price cards and plastic fish.

Blade looked around at all the breakable glass tanks full of water, and quickly hurried through to the other side. He knew from experience that this wasn't a safe place for him to be. One escaped vampire in here, and every fish in the place would be flapping around on the floor before Culder had the chance to stop him.

Culder's safe-house was in the back. He flipped the light on and showed them in. Their new quarters were fairly small, consisting of a basic lab and a combined workshop and armory. Dog-eared movie posters were stuck to the walls and ceiling and the place smelled faintly of garlic and sulfur.

It was nothing like the previous headquarters, but for the moment, it would have to do.

Abigail laid her supplies on top of a bench and leaned back against it, arms folded, as Culder switched on one of the three computers. A media-player dialogue box appeared on the screen, and Culder called up an mpeg video file.

Blade gave him a questioning look. Culder paused, his cursor poised over the play button. "Sommerfield left a video message for you." His voice was matter of fact, but Blade felt a chill go through him as the implications sunk in.

Culder clicked the play button and Sommerfield's face appeared on the monitor. The image was pixelated with digital compression, but it was clear enough for them to see that it was really her. She looked grave, and was pale as though she had been crying recently.

She began to speak, her lip-movements slightly out of synch with the video. "If you're watching this, I'm already dead. If Zoe's alive, I want you to promise you'll take care of her."

The on-screen Sommerfield paused, apparently listening. Then she continued, her voice quieter. "I've been reading her The Oz books every night. We've just started The Emerald City of Oz, the one with the Gnome King..."

Sommerfield's voice cracked and she paused again, wiping at her clouded, sightless eyes. She appeared to take control of herself and changed the subject quickly, her voice becoming low and urgent. "I think I've managed to cultivate a workable strain of the DayStar virus. As a precaution, I transmitted the genetic sequence to Culder, in case our main stock was destroyed."

Abigail turned to Culder, a look of hope on her face. Culder held up his fists, clenched in the air in front of him in a gesture of triumph, then waved Abigail's attention back to the screen as Sommerfield's voice continued.

"In order to achieve maximum lethality, you'll need to infuse it with Drake's blood. If it works, any vampires in the immediate vicinity should die almost instantly."

Blade sat up a bit straighter, listening intently.

"After that, it should only take a few weeks for the virus to spread throughout the rest of the world."

Sommerfield hesitated, as though deciding how to broach the next subject. "There's one other thing, Blade. You need to know that the virus could destroy you, too. Because you're a hybrid, I'm not sure whether your immune system will be able to

tolerate it." She looked away, off-screen. "I'm
sorry," she said simply. "We didn't have time to
properly test it." She glanced behind her again,
then reached out towards the camera. The video
cut to static.

Culder switched off the monitor as all eyes
turned to Blade. As usual, his face was set, impas-
sive. God only knew what he was thinking.

Culder was the first to break the silence. There
was work to do. "Take a look at the plague arrow."

He reached for a refrigerated aluminum case,
snapping it open and holding it out for Blade's
inspection. The glass ampule containing the plague
virus lay inside, resting on a bed of sculpted white
foam. Jutting from one end of the ampule was a
stake-like contraption, giving the overall effect of a
high-tech harpoon.

Culder laid his hand over the case. "I only had
time to fabricate a small batch of DayStar," he said.
"I outfitted it with a compressed gas projectile, so
you should be able to fire it from one of the four-
barrel rifles, or a bow." He smiled wryly, trying to
keep his voice light. "Just make sure the shot
counts, because we don't have enough for a second
try."

Abigail worked with Culder until dawn, attaching
the plague ampule to one of her modified arrow-
heads with clinical care.

When she had finished, she carefully stowed it
away in her quiver and pulled out her portable
laptop. With practiced ease, she highlighted a
dozen songs from her play lists and moved them

across into her MP3 transfer list with a click of her mouse. Plugging the unit in, she hit the download button. While she was waiting, she slipped her earbud headphones in and cued up a track. The blistering intro to Fluke's track "Atom Bomb" poured down the wires into her brain and Abigail nodded approvingly, letting the music fill her senses as she began collecting up weaponry, readying herself for battle.

Behind her, Blade suited up, arming himself with as many of Culder's customized weapons as he could strap to his broad frame, which was quite a few. He loaded silver stakes into the empty slots in his bandoliers and bicep straps, pushing them one by one through the loops in the supple leather. Then he began loading rounds of silver bullets into the clips of his pistols.

Finally, he polished his sword with a gun-rag, buffing the bright metal until it shone like the sun. He sighted down the length of it, checking for nicks, and then took a practice swing that earned him an alarmed look from Culder. He secured it to his back scabbard with a showman-like flourish.

It was important to him that he was properly prepared. Because this was it. The big push. It was a moment he had been waiting for his entire life: a chance to wipe out all the vampires in one go. He could scarcely believe that it was possible, but he knew that he had to try. This time tomorrow, Abigail and this new cell of the Nightstalkers would either be celebrating an incredible, unprecedented victory, or they would be lying face-down in large pools of their own blood.

Either way, chances were that he would die in the process.

His life for the humans. It was as simple as that.

Minutes later, the alley outside the aquarium store vibrated with the roar of a powerful motor. Blade emerged from the back garage astride a Buell Lightening XB12s customized motorbike, revving the handlebar grip, enjoying the feeling of power beneath him. Even laden down with weapons, the bike took his weight with ease, the suspension bouncing responsively beneath him.

As he waited for Abigail, Blade noticed his reflection in the plate glass shop front, silhouetted on the bike by the first rays of dawn. He angled his body slightly, squaring off his broad shoulders and tilting his sunshades down at a rakish angle.

Damn, he looked good on this thing.

If he lived through today, he would probably try and steal it.

A second engine gunned in the darkness of the garage and Abigail rolled into place beside him on her own motorbike, a slightly lighter build of the Buell Firebolt series. She twisted her handlebar grips, the roar of her engine echoing in the close silence of the alley. She was wearing her leather biker jacket and black archer's gloves. Her bow was strapped to her back, along with a single quiver of arrows.

Blade glanced at her approvingly, and then gunned his own engine.

Together, the two motorbikes took off together into the light.

It was time.

SEVENTEEN

Drake sat back on his haunches and regarded the human girl who sat before him with interest.

Zoe stared back at him, her eyes huge in her pale face.

The handcuffs hadn't fitted her, so Drake had bound her to the wall with a length of heavy chain that clinked and scraped as she moved around, struggling to find a comfortable position on the cold tiled floor of the chamber.

Drake cocked his head to one side and sniffed, inhaling her scent, more out of curiosity than hunger. He hadn't been this close to a child before and not eaten it. The girl was so tiny, with delicate features and hair like an angel's nest of curls, spilling over her shoulders in a golden wave. Her arms and legs were painfully thin, with no visible muscle, and her neck was slender as a bird's.

There was nothing to her.

Drake couldn't see how such a tiny scrap of life could even survive unaided. And yet this fragile creature had put up more fight than the other three adults, before he had finally managed to capture her. Drake scratched distractedly at his knuckles, where the long red gouges Zoe had torn in his skin had barely finished healing.

She was a feisty little thing. He liked that.

He watched the child for a moment.

Zoe watched him right back, her tiny chin stuck out in defiance, though her bottom lip was trembling quite visibly.

It was no good. Drake had to find out. "Do you know who I am?" he asked.

Zoe's reply was unhesitating. "You're the Gnome King."

"The Gnome King." Drake smiled. "I like that."

He thought for a moment, the pinwheels in his brain clicking over into new positions. He leaned in closer, curious. "Tell me, child. Do you want to die?"

Zoe was terrified, but put on a brave show, just as her mother had taught her. "I'm not afraid. I'll go to heaven."

Drake laughed, though there was a bitterness to the sound.

"There is no heaven," he told Zoe flatly. "No God. No angels. No happy endings for good little girls." He moved closer to her and looked into her eyes. "The only thing you have to look forward to is nothingness."

As Drake spoke, his pupils widened, until the darkness within them eclipsed the whites. Zoe stared up at him, unable to tear her gaze away. The man's eyes seemed to be getting bigger. She felt like she was being drawn closer to him against her will, until her brain was swimming in the liquid currents of his thrall. She dug her tiny nails into her palm, fighting against the sensation. She didn't know what it was, but she knew that she didn't like it one little bit.

Drake spoke again, his voice soft and resonant. "But what if you could change that?" he continued. "What if you could remain a child forever?" He reached out, running one of his long fingernails along the perfect skin of Zoe's cheek. "What if you could keep this little doll-like face of yours until the sun itself cooled to a cold, hard rock?" He stared deeply into her eyes. "Wouldn't you like that? Wouldn't you accept that gift?"

Zoe blinked, then reached out and calmly touched Drake's cheek. "My friends are coming to kill you."

Three rooms away, King slumped backwards against the pillar, blood streaming from his nose and mouth in a sticky red torrent. He blinked it out of his eyes and looked up dizzily to see Grimwood step back into the light, flexing his enormous muscles as he bounced on the spot like a fighter in the ring.

Life, King was rapidly coming to the conclusion, sucked.

Especially when you were being pounded on by a guy who couldn't find his ass with both his hands, unless he paid someone to hold up a mirror and point.

There was no honor to this. The vampires had caught him, and now they were going to kill him. It was as simple as that, and the bloodsucking freaks didn't have the imagination to do anything else but stand around and watch like big sissies.

It was almost an insult.

Still, it was better than the future Danica had spelled out for him.

King spat blood onto the luxurious carpet and glared up at the two looming figures of Asher and Danica. He was seeing double and he couldn't work out which one of the two female figures was the real Danica. They were both kinda pretty, despite being evil and of course exceptionally slutty. He wracked his brains for a suitable valley-girl vampire joke, but for once, none seemed to come.

He must be in a worse state than he thought.

Instead, he turned and glowered at Grimwood. He may be beaten, but he would be damned if they were going to see him give up. He bared his teeth up at the big vampire, secretly willing his voice not to crack. "Gonna be sorry you did that."

"Nobody's coming for you, King." Asher cut across him, his voice cold, mocking. King stared back at him. The arrogant son of a bitch was enjoying this, getting back at the mortal who screwed his sister and lived to tell the tale.

Well, he had a little surprise for him.

In fact, he had a little surprise for all of them.

King swiveled his head, trying to ignore the strange grating sound his neck made when he moved it. He focused on Asher on his third attempt. "Sure they are. Left them a little trail of digital breadcrumbs."

Danica sneered at him. "Excuse me?"

King glowered up at her. Vampire bitch. He should've killed her when he had the chance. He wiped the trickle of blood from the corner of his mouth and sat up, pointedly ignoring Danica. "One thing you need to know about us Nightstalkers. When you join our club, you get a grab-bag of groovy gift items, including this nifty little tracking node surgically implanted in your body."

"Bullshit." Grimwood sneered, but there was uncertainty in his voice. King could sense it. Was it his imagination, or did this eighteen-stone vampire just glance towards the door like a scared little schoolgirl?

King flexed his wrists behind his back, testing his bonds again. "Scout's honor. One of us gets lost, the others just dial up the satellite and presto, instant cavalry."

Grimwood quickly glanced over to Danica. Some of his bravado was gone. Could this sniveling gimp be telling the truth?

Asher was unmoved. "He's bluffing."

Danica smiled at King, playing along. She didn't believe him for a second, but was interested to see how far he would take the lie. If she knew him as well as she thought she did, this could be entertaining. "Okay, King. Where did they put this tracking node of yours?"

King feigned a fit of coughing and then cleared his throat, motioning to Danica to move in closer. She leaned in towards him expectantly. She could smell the acid scent of fear and hate coming off his skin in waves. King coughed again, then whispered, "It's in my left ass-cheek."

WHACK! Danica slapped his face with the strength of a tree branch whipping in a hurricane. King's head snapped to the side, stars filling his vision. He shook his head like a dog, his voice gaining strength in his amusement. "Okay, it's in my right ass cheek."

Warming up, Danica slapped King again, knocking his head the other way. He couldn't talk to her like that any more. Not in front of the others.

King blinked, trying to focus on her, on anything. "No, seriously...' He considered his options for a moment, his face grave. Then he spat more blood at Danica, aiming for her expensive high-heeled shoes, and gave a wide grin. "It's in the meat of my butt, right below my 'Hello Kitty' tattoo."

This time Grimwood stepped in, swinging a Herculean punch at King's exposed midsection. There was a distinct cracking sound, and King blanched and collapsed forward, gasping for air.

After a moment, he rolled his head upwards, his face white beneath the spatters of blood. He sucked in a painful breath, seeing how far he could push Danica. "Pull down my tighty-whities," he whispered. "See for yourself."

Danica's bottom lip quivered, her eyes starting to sting. Somehow, manacled to a pillar and half-dead, King was showing her up in front of her the others.

"Enough!" she shouted. "It's not funny any more!"

Hanging from the pillar, King lifted his bruised, swollen face, staring up at Danica through blood-shrouded eyes. Danica took an involuntary step backwards as she saw the utter hatred in his eyes. "No, it's not, you horse-humping bitch." He winced as a cracked rib stabbed at him. "But it will be in a few seconds from now."

Danica coughed, trying to regain her composure. "And what happens then, lover?" she said icily.

"Hammer time."

The vampires stared at King in incomprehension.

A slow, knowing smile grew on King's face. "See, that tickle in your throat you're feeling right now?"

Danica coughed again. She blinked repeatedly, and lifted a hand to rub at her eyes. They were starting to sting, as though they were full of grit. She wiped her silk sleeve across them, before glancing over at the others, uncertain. Asher gave a little shake of his head and sniffed loudly at her, his eyes watering.

As one, they both looked towards Grimwood.

The side of his face was smoking.

King went on, his voice light and conversational. "That's atomized colloidal silver you're breathing. It's being pumped into the building's air conditioning system."

Danica stared at him in incomprehension. Then her consciousness expanded to take in the faint sounds of hissing coming from the wall-mounted air-conditioning unit. She looked up, dumbfounded, as the hissing seemed to swell in volume.

As one, the vampires began sneezing and gagging as their hyper-efficient bodies tried to process the silver dust particles lining the insides of their lungs. Asher collapsed against a wall, hyperventilating, while Grimwood clawed frantically at his face, choking and hacking.

With an effort, King pulled himself upright, his legs shaking with the strain. He watched in infinite satisfaction as Grimwood began shrieking, running around in little circles and coughing up blue-tinged flames.

King rested his head against the pillar and looked upwards. "Which means that the fat lady should be singing right about—"

The blacked-out skylight above them shattered.

"Now."

Blade crashed down through the broken skylight, his leather duster swirling around him. He dropped the fifteen feet to the ground and landed in an easy crouch next to King, shielding his face as broken glass poured down around him like silver rain. Then he thumped his gloved hands on the carpet and flipped over into a compact cartwheel, smacking his boot into Grimwood's smoldering face. The big vampire went down hard, unable to defend himself in his panic, dropping in a flail of arms and smoke.

King gave a whoop of delight. He had never seen the legendary Daywalker in action before, and now he had a ringside seat. He almost wished that he had a cigar and a bag of popcorn to finish the job off properly.

Almost immediately, Grimwood was on his feet again, more out of reflex than reason. He shook his head to clear it and lunged at Blade, bellowing like a wounded bear. The other vampires scattered as Blade leapt through the air and caught Grimwood in a flying rugby tackle. The two of them flew backwards, the force of Blade's charge sending them plummeting over the low railings into the lower half of the penthouse.

Taking advantage of the distraction, Danica grabbed Asher and dragged him after her as she fled through the deadly silver smoke, trying to hold her breath as she ran. They had to get out of here before the Daywalker came looking for them. She hoped that it would take Blade a long time to kill Grimwood, buying them enough time to get away.

The two vampires burst out into the darkened outer corridor and tore towards the stairs. As they ran, doors flew open down the length of the hallway and dozens of vampire guards stumbled out into their path, clutching at their throats and gagging. Alarm bells started ringing in every room as the building-wide intruder alarm was triggered, adding to the pandemonium.

In his room nearby, Drake's head swiveled around at the sound of the alarms. He was in the process of dressing, one hand encased in a burnished gauntlet retrieved from his burial armor. The rest of the armor was propped up on a stand nearby, casting eerie human-shaped shadows on the opposite wall.

Drake stretched luxuriously and buckled on his second metal gauntlet. There was only one person he knew of who could get past Danica's tight security. A thrill of anticipation ran through him. Hell, he could use a little workout before lunch. He reached for his sword and strode out of the room past the silent form of Zoe, who watched him go, biting down on her gag.

On the lower level of the penthouse, Blade battled furiously with Grimwood. The two Goliaths demolished furniture and shattered windows as they sparred, bare-fist fighting in a whirlwind of attack and counter attack. For his size, Grimwood was remarkably fleet-footed, striking at Blade again and again as the Daywalker drove him back, trying to find a gap in his defenses. The skin covering half of Grimwood's face was now almost completely dissolved by the effects of the caustic silver. Blade tried to keep his distance, his nose wrinkling in disgust at the stench of burned flesh.

As they sparred, a massed shout went up behind them. Blade spun around to see dozens of vampire reinforcements flooding into the room through the multiple doorways ringing the suite. The vampires were armed with an impromptu assortment of weapons: a bizarre mix of clubs, baseball bats and fire extinguishers.

Blade swore under his breath. He had been foolish to think that the place would be completely unguarded, but now he was beginning to doubt the sanity of their plan. In theory, it was simple. All they had to do was to get near enough to Drake for Abigail to fire the plague arrow at him, and then all of this would be over.

But there was a fat chance of that happening if he had to get through this lot first.

Blade renewed his assault on Grimwood, intent on getting the crazed vampire out of the way before the newcomers got near him. He only hoped that Abigail would get to King in time before one of these bloodsuckers decided to chow down on him. Another death amongst the Nightstalkers would be the last thing Abigail needed, and she was useless to him if she couldn't fight.

The first of the vampire guards reached him and Blade's mind clicked over into single-player mode, scanning the crowd around him to identify the weakest targets. An instant later his body was moving, flying away from Grimwood as he let rip with a powerful roundhouse kick that took out the three vampires nearest to him in a crunch of breaking bone. A skinny med-lab vampire darted up behind him and tried to jump on his back, swinging a chromed dagger, but Blade anticipated the move and reached behind him to grab the back of the vampire's shirt.

The dagger scraped harmlessly over Blade's armored chest plates as he propelled the unfortunate creature over his head, watching it land with a winded thump on the floor in front of him, knocking down another vampire in the process. The creature's eyes barely had time to widen in alarm as it saw the silver stake flying down towards its heart, then it exploded in a burst of black ash, setting fire to the creature pinned underneath.

The heat wave of the double death washed over Blade as he spun away, grappling with a young female vampire who was reaching for her pistol. Blade dispatched her as quickly as the first two, ripping a silver stake from the strap around his biceps and thumping it into her chest, cracking her breastbone. As the vampire shrieked, he grabbed her by the throat and twisted her head off as easily as if he was plucking a ripe fruit from a vine. Blood spurted. For a fraction of a second the vampire's face contorted with shock as she saw her own body fall to the ground minus a head. Then her vision faded to white as a wave of white-hot flames ripped through her senses, turning her head into a mini fireball.

Three other vampires quickly surged forwards to take her place. Blade flipped forward onto his hands and kicked mightily upwards, driving his heels with awesome force into the ribcages of two of the creatures who were slipping around in the decapitated vampire's blood. The vampires actually spun in mid-air before falling back to the ground, their upper torsos lying at an unnatural angle. They did not move again.

Exhaling sharply, Blade flipped himself to his feet and stared around him. A full ten seconds of fighting and he hadn't reduced the vampires' numbers in the slightest. If anything, there seemed to be even more of them than when he had started.

Blade could see at once that he was seriously outnumbered, but he did have one advantage over the vampire goons jostling forward to get a piece of him.

Two advantages, in fact...

Blade whipped out his twin Mach pistols from beneath his leather coat and sprayed the surging mass of vampires with two full clips of hot silver. The room filled with fire and ash as Blade's bullets hit home, taking down over a dozen vampires and blowing plate-sized craters in the walls. The vampires scattered, diving behind furniture and fleeing through the doorways, screaming in panic.

Meanwhile, up on the roof, Abigail peered down cautiously past the lip of the smashed skylight. She saw King bound to a pillar directly beneath her, and gave a gasp of relief. With a quick glance behind her, she tossed the end of a climbing rope through the broken plastic frame and quickly lowered herself to the ground. She rushed to King's side, wincing at the state he was in. Half of his face was one big swollen bruise, and the floor around him was soaked with blood.

She bit her lip in concern. "You alright?"

King peered up at her and shrugged, blood dripping from his face. "Nothing a hot tub of Bactine won't fix."

Abigail sighed with relief. King was fine.

She hit the release switch on his cuffs and they sprang open with a clunk. As King climbed to his feet, Abigail handed him a pistol and a clip of Sundog bullets, then put a hand on his shoulder, her face grave as she prepared herself for the worst. "Zoe?"

King shook his head, rubbing at his bruised wrists. "Drake's got her."

Abigail blew out the breath that she didn't realize she had been holding. Then she gave King a brief nod of thanks and strode out of the nearest door.

She had to find Zoe. She only prayed that she wasn't too late.

Behind her, King stretched his arms out in front of him, trying to get some feeling back into his hands. Then he tucked the pistol into his belt holster and ran after Abigail, trying not to limp.

Abigail entered the darkened hallway outside the penthouse. Glancing around her, she slipped her chrome earbuds back into her ears and cranked up the volume on her MP3 player, tucking the wires beneath the shoulder straps of her bow holster. As the opening bars of Fluke's track "Absurd" thudded into her brain, she unclipped the UV arc from her belt and expanded the telescoping arms with a flick of her wrist. Her senses went into overdrive as she began jogging lightly down the corridor, scanning every doorway, every shadow for signs of possible danger.

After a few hundred meters a vampire tore around the corner and nearly collided with her, retching and clawing at its eyes in a frenzy, smoke pouring from its mouth. Abigail decapitated it with a single diagonal sweep of her UV arc and was on the move again before the body had a chance to hit the ground.

Within moments, more vampires poured out into the corridor ahead and began stumbling towards her. At the sight of them, Abigail's vision narrowed to a single, deadly tunnel, a black fog with a red crosshair at the center. The beat of the music flowed down her spine, hotwiring her reflexes and wrapping her in syncopated warmth as she slashed and kicked her way through the first of the creatures.

Moving into close-combat range, Abigail hit a scary looking female vampire at full speed, stunning it with a single sledgehammer blow to the solar plexus before whipping out her UV arc and slicing its head off. Abigail watched in satisfaction as the severed head bounced off a wall and exploded, blowing a hole in the brickwork. The rest of the creature's body melted away to reveal a momentary, chilling glimpse of gleaming bone beneath. Then that too burst into ash.

Abigail rounded off her sweep by swinging the arc downward and spinning in a full circle, slicing three more vampires into two screaming halves. Then she emptied her rapid-fire stake dispenser into the mass of vampires clogging the corridor ahead of her. Her eyes glinted as she was sucked into a machine-like trance of killing, losing herself into her own live-action shoot-'em-up.

As the dispenser clicked onto empty, Abigail pressed a tab on the side of the gun and ejected the clip. Without missing a beat, she reached down to her belt where a backup was secured. She slammed it into the gun chamber and cocked back the hammer, chambering the next batch, and moved onwards.

Back in the penthouse, Blade battled on, surrounded by a slowly growing mountain of blazing and bleeding bodies. He was already out of ammo, and the vampires were now advancing on him, one by one. Blade dropped to the floor just in time as a beefy vampire dressed in a guard's uniform leaped over his head with a kamikaze yell, then used the move to his advantage, performing a low sweep-kick at ground level that took down two more vampires, snapping their shin bones like breadsticks. Three more instantly sprung up in their place, wielding baseball bats.

This was no good. He couldn't go on like this.

Time to get nasty.

Reaching behind him, Blade unsheathed his sword in a sliding hiss of glinting metal. Three feet of springy titanium rested lightly in his grip, vibrating faintly from the power of the Daywalker's heartbeat thudding beneath his skin.

The telltale click of a safety catch made Blade spin around, using his superhuman speed to deflect the gunshot with the flat of his sword. He then used the hilt to parry two combatants who came at him wielding clubs, screaming at him in Japanese. His sword sliced through the air in a figure of eight and their bodies hit the ground, blood spraying over him like warm rain.

Over by the door, Grimwood dragged himself out of the melee and glared back into the room, watching in fury as Blade sliced his way through his entire night shift of staff. Despite their extensive combat training, the vampires were falling beneath Blade's sword like saplings before a chainsaw-crazy lumberjack. Blade was still outnumbered, but the vampires were all working as individuals, scarcely bothering to check if the way was clear before leaping at Blade with their poorly chosen weapons, eager to get themselves a nip of Daywalker blood.

Useless! They were being picked off like flies!

Grimwood gritted his steel-capped teeth and reached behind him, where an ancient battleaxe was bolted to the wall.

If you wanted the job done properly...

With a snarl of rage, Grimwood wrenched the axe off the wall in a shower of plaster, raising it high over his head as he plunged back into the scrum. Fighting his way through to Blade, he ducked down behind the vampires surrounding him, biding his time. A vampire fell in front of him, dirty yellow sparks spurting from its chest, opening up a clear path to Blade. The hybrid freak had his back turned!

Grimwood saw his opening and he took it, charging forwards and swinging his axe down towards Blade's head with a bellow of triumph.

But Blade was no longer there.

Grimwood blinked stupidly and watched in dismay as one of his own vampire henchmen fell apart in front of his eyes, sliced clean in two by his own axe.

Blade jumped back up as quickly as he had ducked down and advanced on Grimwood, slashing and hacking to make some space around him. The last of the vampires fell less than ten seconds later, joining its comrades on the floor. Blood ran down Blade's sword, staining his gloved hands, but his grip didn't falter.

Then they were once again face-to-face.

With a savage war cry, Grimwood swung his axe down at Blade in a crushing blow. Blade brought his sword up, stopping Grimwood's axe in a shower of white sparks. Then Blade shifted his grip and hooked his sword under the head of the axe. With a savage twist, he flicked the weapon from Grimwood's hands.

Lunging forwards, Blade swung his sword around in a superhumanly fast arc, the blade thrumming through the air. The diamond-ground edge struck Grimwood's midriff with a dull, wet sound, biting into the bigger vampire's waist.

Before Grimwood had time to register what had happened, Blade flexed his powerful biceps, wrenching the sword out the other side of the big vampire.

Grimwood fell to the ground in two halves.

Blade peered down at the gruesome remains of the felled vampire, waiting for him to combust.

But nothing happened.

Then the top half of Grimwood's body twitched, and his eyes opened as he jerked back to life with a gasp. Throwing out his tattooed arms, Grimwood braced his fingers on the marble tiles and pushed himself off the ground in a ghastly parody of a press-up, pulling himself upright. Snarling in defiance, he started dragging what was left of his torso forward like a giant spider, his black, glinting eyes fixed on

Blade. Rearing backwards, Grimwood bunched his muscular arms and sprang up towards the Daywalker, opening his mouth wide to bite...

With a look of profound distaste, Blade caught the thrashing half-vampire by the throat. Holding him as far away from his face as possible, Blade drove his silver-plated sword through Grimwood's chest, puncturing his heart in a single powerful movement.

Grimwood gave a screech of frustrated rage as he felt fire burst from his chest. He reached out towards the Daywalker with disintegrating hands, his claws raking the air. An instant later, the superheated flames roared upwards, engulfing him in a rush of liquid fire.

Blade released the blazing corpse. It dropped to the ground, twitching and jerking. The impact jolted Grimwood's carbonized flesh clean off his bones, leaving behind a charred skeleton that slowly pitched forwards and shattered, showering across the blood-stained floor.

Only then did Grimwood's struggles cease.

There was a sad little clatter as two steel-capped fangs fell out of the dust cloud, landing at Blade's feet and rolling towards him like marbles. Blade gazed down at them thoughtfully. Then he tensed as a sudden cold wave passed over his body, making the hairs on the back of his neck stand up.

Blade knew what that feeling meant: someone was watching him.

Slowly, Blade turned around and looked upwards to see the dark figure of Drake standing on the gantry.

Waiting.

* * *

Outside, Abigail ducked into the thirtieth room in a row, her eyes scanning the darkness with frantic hope. She had tried every single room on the floor and they were all deserted. Her blood chilled at the thought of what might have happened to Zoe.

As Abigail started forwards into the room, two vampire guards turned towards her with a shout. Abigail flung a pair of silver stakes at them, scarcely needing to aim. The guards crumpled to the ground before flying apart in twin whirlwinds of ash.

As the dust cloud settled, Abigail saw the tiny form of Zoe sitting huddled in the corner, her little body wrapped in thick chains. She was alive.

A wave of relief broke over Abigail. Hurrying over to Zoe, Abigail swiftly located the padlock clamped around the chains that bound her. Drawing her e-pistol, she motioned to the little girl to put her hands over her ears, and blasted the lock off. With a cry, Zoe leapt to her feet and threw her arms around Abigail, hugging her so hard that her entire body shook.

After a moment, Abigail stood up and took Zoe's hand, leading her towards the door. "Come on, hon. Lets get you out of here."

Down the corridor, King stumbled out of the medi-lab, pulling the crumpled remains of his shirt back on. Damn, it was cold in here. Hadn't vampires ever heard of central heating? Forget finding Danica. He'd get the vampire bitch later. He had to find Abigail and get the hell out of this place before they all died of hypothermia.

King limped down the gunmetal grey corridor, picking up speed as the feeling slowly came back into his cramped limbs in a painful rush of black pins and needles. He winced, rubbing at his wrists. He hoped that Abigail would appreciate the sacrifices he had made for her, getting all bloody and sweaty like this. Knowing her, she would probably just pat him on the head and give him his next assignment. He wondered how long it had taken her to even notice that he'd gone.

As he rounded the corner, a loud growl came from behind him.

Slowly and extremely carefully, King turned around.

Pac Man scampered around the corner, his tiny black claws clattering on the tiles. At the sight of King, the mutant dog's eyes narrowed and his lips drew back from his teeth as though pulled up by strings.

Swearing, King backed away, his eyes flitting around for something to use as a weapon. This mutt really had it in for him. If only he had his squeaky ball-on-a-string with him...

He carefully edged around the dog, crouching low as though riding a surfboard. He had read somewhere that you shouldn't make eye contact with a growling dog, in case it though you were trying to challenge it.

Or was that with cats?

Bugger it. He was going to have to make a run for it. It shouldn't be difficult to outrun this little canine pipsqueak.

As King tensed himself for flight, Pac Man moved forwards. Two identical Rotweillers stepped around the corner behind him, like evil twins.

King stared in horror. The dogs were built like tanks, square-shouldered and heavily muscled. They growled at him, the sound so low that it seemed to come up through the ground, making King's breastbone vibrate. Their hyper-alert brown eyes locked in on King's face as though it were a target, and their lips drew back, baring row after row of huge, scythe-like teeth, dripping with strings of bloody drool.

King's mouth dropped open.

"Fuck. Me. Sideways."

As one, the three dogs broke formation and hurled themselves at King, barking like crazy as their snouts cracked open and flowered apart, ready to engulf him...

EIGHTEEN

Blade left a sea of still, broken bodies behind him as he climbed the winding steel staircase that led to the upper gantry of the vast atrium.

At the top, the tall, dark figure of Drake stood.

As Blade watched, Drake pulled out a huge burnished iron sword with a flourish. He gave it a nonchalant spin, letting it catch the light. Then he touched the tip to the floor in front of him.

A challenge.

"Are you ready to die, Blade?" Drake called out to him. His voice was low and sibilant, like the purr of a leopard, and yet it seemed to fill the entire chamber, echoing off the walls and raising strange harmonics in the air.

Blade climbed the last step and stood before Drake, feeling a strange sense of destiny. He had killed thousands of vampires in his time, but this was something different. This was Dracula, the ultimate vampire. All the vampires in existence owed their dirty little undead lives to him, the bastard children of a tyrant whose unseen reign had cut a swathe through history, destroying every life it touched.

Blade growled low in his throat at the thought. It was Drake's fault that he had been born a monster, hating what he was and yet unable to do anything about it. It was Drake's fault that he had spent his entire life fighting vampires, hacking and slashing until his fingers bled, knowing that however many he killed today, tomorrow there would be a hundred more to take their place. And it was Drake's fault that his mother was dead, along with Whistler, Sommerfield, Dex, Hedges, and so many more.

And through all of this, he had been powerless to do anything about it.

Until now.

Blade glowered at Drake. "Been ready since the day I was born, motherfucker."

Drake smiled. "Then allow me to accommodate you."

Without hesitation, Drake leapt into the air, performing a perfectly executed back flip off the balcony. He landed effortlessly forty feet down and raised his eyes up to Blade expectantly.

Steeling himself, Blade rushed to the railing and jumped down after him, drawing his own sword in mid-air in a flash of bright metal. He landed directly in front of Drake in a perfect fighter's crouch and straightened, raising his sword. The two warriors faced each other, swords ready, eyes locked, their stances frozen in the classic pose of the samurai.

The message was clear.

Whoever moves first, loses.

Drake cranked his preternatural senses up to the max, studying Blade minutely, gauging the Daywalker's strength. He could hear the tiny plinking sounds as the floorboards under Blade's feet flexed back into shape after the force of his landing and the cellular creaking of the bones in his legs decompressing. Despite hacking his way through an entire legion of Danica's staff, Blade's breathing was steady and his gaze was clear. Drake could smell thirty different types of blood mingling with the sweat that clung to Blade's Olympian physique. There was no fear there, only adrenaline and carefully controlled rage.

A muscle twitched in Blade's leg as a bruised tendon complained. Drake saw the Daywalker's attention waiver for a split second.

He attacked.

Blade felt the movement of Drake's sword before his eye had even registered that it had begun to move. Blade deflected the blisteringly fast swing with a powerful upward strike that made the muscles in his arm quiver. The two swords met in the middle in a blinding shower of sparks.

The battle was joined.

Grunting with effort, Blade twisted his sword away from Drake's with a squeal of metal on metal, the joints in his wrist and elbow stinging from the aftereffects of the mammoth blow. Sweeping around, he advanced on Drake, his eyes glinting with anticipation.

He had been waiting his entire life for this.

Blade parried a second deadly blow, then another, and another, his sword moving faster and faster, until it was clanging and singing like a blacksmith's hammer on sheet metal. Blade's body became a blur of kinetic motion as he cut, slashed and stabbed at the vampire king, driving him back. Drake was fast, but Blade had fought fast opponents before. His mind hummed as he parried Drake's superhumanly fast strikes, glorying in the strength of his muscles, the steely power of his limbs as they whipped and cracked around him like hydraulic pistons. He concentrated every fiber of his being on beating Drake back, using an entire lifetime's supply of hatred to fuel his attack, an electric adrenaline surge driving him to attack again and again, not allowing Drake a single instant to recover.

Drake spun away and snarled at Blade, defensively swinging his sword up in a spinning strike that should have impaled the Daywalker through the heart, but Blade anticipated the blow even before it came and blocked it with a blindingly fast diagonal slash that almost knocked Drake's sword from his hand. Drake had to duck to avoid being decapitated as Blade carried the blow through with a shout, his super-hardened sword blade burying itself deeply in the steel column behind him.

Sweating, Blade tugged hard on his sword.

It was stuck.

Shit.

Drake straightened up behind him, growling. Recovering from Blade's onslaught in seconds, he whirled his sword downwards with inhuman speed, aiming to slice the Daywalker's hands from his body.

At the last possible instant, Blade yanked his sword out of the column and whipped it up in a sweeping arc, blocking Drake's strike and locking swords with him at close range. For a heartbeat, the pair were face-to-face.

Blade's body thrummed with tension as he struggled to hold off Drake, his arms shaking with the effort as he felt the insane strength behind the master vampire's sword. He glared into Drake's reptilian eyes and saw the contempt lurking there, as though he were insect that had to be crushed.

In an instant, Blade realized what the look meant.

The motherfucker thought that he was going to win.

Blade felt a tide of black fury swamp him. He bared his teeth at Drake and snarled at him like an animal, his razor-sharp canines glinting in the artificial light. Then he savagely twisted his sword free with a powerful upward jerk, deliberately slicing open Drake's cheek in the process.

The wound was insignificant, but it stung in more ways than one. Drake screeched in rage as he flung himself away from Blade, flipping himself up onto a high ledge overlooking the atrium. Balancing on the ledge like a giant gargoyle, Drake touched his fingers to the cut and licked mournfully at the lost blood.

Then he swiveled his head towards Blade, his face contorting into a rictus of hate. He felt his features shifting as the cartilage beneath his skin popped and clicked, forming ridges on his brow and cheekbones and pushing out needle-like spines along the length of his backbone.

For a moment, Blade got a chilling glimpse of Drake's true form.

Drake regained control of himself with an effort. His spines retracted with a snap, the skin around them closing up like flowing water.

With a growl, Drake dived down towards Blade, raking his claws across the Daywalker's face in retaliation. Before Blade could bring his sword to bear, Drake whipped around and knocked him sprawling across the atrium with a savage, pile-driver blow. As Blade struggled to right himself, Drake crossed the room in a single bound and grabbed him by the throat, his fingers digging into Blade's windpipe.

As Blade fought to free himself, Drake's fangs began to elongate, pushing out of his skull with a soft whisper, like the sound of razor blades scraping across flesh. Hauling Blade upright, Drake sunk his fangs into the Daywalker's shoulder and bit down deeply, crushing sinew and bone in his powerful jaws.

Blade screamed.

The echoes of Blade's scream resonated through the hallways of the Phoenix Towers. Three floors away, King redoubled his pace, homing in on the sound. He barreled through the dimly lit corridors, searching desperately for an open door, a fire escape, some way of escaping from the maddened hellhounds currently chasing him.

There was none.

King risked a glance over his shoulder. The freaky mutts were gaining on him, hurtling along the corridor towards him without the slightest hint of tiring.

King swore colorfully and drove himself onwards, ignoring the burning ache in his legs as his bruised muscles complained. He had to be near the atrium now. He was sure that it was on this level. If he could just reach Blade or Abigail they could distract the dogs for long enough for him to dig out his gun and blast the freaky fuckers to oblivion, where they belonged.

Legs pumping, King rounded a corner.

Dead end.

King's mind went into overdrive, scanning the short corridor before him. Five feet in front of him were two plate glass windows with a whole lot of empty space beyond. The corridor's walls were completely blank.

No doors, nothing.

He was trapped.

There was the sound of clattering claws behind him as the vampire dogs closed in for the kill, snapping and barking at each other in their efforts to get to King first.

Glancing upwards in a frenzy, King saw a water pipe running along the ceiling above him. He launched himself upwards, grabbing onto the cold metal of the pipe and swinging himself up with all his strength.

The vampire dogs plunged onwards, unable to stop, and crashed through the plate glass windows. Howling, they dropped like stones, betrayed by their own supernatural momentum. They plunged twenty stories downwards into the traffic-clogged intersection below, the Pomeranian yipping all the way down. They were quickly swallowed up by the river of speeding cars.

King spun around the pipe and dropped back down to the floor, cackling to himself. Man, he was good! Jackie Chan himself couldn't have done it better.

He dusted off his hands triumphantly, and turned.

Oh, crap...

Wham! King was hit full in the chest by a hundred pounds of maddened mutant Rottweiler. He flew backwards, limbs cartwheeling, and cracked his head on the glass-covered windowsill before falling to the ground in a heap. His pistol clattered to the floor and slid away from him across the tiles.

Gasping, King raised his head to see one of the Rottweiler twins stalking towards him, hackles raised, lips drawn back from its wickedly curving teeth. King felt the heat of the dog's fetid breath blast over him, evaporating the sweat on his face. Somehow, the vampire mutt had managed to stop in time, avoiding the fate of its siblings.

Time seemed to freeze as they stared at one another.

King's gaze ticked sideways to where his pistol lay several yards from him.

The spell shattered.

The dog lunged at him, its attack all the more terrifying for it being completely silent. King threw his arms up to protect his face as the vampire dog hit him like a ton of wet, furry bricks, crushing him back against the wall. He yelled at the top of his lungs as he saw its mouth open wide, and grabbed the mutt by the scruff of its neck, digging his fingers deeply into the creature's skin in an effort to prevent it from ripping his face off. With his other hand, he groped blindly for his dropped pistol.

The Rottweiler twisted and bucked, jaws snapping closer and closer to King's neck as his grip pulled away, inch by inch. King yelled out in frustration, letting go of the dog's neck and slamming his elbow into its unprotected throat.

The Rottweiler yelped in pain and recoiled, buying King enough time to curl his knees up to his chest. As the dog lunged for a second time, King jammed his booted heels up into the dog's soft belly, bracing a foot either side of the hard bone of the creature's pelvis. Pushing with all his might, he slowly lifted the heavy animal off him.

The vampire dog fought back with incredible strength, lunging again and again, its ebony claws scrabbling on the ground as it fought for purchase. The creature was baying now, in one continuous, ear-splitting sound. King saw the metallic brown of the dog's eyes start to flood with red blood as its snout split apart, ready to feed.

It was now or never.

With a yell, King shoved the dog backwards with all his might and made a grab for his pistol. His fingers closed around the barrel and he rolled over onto his back. He dug the gun into the Rottweiler's furry chest as the vampire dog pounced on him, its teeth flashing down towards his throat...

King pulled the trigger and the Rotweiller exploded in a cloud of thick, choking ash.

As the dust settled, King opened his eyes and spat a mouthful of burnt dog hair onto the floor. He sat up and shook his head.

"Bad dog."

* * *

Several floors down, Abigail crept out onto the gantry of the atrium. Zoe was clinging to her hand, her knuckles white with fear as she listened to the sounds coming from below.

Abigail scanned the area, looking for a safe hiding place for the little girl. She settled on a deep alcove and motioned to Zoe, indicating that she should hide inside. Zoe ducked into the shadows and Abigail reached inside and smoothed her hair back off her face, smiling reassuringly at her. Then she dug a hand into her own belt and slipped a silver stake into Zoe's tiny hand. Just in case.

Then Abigail rushed to the handrail, all pretence of calm gone.

Down below, Blade and Drake whirled around the room like a couple of living tornadoes, smashing furniture and cracking walls in their titanic struggle. Abigail saw that Drake's fangs were locked in Blade's shoulder, and the pair wrestled like fighting dogs as Blade fought to pull Drake off him. The Daywalker's face was gaunt with pain, a long streak of dark blood pouring down his shoulder.

Abigail's heart missed a beat. Here was her chance. Drake was preoccupied with fighting Blade, completely unaware of her presence. She would probably never get a better shot than this.

Scrambling to find a vantage point, Abigail pulled the Plague arrow out of its refrigerated capsule and nocked it into her bow with trembling fingers. Leaning back against the cool stone of a pillar, she tried to line up a shot. She sighted on Drake's shoulder and drew back the high tensile string, holding her breath.

This was it.

But in that instant, Blade swung around, his arm tightening around Drake's shoulders, blocking Abigail's view. With a grunt of exasperation, Abigail shifted position and tried again, this time aiming at Drake's exposed thigh.

The same thing happened again.

It was no good. The titans were moving too swiftly for her to stick to a target. She couldn't get a clear shot, and she couldn't risk hitting Blade.

She needed to approach this from a different angle, and quickly, because from the looks of things, Blade was running out of time.

Oblivious to the presence of Abigail, Blade wrestled with Drake, unable to disengage the vampire's fangs from his shoulder. Drake growled, blood bubbling through his lips as his inch-long fangs sunk deeper into Blade's flesh, locking tightly around the tendons in his shoulder. The harder Blade tried to pull him away, the deeper Drake bit.

Gasping, Blade reached into his bandolier with fumbling fingers and managed to pull out a stake. Wrenching his shoulder to one side, Blade spun the stake around and slammed it as hard as he could into Drake's unprotected ear canal. Drake gave an ungodly shriek and released him, Blade rolled to one side and clapped a hand to his shoulder to stem the flow of blood. He threw a desperate glance across the chamber. If only he could get to his sword...

Drake tore the stake from his head with a howl, smashing it against the wall in fury. He came at Blade full bore, swinging his gauntleted fist towards Blade's head in a murderous blow.

Somehow, Blade managed to duck. Drake's fist went straight through the wall behind, puncturing a steel heating pipe. A thick cloud of high-pressure stream spewed out of the wall. With a guttural cry of rage, Drake reached inside the wall cavity and snagged a fistful of the piping. Flexing his powerful arm, Drake snapped an eight-foot section of metal pipe off the wall as though it were candy cane.

Before Blade could roll out of the way, Drake swung the makeshift club around and cracked the Daywalker across the ribs with it. Blade gasped, blood spurting from his lips. Drake swung the pipe a second time, smashing a hole in the floor as Blade dragged himself frantically out of his way. Driven into a berserker rage, Drake lashed out again and again with the pipe, destroying everything in his path, aiming to crush the Daywalker to bleeding pulp.

Up above, Abigail pelted along the gallery catwalk, desperate to find a vantage point to get a clear shot from. The room rang with a din of echoing crashes as Drake struck at Blade again and again, smashing through glass and steel partitions in his fury. The expensive atrium was a complete ruin, the ashen remains of the slaughtered vampires almost completely buried beneath a sea of rubble.

Even to Abigail, it was clear that the Daywalker was tiring. She watched as he dived out of Drake's way, blood loss and exhaustion slowing his movements. His sword was useless against the destructive range of the pipe, but he kept moving, ducking and dodging, winding Drake into a greater and greater frenzy. Drake screamed in fury as he missed Blade for the tenth time in a row, swiping the top off a priceless marble statue in frustration.

Abigail knew she had to move fast. It would just take one good swing with that pipe and Blade's skull would be crushed like an eggshell.

Panicking, Abigail looked up to see a series of old lighting gantries that spanned the length of the atrium ceiling. An idea hit her. Replacing the Plague arrow in her quiver, she strapped her bow to her back. Jumping lightly onto the handrail, Abigail balanced precariously for a moment, checking the distance with a practiced marksman's eye.

Then she launched herself out into space.

There was a moment of vertigo as she flew outwards across the void. Then her grasping fingertips caught hold of one of the gantry crosspieces. She swung her legs like a pendulum and released her original hold on the crosspiece, grabbing onto the next one. Swiftly gaining confidence, she swung from handhold to handhold like a monkey, moving towards the center of the room. She tried very hard not to think about the forty-foot drop beneath her, concentrating instead on maintaining a regular rhythm as she swung.

It wasn't that hard, really, just like swinging on the hanging rings in a playground.

There was a loud bang and sparks exploded from the rail in front of her. Abigail jumped, nearly missing her next handhold. She dangled there for a moment, breathing heavily, and looked downwards. Two vampire guards stood below, firing up at her with their pistols, trying to pick her off.

Abigail ducked and twisted in midair, unable to escape as bullets zinged around her. She was out in the open, completely exposed. There was a good twenty-yard gap separating her from the other side of the gantry. She would never make it in time.

Abigail sucked in a breath, ready to make a swinging leap for the next handhold. The blood-suckers would have to put a bullet through every single part of her body before she would quit. Too much depended on this for her to give up now, just to save her own hide.

Then the shooting stopped as suddenly as they had started. Abigail dangled one-handed for a moment, nerves jangling, then risked a look downwards to see the two vampires blow up in an explosion of blue light.

Abigail flicked her gaze to the doorway to see...

"King!" Abigail had never been so glad to see anyone in her life. The vampire hunter stood on the upper gantry, laying down cover fire so that Abigail could continue her mission.

Her guardian angel.

But then...

Abigail shouted out a warning, but she was too late. A shadow loomed behind King as Danica stepped out behind him, her skin smoking from the effects of the atomized silver.

With a snarl of rage, the vampiress tackled King, wrestling him to the floor.

King struggled against her, but he was already exhausted, whereas Danica was fresh and out for blood. A human was no match for a vampire, even at their best, and from the look on King's face he knew it. As Abigail watched helplessly, he struggled in her grip and swung up his e-pistol, trying to get a clear shot at Danica's face.

But she blocked his move with the ball of her hand and grabbed the gun by the barrel, twisting it from his grip. In one fluid movement she ejected the clip from the stock, spilling King's Sundog bullets all over the floor. She kicked them out of his reach.

Smirking, Danica tossed the empty pistol aside with a clatter and reached for King. Grabbing the bloodied vampire hunter by his collar, she wrenched back his head and unsheathed her fangs...

NINETEEN

Abigail dangled from the light fitting, forty feet above the atrium. Her head swam as she tried to call up new reserves of strength. She blinked the sweat out of her eyes and glanced down.

Big mistake.

She flexed her knees and began swinging her body back and forth like a pendulum, every muscle in her body aching with the strain. She had to get to the other side and save King before Danica finished him off, once and for all.

Abigail stopped. What about her plague arrow? What if Drake killed Blade and vanished, never to be seen again?

Abigail hesitated, her face twisting in an agony of indecision. She felt her hand beginning to slip as her arm shook with the strain of supporting her entire body weight. With a start, Abigail reached out and managed to grab onto another crosspiece, hanging between the two of them as she got her breath back. The action drove tiny sharp splinters of metal through her leather gloves into the pads of her fingers, and blood mingled with the sweat already running down her arms, slicking her grip.

But before she could move any further, another shot rung out, pinging off the ceiling above her.

Abigail twisted her head downwards. What now?

She cried out in pain as a second bullet thudded into the flesh of her shoulder, spinning her around and nearly making her lose her grip. She caught herself just in time, breathing heavily. The bullet had only grazed her shoulder, but a wave of shock buzzed up Abigail's arm, instantly numbing her hand. Gritting her teeth, she swung herself forward as hard as she could and managed to get a grip on the next crosspiece with her other hand. Sweating, she hazarded a look downward.

Asher stood on the gantry, pointing his old-fashioned rifle up at her. As Abigail watched helplessly, he carefully sighted down the barrel, lining her frantically swinging form up with his electronic crosshairs. He moved the muzzle of the gun a fraction of an inch forwards to anticipate her forward movement.

Then he squeezed the trigger.

Over on the other side of the metal walkway, King fell to the floor as Danica laid into him, felling him with a rapid-fire volley of uppercuts. He'd managed to block her initial attack with a vicious head-butt that earned him a howl of rage and a bone-cracking slap. Now she had him by the throat and was beating the life out of him.

Rolling over onto his back, King wiped his rapidly swelling face with a hand and spat out the cracked remains of a tooth. The lights above him seemed to spin as he tried to focus on Danica. She loomed above him, her eyes shining with anticipation, rolling up her sleeves as though she were just getting started.

King groaned and climbed to his feet, weaving like a drunk. "No offence, Danica, but I've wanted to kill you since the moment we slept together."

Danica raised an eyebrow. "I was that bad, huh?"

King feinted a clumsy punch at her in reply, then lunged downwards and scooped his gun off the floor as she danced backwards, out of reach. He pointed the weapon in her general direction. Danica laughed.

"No bullets in your gun, King."

King smiled a wide and bloody smile. He clicked a button down on the side of the gun, deactivating the magnetic safety lock. Then he straightened up and looked at Danica, his eyes bright with hatred. "Yeah, but here's the real beauty. These babies can be triggered remotely."

Before Danica could move, King pulled the trigger on his e-pistol.

Down on the floor, the Sundog bullets activated with a click and a whine. Within seconds they were glowing white-hot. They exploded, drenching the gantry walkway with a blinding blue flash of UV light.

Danica threw up her hands with a shriek, trying to shield her face from the lethal glow. She wasn't quite quick enough. The smell of burning flesh filled the air and she screamed in surprise and pain. Spinning away from King, she stumbled off through a doorway, smoke billowing from her face and hands.

King let her go. He knew that she must die, but not like this. He wanted her to suffer first. He pulled his last Sundog bullet from its clip and activated it with a flick of his finger, and then loaded it into his pistol.

He would get the vampire bitch later.

This one was for her bastard brother.

Crawling across the breadth of the gantry, King steadied his bloodied hand on the metal railing and aimed at Asher, who was over on the other side, pointing his rifle up at Abigail and firing again and again. Without hesitation, King pulled the trigger.

The Sundog screamed across the atrium, striking Asher dead center in his open mouth. The impact knocked him off his feet, sending him sprawling across the chamber. Asher dropped his gun and clawed frantically at his face, a thin trickle of blood spilling from his lips.

Then, the bullet exploded. Fiery blue light poured from his mouth and eye sockets as his head filled with the deadly UV light. Asher pitched forwards, shrieking and jerking as his skull collapsed inwards and exploded in a mini blast-wave of flame. His headless corpse fell forwards and plunged over the gantry railing, burning up as it fell to the ground.

King sank to his knees in relief.

Job done.

But the war wasn't yet won. Down below them in the atrium, Blade was in the process of dying. Despite the Daywalker's best efforts, Drake was throwing him around the atrium like a rag doll.

Blade sailed up into the air, cracking his head on the underside of the metal walkway before falling thirty feet back to the ground. His senses blazed as the shock of the impact blasted down his spinal column, whiting out the pain of his bruised and torn flesh. Every cell in his body felt jarred out of place,and a deadly exhaustion clouded his mind, making it difficult for him to think, but he knew he had to keep moving.

Groaning, Blade gathered what little strength he had left and tried to roll over onto his side. His body rebelled, a powerful quiver of exhaustion running through him as his abused muscles complained. He felt like his body was moving through thick, clinging tar. The icy throb of his wounded shoulder had faded to a dull ache, but bright blood continued to pump from the deep puncture wounds, sapping his strength and slicking his body armor with warm, sticky fluid.

Blade knew he couldn't take much more of this.

As he struggled to rise, Drake dropped his pipe and pounced on him, dragging him to his feet and slamming him back against a wall. The force of the impact knocked Blade's breath out of him. He was unable to muster the strength to defend himself as Drake hammered a punch into his stomach and then a second at his face, bouncing his head off the wall. Blade's vision filled with blinding flashes as Drake hit him again and again, venting his fury on the struggling Daywalker.

In desperation, Blade lashed out and dug his fingers into Drake's eyes. The vampire roared in pain and threw up his hands, knocking Blade away. Taking step backwards, Drake swung both of his ironclad fists down at the ground, Hulk-style, shattering an entire section of the limestone flooring in a primal display of fury and brute strength. Tiles jumped upwards as the seismic shock wave of the impact rocked the floor, sending waves of two-foot stone slabs flipping up into the air.

Blade was knocked off his feet by the impact. He crashed down onto his back as the floor disintegrated around him. He saw a bright star as his head hit the marble floor and the room blurred and swam around him. Despite his agony, Blade's mind was floating, disengaged from the pain, and he realized with an odd sense of calm that he was going into shock. Black speckles flooded the edge of his dimming vision as darkness threatened to steal what little consciousness he still had left.

Blade took a shuddering breath, fighting to stay conscious as Drake stepped towards him, wielding the leg of a broken marble statue like a baseball bat.

There was only one thing on Blade's mind.

Where the hell was Abigail?

Above them, Abigail swung her lithe body forwards, trying to ignore the pain of her wounded shoulder. Reaching the middle of the atrium at last, she hooked her knees over the central crosspiece in the ceiling, leaving her arms free.

Hanging upside down, she reached behind her and removed her bow from the leather sheath on her back, intent on her mission. There was no going back now. She transferred the bow to her other hand and silently unfurled it. The movement caused blood from the bullet wound in her shoulder to run down her collarbone in a tickling line, dripping into her eyes. Abigail blinked in irritation, raising a hand to wipe the stinging liquid away. But as she did so, the strap slackened on her quiver and a number of arrows slid out, flashing past her before she could stop them.

Abigail grabbed at them in panic, barely managing to snag the larger plague arrow as it tumbled past her. Abigail froze, the arrow clutched tightly in her grip as her pulse pounded in her ears. Sweat ran down her brow as she squeezed her eyes closed, trying to shut out the thought of what might have happened had she dropped it.

A moment later she unfroze, moving in slow motion as she carefully tucked the remaining arrows into her shoulder strap. Drake hadn't seemed to notice the sound of the dropping arrows, intent on his battle with Blade. Abigail nocked the plague arrow into her bow and took a careful breath. She only had one shot at this, and she was going to have to take it hanging upside down.

Blinking blood out of her eyes, she tracked Drake's movements below. She just needed to wait for Drake to turn towards her now, exposing his unprotected chest.

Abigail watched the battle rage on below with bated breath, flinching as Drake lifted Blade off the floor only to slam him headfirst onto the broken tiles. The Daywalker was moving sluggishly now, bathed in blood, his body scarcely moving. As Abigail watched, Drake slammed his shoulder once, twice, three times into the support column above Blade's fallen body, snapping it in two. Abigail muffled a cry of horror as an entire section of the metal walkway collapsed, crashing down on top of Blade's fallen body.

This evidently wasn't enough of a finale for Drake.

Snarling, he leapt on top of the mountain of debris and pulled Blade out of the rubble, dangling his limp form above the floor like a shark on a hook. With a savage grin, Drake head-butted Blade, breaking his nose. Blood spurted and Drake howled in triumph as the body of his foe twitched and shook, unwillingly dragged back into consciousness.

Drake spotted Blade's sword lying on the ground several feet away and let the Daywalker drop as he scooped it up. His eyes glinted as he swung it at Blade in a savage blow clearly meant to slice him in half.

Blade's eyes flickered open at the sound of the sword—his sword—descending, his body jump-started, rolling heavily to the side as the sword buried itself in the debris.

Hissing, Drake wrenched the sword free and swung again.

This time, Blade wasn't quick enough. The sword caught him a glancing blow in the ribs and sliced cleanly through his Kevlar body armor, sending blood spraying into the air. The force of the blow spun Blade around, knocking him off balance. He fell heavily to his knees, blood pouring from his side in a steady stream.

Up above, Abigail's heart beat faster as she watched Drake slaughtering Blade. She couldn't wait any longer. One more minute and Blade would be dead.

She wouldn't let Drake have the satisfaction.

Moving as quickly as she dared, Abigail lifted her bow towards her face. She placed two forefingers under the bowstring, taking the strain, and then carefully released the auto-lock with her other hand. The string quivered as the full force of the drawn bow rested on her injured arm. Her muscles convulsed with the strain, but the arm held. She sighted on Drake as he viciously swung his sword at Blade, missing him by mere inches as the exhausted Daywalker flopped once again to the side.

It was now or never.

Abigail's eyes stung as more blood tricked down into them, but she didn't dare wipe them. Blinking the blood away as best she could, Abigail took a steadying breath and aimed the dark tip of the plague arrow at Drake. She watched as Drake raised Blade's sword high above his head, ready to plunge it down through the Daywalker's exhausted body.

For a fraction of a second, Drake's chest was exposed to her.

Abigail couldn't believe her luck. It was a perfect shot.

She let the plague arrow fly.

The arrow streaked downwards, hurtling towards Drake at over three hundred feet per second. Abigail watched, her heart in her mouth, as the arrow plunged down unstoppably towards Drake's chest.

Then, at the last possible instant, Drake twisted his sword arm fractionally, almost casually, to block the shot.

Ching!

The arrow struck the pommel of the raised sword and ricocheted off, embedding itself in the floor a foot away from where Blade lay.

Abigail sagged, her expression dissolving into despair.

Drake carried through the movement without looking up, plunging the sword down into Blade's side. The tip of the sword punched out through Blade's back, striking the tiles beneath with an audible crack. Abigail bit back a scream of horror as she watched Blade gasp, impaled on the end of his own sword.

Game over.

Drake roared in victory, his features shifting beneath his skin. Then he changed, his human features devolving as blood poured to the surface of his flesh, flushing his skin a deep crimson.

Abigail watched helplessly as Drake's body began writhing and clicking, his skeleton restructuring itself before her eyes. Drake's jaw elongated as massive canines ripped down through his gums, slashing open his lips and driving downwards on either side of his jaw. Steel-strong talons burst through his fingertips in a fine mist of blood and jagged bone spurs erupted all over his body, growing into a suit of razor-sharp spikes. There was a hideous cracking sound as the joints of Drake's knees and ankles buckled, then nightmarishly reversed direction, locking back into place with a gory *clunk*.

Drake turned around, howling, revealing a set of impossibly long fangs that made ordinary vampire canines look like kitten teeth. His pupils began bleeding to red as scales rippled over his skin in thorny waves, plating him with an impenetrable skin of pearly bone armor.

Finally, Drake's true form was revealed.

Seventy centuries of violence and predation in the making, Drake stood amid the ruins of the atrium, pure death given form. His scaled lips twitched upwards into an animalistic smile as he surveyed the destruction he had caused.

And he saw that it was good.

There was a small noise behind him. Drake turned, his eyes narrowing, to see that the puny Daywalker was still alive, crawling weakly towards him through the rubble. Smirking, Drake swung his sword high above his head, preparing to finish the fallen hunter off. His sword sparkled as it sung upwards through the air, catching a thousand glimmering reflections on its polished surface.

Including that of a tiny figure creeping up behind him...

Just as his sword reached the top of its arc, Zoe stepped out of the shadows behind Drake. Before the master vampire could react, she darted out into the open and shoved her silver stake into Drake's thigh with all the strength she could muster.

Drake staggered as the silver scorched his flesh, and turned on her, hissing like a snake. Zoe screamed as the nightmare beast bore down, snapping its jaws as it reached out for her.

But Zoe had bought Blade a crucial few seconds. Summoning up the last of his reserves, the Daywalker pitched his body towards the fallen plague arrow, jutting out of a pile of debris nearby. Snatching it up with numb fingers, Blade dragged himself to his feet and stood there, swaying. Drake's head whipped around, but he was fractionally too slow. Lunging forwards, Blade crossed the few steps that separated them and plunged the arrow so deeply into Drake's chest that its tip punched out through his back in a spray of dark blood.

Drake staggered backwards, furious. Snarling at Blade, he moved to rip the arrow out.

Then he stopped.

Total shock registered on his face as he felt the living poison in the arrowhead get to work. The plague virus seeped out of the broken ampule inside Drake's body, flooding his internal organs like acid injected into his bloodstream. Drake screamed in fury and pain as he felt his insides begin to dissolve, as the virus poured through his bloodstream in an unstoppable, necrotic rush.

Blade sagged to the ground, exhausted beyond measure

Drake dropped the sword with a clang and turned towards Blade, outraged. What had the Daywalker done to him?

Then the plague virus reached Drake's heart. Drake clutched at his chest and let loose an inhuman scream, vomiting up a spray of blood mist. His body jerked as his insides convulsed, burning away in liquid clumps of carbonized flesh. He staggered forwards and reached out towards Blade, his features twisted in agony. All along the length of his body, his bone spurs retracted as his vampiric system went into shock, his bloodstream quickly filling with the decaying residue of dying tissue.

Slowly, Drake sank to his knees. Inside his arteries, the plague virus attached itself to the molecules of his blood, causing them to blacken and expand, exploding every living blood cell in his body. Thin black fluid poured from Drake's nose and mouth in a glistening tide, releasing countless millions of activated virus cells into the air.

Turning his face to the heavens, Drake clenched his fists and screamed.

Up on the gantry, Danica began coughing as she inhaled the first spores of the free-floating plague virus. Tiny dark veins spread across her face like creeping tree roots as the virus tore through her body, destroying every cell that it touched.

She swayed, frowning blankly at the wall.

Then she collapsed, writhing in pain. Colorless fluid began trickling from her mouth as her insides began to decay.

Danica pressed a hand to her lips as she lay help-lessly on the floor, trying to stem the rush of liquid. King's biological weapon! No! Not now! Her fangs elongated, needle-sharp, as the pain and rage tore through her. In desperation she reached out a beseeching hand towards King, who stood opposite her on the other side of the gantry, a look of complete indifference on his face as he watched her die.

Danica's body convulsed and burst into blue flames. She stared at King through the flames, watching as he turned from her dismissively and walked away.

Then Danica died, a final curse stillborn on her lips.

All over the building, the fleeing vampires dropped one by one as the plague virus got to work. They piled up in stacks, shrieking and gasping before bursting into writhing clouds of dust.

In under a minute, they were all dead, leaving nothing behind but ashes.

For the first time in its history, silence descended over the Phoenix Towers.

TWENTY

Amid the silence of the atrium, something stirred.

Slumped against a broken wall, amid piles of rubble, Drake's eyes flickered open, glowing with a feeble internal light. He was back in human form now, his ravaged system unable to provide the energy needed to sustain his demonic alter ego. His insides were stripped almost to a husk, but Drake still clung to his life, his seven thousand year-old body refusing to quit out of sheer inertia, like a car with its engine cut rolling down a hill.

Drake wiped the black slime from his chin as realization crept over him.

Blade had beaten him

He was finally going to die.

Drake's mouth winched up at the corner as he contemplated the irony. Over the millennia, countless thousands had dreamed of this moment, the final downfall of the tyrant who had killed their loved ones, burned their homes, and destroyed their lives. They had come after him in their hundreds, and all had perished.

And now, at last, one of them had succeeded.

This moment should be heralded by cheering towns-people, Drake thought muzzily. They should be waving their flags and punching their torches up into the frosty night air. There should be the cry of dogs and the sound of battle horns blazing across the land, as the message was spread from town to town, city to city.

Dracula had been defeated.

The world was saved.

Instead, there was just the ringing echo of silence, and the gentle trickle of brick dust as a semi-demolished wall began to give way. There was a tiny bleeping sound as somewhere, buried in the rubble, Grimwood's charred watch beeped out its daily reminder to him to feed Pac Man.

With an effort, Drake turned his head towards Blade. The Daywalker lay in a pool of his own blood, lungs heaving as his shattered body fought to keep going. Drake could hear his heartbeat floundering in his chest, the double ba-boom of life skipping into irregularity as the blood ran in a torrent out of Blade's body. The Day-walker's eyes were open, staring sightlessly at the ceiling.

Very soon, he would be dead.

Drake wondered with a stab of detached curiosity whether the hybrid would combust, like a vampire, or remain human when he died.

There was only one way to find out.

Drake settled down to wait.

* * *

Blade stared up at the ceiling, his eyes clouding further as he swam in the black, dizzying tides of shock. He watched idiotically as his own lifeblood spurted from the raw, gaping wound in his chest, pooling around his shoulders.

The blood was so warm... just like a nice, warm bath.

Man, was he sleepy...

Blade's body jerked and he shook himself awake, grasping at consciousness as one might grasp at a bar of soap in the shower. He knew that he was badly hurt, maybe too badly to survive. But despite his savage injuries, a tiny, painful smile crept over the Daywalker's face. He had achieved something far more valuable than his mortal life, beyond anything that a mere human could hope to achieve.

He had taken down Drake, the first, the last, and perhaps the only true vampire to ever walk the earth.

He hoped that would shut King up.

Minutes slipped past.

Drake gazed at the room around him, noting with a hint of surreal satisfaction the sheer scale of the destruction he had caused. Even as he watched, a light fitting plunged down from the ceiling and crashed with finality into the rubble strewn beneath.

A tide of darkness flooded Drake's synapses and he frowned, blinking hard as his vision briefly washed out in a sea of speckled grey. Physical weakness was not something that he was used to, and now the ancient vampire was experiencing all kinds of strange sensations, not one of them pleasant.

Blinking in confusion, Drake turned his head to look at the nearby wall. It seemed to waver in the pre-dawn light, as though reality itself was little more than a mirage. As Drake watched, the ghost of an image formed before his eyes, developing rapidly into an impossibly solid-looking, colorful scene.

Drake gasped as a lifetime of bright images swam over the surface of the wall and paraded before him, as clear and vivid as though he were seeing them for the first time. Drake gazed at them in wonder. He had once heard that one's life flashed before one's eyes as death approached. Of course he had never thought he would have the opportunity to find out, yet here he was.

Drake lay back, readying himself.

This ought to be good...

Villages burning, women screaming... The rich oak smell of gunpowder in the air as his enemies broke ranks and charged at him...

Drake smiled, enjoying the show as it washed over him, filling his mind with a thousand gory images. He had slaughtered indiscriminately, the young, the old, the sick, the wounded—all had fallen beneath his sword, or else by his hands and teeth, their lifeblood sustaining him throughout the years.

And in the end, he had no regrets.

He had enjoyed every last moment of it.

And through all of the pain and death he had caused, the hunters had come, and they had suffered most of all. Drake had made sure of it. He had killed a thousand of them, in a thousand different ways. Why should he not punish them for their impunity? They who thought in their arrogance they could end a life such as his. They deserved to suffer. He saw their faces now, swimming in front of him accusingly.

A royal guardsman, his magnificent uniform streaked with blood, begging for mercy as Drake bound him to his horse, ready to hurl man and animal off the battlements.

A Turkish boy warrior, praying to his gods for forgiveness as Drake tipped a vat of boiling oil into the well the boy had chosen to hide in.

A Spanish conquistador, nailed to a tree with tears dripping down his face as Drake made him choose the order in which his seven young children must die...

And now, Blade. An African American dressed in leather and steel, the whisper of his vampire blood calling to him even as he plotted with the humans to kill his own ultimate ancestor.

Drake frowned. It was a contradiction too great to be coincidental. Where had he come from, this hybrid warrior? What circumstances had led him to become what he was? Even to the humans, Drake knew that Blade was seen as a monster, a killer. If the human authorities ever discovered his secret they would undoubtedly imprison him, perhaps even kill him, for it was one of the follies of mankind to destroy what it did not understand.

No matter.

Blade had succeeded where the others had failed, and given his life to save humanity—a race who hated him. It was a bitter irony that even Drake could respect.

Drake coughed weakly, black fluid trickling from his wounds. Part of him, a very small part of him, had always known that the day would come when he would lose. An even tinier part of him had wanted it, crying out from the darkness of his soul and begging for his final release into the unknown abyss.

If he was honest with himself, it was this tiny piece of darkness that had driven him to ever-greater depths of inhumanity, like a spoilt child testing its parents with ridiculous demands. But the day finally had come when Drake had realized that no matter how far and how hard he pushed the human race, it did not, as yet, have the strength to fight back, or at least not in a way that could truly threaten him.

And so Drake had allowed himself to become a monster. Yet within his glorious excess, Drake now saw that he had been missing something important. He had thought the human race foolish in their defiance of him, but that it was that very foolishness that had kept them going, even when logic told them they were beaten.

Drake could see it now, in a way that he had never understood before. He had given the humans every opportunity to surrender to him over the years, to bow down and accept him into their hearts, while taking his blood into their bodies and souls. Although they were not perfect, they could become so by embracing him and his kind. They would become vampires, perfectly designed to withstand the passing of the millennia as they now lived through the changing of the seasons. With that one change, they would lose the one thing that drove mankind onwards, through peaks and troughs of frantic creativity as they desperately sought to build, to invent and create so that they wouldn't have to face up to the thing they feared the most: the moment of death.

But no. They wouldn't give in. They had fought back with their fists, axes, spears, arrows, swords, and guns, unwilling to change what they were, even if it meant dying in the process.

And finally, after thousands of years, they had succeeded. Their technological prowess had finally overtaken the strength of their feeble bodies, creating a weapon so powerful that it could wipe out even him, the incarnate creator of the entire vampire race.

And with that brilliant burst of creativity, they had finally shaken off their humble origins and stepped right up to the top of the food chain, to claim what they thought was rightfully theirs—complete domination of the planet.

But in the end, it had taken the sacrifice of just one man to make their dream a reality.

Drake's eyes moved back to Blade's prone form, lying motionless amid the rubble. The Daywalker's lips were pale, his sweat-drenched body coated in a fine layer of dust. Drake turned his head stiffly to the side to look more closely at Blade's face. "Well done, hunter," he whispered. "Well done."

There was no reply. Drake sagged weakly back onto the broken tiles, his body shuddering as his lungs began filling with carbonized cellular matter. He fought for breath, his chest heaving. "You fought with honor... just as I knew you would."

Blade gave no indication of having heard him.

Drake turned his head and saw something lying nearby, half buried under a broken statue. It was a charred vampire skull, black and fragile as a dried leaf. He reached out for it, his burnished iron gauntlets scraping over the tiled floor. As his fingertips touched the top of the skull, it began to disintegrate. Drake watched, mesmerized, as the whole thing caved in on itself, black granules running outwards onto the tiles like a dried up sandcastle crumbling beneath the waves.

Drake gave a faint smile. For all of their boasts about being superior to humanity, the vampires had only gone and followed in their footsteps. They had recognized that they were weak, and had tried to improve upon themselves using technology. They had dragged their ultimate father from his self-imposed grave, hungry to unlock the secrets of his blood, and in doing so, they had sealed their own fate.

A strange sound intruded on Drake's hearing—the distant wail of sirens. With an effort, Drake lifted his head. Although the sound was unfamiliar to him, it was not difficult to guess what it meant. He turned to Blade again, his voice droll, almost conversational. "The humans are coming for you, you know." He chuckled, a strange sound that quickly turned into a strangled wheeze. "In their eyes, you and I are the same..."

The vampire king's voice tailed off. They were not the same. Blade's existence had purpose. Blade had honor.

Drake no longer had either.

Drake took a last, gasping breath, resigning himself to eternity. "Allow me one last indulgence, then. A parting gift..."

Drake turned his head to face Blade, his eyes locking with the Daywalker's.

A moment later, Drake died.

A deathly hush hung over the atrium as the dust slowly settled, drifting down over the fallen bodies like a shroud.

Then the sound of running feet filled the corridor outside. The main door flew open and Abigail and King pounded into the room, moving as quickly as their injured bodies would allow them.

They rushed to Blade's side. Abigail grabbed hold of Blade's hand, while King shook his great shoulders and called his name. But they were too late. The Daywalker was dying, fading fast, his blood pouring from the bone-deep wounds in his chest and side.

Of Drake, there was no sign. The vampire king had gone.

Abigail stared down at Blade. He lay stiffly amid the ruins, his breath coming in short gasps as the life flooded out of him, drop by glistening drop. He was so badly beaten that it was hard to tell where one injury ended and the next began. His face was ashen with blood loss and sweat coated his forehead, trickling down and mingling with the blood matting his dark hair.

Abigail felt tears blur her vision, and for once she did not wipe them away. Blade had sacrificed himself for them. Not just for her and King, but for the rest of humanity. A race that had never given him anything besides pain, and here he was, bleeding to death like a stuck pig because he cared so much.

Blade's body shuddered, air whistling out of his punctured lungs as he fought to breathe. Abigail flinched. She'd seen enough of death for one day. She found himself wondering whether she should say something to reassure the Daywalker, maybe say some last rites or something. Because from the looks of him, the big guy didn't have long left.

No human could take a beating like that and live.

Down on the floor, Blade's eyes lost their focus as he looked through Abigail and King, through the fading and transient shapes of his own world, until all that was left was the sound of his own slowing heartbeat, pulsing long and loud in his ears.

The world swam and he felt like he was falling backwards through the earth, his mind shrinking and expanding at the same time, dragging him unstoppably downwards into a black hole of nothingness. Blade felt his pain and confusion fade away, to be replaced by a warm, glowing feeling that enveloped him like a haze of liquid light.

For the first time in his life, he felt complete.

Abigail called out to Blade, shaking him, but he couldn't hear her any more. The world dropped away from him in a dizzying whirl of darkness, pulling him down beneath the swirling currents of oblivion.

As his eyes closed, Blade gave the faintest of smiles.

They had done it.

They had beaten Drake, and with him, the rest of the vampire race.

They had won.

And with that thought, Blade's world faded to black.

TWENTY-ONE

It didn't take long for the authorities to arrive. As dawn broke, the city police descended in full force, alerted by the silent alarms tripped throughout Phoenix Towers. They were shortly followed by the FBI, the fire department, and oddly enough, the local canine control squad.

As the red orb of the sun rose on the horizon, Cumberland and Hale swooped in on the scene in their FBI helicopter. There had been reports of disturbances within the towers just before the alarms went off, and two local witnesses had phoned the cops after seeing a man fitting Blade's description enter the building. It was too much of a coincidence to ignore, and at this stage in their careers, the two of them couldn't afford any more slip-ups.

The choppers touched down on the plaza and Cumberland and Hale disembarked. They saw a riot-sized convoy of police and FBI vehicles converging around them in a blare of lights and noise, and hurried to pick up their gear. Barging their way through the gathering crowd, they drew their guns and rushed towards the entrance to the Phoenix Towers, tailed by dozens of FBI agents and officers. If Blade was in there, the two agents wanted to be the first ones on the scene. They had already lost Blade once, and weren't about to let it happen again.

Inside the building, the first rays of sunlight shone through the smashed blinds of the penthouse, setting the scattered vampire corpses ablaze. By the time Cumberland and his men reached the room, there was nothing left but a series of body-shaped piles of ash lying on the shattered marble tiling.

Cumberland stood at the entrance to the atrium as his men fanned out around him, unable to believe what he was seeing. The place looked like someone had gone crazy with a wrecking ball. The shattered walls creaked alarmingly as the agents crunched their way through the piles of debris, looking for signs of life. Smashed statues lay broken on the floor, and one of the walls looked like someone had opened it up with a giant can opener.

Otherwise, the room was empty.

Cumberland sneezed explosively, holding a scented tissue to his nose. He was glad he wasn't the one writing up a report on this mess.

As he stood looking around him in bewilderment, a shout went up from the back of the atrium and Cumberland rushed forward, pulling out his handcuffs in a blaze of joy.

They'd found him!

At last!

Cumberland ran round the corner, skidding on the thick cloud of unusually colored dust that covered everything.

Then he stopped.

Very, very slowly, he put his handcuffs away. Then he sat down heavily on a smashed statue plinth and stared at what lay before him, his shoulders sagging in defeat.

Blade's motionless body lay at the back of the atrium, half-buried in a mound of rubble. His eyes were clouded in death, his body cold and stiff.

The FBI had finally got their suspect.

But not in the way they had wanted him.

Later that night, Cumberland and Hale stood glumly around the autopsy table at the FBI morgue. They watched with heavy hearts as a trio of medical examiners carefully lifted Blade's battered body onto the table. There was little hope left for their investigation. Whistler was dead and now Blade was out of the picture too, taking with him a lifetime of unsolved crime leads and three years of the detectives' lives. All they could hope for from today was to get a few DNA samples, which they would then try to match against those they already had on file.

Agent Cumberland was not an unkind man, but nobody would ever describe him as being "nice." He believed that people should have to face justice and pay for their crimes. The way he saw it, the criminals in body bags hadn't paid for anything—they'd just died, the only sure way to escape the clutches of the FBI.

Cumberland stuck his hands into his pockets, watching as the chief examiner switched on a bank of chrome overhead lights and pulled his mask over his face. Picking up a scalpel, he leaned down towards Blade's corpse, ready to make the first incision.

But as the scalpel touched Blade's bare chest, the Daywalker's skin began to crawl, as though a whole army of ants were marching beneath it. The chief examiner jumped back in alarm as the body on the table began to jerk and jump violently, in a ghastly parody of life. There was a series of wet pops and cracks as the subdermal cartilage in Blade's body began to loosen and shift. At the same time, the melanin began to drain from Blade's ebony skin, lightening it until it was almost completely white.

The medical staff dropped their instruments and backed away as the corpse's face restructured itself before their eyes, bones shifting and flattening into an entirely different formation. Simultaneously, Blade's heavy, muscular limbs flexed and contracted like those of a plastic doll thrown into the fire, becoming shorter and more compact.

And then the transformation was complete. Cumberland strode forwards and stared down at the body on the table in shock, unwilling to believe the evidence of his own eyes. Behind him, Hale dropped his clipboard and backed away until his head hit the back wall, gibbering faintly.

In less than thirty seconds, Blade's body had completely changed from that of a tall African American to the body of a shorter, more muscular Caucasian man.

His mouth hanging open, Cumberland sat down onto a nearby stool and put his head in his hands, picturing the faces of his colleges as they read his final report on this case. He looked up at Hale, catching his eye. For the first time in their partnership, the two FBI agents shared a single thought.

Case closed.

TWENTY-TWO

Blade stood on the cliff top, staring over its edge to the sea beyond. It was a bright summer's morning, a couple of hours after sunrise. The yellow sun hung low in the sky, slowly growing in warmth. A stiff breeze stirred the scrubby bushes that clung to the cliff top, making the tiny red flowers dance and filling the air with their perfume.

Blade inhaled a lungful of sea air, breathing in so deeply that his bandaged ribs creaked. He could smell the fresh green scent of the sea: brine and seaweed, and a faint tang of the earthy peat moss growing beneath his feet. It was a good, clean scent. Blade felt it sweeping through his system, blasting away the stench of gunpowder, blood and death. He felt like he had never truly smelt anything before, as though he had been buried underground for the last thirty years.

Which, in a way, was true.

The plague virus hadn't killed him. The human genes within him had won out in the end, and Blade had recovered from the plague's effects as quickly as if it were a minor bout of flu.

In the weeks that had followed his epic battle with Drake, the vampire plague had spread throughout the rest of the world, as unstoppable as a cold virus. The humans had helped it spread, just as Sommerfield had predicted they would, carrying it on their bodies and clothing by train, ship and plane across the entire globe, from Mexico to Mozambique. Any vampire who so much as crossed paths with an infected human perished in minutes.

Within weeks, the war had been won.

All the vampires of the world were dead.

Blade turned his face into the breeze, cautiously letting himself enjoy the sensation. His memory of his battle with Drake was more than a little hazy, but he remembered the vampire king's last words to him, and had seen what he had left behind. Drake knew the authorities would never stop until they caught the Daywalker, just as the hunters had never stopped in their quest for him. Realizing that his own people were doomed, Drake had chosen to give Blade a gift.

Freedom.

And with it, came a second chance at life.

Closing his eyes, Blade let the sunlight wash over his face, filling the inside of his eyelids with a comforting red glow. He listened to the sounds around him—the rumble and splash of the sea, the white gulls bickering in the air above him, the drone of an airplane passing in the distance.

Today was a very special occasion for him, one of many that had marked the long weeks of his convalescence. This morning, for the first time in nearly twenty years, Blade had ventured outside without wearing his body armor. He stood unprotected on the cliff top, reveling in the sense of freedom. His trademark sunshades were gone, as were his leather duster, black combats and weapons belt.

He didn't need them any more.

Blade felt curiously exposed, almost giddy with the unhampered lightness of his body, nothing more than an airy cotton T-shirt between him and the elements. He was dressed in newly purchased casual clothes, with a cellphone strapped to his waistband rather than his usual Mach pistols. To a passer-by, there was nothing to distinguish Blade from any other early-morning walker, out enjoying a coastal walk before the tourists descended.

Nothing, that was, apart from the sword.

Blade lifted it up and held it out before him, admiring the way the light glinted and sparked off the hilt. It really was a work of art. Its tempered blade shone silver in the sunlight, flowing elegantly into the strong, tapered hilt, its circular guard faintly blackened and worn by years of heavy use, of slicing through bone, flesh and sinew, cleaving heads from shoulders and hacking limbs from burning corpses.

Blade blinked and rubbed his eyes with a bare hand, setting after-images of the sun swirling on the insides of his eyelids. He had a thousand memories tied in with the weapon, memories he no longer needed or wanted.

Yet he was really going to miss this sword.

Below him, the surf sparkled and foamed, the water an iridescent shade of turquoise.

Blade ran his sleeve down the length of the weapon, buffing the hilt to a high shine as though scouring his fingerprints from it. He gave it a last, extravagant flourish, cutting the sunlight into ribbons and scaring a blackbird from a nearby bush.

He turned and pitched it into the ocean, as hard as he could. The sword sparkled in the sunlight as it spun end over end through the morning air. It hit the water with a splash and sank quickly into the deep, clear depths of the ocean.

Then Blade turned and walked away, over the horizon, and into legend.

EPILOG

Night was falling as Abigail's newly converted Land Cruiser pulled up to the curb in the industrial district of the city. Loud music boomed through the smoggy night air as she moved swiftly across the sidewalk towards a bar known as The Slaughtered Lamb, a local punk dive wedged into a crowded block in the meatpacking district.

A burly doorman stood outside, checking customer IDs. His name was Lucius, and he was having a very, very weird night. A burst of hillbilly thrash metal blasted through the shuttered wooden doors, making the oil-slicked puddles dance in the street.

Abigail walked straight up to the doorman, making no effort to hide her approach. King joined her a second later, grinning. The pair of them were heavily armed and clad entirely in reinforced black leather. They meant business and didn't care who knew it. Customers queuing for entry eyed them in alarm.

The line slowly dissolved, melting away into the night.

Abigail saw the instant flash of fear and recognition in the doorman's eyes and smirked to herself, mentally checking off a box in her head. She watched as King stepped up to the doorman, smiling pleasantly. "Evening, Lucius."

Lucius swallowed, his eyes widening in alarm as he took the four-barreled shotgun resting in the crook of King's arm. "King. What the hell are you doing here?"

King watched as Abigail peeled away from him, the very picture of innocence as she casually wandered off down the side alley adjoining the bar. King eyed the door to the bar. "Just a little sport hunting..."

Ten seconds later, they were inside the club. Within the dank-walled interior, the music was so loud it was almost a physical presence, blasting from the five-foot high Kelly amps like a sonic tsunami. The drinks on the bar rattled in time to the music, giving their own acoustic interpretation of the song. Onstage, a rough-looking band belted out a cover version of Sam and the Sham's "Little Red Riding Hood."

King strode through the crowd, his eyes scanning the customers queuing at the bar and moshing on the dance floor. The place was packed with locals, a seething throng of street racers, punks and off-duty meat-packers. In the corner, a dour-looking barman poured colored drinks from strangely shaped bottles, scratching at his stubble in the heat.

Lucius bounded alongside King as he ploughed his way through the masses. The burly doorman was sweating, the whites of his eyes flashing in the dim light as he threw urgent glances back towards the barman. "Ain't no vampires left, King. So who d'ya have to hunt?"

King paused at the bar door, considering this. "That's an interesting question, my friend. And I've got a question for you in return."

Motioning for Lucius to go first, King pushed his way through into the back, heading towards the restrooms. They had not gone far before an unearthly roar echoed along the dank passageway, drowning out the thudding music.

King drew his shotgun, giving Lucius an accusing look.

Before Lucius could speak, the door to the men's room slammed open, rebounding off its spring-loaded stoppers. Abigail flew out and hit the wall headfirst, falling to the ground in a heap. She was on her feet again in an instant, drawing a foot-long knife from beneath her coat with a kamikaze war cry.

King raised his four-barrel gun, taking aim at the empty doorway.

Then...

A hideous were-creature barged out of the men's room. Roughly humanoid in shape, it stood over seven feet tall and was covered from head to foot in thick, shaggy fur. The remains of a blood-soaked Stray Cats-style suit hung in tatters from its bestial form, random shreds caught on razor-sharp black claws.

It did not look like it was having a good day.

King cocked his rifle and nudged Lucius, gesturing towards the creature. "What do you get when you cross a vampire with a werewolf?"

At the sound of King's voice, the were-creature whipped its huge head round and glared at him, beady black eyes glinting in the half-light. It snuffed the air for a moment and opened its mouth and howled at King in a fetid blast of noise, strings of bloody saliva hanging from its jaws.

King smiled grimly. "A fur coat that sticks to your neck."

There was the sound of slamming doors as Lucius fled through the club. King motioned for Abigail to cover his back, then turned to face the beast. He jacked a solid-silver round into his rifle and looked up at the monster, poising his finger on the trigger. "Don't you know that fur is murder?"

He fired his weapon point-blank into the mutant creature's face as it leapt at him, its muzzle splitting open to reveal row upon row of wickedly curving hinged fangs.

Vampires the world over may be dead, but for the Nightstalkers, the fun was just beginning...

ABOUT THE AUTHOR

Natasha Rhodes is an upcoming writer and film-maker from Kent, England, who currently lives in Los Angeles. After graduating from Film School, she worked on various low-budget action/horror movies before turning her hand to SF writing. Her hobbies include sleeping, eating, surfing and attempting to teach her pet iguana not to eat the wallpaper.

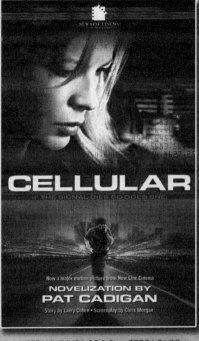

ISBN 1-84416-104-8 $7.99/ £6.99

In her most desperate hour, kidnap victim Jessica Martin uses an old smashed-in telephone to connect to an unknown number – a call that could be the difference between her family's life and death.

On the other side of town, when his cellphone rings, Ryan is thrown into a deadly high-stakes race as he searches for the kidnapped stranger. But with both time and his cellphone battery running out, Ryan's chances don't look good!

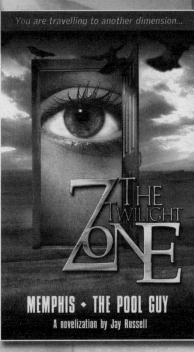

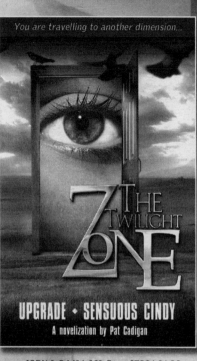

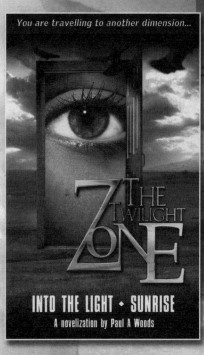